Dear Jessica —
A private
with the bro-
Enjoy!

Make Me An Offer

by

Jessica Dee Rohm

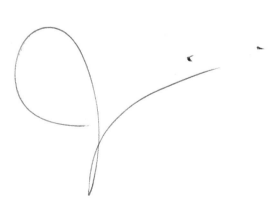

First published by AuthorHouse 07/21/04

ISBN: 1-4184-0704-6 (e-book)
ISBN: 1-4184-0705-4 (Paperback)
ISBN: 1-4184-0706-2 (Dust Jacket)

Library of Congress Control Number: 2004091712

This book is printed on acid free paper.

Printed in the United States of America
Bloomington, IN

To Eberhard

And

Lucas and Olivia

Chapter One

When Camilla Madison went for her interview at *Marry Well* magazine shortly after graduating college, she thought the whole adventure would be a lark. How frivolous and absurd, really, was the concept of a monthly journal designed to teach women how to catch and keep a rich man. Life had taught Camilla that rich men only brought trouble, not happiness. But Alyson Strong, the magazine's founder, was as serious about her concept as Rose had promised. Today, Camilla could only reflect back on Alyson's rise with admiration and awe.

From puberty on, Alyson had engineered her future by strategically seeking out people and places that would expose her to wealthy men. She grew up in modest circumstances in small-town Kentucky where her salesman father and socially ambitious homemaker mother had taken pains to teach her that it would be just as easy to fall in love with a rich man as a poor one.

While Camilla had sweated over Jane Austen and George Eliot, politically correct feminist studies, Alyson was wrapping up her MBA at Columbia Business School, having decided that her career path should lead her directly toward her ambitions. Sometime during her junior year, the light bulb flashed, and her vision materialized as if it were a Polaroid print. It was during her kick-off presentation to the Student Business Plan judging committee, sponsored by Columbia's Center for Entrepreneurial Studies, that Alyson finally unveiled her idea for *Marry Well*. Striding across the stage, she clicked the remote for her PowerPoint presentation as she described a magazine that would fill the gap between *Cosmopolitan* and *House and Garden*.

The astounding figures Alyson presented to the committee — made all the more memorable by the gyrations of her own — included current advertising revenues for the industry of $18 billion and a demographic profile of *Marry Well's* projected target audience, showing a median household income of $56,167.

Of her target readership audience in New York and elsewhere, which she calculated to be 1,595,384 plus-or-minus searching female souls, Alyson found that 3.5 percent were widowed, 19.6 percent were divorced, 12.1 percent were separated, 42 percent had never been married, 8.6 percent were living with an unmarried partner, and the remaining 14.2 percent were married but looking to upgrade to a better model.

Few of the judges at Columbia saw the merit in yet another magazine during a time when so many were folding, but the underwriter of the Student Business Plan contest, which provided endorsement and funding to the winning new venture, believed in her, and tilted the jury in her favor. Not so coincidentally, he was her first featured centerpiece interview, which became the prototype for the magazine's signature column.

With $50,000 of seed money, and a potent ally in Harry Wong, Alyson started her business from an office in the Puck Building at 295 Lafayette in New York City and became an infamous success in publishing. The editorial content of the glossy monthly magazine was geared to the 20-to-50-year-old female who needed foolproof ploys to catch and wed a rich man.

Now in its ninth year of an extraordinary ride (for the greater part of which Camilla had been along), *Marry Well* far exceeded its original goal, capturing a loyal subscriber base of nearly 1.8 million from places as far away as Helsinki and the Falkland Islands. A recent reader poll attributed 16,379 unions to *Marry Well's* wily advice.

One of Alyson's ingenious pitches to advertisers was to emphasize that capturing readers during the "hunt" period guaranteed their loyalty during the lucrative "kill" time of their married lives. When Camilla asked her during that first interview what this meant, Alyson explained that the hunt was looking for a husband with more money than a wife could spend and the kill was marrying him and spending as much of it as possible. She supported this theory by citing a recent study by *Modern Bride* magazine and Roper research, called "Your New $100 Billion Customer … the Engaged Woman." A *Reuters'* report, entitled "Targeting the Single Female Consumer," identified that "independent, ambitious, solo females share one common goal — to marry well."

Central to Alyson's creative inspiration was her feature on a wealthy prominent male — an empire builder, media mogul, Wall Street tycoon, tech-tiger and the like. She would always conduct these interviews herself. She called the column "Him on Him" — because every man's most important subject was, after all, himself.

Marry Well included regular columns on plastic surgery and dermatological procedures ("Dr. Fizer's Fix-It Shop"), fashion ("Flash in the Pan-ts"), beauty ("Make-Up or Break-Up"), careers that attract but don't threaten men ("Job Magnets: Rebel, Don't Repel"), legal advice from well-publicized jurists in topics such as pre-nuptial agreements and marital law ("Torts for Tarts") and divorce gossip ("Dish Wish").

Due to Alyson's temperament, and the natural transience of employees in publishing jobs, columnists and their ideas came and went with the wind. Only two writers had survived from the beginning, Camilla and her friend Rose Manna, and one member of the administrative staff, Chuck Maynard, who was Alyson's treasured director of advertising sales.

"Be Choosey ~~Who~~ What You Put in Your Mouth," Rose's mouthwatering column on food and dining, attracted a following with discerning taste. Camilla, who grew up in tony Palm Beach, invented a decorating feature headlined "Pillows of Society," that was often quoted by interior designers about town.

Rose and Camilla's columns had the more loyal followings but, based on the volume of letters to the editor, the most popular column remained "Him on Him," which Alyson still wrote herself. After year three, she had shamelessly added the subtitle "A Beditorial," coining a new term, which had shown up in every Webster's Dictionary edition since. She claimed the name just "came to her" while she was busy conducting primary research with one particularly attractive man of the month. The "Him" was always preferably a bachelor, although Alyson made few distinctions between the available and the married, when push came to shove.

"Relationships are fluid," Alyson was wont to explain.

Her spicy "Him on Him" columns revealed an intimate view of her high and mighty subjects, which in turn sparked interviews for Alyson herself with Barbara Walters and Oprah, each eager to learn how Alyson managed to get such powerful men to divulge so much.

But Alyson never told. Next to the recipe for Coke, she considered this information to be the best-kept secret in the business world.

Alyson wasn't fashion model beautiful, not nearly as pretty as Camilla for example, but she was glamorous and cunning, funny and flattering. Memorably tall at nearly six feet, she colored her hair soft blonde with subtle highlights. Large white teeth, which she flashed at moments to maximize their effect, underscored the slightly equine shape of her face. When she spoke, it was with perfect diction and a studied Southern drawl.

She made the most of her raw materials, taking Willy's grueling exercise class at Lotte Berk seven days a week, religiously plumping her lips with collagen injections at Dr. Fizer's, bleaching her teeth, wrapping her nails, waxing and buffing, and dressing stylishly and provocatively at the same time. Dr. Wontell had augmented her already ample breasts (which were often discussed at Park Avenue dinner parties) when Alyson was supposed to be in Acapulco on holiday.

Jean-Yves Ferret, whom she had featured in an early issue, cut her hair himself, first at her bachelorette pad at the San Remo and, after she married, at her apartment at River House. Graciously, Alyson had once arranged for Camilla to get her hair cut by Jean-Yves, too. But Camilla walked out after waiting two hours for the hairdresser to the socialites to stop talking on his LG phone.

Juan de las Heras, one of the only heterosexual interior designers in New York, another former *Marry Well* centerpiece and Alyson fan, had decorated both her unmarried and married abodes.

Alyson's energy was legendary in the publishing world. She barely slept four hours a night, often returning home at one or two in the morning after her forays into Manhattan's social whirl. The alarm roused her at six, providing time to secure her center spot on the faded blue-green carpet in the Lotte Berk townhouse on 67th Street. Such precautions weren't really necessary — ever since she had featured Willy in her column, he protected her spot as if it were the board chairman's box at Carnegie Hall.

When she turned 35, she had decided to practice what she preached and managed to snag the newly-widowed Walter Strong of San Francisco, whose net worth was estimated by *Forbes* magazine to be in the $400 million range, mostly from real estate and a couple of magazines that he had bought for fun. She met him by pretending that *Marry Well* might be for sale — but only after his secretary had declined several interview requests on his behalf, despite Alyson's promise to put him on the cover.

In fact, he hadn't seemed susceptible to any of her usual ploys, which taxed her resources and challenged her imagination. Finally, after the usual flattery, seduction, and glamour failed to clinch the deal, Walter fell for her because of her intellect, and because she could finish *The New York Times Magazine* crossword puzzle without cheating (as far as he knew).

To Alyson, the marriage was another stepping-stone on the road to success.

Walter Strong — like his friends Henry Kravis, Evelyn de Rothschild, and Conrad Black (oh, poor Conrad!) — had always preferred brains to just beauty; his idea of a trophy wife was a woman you still wanted to talk to after sex as well as during foreplay. Walter had been 47 when he married Alyson. His first wife had died five years earlier of breast cancer, and his only son Rex, now 17, had come with him to New York, where the Strong family claimed to have had real estate interests since Peter Stuyvesant's day. Alyson's stepson was finishing high school at Collegiate, and would be starting at Columbia College in the fall, where he had been accepted early decision.

After tying the knot, Alyson seemed changed — for a while. But even getting married well didn't cramp Alyson's style for long, and she was soon back to scouting talent for her beditorials after a hiatus of only a year.

Alyson was always first to arrive at *Marry Well*, and Camilla used to rush to be second, eager not to miss Alyson as she regaled her editorial staff with effusive reports on the prior evening's events.

"I'm my own best scout," Alyson would brag, ostensibly attending these functions to line up her next showcased "Him on Him" star.

During this particular Monday morning's oration, Chuck took copious notes about where Alyson had gone and whom she had met over the weekend, to use as fodder in his sales pitches and strategic leaks to syndicated gossip columnists Richard Johnson and Liz Smith. Advertisers loved name-dropping; they seemed to think that the rich and famous people Alyson knew would tout their products if the ads appeared in *Marry Well*.

In contrast to Alyson's frenzied life, Camilla's was changing — especially since she had found out she was pregnant seven months earlier. Now Camilla took it slower in the mornings, and this Monday morning — September 15th to be precise — she happened to arrive in the middle of Alyson's daily sermon.

"This weekend, I was invited to the Tour de Farce Tennis Match at Teddy Ruckensayer's estate in Easthampton," Alyson reported. The air seemed to flutter around her, like it does around the palpitating wings of a hummingbird, when she told her stories. "Price of entry: net worth $100 million and up."

"Then how did you get in, Alyson?" Chuck teased with a wink. Only Chuck talked to her like that; after all, he was responsible for bringing in most of the revenues and therefore had earned a special place in Alyson's heart.

"Oh, I didn't *play*, silly," she retorted. "I was the prize."

She was sporting a new necklace that she announced had been given to her by a future "Him on Him" whom she had interviewed in Florida the Friday before.

"Is that ethical?" Rose asked. It was what everyone had been wondering too.

"If the mayor of New York can date the governor's aide, why can't I accept a token of appreciation from a friend?" Alyson asked.

"It is gorgeous," Camilla said.

Alyson preened while they admired her loot. "He said it looked even better on me all by itself."

"You mean …with nothing else on?" Chuck asked, a gleam in his eye.

"Precisely."

Alyson's marriage to Walter had proven to be a boon to her business. Introductions to his friends broadened her contact base, and encouraged her to spread her entrepreneurial wings. She learned to seek new opportunities for her popular *Marry Well* brand — such as *Marry Well's E-Male*, her wildly successful digital dating service — as well as hunting new subjects for her overwhelmingly popular "Him on Him" column.

As the economy plummeted, however, so did the fortunes of her wealthy subjects. She lately complained that a man's virility was so tied to his net worth that if the stock market didn't rise soon, neither would anyone she knew. "A hard man is good to find," was one of her favorite sayings.

With technology, big industrials, and financials in the doldrums, Alyson had to resort to looking beyond New York to find her subjects. This shift in strategy took Alyson from Wall Street to Main Street. "A girl's gotta do what a girl's gotta do," she explained.

In trying to convey her boss's essence to outsiders, Camilla often likened Alyson to Lord Byron, as described in his most celebrated epithet: *mad, bad, and dangerous to know.*

Alyson was even more outrageous now than she had been when Camilla started working there seven years before. She'd assumed that the initial calming effect of Alyson's marriage would last, but this morning it sounded again as though Alyson's pendulum had swung even farther in the opposite direction. At the end of the week, Camilla would go on maternity leave for six months; she wondered if she'd miss Alyson's tales while she was gone or find the break a welcome respite. Maybe it was her hormones raging, but right now she was growing weary of Alyson and everything she had come to represent.

Camilla returned to her office; where she had little to do since turning her column over to her maternity leave substitute, Prissie Easton, who would write "Pillows of Society" while Camilla was out. Folded hands over protruding belly, Camilla felt the baby kick, which brought a smile to her lips and tears to her eyes as she thought about her parents. She remembered all the trauma she'd had to overcome to get to this enviable place in her life — if only they had lived to see their first grandchild.

She wished that she could see her father again, to tell him everything that had happened, and how she had forgiven him. Replaying Malcolm Merewether's words of wisdom in her head, she remembered how her teenage self had perceived them as parental platitudes to be ignored.

On that day years before, she remembered looking up into a sparkling blue gaze so like her own — "swimming pool eyes" her mother Tina called them. Camilla had dressed carefully that morning, in a lime green and bubblegum pink Lilly Pulitzer print shift with matching sandals that she'd bought on sale at C. Orricco's with her babysitting money. Her father had urged her to look her best for her meeting with Richard "Rocky" Faber, who was also Malcolm's biggest client and personal friend.

Rocky Faber had invited 14-year-old Camilla to lunch to advise her on her future. Since Palm Beach Day School ended in ninth grade, she would have to leave her beloved island paradise for a suitably academic East Coast preparatory school to ensure that she would get into a good college.

It was all in "The Plan" that her parents had for her, a plan from which they never wavered.

"No one in this county is better connected than Rocky," Malcolm reminded Camilla, as they waited together on the portico of the Merewether home at 115 Seaspray for Rocky Faber to arrive. He leaned over and straightened the pink bows on the shoulders of Camilla's dress. "He's on the board of trustees of Hoskins, darling. One word from Rocky and you're in — it's one of the best prep schools in the country."

As her father spoke, Camilla noticed how paunchy and gray he had become. The Christmas cacti in painted clay pots that surrounded them were in full bloom, reaching toward the bright November sunlight with outstretched leaves. One bud remained, flanked by fading flowers on their last legs.

At the time, she had been as hopeful as her parents that Rocky could open the door to her future. Camilla remembered how she couldn't wait to go off to school, to be someplace new and exciting. Malcolm had been badly burned early in his career as a Palm Beach real estate broker when he had worked with a big customer for over a year, only to have the man buy a $14 million oceanfront lot from another broker the one weekend Malcolm had gone fishing. Since that experience, he treated every deal as one would a baby — he never left it alone until it was put to bed. Even then, there always seemed to be another one crying for attention.

Selling had become a dialect for him, as well as a way of life.

"He'll be a terrific contact for you, Camilla, especially when you get ready to take over Merewether Realty in a few years —"

"Dad, I'm still a kid —"

"Ah, Camilla, time evaporates," he said, looking at his watch, "and the older one gets, the faster it disappears."

It was no secret around the Merewether household that if it hadn't been for Rocky's loyalty to Camilla's father's firm, Malcolm might have been out of business a decade before.

Then Malcolm had smoothed his daughter's sun-streaked blond hair and took her right hand gently in his. "You are a beautiful young woman, Camilla." He lovingly stroked her cheek and gazed into her eyes, telling her that her fair complexion was as translucent as the inside of an oyster shell.

"That's enough, Dad!" Her father was embarrassing her.

Rocky Faber drove up to the Merewethers' pink stucco house covered in fuchsia bougainvillea, at 11:30 sharp, in his white Mercedes with the top down. He must have been her father's age at the time — early forties or so — but he looked younger.

On the few occasions she had seen him over the years, he'd had a bookish appearance, more like she imagined a college professor than a

11

wheeler-dealer, which is how he had always been described. His once-blond hair was still yellow, but more like the faded edges of one of her father's volumes of Hawthorne or Poe. He was casually dressed, in khakis and a washed-out brick-red polo shirt with the three-letter logo PGA, for Professional Golf Association, of which he was a charter member. He was tall, at least 6-foot-3, and youthful, although his skin was parched and leathery from too many days in the sun.

On the drive across the Middle Bridge that day, Camilla noticed how the wind gusting across Lake Worth hadn't disturbed Mr. Faber's hair while it played havoc with her own. The loose strands kept getting stuck in her Bonne Belle cotton candy lip gloss, forcing her to hold her hair back with her hands, with her elbows up in the air.

She noticed Rocky diverting his gaze from the road to look at her, and she felt self-conscious, wondering if she had forgotten to shave under her arms. But he put her at ease by asking questions about her aspirations, of which she had many, as a young woman should. He had seemed so gentle and kind.

"Well, Dad wants me to join him in the real estate business...but I want to be a journalist," Camilla declared.

"And have you thought about how you would get there?" Mr. Faber asked.

"Not really," she admitted.

"Well, maybe I can help you."

"That would be great, Mr. Faber."

"Rocky. Call me Rocky — everyone does."

The exclusive Palm Beach Yacht Club is located on Flagler Drive along the shore of a lagoon called Lake Worth, directly across from the island of Palm Beach. Since her parents weren't members, she had never been there before. From where she and Rocky were seated, Camilla could see the imposing yachts lolling in their slips — crisp bow pulpits, sleek teak railings, colorful canvas canopies with pristine piping — all vacant and lonely on a winter weekday afternoon.

How impressed she had been! She remembered the army of red flags on white boats, waving to her in the wind.

Fighting her nervousness, Camilla had fiddled with the napkin in her lap, folded her hands, and tried to admire the view across the lagoon, of the twin belvedere towers of The Breakers Hotel eclipsing the low winter sun, just a few blocks north of where she and her father had just stood.

"What schools are you considering?" Rocky asked her, which she had thought at the time was meant to put her at ease.

"My guidance counselor has advised me to aim high —"

"Your father says you're a straight-A student, tennis star, captain of the soccer team, editor of the school newspaper —"

Camilla blushed. "Dad has a tendency to brag. Anyway…I've applied to Andover, Exeter, Taft, Groton, and Hoskins." She straightened as she inched forward to the edge of her seat. "Would you consider writing a letter of recommendation for me? Hoskins is my first choice."

Rocky paused to regard her in a fatherly way. "I admire a girl who is aggressive about what she wants. You get nothing if you don't go for it."

With a tap of his index finger on the rim of her glass, Rocky indicated that Camilla should join him in a glass of wine, which he told her perfectly complemented the Florida grouper, just caught that morning and delivered by the fishermen to the club's back door. She hesitated only slightly before sipping, because she trusted that he, like her father, would never steer her wrong, and she had a healthy 14-year-old's feisty vein of curiosity. Although she looked her age, the club's staff turned a blind eye and served the wine, because not only was Rocky a member of the club's board of overseers, but he was chairman of the club's Christmas gratuity fund as well.

The alcohol made her giddy, and relaxed enough to call him Rocky. She was grateful for the letter he agreed to write for her and tried to show her appreciation by smiling broadly, especially since she had finally had her braces removed a month before. After she scraped the last of her ice cream off the bottom of the bowl, as was her habit, she rested her elbows on the table, despite her proper training, and she asked him about his job and his wife and his golf and his boat.

"Would you like to see my yacht?"

"Okay," she innocently replied.

Even now, so many years later, she chastised herself for having been so blind. Wine, yachts, intimate conversation — she was only 14. What had she been thinking?

The main deck of the yacht had several sectional seating areas, all upholstered in stiff white leather. The bow and aft areas had immaculate mattresses laid flat for sunbathing. While Camilla had seen many boats before — speedboats, rowboats, and canoes — Rocky's yacht was something new.

There was a wet bar, icemaker, refrigerator, a blender for frozen drinks, and other items one would expect to find in a full-service kitchen in a home, except here everything was in miniature. A stereo system was built into the lacquered rosewood paneling beneath the seats. The steering wheel was surrounded by high-tech controls and equipment — a compass, radar and VHF, a chart plotter, a fancy navigation system — and Rocky explained that boats operated like airplanes, autopilot and all.

Rocky pointed Camilla downstairs toward the galley, brushing up against her as he cautioned her not to bump her head. She remembered now how acutely aware she had been of his proximity to her in the cramped stairwell. He had a sour smell, perspiration mixed with wine.

Camilla had marveled at the cleverness of the yacht's design, so much more sophisticated than the sporty sailboats and catamarans that her friends from school had owned. Everything was so compact, and the hardware was ingenious; it was impossible to open any of the cabinets or doors because the handles had some automatic locking device that kept them from flying open when the boat rocked or swayed. She was about to ask Rocky to show her how they worked, when he excused himself, explaining that he needed to visit the "head."

"Head?" she asked.

"The bathroom," he explained, in a patronizing tone.

Of course Camilla knew what the head meant; she was just nervous.

Camilla continued to explore while he was gone. Each of the two guest staterooms had a marble-floored head en suite, with a full stall shower. She heard the door unlock to the master head as she stood in the master stateroom cabin looking out one of the portholes at the sky. She turned around to ask Rocky if the head had a tub and saw him standing there, stark naked, with what she presumed was an erection, although she had never seen one before.

She stared.

"I've wanted you ever since I first met you," Rocky said, taking a step closer.

"I was six," she responded, dumbfounded.

"Yes, I remember."

For what seemed like hours, she froze fast to the spot where she stood. When she had finally reacted, she darted for the door, but Rocky slid in front of her and slammed the stateroom door shut. She jiggled and jerked the knob, encountering the tricky locking device, which she doubted he would decipher for her then. Smiling his yellow smile, devoid of its trademark charm, he grabbed her long hair with one hand and fondled her bottom with the other, pressing his naked body against the sheer cotton fabric of her shift.

Camilla had known this man most of her life and couldn't believe what was happening. She turned the white-gray color of cold ashes with fright. Options ran through her head — screaming, biting, kicking, crying — but they were alone on the yacht and he was much stronger than she.

"I could have any woman I want, you know, but I chose you," he breathed into her ear.

She opened her mouth to protest, but gagged instead, on the acid bile of terror that had risen from her stomach to her throat.

He tried to kiss her, forcing his tongue between her parted lips, but she bit it and kicked him in the shin as hard as she could. The soft leather straps of her sandals did nothing to support her attack and her uncalloused toes were hurt more than his hard shin by the force of the contact between them. She dug her teeth into him as hard as she could, on his right biceps, but his developed muscle resisted the pressure of her bite. He tasted of salt and aftershave infused with clove.

The taste of clove still made her ill.

Annoyed, Rocky abandoned any pretense of romantic intention, and pushed Camilla down on the thin cabin bunk, tearing off her white cotton panties and throwing them on the floor.

Then he pushed himself inside her, holding her wrists down with his elbows and her legs apart with his knees.

At that moment it had seemed as if she was outside herself, watching. She'd had to disassociate in order to survive. What was happening to her was being done to someone else, a girl she knew, whom she cared about, but who was too far away to reach.

The first thrust felt like a dry wooden rod. A scream escaped her lips. The second thrust punctured something and drew blood, a warm rivulet of sticky stuff that trickled down her thighs. A third brutal thrust and it was over. She felt him quiver, and pull out, making a small suction noise as he did so, like her mother's kitchen sink.

Camilla had tried to scream then again but nothing came out. She felt no pain afterwards, only intense disgust; she could no longer smell his sweat or taste his clove aftershave or the sour wine on his breath, all of which had overwhelmed her before.

The only information that her battered senses transmitted to her brain were two images: a strawberry birthmark the size of a dime but shaped like a heart on Rocky's left shoulder and, in the corner, a photo of Rocky's family, happy and sun-tanned, seemingly laughing at her misfortune.

When it was over, he dressed quickly, pulling his socks on first. "You provoked it, you know. It was your fault," he said.

She felt a dull throbbing in her temples and heard her own heart thumping in her ears like drums.

"That should be a lesson to you, and girls like you, little teases," he had said. "If you intend to dine and drink with a man, to lean into him when you speak, to wear a dress with your legs naked and no bra underneath, then you should expect to deliver on your promise."

Camilla had cowered and flinched at his words. As he buckled his belt, he warned her not to say a word to anyone, because he would deny it and say she was a lying, troubled teenage girl. She knew if he did, that people would believe him, because of who he was, and who she wasn't.

"If you dare breathe a whisper to anyone, not only will I destroy you, but I'll bankrupt your father in a minute." She thought he could, and she believed that he would.

Camilla was terrified, although her inner fire was stoked. She knew she had been wronged, and that she couldn't tell a soul, that it would be up to her to salvage what was left.

Rocky then told her to wash herself off in the master stateroom head. As her tears disappeared in the shower steam, she scrubbed herself in a perfunctory way as she often had after a soccer game or tennis tournament. Then she got dressed, and walked quietly to the Mercedes, where they listened to classical music, while the late-afternoon winds blowing off the water blasted frigid air on her violated body, all the way home. They never spoke another word and as they pulled up in front of her house, she faced him squarely, narrowed her eyes, and spat right in his face.

When 60 days had passed and Camilla still had not gotten her period, she knew.

She then went to Lewis Pharmacy on South County Road after school, telling the clerk behind the counter whom she recognized from her mother's garden club group that she was acting on behalf of a friend, and bought a Clear Blue pregnancy test. Later, just as she had expected, both the square and the circle showed a blue line, corroborating her worst fear: Rocky had impregnated her. She vomited into the bowl.

All she wanted was for him to die. But a steely inner compass, with poles of right and wrong, made her fight. Bouncing back, determined and focused, she devised a plan.

A week after she had made her decision, Camilla had come home from school to find her mother in the kitchen, doing a crossword puzzle and drinking a tall glass of lemonade. There was a stack of letters on the counter near where Tina sat.

"Darling, you did it. You've been accepted by Andover."

"That's great, Mom, really great." Camilla recalled her forced smile.

"You don't look happy. Are you disappointed about Hoskins?"

"Mom, how about a walk on the beach?"

Her mother looked up. "Now?"

"Now."

Without another word the two, one an older woman and one no longer a girl, left. After 15 minutes, as they approached the busiest part of the beach where it intersected with Peruvian Avenue, Camilla said, "Mom, I'm pregnant."

Tina Merewether stopped in her tracks. "Are you sure?"

"I took one of those over-the-counter tests. It was positive."

"I always thought when you started having sex…" Tina said, "…you would tell me, that we could discuss — what precautions you should take."

"If it makes you feel better, so did I. Let's just say, this took me by surprise. And, before you ask, no the father doesn't know and it's not important who he is."

"Don't you think he's entitled to know?"

"No."

"Darling — how long?"

"About two and a half months."

Tina swallowed hard. "Too late for Mifeprex, you know — the abortion pill. But, if you choose to..." she swallowed hard "...terminate, a regular abortion is still possible."

Camilla thought about the baby as a part of her, as a living person. Her mother's suggestion shocked her because even though Tina had married an Episcopalian, she had thought her mother's Catholicism was more deeply entrenched than that. Certainly, Camilla's was. "Mom, I can't do it — I'm going to have it, and give it up for adoption. But I need your help, I want your promise to find a good, loving home for my child."

"Camilla, please, let's think this over —" Tina protested, but Camilla could sense her mother's relief.

"No, I have thought this over. I've thought about nothing else for the past week; my mind is made up. I'm having the baby, we'll find a good home, and I'll move on with my life."

"Are you sure? Being pregnant is so...public. And adoptions...why sometimes they publish them in the Shiny Sheet." The locals called the *Palm Beach Daily News* "the Shiny Sheet" because its paper was glossy and slick.

"Yes. I've thought hard about that. I've researched it thoroughly. Mom, we'll just have to go out of state — for a while."

Tina seemed to look at Camilla differently than she ever had before. Without judgment, or sympathy, just…acceptance.

"I'll start discreetly asking around. I know an attorney who specializes in family law," Tina said. "Ever since you were five, when your mind was made up it was immutable —"

"And one more thing…whatever you do, don't tell Dad."

Camilla had felt her mother stiffen, although they continued to walk arm-in-arm.

"It will take some doing to keep something this big from your father. Are you afraid of what he might do?"

"Yes," Camilla said, although deep inside she was more afraid that if her father found out who had done this to her he might feel guilty, or he might blame her, as Rocky had.

"We'll go away for the summer. Maybe Nantucket, where we won't run into anyone we know…" Tina grew serious. "You won't be able to see Dad for three months."

Even though part of her had longed for her father's comfort, the idea of him looking at her the way he had on their porch that day of the rape was too much to bear, pushing her — albeit in his innocent way. She still loved him, but she thought then that she could never view him the same — as her protector, her Dad.

If only she could see him one more time, explain it all now, with perspective, forgiveness and love.

When she had been a naive 14-year-old girl, she couldn't. She had closed up, like a morning glory at dusk, and said to her mother with finality: "If it has to be three months without Dad, then it has to be."

21

A determined Camilla carried that baby to term; her labor had begun at lunchtime on August 31st, 40 weeks from the day she was raped. She had asked to be put to sleep to numb the pain. The truth was she was afraid to know her baby, to love it, and to be unable to give it up. What she had never anticipated when she decided to go forward was the synchronicity of mother and child — a rhythm so visceral she knew she could never forget it.

She refused to name or nurse the baby boy. Tina assured her that the adoption had been arranged through a lawyer she trusted. A very fine family, far away from Florida, would take him and he would want for nothing.

At the time it had seemed such a sensible solution. In her naiveté, she imagined herself as a favored aunt, who would send presents at Christmas and visit whenever she could. "You must give me their address and phone number, so I can be sure to stay in touch," she had instructed her mother as the nurse took her baby away.

Tina couldn't give Camilla the address because she didn't know it. In fact, the adoption file would be sealed at their lawyer's request for 15 years, and secrecy was a condition of the private adoption contract — the adoptive parents didn't want to risk the birth mother changing her mind. But Tina promised Camilla that on her thirtieth birthday, if Camilla still wanted to know, that she would contact the lawyer on Camilla's behalf to find out the name of her son's adoptive parents — and maybe someday they could know one another at last.

Camilla asked to say good-bye. Her son had blue eyes and blond hair. On his left shoulder, he had a strawberry birthmark, like his father's, shaped like a heart.

Before Camilla's sadness overwhelmed her day, Rose stuck her head in the door. "Hey, Camilla. What planet are you on?"

And because Camilla had had enough of lies, she said, "Babies."

Although Rose knew Camilla well enough to know that wasn't the whole story, she didn't push for more.

Chapter Two

In Camilla's fantasy life, she would have refused to meet with Rocky, or rejected his offer to show her his boat, or been brave enough to expose his crime — choosing to keep their baby and raise him herself. But in reality, she took an entirely different path. Broken-hearted, she watched her son spirited away to his new parents while she, still a child herself, got on with her life.

Phillips Academy, known colloquially as "Andover" after the Massachusetts town in which it was located, offered Camilla both the anonymity and opportunity she was seeking. The 500-acre campus was twice the size of downtown Palm Beach, and the hundreds of students she met there, from 42 states and 26 countries, posed a sharp contrast to the 18 young Anglo-Saxon men and women who had made up her class at Palm Beach Day.

The academic demands and rigorous program distracted her, most of the time, from the excruciating ordeal she had just endured. But during quiet moments in the stacks of The Oliver Wendell Holmes Library, or while she was jogging around the Sarota Track, or while she slept, she was haunted by flashbacks of the rape and paralyzed by her guilt over having given up her son. These twin memories would plague her for years to come.

Camilla focused on her studies, avoiding Friday night dances in George Washington Hall and forays into Boston's nightlife, a mere 21 miles away. Rumors spread that she was a lesbian, based on her constant refusal to date the young men at school; finding the fiction convenient, she never confirmed or denied the whispered suspicions. Instead, she graduated in the top ten percent of her class and got into Barnard College in New York City.

In busy Manhattan, Camilla took another giant step away from her past. Her world got larger, filled up with museums and musicals, people of all colors and nationalities. The students milling about the campus outnumbered the entire 9,814-person population of Palm Beach three-to-one.

The energy of Manhattan both excited and preoccupied her — for a while. She pursued her passion for journalism and became editor-in-chief of the *Barnard Bulletin,* a respected campus newspaper. Her decision to permanently abandon Palm Beach and settle on New York's Upper West Side sat uneasily but determinedly on her chest.

By junior year, most of her classmates were in steady relationships with a member of the opposite sex, but Camilla still avoided dating. She was becoming increasingly anxious and aware of how lonely she was as her college years progressed. Perhaps that was why she was drawn to a lecture in Barnard Hall being given by Dr. Doris Sanger, a consulting psychiatrist to Barnard's Center For Research on Women, where Camilla became transfixed by the charismatic doctor and what she had to say. The subject of the lecture was *Trauma in Adolescence.*

Dr. Doris Sanger looked to be in her early fifties, with shaggy hair that had obviously gone white but which she wore tinted a shocking cobalt blue. Her cheekbones were high and prominent, her nose aquiline, and her round, hazel eyes shone bright under heavy eyelids set into pure white opaque skin. She was trim, and wore striped trousers and a vintage peasant-style blouse that had recently come back into vogue. She gesticulated wildly when she spoke.

"The brain of a young person, particularly during the high school and college years, operates differently than that of an adult. The *amygdalae*, the part of the brain responsible for human emotions, are stimulated by the onset of intense hormonal activity. From ages 15 to 22, the *amygdalae* rules, rather than the *cortex* — the thinking and reasoning part of the brain that prevails in adults — or the *brain stem*, the part of the brain that controls bodily functions, which dominates in young children."

She used a lighted pointer to indicate which section was which on her acetate overhead slide.

"The amygdalae's dominance can override clear thinking, making teens push boundaries, sometimes resulting in situations that spin out of control. Drug overdoses, alcohol toxicity, and rape..." she seemed to look at Camilla when she said this "...happen more often, with severe repercussions, than many may think.

"Teens and post-adolescents tend to suffer from hyperactive feelings. A recent study conducted by NIDA entitled *Neurochemistry in Young Adults,* logged an average of 28 emotional shifts in adolescents and post-adolescents during a 12-to-18-hour alert day, as compared to an adult's one or two changes. That is partly why trauma and loss during this period affect individuals in this vulnerable stage very powerfully, why trauma in adolescence can never be swept under the rug. Why it must be confronted and dealt with."

Something was stirred in Camilla. After the lecture, she dashed up onto the stage, "Do you see patients?"

Dr. Sanger stood so close that Camilla could see the green flecks in her otherwise golden-brown eyes. Camilla knew she was being assessed, but waited patiently for the verdict. "Yes. Here's my card. Please call for an appointment."

Camilla started seeing Dr. Sanger regularly during the spring of her junior year. During these sessions, she revealed for the first time the painful details of the rape, and the powerful inhibiting effect it had had on her ability to sustain a normal social life. She gradually became less ashamed, confiding not only in Dr. Sanger, but also in her roommate, Rose Manna, an outspoken firebrand from Venice Beach, California.

Rose usually wore her frizzy persimmon hair tied back in a red paisley bandanna, the kind people put around the necks of Labrador retrievers. Her face was loaded with freckles, patterned like the Milky Way; her light green eyes were the color of new spring leaves. She and Camilla were similarly built, slim but curvy. Before long, Camilla told Rose everything — almost.

Rose eagerly returned Camilla's confidences, divulging how her mother and father owned a video store on the Venice boardwalk, where they spent twelve-hour days making three-dollar sales. Rose told Camilla how when she had gotten a square meal, it was usually from McDonald's, leading her to become an accomplished cook by the age of 12. And how she sought the love she lacked at home from boys she met outside. Camilla listened to Rose's tales of promiscuity in awe and with a bit of envy.

But as much as Camilla trusted both women, she could never bring herself to tell either Dr. Sanger or Rose about the child she had abandoned.

One night, encouraged by Rose, Camilla slept with a guy from Columbia College who was auditing her political science class. She gulped down half a bottle of Southern Comfort to repress her inhibitions but still felt nothing during the brief and sweaty coupling. The entire experience was like reading a book on an airplane; she lost herself in her own head to block out the unpleasantness around her.

For a long time, Camilla denied that her past had lessened her receptivity to love. She was sure she just hadn't yet met the right man. She tried to reassure herself with this theory as she approached the end of her college years and drifted out of therapy with Dr. Sanger, when it became clear that she was getting too close to the truth.

Following graduation in June of 1992, 22-year-olds Camilla and Rose shared a one-bedroom townhouse apartment off West End Avenue on 76th Street. It was a six-flight walk-up that they decorated with flowered sheets stapled to the moldings and with furniture from flea markets. They'd had a ball — exploring the rich variety of thrift shops and ethnic restaurants, sidewalk sales, and free concerts on summer nights in Central Park.

Together they landed those first jobs at the then-upstart magazine *Marry Well.* Rose convinced Alyson Strong, *Marry Well's* founder and editor-in-chief, to let her develop a column about food, emphasizing its power in the realm of seduction. Camilla, whose Palm Beach polish and privilege were immediately detected by the perceptive entrepreneur-publisher, was charged with creating a column on interior design.

Alyson Strong, just a few years older than the two recent grads, was a demanding boss. Although Camilla had aspired to serious journalism — not writing decorating tips for the prospectively rich, nearly famous, and recently married — she loved her job. It was fun and challenging, and Alyson was a dynamo — outrageous and full of life. Camilla had picked up the necessary New York savvy by watching Alyson. She also enhanced her professional knowledge by taking courses at the New York School of Interior Design.

Just when it seemed calm waters were prevailing, Camilla's boat capsized again when she was 29.

The shrill sound woke her up at one A.M., dragging her back unwillingly from the depths of a dream. The telephone startled Rose, too, who covered her head with a pillow as Camilla reached over to pick up the phone that rested on the nightstand between their beds.

"Hello?"

She swung her feet onto the floor and turned on the light. It was an early autumn evening, still balmy and warm, but the news made her shiver.

Rose sat up as Camilla held the phone in her hands. "What's wrong? Who called?"

"The police. My parents… are…dead. Their car crashed through the barricade on Flagler Drive and sank to the bottom of Lake Worth."

The next morning Rose called in sick to *Marry Well* for both Camilla and herself. After hanging up with the office, Rose called Dr. Sanger. Although it had been seven years since Camilla last had seen her, the blue-haired Doris Sanger was the only psychiatrist whose name Rose knew, and she remembered how much she had meant to Camilla before.

Rose brought Camilla to Doris Sanger's apartment later that morning. In Doris' office, a desktop computer was surrounded by loose lined canary yellow pages covered in handwriting, and tattered manila file folders. Camilla felt dazed and numb, but managed a small smile for Dr. Sanger.

"Come back in an hour," Doris said to Rose, and then she explained to Camilla that she had retired from private practice to dedicate herself to research on the psychological trauma of rape victims. "You were my inspiration," she said to Camilla.

Camilla saw Doris every night after work for a month following her parents' funeral. All day long she repressed her grief, knowing that Alyson would consider it self-indulgent, but in the evenings, she broke down and let her feelings flow. The women bonded again as Doris supported Camilla through her crisis. Lurking beneath Camilla's sadness was a fear that her parents' death was punishment for something that she had done.

"Nonsense," Doris declared. "Life is full of ups and downs. Just when things look most bleak, something wonderful can happen. Why, just look how far you've come in the last ten years!"

When a Mr. Robert Madison called the apartment the following week, Rose answered and asked him what he wanted.

"This is a private matter concerning Ms. Merewether's parents' estate."

"I'm not sure she's ready for this... She's not materialistic. Never once have I heard her mention an inheritance."

"I understand. But she needs to know what's in the will. Can you bring Ms. Merewether in?"

Camilla, who had pieced together the gist from Rose's comments during the exchange, said loudly: "I can't, Rose, I can't."

"You heard that. She's distraught. Could you come here?" Rose asked.

There was a pause. "It's unusual…but I suppose I could. After work tomorrow?"

"Yes, that will have to do."

Robert Madison arrived shortly after dusk. He was so good-looking, long and lean, with direct blue eyes and bristly light brown hair cut short and fashionably styled to stand up with the help of Sumo hair wax, like a patch of freshly laid sod. He wore a loose-fitting dove gray suit, with a pale pink shirt, and a silver and black striped tie. The black Gucci loafers on his feet were scuffed just enough to take the new-edge off without making them appear dirty or worn.

Camilla had grown pale and gaunt from grief. Through eyelids swollen from crying, her glassy gaze settled beyond Robert and Rose, giving her the appearance of a sleepwalker or a ghost.

Robert reached into his briefcase and withdrew several objects: a wrapped gift, a letter, and a thick sheaf of official-looking documents. "Ms. Manna, could you excuse us please?"

Rose indignantly backed away, into the bedroom, where she kept the door ajar.

"Camilla, I grew up near you — in Jupiter. I attended Rosarian Academy while you were at Palm Beach Day. I met your parents five years ago at a cocktail party."

"Were our families friends?"

"No. I've been estranged from mine for years. I met your parents at a reception for one of Richard Faber's new projects —"

The mention of Rocky's name made Camilla wince. "Is he an acquaintance of yours?"

"I've never met him. A friend invited me to attend. Anyway, your father confided in me that since you left Palm Beach to attend Andover and then college in New York, you'd rarely returned. He respected you enormously, Camilla. Although he was...disappointed...he understood that children make their own way —"

At this, she started to cry again. Robert put his arm around her to comfort her. "I'm sorry," she said.

"It's OK." He was patient and gentle. When she paused, he added, "Your parents appointed me estate lawyer and co-executor with you of their wills — only for a couple of years, until you turn 31, of course. They said you would know all you needed to know by then. They wanted someone near where you chose to live to be there for you."

That would have been just like her parents, to thoughtfully consider what would be convenient for her. Robert wiped the tears from her eyes with a clean tissue; with his other hand, he passed her the letter. Camilla blew her nose and then tore the envelope open. It was in her mother's elegant script. It explained who Robert Madison was, that if she were reading this note they must be dead, that Camilla had been their gift from God, that they would watch her from heaven, and that she must be strong and move on.

The stationery fell from her fingers to the floor.

Robert handed her the gift.

"Is this from my parents too?"

"No, this is from me." He looked at her with kind, open eyes. "Your face is flushed. Are you feeling OK?" He was squinting at her.

She smiled. "I'm just embarrassed."

The package was oddly shaped and poorly wrapped, slapped together by an inexperienced hand. Camilla opened it slowly. It was a snow globe of Times Square; in it, a snowman tried to catch the New Year's ball. She looked at the giver quizzically.

"I know it's hokey, but I didn't want to come empty-handed. I expected you to be in mourning; I thought maybe it would cheer you up. Look to the future, not to the past."

"It's lovely. Thank you."

"Let's not discuss these papers now — I could come back in a few days when you've had some rest?"

"Yes, I'd prefer that."

Rose, who had apparently been listening to everything through the bedroom door, emerged as if on cue to see Robert out. "Cute," Rose said to Camilla when Robert had left. Her levity under such circumstances made Camilla smile.

Three days later, Robert returned. He explained the contents of her parents' wills with extreme care. As co-executors, together they would be responsible for investing her inheritance, most of which was tied up in the house on Seaspray, the remainder in stocks and bonds at Palm Beach County Trust.

"What about the house, Camilla?" Robert asked.

"Sell it."

"Are you sure?"

"Yes, I'm sure. I'll never go back there now."

"We've already had a query —" Robert said.

"So soon?"

"Ummm. Jeb Ramsey," he said looking at his notes. Then, shaking his head: "Some people read the obituaries every day, looking for… opportunities —"

The ambulance-chasing sound of that made her stomach queasy. "Oh, them. They've always loved the house. Sell."

"Don't you want to know how much?"

"I don't care."

The house was sold for $1.8 million in February of 2000, practically on the day that the first great bull market peaked, and a week before Camilla turned 30. After expenses were paid and the proceeds were added to the stocks and bonds, Camilla was left a minor heiress with approximately $2 million to her name. Robert and Camilla together decided to let her father's money manager at Palm Beach County Trust—one of his buddies from the Rotary Club—continue to oversee her finances while she concentrated on her career and recovery.

Most of her acquaintances from Andover and Barnard had begun to marry, move away, or fall by the wayside — victims of fast-changing friendships and lives so typical of people entering the fourth decade of life. The fear that Rose would follow the others reactivated her feelings of emptiness. It made her long more than ever for a lasting relationship with meaning, one she could invest in and trust.

Camilla came to lean heavily on Robert during the year following her parents' death. They grew closer, through common interests, like off-Broadway shows and Thai cuisine. He, Doris, and Rose became her extended family, offering unlimited support throughout her bereavement and recovery, slowly replacing the family she had lost.

One morning, Rose asked, "Have you slept with him yet?"

"Of course not. You'd be the first to know."

"Why not? It's been a year."

"It hasn't exactly been your average year, has it?" Camilla asked. "He's just gentle and sweet, we're friends…I guess he's taking his time."

"I hope he's not a fundamentalist — it doesn't sound normal to me," Rose said.

Camilla sighed.

"How do you define normal when it comes to sex?" Camilla asked Doris the next day.

"I would say a satisfying fulfillment of physical need between two people who love each other," Doris said, after brief reflection.

Camilla had not yet recovered completely from her past to allow herself to fall in love. But the loss of her parents brought out in her a fierce need for family, and she ached for the child she had lost. At 30, she had begun to feel haunted by the tick of her biological clock.

"I want to get married and have a family," she said.

"Then you will," Doris replied.

A few weeks later, Camilla decided to seduce Robert. The menu she planned — swordfish Diablo and lentil rice — was accompanied by a smooth bottle of Domaine Ott rosé. She splurged and bought him a silk bathrobe, and tucked a package of condoms into the pocket. The selection of his favorite band, The Offspring, played on the stereo in the background while she massaged his feet after the meal.

Robert turned out to be the antithesis of her only other experiences with sex — there was no roughness or urgency in his style. There seemed to be something he was holding back, but his reticence and tenderness suited her bruised psyche just fine. It wasn't very — "passionate," as Rose would say — but maybe that would come in time. When it was over, Robert held her in his arms and said nothing.

"Robert, is something wrong?" Maybe she wasn't very good at whatever women were supposed to do to men?

"Nothing's changed," he said. "We're loving friends. Confidants and pals. That's what couples — even husbands and wives — should be." He kissed her nose.

"Two people who love each other…" she repeated what Doris had said.

"That's right," Robert agreed.

After six months of courtship, Camilla asked Robert to marry her, telling him how badly she wanted a child, without confiding in him about the one she had lost.

Rose was against the marriage. "It sounds like a life of vanilla pudding to me. Where's the spice, the…lust?"

But never having tasted the tangs of which Rose spoke, Camilla found it easy to rationalize them away. Companionship and a child were things she could count on and control.

The morning of her wedding, a spectacular sunlit day, Rose made one last attempt to dissuade Camilla from going through with her plans.

"Do you believe I'm your best friend?" Rose asked.

"We will be best friends forever."

"Then here's my last best friend bulletin: Don't marry Robert."

"One thing has nothing to do with the other. Robert will never come between us."

"Oh I know that," Rose replied. "The marriage is cursed, Camilla. It is inauspicious." Rose was a serious disciple of astrology, numerology, and other sciences of the pseudo kind. In other ways she was so… practical… that Camilla had chalked those interests up to Rose's being from California.

"Now how do you know that?" Camilla asked Rose, thinking it better to humor her than challenge her beliefs.

"Chakrapani did your charts," Rose proclaimed, whispering as if a stranger might hear them.

"Rose, please, I can't plan my life by what your astrologer reads in the stars."

"The stars never lie," Rose said.

With finality, Camilla said: "I love you Rose, but I want this. I want a family."

So Camilla married Robert.

As the novelty of her new life began to wear off, the most wonderful thing happened — she got pregnant again!

The Future was the name of the chic new rental building where Camilla and Robert Madison lived. As Camilla strode past the dog walkers and nannies in the lobby of the building, she caught sight of her immense self in the tinted-mirror walls. She knew that her self-image was more diminished by her unchallenged mind than her horizontally challenged body; since starting her maternity leave a month earlier, she was at a loss as to how to fill her day. She imagined that once the baby arrived, the remainder of her six-month unpaid leave — the best deal she could negotiate with Alyson — would fly by faster than she cared to imagine.

"Six months!?" Alyson had screamed upon hearing Camilla's request. "No one, I mean NO ONE, has ever asked for more than two."

"Alyson," Camilla reminded her boss, "I'm the only female in the magazine's existence to have a baby, and one of the few to last more than nine months in her job."

"I didn't know anyone was keeping track. Do you notch your belt too?" Alyson retorted. "All right...six months, unpaid. But no extensions...or you're out!"

Camilla was still thinking about Alyson as she put her key in the lock and opened the door to her apartment. The jagged steel skyline view and palette in shades of shadows confronted her with some of the things she disliked most about New York — it was sharp, cold, and gray.

She stood at the window watching the November rain pour, as if someone had decided to turn all the swimming pools in Palm Beach upside down at once. At least there it was warm when it rained; here, in New York, it was cold rain, "pre-snow" she called it, without any of the magic of the white flakes she had fallen in love with when she first saw them at age 15.

Looking around the apartment, she wondered where the baby would fit when it arrived. Camilla had suggested moving, but Robert had been resolute: They could not afford a new place until she returned to work, so for now they would just have to make do.

"A baby can sleep in a drawer," he said, not looking at her when he said it.

It wasn't that Robert wasn't successful on his own. He was a seventh-year associate with the law firm of Irwin & Sanchez, just a step away from partner, not bad for 35. He was smart and he worked hard, lately incredibly hard, sometimes through the night. His prudence and frugality had begun when it became apparent that her inheritance had all but vanished, due to mismanagement by her father's old proxy from the Rotary Club.

Camilla naturally presumed that her father's stockbroker would conservatively invest her fortune, which he did, at first, in blue chip stocks, New York State tax-exempt bonds, and U.S. Treasuries. But once Robert and Camilla married, he viewed Camilla as financially secure, and switched strategies without her knowledge, reinvesting her funds in Nasdaq darlings like Akamai and CommerceOne, CMGI and Exodus, the latter a foreshadowing of her portfolio's fate. Those shares were already depressed at the time, in early 2001, and according to him, had nowhere to go but up.

Camilla should have known from experience that her father's judgment of people could be seriously flawed.

Now her one-time fortune had dwindled to a mere $157,280, but once more sloughing off the dead cells of fate, she reassured herself that there were lots of people worse off than she. Just the same, she had decided to fire Palm Beach County Trust and move the management of her account to New York, as soon as she was settled with the baby. She had started collecting brochures from brokerage firms and data from the Internet, on Morningstar rated mutual funds and MBIA insured bonds. Things would turn around, they always did, and when they did, she'd be ready.

39

She and Robert were far from destitute; they were relative newlyweds, with a baby on the way — a baby she could keep.

Thinking about her lost son made her feel guilty. Camilla had always intended to tell Robert about Rocky, and that other long-ago child, but had never found the right moment. Perhaps after their own baby was born. Yes, then she would tell him everything.

Maybe it was this guilt that made Camilla dial Robert's office, only to be disappointed by voice mail. For 20 minutes, she tried his cell phone and his business line, compulsively hitting the speed dial, urgently needing to hear his voice. With each ring that passed unanswered, her panic grew.

At Doris' suggestion, to make Camilla feel secure following her parents' death, she and Robert had made an agreement — he'd always call if his plans changed. If he didn't call, he knew she'd assume the worst. Because, unlike some people, they both knew that the worst could really happen to them.

The thought of losing Robert, too, was almost unbearable.

Camilla braced herself against the sofa arm and anxiously dug her fingers into the velvet nape while she thought about what she should do next. She felt the pressure of the baby's weight on her bladder and as she stood up to go to relieve herself, her water broke, seeping down her pants and onto the floor.

Camilla called Robert's numbers again, confirming that he was unreachable. She thought about calling all the hospitals, to inquire about accidents, but felt a sharp pain in her abdomen, so called her doctor instead, telling his service that it was an emergency. Finally, she gave in and called the one person whom she knew she could trust.

Rose's cell phone rang as she was in the checkout line at Fairway Foods. To answer it, she'd had to jostle her goat cheese and broccoli rabe, with which she intended to make a healthy quiche for supper from a recipe she found in the food section of *The New York Times.* In the process, she dropped an organic sheep's milk yogurt, which splattered on the floor nearby.

"Shit!" she screamed into the receiver.

"Rose, it's me," Camilla said.

"Hold on."

An elderly woman who stood behind Rose on the line wagged her finger, furious at Rose, who apologized and stepped out of the line to talk to Camilla.

"This better be important," she said. "You just set my dinner back 40 minutes."

"It is," Camilla said. "It's the baby. My water broke."

"Where's Robert?" Rose asked.

"I don't know. I can't find him," Camilla answered. "Rose, I'm worried."

"Hang on, honey. I'm on my way," she said, dumping her ingredients in the reject cart by the register as she dashed out the door.

While Camilla was waiting for Rose to arrive, she tried hard not to think she was cursed. If she lost Robert or their baby or both she just didn't know what she would do.

The doorman buzzed, but before Camilla could say, "Send her up," Rose was at her door.

"Let's go," Rose said. She had brought Camilla a bagel — oat bran and whole wheat — from H&H, near where they used to live.

41

"I'm scared, Rose," Camilla said.

"I know, honey. It's OK now. Eat. You'll feel better." Rose thought food fixed everything.

Camilla's face contorted. "Eating is the last thing I can do."

The cab ride up First Avenue was stop-and-go. Camilla grimaced as the cab hit a pothole.

"You OK?" Rose asked.

"I think so," she said. But she was unconvincing; in truth she was worried for the baby, because her water had broken a month too early.

"Rose, I have to tell you something," Camilla said as they pulled into the horseshoe driveway in front of Riverview Hospital. And she told her about the promise Robert had made and how he had always called her before when his plans changed. Tonight, Robert wasn't where he was supposed to be and she had no idea where he was.

"Camilla, honey — I'm sure he's fine. He's a Young Turk... They have to work all the time. And remember, he's not expecting the baby until next month."

"You're probably right. He's probably just out to dinner with a colleague."

"Sure," Rose agreed.

But they were both worried now.

Camilla's obstetrician, Dr. Rosenkrantz, was waiting for them in the Riverview Hospital emergency room. While he negotiated for an examining room, a large, young African-American girl was rushed into the ER in labor. She was treated badly, Camilla noted, as soon as it became apparent that she had no health insurance.

There was so much commotion in the ER — a stab wound, an Alzheimer's case, an accident where a woman got crushed by a souvlaki cart that had detached from the hinges of a car speeding through an intersection — that it took Dr. Rosenkrantz 20 minutes to get Camilla on a gurney. By then, active labor had begun.

As two green-clad orderlies rolled Camilla away, Rose continued to call Robert's numbers. She left messages at the office, on the cell phone and on the apartment's answering machine, the only possession Robert had actually brought to the marriage.

"You'll have to turn that thing off now," a passing intern told Rose. "It interferes with the equipment."

Rose followed Camilla into the examining room, a sterile dormitory-like chamber with lots of high-tech machines, and held her hand as Camilla was hooked up to the fetal monitor and IV drip. Camilla dug her fingernails into Rose's palm, but Rose's face remained placid and calm.

The technician had been double-checking the sonogram screen while Dr. Rosenkrantz examined her. Now they both stared at the monitor.

"Camilla, the baby is in distress. Just sit tight while I try to secure a delivery room."

Merry Rose Madison was born at 11:08 P.M. on November 8th. On the sly, Rose consulted Chakrapani, who declared the date to be high on his rating scale of auspicious birthdays. Rose asked whether the repetition of the numbers eleven and eight in both the date and time of birth were fortuitous. Eleven, he explained, has the quality of enlightenment and eight of material success, but that this was irrelevant. What really mattered was that Jupiter was in the 4th house.

When Dr. Rosenkrantz first held her daughter up in the air, Camilla had a momentary attack of panic, because the beautiful blue-eyed baby made not a single sound.

"Is she healthy?" an exhausted Camilla asked.

"Her Apgar score is a nine," the doctor replied. "Almost unheard of for a preemie."

"Will that help get her into college?" Rose asked.

"Maybe nursery school," Dr. Rosenkrantz replied. "Which in New York City is much harder than the Ivy League."

Then they all looked at Merry who, against all odds, gave them a wide toothless smile. She was bathed and swaddled by two jolly nurses and taken away to the nursery as Camilla was wheeled into recovery. Camilla was dazed and exhausted. Her joy at having delivered a perfect baby was spoiled by her mounting concern over Robert. In her sleep, she had horrible dreams about bombed-out houses and yachts moored offshore, refusing help to the refugees.

Rose had gone home to sleep, and when Camilla woke up the next morning, it was Robert who was holding her hand. He kissed her gently. He smelled sweaty and yeasty, like beer.

"I'm sorry," he said. He looked contrite.

"What are you sorry for?" Camilla asked, relieved and enraged at the same time.

"That I wasn't here for…"

Before he could finish, Camilla interrupted. "Where were you?"

"I was out with clients. My cell phone didn't work in the restaurant."

"What restaurant?"

"Why?"

Camilla wanted to remind him of his promise to always let her know where he would be, and how frightened she had been when he hadn't called and couldn't be reached. But she held back. She could give him the benefit of the doubt, and assume he had forgotten his word. But she knew him too well — he had been out of touch because he wanted to be. Even when they occupied the same room, he could be absent. Where had he been? Where, in fact, was he now?

"I was worried sick, that's why."

"Nothing to worry about. Here I am," he smiled, his even teeth looking as if they had been made to order.

"Robert," she said, "have you seen her?"

"Yes. I've held her. She looks just like you." He smiled.

"Funny. I think she looks like you," Camilla said.

"Well, yeah. But I can tell she has your character."

The nurse brought the baby in for a feeding. Merry was eager, and her bright eyes darted around taking in everything while she sucked; unlike some babies Camilla had seen who closed their eyes and drifted off.

"See what I mean," Robert said. "She misses nothing — just like you."

Camilla doubted that; her life had been clouded by missed cues and missteps.

"That is a skill I learned in New York," Camilla said, fleetingly thinking of Alyson. "I doubt very much I had it as a baby." She squeezed his hand; despite their differences, she still cared deeply for him. He was her husband, the father of her child, her loving friend. "Robert?"

"Yes?"

Camilla felt his uneasiness; he was trying to be kind, gentle, and attentive but she could tell something was bothering him. He kept avoiding her eyes, looking at the door. "Is something wrong?" she asked.

He tried to conceal his tears, rubbing his eyes with his thumb and index finger, making them even more bloodshot than they already were. "Allergies," he said unconvincingly.

"In November?"

As they had planned for months, Robert brought his pajamas and would spend the night. Dr. Rosenkrantz had arranged a private corner room with a full bath, one of only two on the maternity ward at Riverview. Robert slept on a cot, and the next morning, the three of them — Camilla, Robert, and Merry — watched *Friends* reruns and counted the bouquets of flowers and colorful balloons attached to jelly bean-filled baby bottles that started to arrive.

Doris Sanger had sent irises the color of her hair, with a cryptic note that read: "Happiness is relative."

"What do you think she means?" Camilla asked Robert. He shrugged in reply.

The view from the bed was out toward Roosevelt Island across the East River. The stormy night skies had turned to a glorious sunny day so bright that Camilla could see the particles of moisture lit up like sparklers against a wall of cerulean blue.

The doctor came in to make his rounds around two P.M., declaring mother and child well. Robert had showered and dressed while Camilla was being examined, and now he interrupted the doctor, in an awkward and hurried way, to plant a kiss on Camilla's forehead. When she looked up at him, his eyes were again filled with tears.

"I'll call you later," he said as he walked out the door.

"Young fathers these days are very emotional," Dr. Rosenkrantz observed. "In my day, they exhibited bravado and passed out cigars."

Camilla thought it was supposed to be the mother who exhibited hormonal swings of emotion.

"Whatever happened to that other mother, the young one, who was admitted at the same time as me?" Camilla asked, curious and concerned.

"Which one?" he asked.

"She was alone, and scared. She was underdressed, for the weather, in a red t-shirt and jeans —"

"That mother is still in labor," Dr. Rosenkrantz said.

"Still? How awful."

"She's a staff patient, Camilla. And she's uninsured. She'll be assigned to the teaching ward, and I imagine it will be the residents who deliver her."

"Doctor? See those flowers over there? The blue irises? Please ask the nurse to take the card out and deliver them to her. Tell her they're for good luck. From a friend."

Rose called her from the office at four and Camilla told her in awe about all the flowers and gifts they had received, so quickly, even from Doris. Rose admitted that she had e-mailed the news to all Camilla's friends as soon as she had gotten home the night before. "You are loved by many," Rose said.

"Guess so." But she didn't feel it.

Robert called that evening from the office to say that he had to work late, again, and wouldn't be by. He would be sleeping at home because he found it difficult to function during the day after the noise and commotion on the maternity ward at night.

"I'm working on a big case," he said. "When will you be coming home?"

"I guess I'm lucky. Because of the premature delivery, Merry and I get to stay four days. Other new mothers get thrown out after 48 hours." She wondered if the young girl was still there.

On the second day, Camilla was encouraged to walk around to get her circulation flowing. It was painful to move, but she put on her slippers and new mauve robe and shuffled slowly down the hall. In the center of the maternity ward, there was a large open room and she saw the girl from the ER in a stainless steel bed, hooked up to an IV. Even from the linoleum-clad hallway, she could hear sobs ricocheting off the sterile white walls. Camilla hobbled in as best she could.

"Hi there." She gripped the metal bed frame. It was ice-cold to touch. "I'm Camilla. I just had a baby too." The girl stopped crying. Camilla rested a hand on her shoulder. "What's your name?" she asked.

"Chantal. My name is Chantal." Camilla noticed the irises on the nightstand near the bed. The petals had started to curl.

"That's a beautiful name. It sounds French."

"Have you had your baby?" Chantal asked.

"A baby girl. We're calling her Merewether …in honor of my parents," Camilla said. "And you?"

Chantal started weeping again. "It died. Stillborn."

Camilla wondered if that long labor had anything to do with it. "Oh, I'm so sorry, Chantal. How old are you?"

"Sixteen," Chantal said.

Camilla remembered when she had been about Chantal's age and pregnant. Then, it had seemed that no one in the world was as unlucky as she was. But she'd had her mother, and the beautiful tranquility of a Nantucket summer, and superb prenatal care, and health insurance — and her baby had survived. He was cared for and loved by a good family, *somewhere*.

"You can be a mother many times over. God works in mysterious ways. Things that may seem horrible at first can turn out to be for the best. Does the father know?"

"No one knows. I come from Washington DC. I ran away when I found out, and I've been living with my cousin on 106th Street ever since."

The nurse stood at the foot of the bed and eyed Camilla suspiciously. "Listen, Chantal. Give me your phone number. I would like to call you if you don't mind."

"We don't have a phone. But you're real nice to offer."

Camilla borrowed a pencil from the nurse and wrote down her number. "Then you call me, Chantal. Soon as you're up and about."

Later, when Rose came by for dinner, they invited Chantal over to Camilla's room and ordered in Chinese food from Foo King, Rose's favorite restaurant downtown. Poor Merry got indigestion from the garlic in Camilla's breast milk, and Camilla felt awful the next day. But she and Rose agreed that the Chinese picnic did wonders for Chantal's spirits. Camilla went to visit her room again the next morning, but the bed Chantal had occupied was empty as a grave.

Robert called at 9 A.M. and not at all the next day. Camilla was devastated by his neglect, making up excuses for him ranging from his big case to his insecurity about his fathering skills. Rose didn't even ask where he was when Camilla called and asked Rose to pick her and Merry up to take them home. Rose just showed up, with a car baby seat in tow.

As soon as they walked into the apartment, Camilla knew that something was changed. The air was stale, as if no one had been breathing it for days. In the bedroom, Robert's closets were empty and his vacated dresser drawers were left askew.

"He even took the toothpaste," Camilla said, looking through the bathroom door, noticing that the large box of condoms was gone too. "And it was the only tube."

Then she spotted the note leaning up against the bowl of five-day-old rotten fruit on the table in the corner.

Camilla read it, then handed Rose the note:

Dear Camilla –

While this may seem the worst time to tell you, there could never be a good time and I think it best if you and the baby have a clean start. I'm not the father you want for your daughter anyway. It's not you…it's just that I've met someone else. We are in love and moving away. I will always care for you and I hope that someday we can be friends.

I cannot tell you how sorry I am.

Robert

Camilla sank into the couch. She lifted Merry from the car seat and held her in her arms, kissing the soft spot on her head. The baby was asleep and blissfully unaware.

"What an asshole!" Rose said.

"What do I do now?" Camilla asked.

"Is your name on the lease?" Rose asked.

"If it is, I didn't sign it," Camilla said.

"Then let's pack."

While Merry slept in her car seat, Camilla moved like an automaton, throwing only her most important possessions into the suitcase Rose had laid out on the bed. A photo album, with pictures from her childhood in Palm Beach, brought back distant memories — biking to school, Sunday brunches after church, walks on the Lake Trail, and especially the tall, stalwart trees on Royal Palm Way that she had secretly named after the Roman emperors. It all seemed now like a tale she had heard rather than a life she had once led. *Happiness is relative…*

Between two sweaters she placed her graduation picture from Andover, where she imagined her classmates from there as happily married mothers with husbands who never let them down. The scrimshaw trinkets and lobster bibs from Nantucket and Boston, where she had spent her summers engaged in study programs and part-time jobs, reminded her of how much promise she'd once had.

Rose held up their Barnard College yearbook. "Maybe Merry will carry on the tradition?"

"I hope her life is nothing like mine," Camilla said.

To honor Camilla's wedding two years before, Alyson Strong had sent a wedding gift, and she found the note among her things. The gift had been a yearlong subscription to *Marry Well* with a prescient message penned in Alyson's indomitable style: "I can tell you haven't been reading our pages religiously …better luck next time!"

Camilla showed it to Rose who threw it in the trash.

Camilla picked it out. The note landed in purgatory — neither the suitcase nor the garbage, but her pocket instead.

"Is that everything?" Rose asked Camilla.

"Everything I can carry." She glanced in the direction of her mother's heirloom silver, Bernardaud china, and Baccarat crystal, boxed and stacked in the closet on the top shelves, and the wedding gifts from all their acquaintances, which she'd have to come back for.

That little suitcase held everything else — her whole portable past, her entire life up until that point — not much at all.

Chapter Three

The only reason Camilla now got up in the mornings was Merry. Otherwise she would have buried herself under the down comforters and willed herself to stop breathing. Rose's declarations that Robert wasn't good enough for her, or that his was a case of arrested development, fell on deaf ears and a cloud of depression. She was convinced that Robert didn't love her because she wasn't lovable; Rocky had raped her because she deserved it; her parents had been killed as her punishment for being raped; and she had been deprived of ever knowing the fate of her first child by the timing of her parents' death.

It was almost too much to bear. She felt like Job.

Her post-childbirth stomach was distended and her arms and legs still bloated, appearing more like the underbellies of beached seals than the limbs of a human being. Her breasts felt like water balloons and her nipples were raw and cracked from her struggle to breastfeed Merry. She developed a fever, and only through sheer determination and a washcloth filled with chipped ice that she sucked on every time she nursed her baby, did she get through the milk fever to the point where the fluid flowed freely and Merry was sated.

Camilla wept for weeks and barely ate a thing. Rose prepared macrobiotic and ayurvedic recipes such as basmati rice with ghee and kapha fava beans over tofu, and reminded her that she needed the vitamins and calories for Merry. While Rose was at work, Camilla slept when the baby slept, and the rest of the time, she watched TV and flipped half-heartedly through back issues of *Marry Well*. Under the masthead, she regarded the magazine's mission — *to focus on the most pressing, important, challenging and satisfying aspect of a woman's life...to Marry Well* — with contempt.

Alyson Strong had called once, when Camilla didn't return to work as scheduled. She was unsympathetic to Camilla's vague explanations, asserting that the motherhood bug, which carried a disease that ravaged the ranks of well-educated and talented women in plague-like proportions, had bitten Camilla. "We have a job to do here, Camilla. You can't expect us to wait," Alyson said, her voice straining with impatience.

Apathy prevailed and Camilla said: "A girl's gotta do what a girl's gotta do." The irony of the quote seemed lost on Alyson.

The 400 extra calories a day that Camilla burned by nursing Merry, and the Spartan diet that she had unintentionally placed herself on, returned her to her pre-pregnancy size in months. She knew she should take Merry out for a stroll in Riverside Park or down Broadway, but she couldn't motivate herself to move, using as an excuse that the blustery air wasn't good for a small child. Christmas came and went, as well as the New Year; if Rose hadn't planned a small party, the holidays would have passed without notice.

Rose bought Merry a toy stove and a set of green plastic pots. For Camilla, she found a needlepoint pillow that read:

"Women are like tea bags. They only know how strong they are when they're in hot water."

"I should call you Chamomile, like the tea," Rose said.

Camilla smiled weakly. "Don't you dare!"

Although she appreciated Rose's effort, she still felt wretched. If only a big white sanitation truck would roll by and whisk her away. But then Merry would wake up and need her, giving her a reason to live after all.

Camilla came to think of herself as a hibernating bear and of Merry as her cub, whom she had to protect with a fierceness kindled by the fire deep within her. This drive was what eventually turned her around, providing both the warmth and energy to thaw her paralysis. Slowly, slowly she became ready to reemerge.

Finally, one freezing Saturday morning in February, shortly before Camilla's 32nd birthday, Rose sensed that the tipping point had arrived. She pulled Camilla out of bed, washed her face and dressed her in her own clothes, a morose black turtleneck and jeans, which for once suited Camilla's predisposition just fine.

"Camilla, enough. We're going out."

"Where to?" Camilla asked, uninspired.

"We're going shopping. Let's go to Zabar's and Fairway. Then we'll eat lunch, at Isabella's, frittatas with red bell peppers and chives. And then we'll take Merry to the Museum of Natural History," Rose said.

"Really Rose, that sounds exhausting. And Merry, she's too little —"

"Nonsense. She needs the stimulation. And you've moped around long enough. Merry is the only good thing to come from your marriage to Robert Madison and you get to keep her. Think how lucky you are."

Lucky? She was anything but lucky.

But maybe Rose was right. It was time, as her mother's letter had advised, to be strong and move on. She'd start by calling Doris Sanger as soon as the weekend was over; she was willing to let Doris help her again.

Rose took the handles and Camilla grabbed the wheels of the Peg Perego stroller Rose had bought as a baby gift, as they backed down the six flights of stairs. They moved slowly and carefully, giving Camilla's senses time to absorb the tiny piece of torn carpet on the stair, the waterlogged wallpaper on the ceiling, the chipped wood on the banister.

"Who are your neighbors now?" Camilla asked.

"The studio across the hall is for sale," Rose replied. "My friends Cody and Felix live on the fifth floor below. I see most of the other owners from time to time, young singles or couples — and old Mrs. Crenshaw. Remember her? She's still renting 2A— but we hardly speak. Why do you ask?"

"Curious really. Seems the place is falling apart."

"You miss nothing, I see. Everyone works. No time for repairs."

When they exited onto West 76th Street, Camilla squinted from the brilliant mid-winter sun. Merry laughed, her first laugh, which made both Camilla and Rose comment at once: "She's true to her name!" And she laughed again as if to prove the point.

"Rose, what am I going to do?"

"I don't know," Rose replied. "But you've got to come up with something. You've always been my role model, Camilla. No matter how many times you get kicked down, you always seem to get up again — stronger, better, with new ideas."

"This time it's different," Camilla said.

"Why is that?"

Camilla couldn't think of a single real reason, so she stated the obvious excuses: "No parents, no husband, no job —"

"So?" Rose replied.

On the scale of catastrophic events — war, cyclones, murder, rape, parents dying in car crashes — having your husband leave you rates pretty low. "I get your point, Rose."

"How are your finances?"

"Since November they've dwindled down to just $150,000. At this rate, I'll soon be broke."

"Don't worry about that. You can stay with me as long as you need to."

"I appreciate that, really…but I know what you earn and you can't afford a wife and child."

They walked silently for a few blocks, lost in thought and the blaring of the traffic on Broadway.

"I can ask Alyson. She might take you back," Rose said.

Camilla's face brightened; then darkened again. "I doubt it. You know how she is. If you disobey her, she treats you like she's a lover scorned. And to not return after maternity leave…that reinforces every prejudice she has. Besides, Prissie Easton got my old job. She's good too."

"What else could you do?"

"That's not the problem — I can learn anything. It's Merry. And balance. She has no father, so I need to — want to — be present."

"OK. Let's analyze this. First, you need to make money, right?"

"Wrong. First, I need to be accessible to Merry. Second, I need to make money." She would show Robert Madison that she didn't need him.

"And…?"

"That means I need a job with high income potential, complete flexibility, no travel, no limits for growth, no advanced degrees —"

"Camilla, that job doesn't exist," Rose said. She tucked the blanket a little tighter under Merry's chin.

"I admit it sounds like a long shot," Camilla said, feeling glum again.

"Look, I don't like numbers or computers or sales. I like to cook. But you've got the skills to make tougher career choices."

"But writing about decorating is the only thing I know."

"What about your dad's business? You're always telling me how much you learned from him."

Camilla had picked up a lot from her father; she was comfortable with numbers and sales. Being comfortable and being in demand, however, were two different things.

By the time they got to Isabella's on 77th Street and Columbus, Merry had sunk deep into her baby blankets in the stroller and was fast asleep. Only her translucent eyelids and pink hat, with a fluffy pom-pom almost as big as her head, peeked out.

The restaurant was a blinding vision of bleached wood and bright lights. Camilla started to feel alive again for the first time in months.

Merry opened her eyes and looked around, taking in the activity around her. Rose had been right; Merry needed the stimulation. Camilla vowed right then and there to take her everywhere she could.

"Do you miss him?" Rose asked Camilla.

"Robert?" Camilla shifted uneasily in her seat. Her ego had been bruised, her self-esteem shot. There had been moments during the past three months when she had been in true despair. But, if she were honest, it wasn't Robert she missed. It wasn't Robert she wanted back; it was her own life. "Not anymore," she concluded.

The conversation broadened to include movies and books and theater and people; all of which Camilla has missed during her isolation. After another hour, they paid the bill and bundled up against the frosty winter air. Camilla stood tall and stretched.

"Rose, do you mind if we skip the museum and stop by The Future? I need to check for mail and pick up a few things from the apartment."

"No, honey. Good idea. Let's walk. It'll do us both good."

They entered the Park beside Tavern on the Green and walked east and south, passing the Children's Zoo and Wollman Rink on the way. They continued downtown on Fifth Avenue and past the windows of Lord & Taylor, with its motorized cupids dancing behind the glass, making Camilla realize that it was almost Valentine's Day — where had the New Year gone? She hadn't noticed it passing at all; she looked back on it now as an opportunity to celebrate that she had let go by.

"I'm looking at this career thing the wrong way, Rose," Camilla said. "Rather than trying to dream up the perfect job and then find it, I should be sourcing opportunities and needs in the marketplace and then invent the job that fulfills them best."

"I may be a half-baked cooking editor, but whatever are you talking about?" Rose asked.

"I'm not sure yet but I know I'm on the right track."

Once back in The Future, most of the mail was for Robert, so Camilla decided to leave it behind in case he called the building to have it sent. There was a letter for her from a lawyer — Bernard Grossman — asking that she call to work out a suitable settlement to facilitate the divorce. The form letter stated in the reference line that Case # 34025 was called Madison vs. Madison.

In the apartment, she sadly noticed that the only legacy Robert had left was the Panasonic answering machine he had come to the marriage with. Rose and Merry were looking out the window at the skyscraper view when Camilla pressed the button on the machine.

"Camilla, hi, it's me Chantal," said the first message. There were three more like it, the last left over a month before. Camilla saw how Merry smiled every time she heard the sound of Chantal's voice.

"How awful," Camilla said. "She must think me so insincere. As if I cavalierly said 'Let's have lunch' or something, without really meaning it."

"Why don't you call her? She left her number at work, didn't she? Some day care center."

Camilla played back the messages and wrote down the information. Little Tots in East Harlem. "Yes," Camilla said, "I'll call and explain."

The last message was from Doris, who was off on a trip: "I'm attending a human rights symposium on the West Coast. Hope you and Merry are well. Will call again."

Then she took a deep breath and packed up what she had really come to get. The silver-plated tea set, the Steuben candlesticks and Tiffany serving trays, all the wedding gifts of value, which, when added to her diamond engagement ring and gold wedding band, would probably raise a tidy sum from the man with the beard on 47th Street. At the last minute, the only items she couldn't part with were those that her mother had left her, the family silverware, china, and crystal.

"Camilla, don't —" Rose started to say when she realized her friend intended to sell the valuables she was then packing up.

"Why keep this stuff now?" Camilla asked. "It's tainted. And, besides, we could use the money."

When Camilla settled into the taxi with Merry snuggled in her lap, she closed her eyes. She had gone through a range of responses to her abandonment — depression, humiliation, and anger — but they were passing now. In truth, Robert Madison hadn't been the one for her. She had her baby to love and protect, and she had to find a place in the world where she could realize her own hopes and dreams, and maybe somewhere along the way, there would also be passion. It was time to get on with her life.

Camilla sent an e-mail to Alyson Strong at *Marry Well* as soon as she got home. As difficult as she could be, Alyson had always thought highly of Camilla and had never hesitated to praise her work. Camilla asked to see Alyson, and hinted that she was looking for a job, but wanted to explain her circumstances. Next, she made a list of the people she needed to call in the morning: Chantal; the real estate agent for the studio next door; Robert's lawyer; Doris; and Irwin & Sanchez about the medical insurance. And then she tapped out a list of the income she would need to cover her expenses. By the time she gave Merry her midnight feeding, she was spent.

"Be a good baby, Merry," she said as she looked into her child's spirited blue eyes. "Please sleep through the night."

And she did.

Rose whipped up a cream cheese omelet for breakfast, with sliced strawberries on the side. Camilla and Merry wandered sleepy-eyed from the bedroom, roused by the smell of butter bubbling in the pan and water gurgling through freshly ground coffee beans in the cone of the automatic drip.

"I'm in a bit of a hurry, so you'll have to do the dishes alone. Alyson's coming back from Florida and called a meeting for nine," Rose said as they finished eating.

"What was she up to in Florida?"

"No one knows for sure, but we suspect it has something to do with Mr. Diamond Necklace."

"Still? What does her husband have to say?"

"He's been out of town, but if you ask me, he's too sharp not to notice something's up. Maybe their marriage is strictly business."

Camilla put down her fork. She lifted Merry out of the stroller seat where she had placed her. She held her close and said, "What benefits could he possibly be getting out of the relationship, to make him stay if he knows?"

"Beats me," Rose said. "She's smart, exciting, connected. She's a trophy wife. Maybe sex isn't his thing, so he lets her get it elsewhere."

Camilla knew that despite the popular image of men as lustful creatures, many men just didn't like sex much. Like Robert, for instance.

"Rose, I called the broker for the studio next door."

"What for? We have plenty of room."

"You haven't slept in weeks, except for last night. With your orange hair and black rings around your eyes, you look like a raccoon dressed up for Halloween."

"Thanks a lot."

"A beautiful one, of course."

"How do you plan to pay for it?"

"I'm going to sell what's left of the NASDAQ stocks — they've moved up three percent since I last checked — and I got $10,000 for the wedding presents," Camilla explained, watching Rose's face register relief. They both knew the worst was over.

"You have been busy," Rose remarked.

"That's not all. I called Irwin & Sanchez too — Robert has relocated to the Los Angeles office," Camilla said.

"Weren't Tasmania or Siberia available?" Rose asked, angrier with Robert than Camilla had ever been.

"Well, the good news is Merry and I are still covered by medical insurance. As long as we're legally married that is."

"What do you mean by that?"

"I called Robert's divorce lawyer today, Mr. Grossman. He offered me $2,000 a month in alimony payments and child support."

"How much does Robert earn?"

"His salary is $210,000, plus bonus."

"What? And they offered you $24,000?"

"Grossman referred me to *New York* magazine's issue on 'How to Live in New York on a Shoestring'. He said: 'Take it or leave it…' or I could get a lawyer and 'maybe in five or six years he'd see us in court.'"

"Let's get a big shot divorce lawyer. I'll ask Alyson. She knows them all."

"Do you know what that would cost? And Robert and I were only married for two years. No, Rose, my mind is made up. I accepted the offer, plus guaranteed health insurance, a lump sum settlement of $25,000 — that's half his 401K — and life insurance, with Merry as the beneficiary."

"Great! We can poison his soup —"

Camilla laughed with Merry close behind. "I've decided to cut my losses and move on, Rose. It's better that way. Better for me and way better for Merry."

"What about visitation rights?"

"Grossman advised him to waive them in exchange for a quick financial settlement."

"The bastard doesn't even want to see his own child?"

"It would only 'complicate his life,' according to Grossman. I discussed it with Doris last night. She said it's sad but not unusual. That four out of ten children in America — more than 23 million — grow up without fathers, and as long as they receive love from other sources, they turn out OK."

The real estate agent was 25 minutes late for the appointment. She caught her too-high heel on the loose piece of carpet on the stairs and Camilla heard her swearing through the door. Deirdre Tortile from The Griffin Group real estate firm broke the nail on her index finger on the intricate zodiac door-knocker Rose had hung, so the first thing she said to Camilla when Camilla pulled open the door was *"Stupid!"*

"I mean my nail," she explained, holding up a jagged acrylic tip. "Not you."

"No problem," Camilla said.

"You the babysitter here?" Deirdre asked, eyeing Merry curiously.

"This is Merry. I am her mother. My best friend Rose lives here," Camilla replied. "We used to live here together before I got married. Then when the building went co-op, Rose bought our old apartment at the insider's price."

"I hope you're not expecting that same discount. Those days are gone, along with short skirts and IPOs."

Deirdre went to tickle Merry under the chin but must have scratched her instead because, uncharacteristically, Merry let out a howl. Deirdre recoiled, especially when it became obvious Merry needed a diaper change immediately. She suggested that they meet across the hall in five minutes.

Once inside the apartment, Deirdre turned on the lights and positioned the portable tape recorder on the kitchen counter. She pressed the play button with one of her good nails and adjusted the volume so that the forest sounds of chirping birds and rustling leaves would drown out the traffic noises once she opened the sole window to air the place out.

"I'm so sorry I was late," Deirdre said. "The traffic was awful." Camilla guessed that she was in her mid-forties, with wavy auburn hair cut just below the ears. She was wearing a brown wrap-around cotton knit dress, à la Diane Von Furstenberg, which accentuated every lump. A safety pin held the v-neck together, revealing Deirdre's feeble attempt at modesty.

It didn't take Camilla long to look around, the apartment was so small. "How much does the owner want for this place?" Camilla asked.

"It's a sponsor unit. The owner turned the building into a co-op on a non-eviction plan. The rent-controlled tenant moved out a few months ago." Camilla knew from her father that "sponsor" was a fancy name for "owner." "Because it's a sponsor unit, you're not subject to the usual co-op board restrictions, for instance, you can finance up to 90 percent."

"How much are they asking?"

"Some buildings don't allow babies, pianos, dogs, even smoking now —"

"What did you say the price was?" Camilla looked at Merry fussing in her arms. She was not smiling.

"Not to get personal or anything, but I don't see a wedding ring. Are you still married?"

"Separated."

"Are you employed?"

"Is it legal for you to ask me these questions?" Camilla asked.

Deirdre flushed. "The listing price is $190,000. The release price is $180,000 — that's the price the sponsor's bank will let him sell at. The monthly maintenance comes to $845.15 a month. A steal!"

"Can I work at home?" That was always an option Camilla wanted to leave open.

"Short of dealing drugs or turning tricks, you can do what you want."

Camilla did some rough calculations in her head: $150,000 in stocks, $25,000 from Robert, and $10,000 from the wedding gifts. "I'll take it."

"You have $180,000?"

"Not today...but I will —"

"Listen, you're a nice girl. I like you. But I can't tie up an apartment waiting for you to get turned down for a mortgage. Go get the money and if this unit isn't sold yet, I'll draw up a contract." The soothing nature sound tape was over and the recorder clicked off so loudly, it sounded as if a tree fell. Deirdre put the tape player in her purse.

"Are you so strict with all your customers?" Camilla asked.

"Not if they have cash. Cash is king," Deirdre said as she double-locked the door behind her. Before she left, she smiled supportively at Camilla, reaching into her purse for a pen and scrap of paper "Here. Call this number and tell John Confrere that I sent you. If anyone can get you a mortgage, he can. I'll do my best to hold the apartment until I hear from you."

Camilla heard her swear again as Deirdre caught her heel on the rug on the stairs for a second time. She had an edge to her, but Camilla liked her anyway. It struck her that Deirdre Cortile was the type of person who said what she thought, tough but good-natured. She felt she could trust her; but then again, if she wanted to live next door to Rose, what choice did she have?

That morning quickly turned into a beautiful March afternoon with the promise of spring in the air. Camilla carried Merry and the stroller down the six flights of stairs and decided to walk through Central Park to the JPMorgan Chase branch on East 46th Street, where John Confrere worked. Camilla ate a pretzel on a bench in front of the carousel, while she watched it go round and round. A plan was spinning in her head, and when she saw a young girl reach for the golden ring as her carousel horse rode by, she realized it was time for her to do the same.

With renewed energy, she proceeded to JPMorgan Chase. On the way, she noticed several homeless people warming themselves on steam grates and picking through garbage pails for redeemable bottles and cans. They had jobs to do, purpose in life, favorite haunts, and enjoyed beautiful weather just like everybody else.

"Excuse me," Camilla said, as she approached a serious-looking man, about 35, with thinning hair and a scratchy moustache, who was sitting at the desk with a sign that said "Mortgages." "Are you John Confrere?"

He searched her face, looking for clues. "Have we met?"

"No. Deirdre Cortile from The Griffin Group sent me."

Recognition registered on his face. "Have a seat."

John's phone rang and Camilla heard him discussing fixed-rate mortgages and amortization schedules. When he finished his call, he turned his attention back to her.

"I'm interested in buying an apartment. A studio in a co-op, it's a sponsor unit. Deirdre says I can have it for $180,000."

He whistled. She had also found it hard to believe that one room could cost so much.

"I'll need a mortgage —"

"How much do you need to borrow?" he asked.

"Maybe I'd better fill you in on my situation first, then you can tell me how much I'm eligible for." For the next 20 minutes, Camilla described her predicament to John. She told him about Robert, and her finances, and Rose. He listened attentively the entire time, with his hands folded on his desk. Camilla noticed that his fingers were long, his knuckles square, and his cuticles perfectly groomed. When she was done, he fiddled with his calculator, after which he informed her that her net worth was $185,000 and change, a fact of which she was already aware.

He looked at her kindly and said, "You have enough cash to qualify for a mortgage of at least 50 percent. What did you say you did for a living again?"

"Right now, I'm considering my options: I could go back to writing — I'm seeing my former boss tomorrow —"

"So you don't have a job?"

"Not yet."

"Listen, Ms. Madison. With alimony and child support payments of only $2,000 per month, of which a portion goes to taxes, I don't see how you could carry a mortgage, monthly maintenance charges, insurance, child care —"

"John, please call me Camilla. I know. I need your help in determining how much I need to earn, and how to package myself in a loan application.

Then leave it to me — I guarantee you that by the end of this month, I'll have what I need to proceed." She hoped what she was saying was true. Alyson had been reluctant to meet with her, putting her off for days; but with Alyson, she knew that was probably a deliberate ploy to establish the balance of power early.

The time gap turned out to be a boon. Alyson's delay had inadvertently given Camilla the time she needed to formulate a plan, a market-ready opportunity, a big idea — something that she hoped Alyson would feel *Marry Well* couldn't do without.

Camilla watched John drum his long fingers on the desk while he weighed what she had said.

"I believe you," he said. "I'll do what I can. Did you bring proof of your assets?"

The question made Camilla realize that as of her 32nd birthday two weeks before, a milestone that passed uncelebrated, she had been sole executor of her parents' estate for a whole year without exercising her power. "Would it help if I rolled them over into a JPMorgan Chase account?" she asked, smiling because she knew it would.

He smiled back. "I would say that should clinch it."

John and Camilla worked together for over an hour. A young woman from JPMorgan Chase's investment department, who drew up the papers necessary to liquidate Camilla's remaining stocks that were still at Palm Beach County Trust, joined them. They decided to roll half the money over into insured CDs, the other half into a money market account. She deposited the proceeds from the sale of her wedding gifts into that account as well. Then John went over her options for financing the apartment, and recommended that she finance 50 percent of the purchase price plus the closing costs — $94,000 — under a 3/1 adjustable-rate mortgage, which at the moment carried an interest rate near a 45-year low.

"Why so short a period?" she asked

"I can tell that within three years you'll be moving on to bigger and better things than a studio apartment in a six flight walk-up. Right now, we want to keep your overhead as low as possible," John explained.

Encouraged by John's support, Camilla said, "Let's go forward."

Merry started to fuss and Camilla picked her up, slipping her breast out of her bra to let Merry nurse. John looked away.

"May I use your phone while you finish the paperwork?" Camilla asked.

"Of course," he replied, avoiding looking up.

Camilla called Little Tots to learn that it was Chantal's day off. She had phoned twice before, only to be told that Chantal was busy and she should call back another time. Then she called Deirdre Tortile. "John," she whispered while she waited for someone to answer, "is the mortgage enough of a sure thing for me to put in a bid?"

"As soon as you sign the breast — I mean, rest — of the papers, I can print out a pre-approval," he said, as he turned the color of a poker fresh from the flame.

"Deirdre — it's me, Camilla Madison. I'm submitting an all-cash offer of $180,000 for apartment 6B."

"But —"

"No buts, Deirdre — cash is king."

Chapter Four

For her meeting the next morning, Camilla wore a conservative blue suit. The thought of seeing Alyson again both excited her and made her nervous. With Alyson, one never knew what to expect.

The elevator opened directly into the reception area of *Marry Well*. It hadn't changed much since Camilla had seen it last. There were three new "Him on Him" framed spreads lining the walls, and pictures of Alyson with Steven Spielberg, and Alyson with Colin Powell that hadn't been there before. But behind the circular reception desk, there still hung a corset that had presumably been Martha Washington's, a lace thong of Jane Fonda's, a silk garter that Princess Di had worn on her wedding day on loan from the fashion collection at the Met, and one of Alyson's own satin teddies in electric blue — something old, something new, something borrowed, something blue — all of which had belonged to women who had married well. (How a marriage ended didn't concern Alyson one bit.)

On her way back to Alyson's office, Camilla passed *Marry Well's* test kitchen, where Rose prepared the dishes she wrote about in her column; it was empty because Rose had called in to say she'd be working from home, fine-tuning her column — while she surreptitiously watched Merry for her friend. Camilla embraced a couple of her ex-colleagues, Rabia Rubenstein and Harry Clark, as she passed their desks, both of whom seemed delighted to see her again.

Alyson stood in the doorway of her office; her pelvis thrust forward and her hands on her hips. Prominent bones showed through Alyson's Betsey Johnson scarlet dress and her long thigh flirted through a foot-long slit up the front. She had a necklace made of diamonds the size of hail pellets around her neck, which Camilla assumed was from Alyson's Florida friend, a.k.a Mr. Diamond Necklace.

"Well, well, well...if it isn't the prodigal daughter," Alyson said, air-kissing the space around Camilla's ears. "Come in."

Alyson's desk had been custom made to resemble a bed. The wall behind it was upholstered in coral flowered chintz, like a headboard, and plaster pillows painted in the same pattern as the chintz were attached to the desktop on both ends. The chairs facing Alyson, on which she motioned for Camilla to sit down, looked like bidets — with solid yellow cushions where the bowls ought to have been.

"You're looking well, Alyson. Life must agree with you."

"Everyone agrees with me, Camilla. You should know that." At that point, Alyson stood up and walked around, sitting on the bidet-chair next to Camilla. "I know you're here to beg for your old job back — I heard the marriage went bust. But I've got two problems: first, Prissie Easton is doing a fabulous job on the column and, second, I never hire back anyone for the same job. If I set that precedent, the whole staff would think they could come and go as they pleased."

Camilla was prepared. "I know all that, Alyson. I've got a different idea."

At that, Alyson, who had moved back to her own desk and was about to compulsively check her e-mail, gave Camilla her renewed attention. "Camilla, you know I think you're bright and talented. And I like you — I really do — or I wouldn't have agreed to meet." She paused dramatically before she pounced. "So what's your idea?"

Camilla saw Alyson's eyes brighten at the suggestion of something new. "It has to do with an opportunity I see in the marketplace —"

"Funny you should use that phrase. Since you left the magazine, I've been concentrating on developing new businesses, seizing market opportunities as they arise — to capitalize on the *Marry Well* franchise."

"So I've heard. Rose told me the dating service is a hit, and that you've licensed the *Marry Well* name to a chain of spas —"

" — And a perfume, a line of diamond engagement rings, a California sparkling wine, and —"

"Is there anyone you say no to, Alyson?"

"Of course. I'm very discerning — I've turned down cookware and baby clothes. What are you thinking of?"

"Have you noticed that during the past few years the residential real estate market has gone through the roof?"

"Of course. Low interest rates, safe harbor investment — Manhattan isn't growing larger; you can't plant more land the way you can print more stock shares," Alyson said.

"So you know what I'm talking about. Think about the demographics of your readership — divorcees, soon-to-be-marrieds, widows — and what they all have in common, and one of the things that consistently comes up is real estate: they're all going to move sometime soon."

Camilla could see Alyson was intrigued, despite herself. She had the honed antennae to recognize good ideas and the motor to drive them forward. In some ways, she and Alyson were alike: two sides of a coin called luck.

"Go on —" Alyson said.

"So here's my idea: I start a real estate column for the magazine, writing about fabulous and sexy apartments and townhouses that are on the market. I'll do one feature per issue — sassy and stylish — just like I did for decorating. My dad was in the business. We owned our own brokerage firm in Palm Beach. I grew up around expensive real estate. I know how it works. I can speak the jargon. Sure, there are some differences between New York and Palm Beach, co-op boards for instance, but I'm a quick study."

"Hmmm…I could see Chuck selling advertising against your editorial; he can hit up all the real estate developers and brokerage firms for color space ads — do you realize how profitable they are?" Alyson asked.

"I checked it out — your competitors are getting $24,000 a page."

"At least." Alyson was on the edge of her seat. Camilla could tell she was hooked.

"I thought I'd give the residences ratings, like movie reviews, maybe use diamond engagement rings as the symbol. Two rings for privacy, three rings for sex appeal, that kind of thing. Eventually, I envision the *Marry Well* rating to be like the *Good Housekeeping* seal of approval."

"It's a clever idea," Alyson said, more reserved now, fondling her diamond hailstones and uncrossing her long legs. Camilla knew she would restrain her true enthusiasm as a negotiating tactic.

"I know," Camilla beamed. "How much?"

"How much what?" Alyson asked.

"How much will you pay me?"

Alyson shuffled some papers on her desk, as if the answer could be found there. Camilla knew she was stalling. "Fifty thousand, plus expenses."

"I was hoping for more," Camilla said firmly. She had been earning $65,000 when she left on leave.

Alyson's mascaraed eyes narrowed into slits. It was she who set the terms. "No can do, Camilla. It's 50 or I get someone else."

Camilla was taken aback. "Someone else to execute my idea?"

"Only as a last resort."

"Can I sleep on it?" Camilla asked, feeling slightly trumped.

"Of course. I'll expect your call tomorrow morning."

While Camilla was busy replaying the meeting in her head as she waited for the elevator, the doors opened and a tall handsome teenager bounded out. He bumped into Camilla, causing her to drop her purse and papers all over the carpet. They bent down simultaneously, banging heads, as they both tried to pick up her things.

"Oops," the student said, rubbing his head. His raucous laugh was so endearing, Camilla couldn't be mad.

"It's OK. I've got it —"

"Thanks," he said and he rushed past her to the receptionist's desk.

"Rex! You're late. Don't think just because you're her stepson she'll cut you any slack. If you want that summer internship, you'll have to hustle like everyone else," Camilla heard the receptionist say, in a teasing tone, as the elevator doors closed behind her.

The downtown office of The Griffin Group, where Deirdre Tortile worked, was right around the corner from *Marry Well.* Camilla decided to stop by and check on the contract for her studio apartment. It was lunchtime, and she was starving, so as soon as she apologized for dropping by unannounced, she asked Deirdre to suggest a restaurant nearby, as she was sure all her old haunts were long gone.

At Deirdre's insistence, they went to a born-again coffee shop with a new age menu; Camilla ordered a Chinese chicken salad and a mango milkshake and Deirdre had a papaya bran muffin and coffee.

"Is that all you're eating?" Camilla asked.

"Constipation. We brokers call it strange potty syndrome — it's an occupational hazard — must be all the information we withhold."

"So — what goes into these infamous board packages?" Camilla asked, eager to change the subject. "Where I come from, there are no such things."

"They used to be a peculiarity to New York, but I hear they're becoming more popular elsewhere. These days, people everywhere want to know who their neighbors are going to be. Anyway, since you're buying a sponsor unit, the board package is just a formality. But still, you want them to rubber stamp it, not to cause any trouble."

"What kind of trouble could they cause?" Camilla asked.

"If you have any skeletons in your closet, you'd better tell me now." Camilla chewed to buy time. "Listen, Camilla, if we're going to work together, we have to tell each other everything. Think of me as you would a lawyer — client confidentiality and all that rot. These boards are B.S. anyway — a good broker knows how to get around the rules."

"I just want the apartment, no trouble."

"I know. So — who do you know?"

"My best friend Rose lives in the building."

"Is she on the board?"

"No, but she's close to Cody and Felix, her neighbors downstairs. Cody is board president. Rose has already talked to him — he's having an April Fool's Day party in his apartment and they've invited me."

76

"That'll help. But I mean who do you know who *counts* —"

"I beg your pardon?" Camilla sputtered.

"Look, you'll need at least three letters of reference from people who live in other co-op buildings, the snootier the better — you know: Park Avenue, Fifth Avenue, Central Park West. If they don't know you well, they should be willing to pretend they do. I'll write the letters for them, you just get them to put them on personal stationery and sign. Do you have a bank reference?"

Camilla thought about her new investment advisor at JPMorgan Chase. "I think so…"

"Excellent! Closing costs — transfer taxes, flip tax, recording fees, title insurance — usually add about four percent, unless of course the purchase price is more than a million, in which case you'd have to worry about mansion tax —"

"Mansion? Hardly. How many square feet is it anyway?" Camilla's head was spinning.

"About 650."

Camilla devoured her lunch while Deirdre picked on her muffin in between taking calls on her cell phone. Yes, she could show 205 East 58th Street at three. No, Four Sutton Place was not sold, but there was a contract out. Yes, Eloise Wrestler got turned down by the board of 720 Park; "Why? Why?" the caller wanted to know. Because her last ex-husband's ex-business partner's ex-girlfriend was on the board and had heard through the ex-chain that Eloise smoked in bed and had a Pekingese who pooped in the elevator.

"My, you sound busy," Camilla remarked.

"I've got 22 exclusives and seven buyers at the moment," Deirdre said.

"Do all those deals close?"

"I wish…" She rolled her eyes. "It goes like this… it's usually the wife shopping for apartments. Her husband makes the money and, more often than not, when you're talking about the kind of money that can buy a townhouse or co-op for many millions, you're talking about a guy to whom money and power are important."

Camilla thought about Alyson's "Him on Hims."

"Anywho…as I was saying… So the husband, who's usually got a young mistress on the side, pushes his wife around, or at the very least neglects her. She's frustrated and unhappy, but she can't leave him because she'd give up her status, her luxury life, her fancy clothes, and her charity board positions. She shops for revenge, sometimes for expensive apartments. In fact, I've had one customer for three years who gets all dressed up in her Prada outfits every Wednesday, lets me buy her lunch, and we look at apartments all afternoon. It's a kind of voyeurism too."

"Will she ever buy?"

"Who knows? But by now I've invested so much time, I'm afraid to let her go. She knows it too, and revels in it. She's seen a couple of places she's liked, and brought her husband back for a look, but he always finds something wrong with them — the view, the light, the closets are too few, the toilets are too small, the kids' rooms are too close to the master. By putting down her choices, he puts her down as well."

There were many forms of violation, thought Camilla as she listened to Deirdre speak.

"Sounds downright sick and abusive," Camilla said.

"It is. So whom does she abuse in return? Her housekeeper and her real estate broker — the two people dependent on her to make their livings. And the two job categories that are easiest to fill — let's face it, we all have access to the same listings"

"What if," Camilla said, "you had something unique to offer?"

"Like what, honey? A chauffeured Bentley to schlep people around in? That's been done."

"Why do you take it?" Camilla asked.

"Where else can I make this kind of money and keep my own hours?"

Camilla mulled the point — high income potential, complete flexibility, no travel, no limits for growth, no advanced degrees … "Pardon my bluntness, but what kind of money do you make?"

Deirdre was taken aback. She clearly didn't want to answer, even though the percentages were public knowledge. "Check!" she shouted, index finger in the air.

"If I recall, residential real estate commissions are six percent in New York — right?" At least that's what John Confrere had told her.

Deirdre still didn't answer.

"Didn't we agree to tell each other everything?" Camilla asked.

Deirdre eyed her shrewdly, "Six percent gross, unless it's a sponsor sale, then it's four. Rentals are between ten and fifteen and they're quick cash."

"That's obscene," Camilla blurted out. She had vaguely remembered that her father had gotten only one percent from Rocky.

"I don't end up with six in my pocket," Deirdre said. "Three goes to the co-broker's firm, and I have to split the rest with Griffin — 65 percent for me and 35 for them. Griffin's sales last year exceeded $4.2 billion."

"Still…15 transactions, times $180,000, times 3 percent, times…"

"Honey, yours is a baby deal. I sold 30 million dollars worth of real estate last year."

"Wow — that comes to…" Camilla was scribbling on her napkin.

"$585,000." Deirdre grabbed the check when it came. "Lunch is on me."

That night, Merry slept straight through while Camilla tossed and turned for hours. When she finally dozed off, she dreamed that she was on the shores of New Jersey. She could see a pot of gold on the other side of the Hudson River, but she had neither a boat nor a paddle. If she could only figure out how to get there, the pot could be hers, and she and Merry would be home free.

As soon as Merry went down for her morning nap, Camilla called Alyson, who had someone in her office but took the call anyway.

"Is this Ann Lowther?"

"No, Alyson, it's me — Camilla."

"Oh, Ann Lowther is the other person I'm considering to write the real estate column."

"Alyson, we need to talk. In person."

"What for? A simple yes or no will do."

"Yes, then. I will write the column. But it's not so simple —"

"Let's get one thing straight, Camilla: I make the rules. And if this is about salary —"

"I'll take fifty," Camilla said.

"Just like that?" Camilla could tell Alyson's curiosity was piqued. "Can you come in at noon?"

Camilla looked at Merry sleeping on her bed. If Rose couldn't watch her for an hour during her lunch break, she could always call back and reschedule Alyson. "Sure."

"See you then."

Rose agreed to meet Camilla and Merry around the corner from the *Marry Well* offices shortly before noon. The two friends decided that Camilla would pass the stroller to Rose, who would take Merry for her first long walk around Soho. She told Camilla that they would go to Dean & Deluca's gourmet store and not leave until Rose had properly introduced Merry to the thorny artichokes and purple eggplants, waxy star fruit and orange kumquats. Then she would wait for Camilla at Foo King, where Rose went almost every day for what she claimed was still her favorite "gourmand" cuisine.

Approaching Alyson would take some finesse, Camilla knew; she guessed she would fare best if Alyson thought that the proposal Camilla intended to make was Alyson's own idea. Camilla stepped off the elevator, rehearsing the lines she planned to deliver, when the receptionist interrupted her train of thought: "You here to see the boss?"

"Yes, I am."

Alyson appeared as if on cue and led Camilla into the glass-enclosed conference room down the hall. "Forgive me if I'm a little draggy today. I went to the wrap party for *Law and Order* last night, and Hugh Jackman stopped by late, after his curtain, and then there was this fabulous party, and then —"

"Sorry to interrupt, but I know you're busy and I've got an idea to discuss that might take some time." Alyson reared her head indignantly.

"I was up most of last night thinking; I have a joint venture to propose. Or shall I say, an elaboration on my column idea," Camilla said.

Alyson was about to say something, probably clever or flip, but she must have detected Camilla's seriousness, because she settled down and kept quiet.

"We both see the opportunity. I'll write the column about the amazing palaces of the rich and famous people you feature in your magazine. I've got loads of ideas about how to tie my column into other sections — for example, how about photographing your "Him on Him" subject, in his apartment for sale, cooking his own recipes on his Viking range, and featured in an article by Rose?"

"Viking would pay big bucks for that — not to mention the revenues for product placements in the photos!" Alyson said.

"But I think we should take it a step further." Alyson looked suspicious. "Alyson, I'll bottom-line it for you. How about actually *selling* real estate? Marry Well Realty? We would be different from the usual brokerage firms out there because we would cater to clients going through life changes — marriages, divorces, career moves, relocations. To paraphrase from your masthead: Get 'em during the 'hunt', and keep 'em for the 'kill'."

"This is a magazine, not a real estate brokerage firm," Alyson said, transparently buying time to think through the suggestion. "We're not set up —"

"I could work from home. I plan to write my column from there too."

"No, no, no. That would never work. You'd need a license, a database, listings—"

Camilla paused. "These are the details of the joint venture we'd need to discuss only if you agree with the idea."

Alyson was mock livid. "So you'd use *Marry Well's* reputation and cachet, and you would contribute exactly what? Experience? No. Capital? No. Do you want to get paid to stay at home and…knit? Where's the 'joint' in this venture?"

Camilla had anticipated a reaction like this. After all, she had worked for Alyson for seven years, and knew that she tended to see everything through a lens of self-interest. "I'm creative and hard-working. You'd own half the business, Alyson; I'd do the work. It would operate on the same financial basis as other real estate firms — eat what you kill. As an active broker, I only get paid if I produce; you'd get your half of the profits without lifting a finger."

"If I remember the principles of finance from my Columbia days, half of nothing is nothing."

"As you pointed out last time we met, the marriage went bust, and I've got a child to feed. I've got incentive, and in New York real estate, half of a modicum of success could be quite a lot." Alyson seemed unmoved by Camilla's personal problems, so she decided to appeal to her greed, throwing in: "The Griffin Group's sales totaled $4.2 billion last year."

Alyson's eyes widened. "Those commissions are hefty. I remember what I had to pay when I sold the San Remo —"

"Six percent of the gross sales price," Camilla said, lingering on the word *gross.* In the magazine publishing business, everything was based on net; it was Alyson who was used to paying enormous commissions to advertising agencies, and Camilla remembered that she had often complained about it bitterly.

Alyson leaned back in her chair and regarded Camilla closely. It was clear she was calculating her potential risks and rewards. She wore a poker face so that Camilla could not tell which way she was leaning.

"Can you do both the column and sell real estate?"

"They go hand-in-hand. As a broker, it would be so much easier to gain ready access to apartments I might review — as long as we're careful to disclose my true purpose to the owner. As a writer, I might get first chance to pitch a big exclusive. We then showcase the property in the column, as well as other brokers' listings to retain *Marry Well's* integrity, and generate new revenues for the magazine through the ads and..." She caught her breath. "... a new profit center for you from your share of the commissions I generate."

"I'll have to have my lawyer look into what's required to start a real estate subsidiary," Alyson said. "I know from my husband that in order to become a licensed real estate salesperson you need to be sponsored by a broker. Only after nine months under a broker can you become one yourself."

Camilla was chagrined; she hadn't known about broker-sponsors — her father had always been on his own — but she couldn't let her ignorance show. If Alyson had to set up a new company and get a broker to head it, months, maybe years, would pass. And another layer of management between Alyson and herself could cause problems and waste time.

"Could Mr. Strong's firm sponsor me and Marry Well Realty? That would save time and money. Keep it all in the family, so to speak," Camilla said. She had often heard Alyson say about the rich men she had dated: "His money's my money and my money's my money too."

Alyson clicked her tongue on the roof of her mouth. "Yes...now you're talking. I like it, Camilla. I like it a lot. I'll talk to Walter tonight."

Merry gurgled with glee when she saw her mother walk into Foo King. She was nearly six months old — verbal and lively. Camilla picked her up out of the stroller and kissed her ears; Merry grabbed her mother's nose with her two-inch hand and squeezed as if she were honking a horn.

"So how'd it go?" Rose asked.

"We have a deal!"

"No way. I can't believe she went for it. She's not one to share the pie."

"She's really smart, Rose, you know that. I'm bringing her incremental revenues without her having to put up any money, do any work, or take any risks. I get instant credibility by being able to use the *Marry Well* name, a broker/sponsor for my real estate license..." She lingered on that to accentuate her newly-acquired knowledge. "...exclusive access to a first-class customer list, a leg up on getting high-end exclusive listings. It's a good deal for me too."

"Those are the only ones that work, I suppose," Rose said.

"Right — it's a potential gold mine for everyone."

The restaurant started to fill up. It was a Formica-laminate and stainless steel world with linoleum floors and red plastic banquettes. An earthy woman behind the counter—which was designed to look like the Great Wall of China—waved at Rose, who smiled back. "That's P'nina," Rose said.

P'nina Ching came over to their table and gave Rose a big kiss. She pinched Merry's cheeks gently, calling her a "shayna maydeleh." Seconds later, P'nina's husband, Lee, emerged from the kitchen and threw his arms around Rose, saying: "Long time, no see."

"Lee, P'nina...allow me to introduce my best friend, Camilla Madison and her baby, Merry," Rose said.

"P'nina, make them feel welcome. Sit, sit with them." He shoveled his wife's ample bottom with his small, bony hands, toward a corner booth, "What can I get you?" he asked as he placed a small bowl of fried noodles and a plate of plum sauce on the table.

"Vegetarian stir-fry," Rose said.

P'nina grinned as Lee disappeared toward the kitchen.

Merry was contemplating a piece of fried noodle with the seriousness of a paleontologist examining a shard of bone.

"Such a beautiful baby," P'nina said.

"Do you have children?" Camilla asked.

Tears welled up in P'nina's eyes. "I am a Russian Jew, Lee is Chinese-American. My husband says children of a mixed marriage have too many problems," she answered. She seemed eager to change the subject, excusing herself to greet another customer.

Camilla knew that six degrees of separation was a proven formula, so she moved next to Rose on the banquette to avoid being overheard.

"I didn't ask for a contract," Camilla said quietly.

"Maybe you should talk to a lawyer about drawing one up," Rose whispered back.

"Do you think I can trust Alyson?"

Rose looked around before answering in a hushed voice. "Trust her? Would you stick your head in the mouth of a lioness?"

Camilla thought about what Rose had said. In all the years she had known Alyson, she had seen her tough and ruthless, but never explicitly dishonest. Her ethical lapses extended more into the personal side of her life.

Although she found it hard to believe that anyone could live with dichotomous values — i.e., be true in the boardroom and untrue in the bedroom — Alyson's reputation in regards to *Marry Well* was spotless. *Marry Well* was Alyson's baby. And besides, she was afraid that if she asked Alyson to sign a contract, the whole deal would be off.

"Only if she brushed her teeth," Camilla laughed.

"Our lioness bleaches hers," Rose replied.

They were both laughing now. "Seriously," Camilla said, "I have to trust Alyson—"

Merry let out a peal of laughter and clapped her hands, which had gotten into the dish of plum sauce, and were disgusting. "Aly-son," she said out loud.

"Holy guacamole," Rose shouted, "I think she just uttered her first word."

They fussed over Merry a while longer, trying to get her to say chopstick and noodle and Rose and Mama, holding things up for her to see, and pointing at each other as they said their names.

Finally Camilla conceded. "It's three o'clock, Rose. You'd better get back before we're both unemployed."

Outside, Rose spotted a newsstand and crossed the street to buy a *New York Times*. "There's something I want you to read."

Camilla skimmed the headlines on the first page. Rose pointed to an article about the Human Rights Symposium on Women's Issues.

"Isn't that where Doris was?" Camilla asked.

Rose sat down on a bench; gently rocking the stroller, hoping Merry would fall asleep. "Yes. I read it this morning. This year's topic was crimes against women. The article states facts like a woman is raped in Pakistan every two hours, and one is gang-raped every four days, yet only 321 cases were reported last year."

"That's awful, Rose. Does the article explain why so few cases are reported?"

"No. I thought maybe you could tell me."

There were, Camilla knew, many reasons why a woman wouldn't report a rape, but somehow she hadn't related her own circumstances to other victims before. Perhaps that was the nature of this crime, in which each sufferer felt her plight was unique; that each woman thought it was her own fault.

"I wonder if victims of all crimes feel guilty?"

"If they do, they shouldn't," Rose said.

"Rocky said it was my fault, that I provoked him," Camilla said.

"He did it, Camilla, because he knew he could get away with it. He held all the power — over you and your family. It's the same in Pakistan, these men know they'll get away with it."

"Are you saying that men are corrupt?"

"Not just men, Camilla. People with power. It just so happens that in most societies, it's only men who have power. But where that's changing, like here, women can be just as bad. Look at Alyson —"

"Aly-son," Merry muttered from her stroller as she nodded off to sleep.

Camilla walked around Soho after Rose went back to work; it would be useless, she knew, to try to lift a sleeping baby from a stroller, hail a cab, fold the stroller, and get it and the diaper bag into the back of a taxi without waking Merry up. She would just pass time until Merry's nap was done. She seemed to notice happy couples on every corner, arm-in-arm, laughing and kissing.

Romantic scenes made her sad. She wanted to be loved like that, but of the three men who had entered her life, two had hurt her badly, irrevocably, she thought, and one was no more memorable to her than an airplane paperback. She wondered if the heart was like a plate — shattered once, shattered twice, it can be glued and re-glued, but it's never really whole again.

Just as Merry opened her eyes, Camilla spotted a free cab. The taxi arrived at Little Tots at 5 P.M., when the moms and dads were starting to arrive to pick up their children. Camilla and Merry stood to the side as the day care center cleared out, counting the colors and types of uniforms that the parents wore — brown for the UPS men, blue for the postal workers, green for the hospital orderlies, gray for the doormen, and pink or white or blue for the housekeepers who worked a mile downtown but a world away.

It was a game Camilla had started to play with Merry, pointing to colors and objects, and saying their names.

They spotted Chantal sitting on the floor in the block corner, surrounded by four toddlers who were racing toy cars through her hair. Chantal sat with her back facing Camilla, and her arms around two of the children; she wore the same red t-shirt she'd had on at the hospital. She turned around when she heard Camilla approach, but her smile faded when she saw who it was.

"Chantal...I can explain."

"You don't need to explain anything. I understand."

"No, you don't. Please, when do you get off?"

"I've been off for half an hour. I just stick around because I like the kids. There are always some folks who can't get off the job on time."

"Why don't you let Merry and me take you to dinner? We can go anywhere you like."

Chantal looked at Merry and kissed her little cheeks. "She's twice the size!"

Merry kicked her feet and waved her arms. She bucked like a baby bronco; if she hadn't been strapped in, she might have fallen out of the stroller and flat on her face.

"She likes you," Camilla said. Merry went into a long monologue of coos and clucks. She was trying hard to speak.

"Okay," Chantal said, motioning her head in Merry's direction, "She talked me into it."

Chantal led them to a hole-in-the-wall establishment called Mabel's. Since Merry was still breast-feeding, she got to enjoy the baby back ribs and jerk pork, collard greens and fried plantains secondhand. Judging from the belch she let out after nursing, she seemed to enjoy the meal as much as Camilla did.

"I'm so sorry, Chantal. I can imagine how you felt when I didn't return your calls."

"I'm getting used to rejection," Chantal said, in a self-deprecating rather than self-pitying way.

"I was so depressed I didn't want to talk to anyone. But I didn't even get your messages until last week —"

"I understand. I had that post-partum thing too. And I don't even have a baby to show for it."

"In my case, it's worse than post-partum depression." She told Chantal about Robert leaving her for someone else.

Chantal shook her head sympathetically. "I'm sorry for you, Camilla. That's a rotten thing to do."

"What about you? Have you told the father what happened?"

"I can't. I can't ever go home again."

"Why not, Chantal?"

"'Cause the father was my mother's boyfriend. He's real mean. He just forced me while my Mom was at work…if you know what I mean."

"I know what you mean."

Doris had written an article for *Parents* magazine about the vulnerability of young girls to the advances of boyfriends or second spouses of their mothers. In it, she had advanced her theory of The Oedipal Triangle, in which the mother is a silent partner in the crime.

They both watched Merry play with a buttermilk biscuit while they sat with their private memories.

"Chantal, how's the job? The children seem to love you."

"Yeah, the kids are great. Problem is…sometimes the owners pay me and sometimes they don't. There aren't many jobs when you're 16 and uneducated like me."

"Chantal…you gave me an idea. I'm going back to work soon — I've got to. I'm going to need some babysitting help with Merry."

"I don't know…"

Camilla could tell Chantal still didn't trust her. "I promise to pay you every Friday, no matter what."

"I still don't know…"

"Three hundred dollars a week."

"That sure would make my cousin happy. She's complaining all the time about how much I eat."

"Meals included!"

Chantal was grinning now; Camilla knew she made her feel needed.

"When do I have to start?"

"One condition —"

Chantal's expression deflated. "What's that?"

"You have to go to school too. We'll go to the high school together; I'm sure they'll work with us on a schedule to suit my needs and yours."

"Naw, I can't register. I tried. They told me to go back where I came from."

Camilla pursed her lips and said: "I've got it. You can finish high school online — high school equivalency — I read about it in the newspaper."

"I can't afford a computer —"

"Don't worry about that. Rose has a computer you can use. She got a new laptop from her job."

"You're awfully nice, Camilla."

"What goes around comes around, Chantal."

There was something about Chantal that made Camilla feel confident. Mother's intuition gets less credit than it deserves. Since giving birth to Merry, Camilla could feel tiny vibrations, like those made when a violin bow slides across the instrument's strings, which sang to her and told her what to do.

Although they came home in good spirits, especially Camilla, who felt full of hope, Merry had a colicky night and Camilla slept poorly. The jack hammering persistence of the telephone woke her. It was nine o'clock and Rose was already gone. Camilla rolled over to answer the phone, nearly smothering Merry, who was snuggled asleep, tight against her ribs.

"Camilla Madison," she answered, figuring that at that hour it had to be business. "We got the commitment letter. Now it's official!" It was John Confrere.

"I hope this isn't an April Fool's joke."

"No kidding!" he said, as excited as if it were he who got to keep the money.

"You're the best! What happens now?"

"Deirdre can send in the board package, there will be a courtesy interview, and then you can close. Do you have a lawyer?"

"A lawyer? In Florida, the title company handles the closing."

"And most of the 49 other states as well. But in New York you need a lawyer. There are 32,000 licensed attorneys in New York City and they need something to do."

"I only know one lawyer," she said, thinking of Robert's divorce lawyer, Bernard Grossman.

"Is he tough, fast-talking, and mean?"

"Do you know him too?"

John laughed. "Probably not. But that's what you need."

"OK, if you say so. I'll call him today."

"Camilla, have you started your job yet?"

"Not yet. But I'm getting everything in place. I've hired a babysitter for Merry, and I'll have my best friend Rose next door, plus I've got a blockbuster idea...I only hope I can pull it off." So she told John about Marry Well Realty and all that she hoped to achieve.

She could tell he was impressed. "I knew you'd be going places, Camilla. It's only a matter of time."

The party invitation from Rose's neighbors Cody and Felix said that it was to be a costume affair. "Come as Something You're Not" was embossed in silver on a red card with the words "April Fool" printed in large letters.

Rose wore a T-Rex suit because it was the most ferocious carnivore ever born and she was, she claimed, the most avid vegetarian. They dressed Merry up in yellow, as a tennis ball. And Camilla, bemoaning that she couldn't be what she wasn't because she still wasn't sure what she was, dressed up as Alyson — high heels, cell phone, mock jewels and all.

Cody and Felix had bought both apartments on the fifth floor, converting the back studio into their bedroom and the front apartment into an open entertaining space. Camilla was amazed at how much could be done with so little. They were both in the advertising business; Cody was the account director for Spunkette Shampoo at BBD&O and Felix an art director at LLN&G, a smaller shop downtown.

The main ingredient in the sparely decorated apartment was style. A faux limestone doorframe had a concealed light in its pediment, making it glow like the moon. There was a matching console table next to the doorway that was crammed with antique English snuffboxes, which smelled mildly of hashish. A relief sculpture of a naked man with a clamshell concealing his genitals was hanging over the collection.

The focal point of the minimalist living room was a carved marble chocolate brown chimneypiece on which sat a Giacometti-style figurine. A wood and iron campaign bed upholstered in mattress ticking provided seating in lieu of a sofa, and on the large glass coffee table sat a Mackenzie-Childs platter, holding colorful and crispy crudités. There was no rug on the highly polished herringbone floor.

In a shellacked box sat a dozen or so "blunts," which Camilla knew were hollowed-out cigars filled with marijuana and dipped in embalming fluid. Although she had never seen them before, she remembered what they looked like from a special on CNN.

Bach was playing on the stereo and Cody walked over to introduce himself and offer Camilla a glass of wine. He welcomed her to the building, which she took as a good sign, and asked her who she was supposed to be.

"I'm dressed up as my boss," she said. "And you?"

Cody was wearing a monochromatic suit and tie. "I'm a heterosexual."

There were many young professionals there that evening, several from the advertising world, but clients as well. There were doctors and lawyers, aspiring actors and publicists, and Cody and Felix's relationship counselor who, upon meeting Rose, asked if she and Camilla were gay.

"We certainly love each other, but not in a sexual way," Camilla said. Sometimes she wished it could be that easy.

She joined a couple on the campaign bed and they embroiled her, like the ping-pong ball in a match, in their spat. One partner complained of the other's infidelities, while the other defended his own. Then the unfaithful one, ashes an inch long on his cigarette and about to fall off, toppled over onto the floor, having had one too many, ending the game with a preemptory thud.

Camilla held 20-pound Merry in her arms, but her shoulders were beginning to ache, so she moved from the campaign bed to a chair with a back facing away from the window. Felix positioned himself across from her and asked what she planned to do for a living once she was settled in her new place. She told Felix about her column and, swearing him to secrecy, about her idea to expand it to real estate brokerage as well. Eventually, she told him, she hoped to add management and leasing too.

Felix was a perky sort, small and friendly. His ears stood away from his head, like a cartoon mouse, in a way that gave the impression he was listening to every word that was being said. He had a light smattering of freckles across his nose and sandy eyebrows arched like upside down letter U's.

"Interesting, very interesting. I can think of a possible client for you right off the bat."

Camilla's radar spiked. "Really?"

"Our friend Dennis will be moving back to New York from the West Coast by the end of the year. He's an actor — maybe you've seen him? Dennis Meehan, he was on *The Young and the Penniless*."

"Sorry, I've never seen it."

"Anyway, he'll be looking for a place for him and his partner to live — probably Fifth Avenue, he's a real snob now that he's a star." Felix reached in his pocket and handed Camilla a card. "E-mail me your contact information and I'll have Dennis call you when he's coming to New York."

"You have no idea what this means to me." Camilla said, knowing that she'd need to drive business of her own if she wanted Alyson to take her seriously. If all the leads came from Alyson, the "partnership" wouldn't stand a chance.

Chapter Five

Alyson had arranged for Camilla to meet with her husband, Walter Strong, to work out the details of Marry Well Realty's launch.

"He's squeezing you in, Camilla, so make the most of your time together," Alyson said.

It struck Camilla as strange that she had never met Alyson's husband before, reinforcing Rose's suggestion that the Strongs led very separate lives. Whenever Camilla thought about what she would want from a marriage, the image was more than she'd had with Robert. She believed that somewhere was the missing part of herself, and that when she met him, the two parts would be joined as one.

Walter Strong's company, West Coast Properties, occupied the top two floors of a brand new office building on Times Square that he had developed and built. It had no number; it was simply called West Coast Tower. Camilla entered the four-story lobby and advanced through security, where she had to show photo ID, empty the contents of her pockets on the counter, have her photo taken, and be frisked by the only female guard on duty, before being given a badge with an embedded security chip that would allow her access to the penthouse floors.

She walked around an enormous bronze sculpture called "Nude with Horse" by California artist Robert Graham, and observed two brightly colored, abstract canvases by painter TAZive. At the elevator bank, she was instructed to speak her floor number into the microphone and swipe her badge; once cleared, the elevator would whisk her upwards to the West

Coast Properties reception area on 64, with access to any other floor strictly denied.

The reception lounge for West Coast Properties could best be compared to a private club. Elegantly dressed hostesses served drinks and hors d'oeuvres from sterling silver trays. In each of the four corners there was a video screen, set to CNBC, but with a remote, headphones, and a pile of first-run DVDs stacked neatly nearby. The soundtrack from the original *Mission Impossible* was playing softly on the stereo, and the coffee table was strewn with every highbrow business magazine imaginable. Discreetly tucked away in a cubicle by the conference room were a fax machine, Internet connected laptop, and six prepaid, disposable cell phones for guests who may have forgotten theirs.

Walter personally came out to greet her, which surprised her, and within minutes she began to glean what had made him so successful. He wasn't tall; in fact, she was sure he was several inches shorter than Alyson, but he was handsome, warm, and very charismatic. He shook her hand firmly, taking it in both of his, while he looked directly into her eyes. She followed him down the long hallway to his office, noting the beautiful cut of his simple navy suit and that he had not one gray strand in his conservatively cut dark hair.

His office didn't have a desk; it looked more like a living room in a private home. The walls were paneled in antique wood, or at least the best replica she had ever seen, and the soft velvet sofas were the pale green hue of beach glass. There were several comfortable armchairs, bold bright paintings by Eric Salle and Julian Schnabel, a Persian rug on the floor, and a wood-burning fireplace — a marvelous and unexpected surprise in a modern skyscraper such as this.

The only thing Walter's office had in common with his wife's was that everywhere one looked, there were snapshots of Alyson. Camilla noticed a small grouping of framed photographs — a woman, and a boy at different ages — on a glass shelf by the window. She presumed they must be of his first wife and child.

"Alyson insisted I meet with you — she tells me you're a budding entrepreneur. We like those around here," Walter said, smiling. She noticed a solid brass block on the coffee table that had a quote from Publius: "No one knows what he can do until he tries."

"I don't know how much Alyson has told you about my idea. At first it was just to write a real estate column, but I'm trying to buy this apartment, and I realized how much brokers in New York earn, and I started to put two and two together—"

"Don't undersell yourself. The late Charles Revson — you know who he was?"

"Founder of Revlon Cosmetics?"

"Exactly! He said that there's no such thing as an original idea: to be successful, you need to be able to cherry pick the ripe fruit of others' ideas and package them in an original way. It's the ability to market and sell that will make you money."

"In that regard...I'm an unproven quantity as well. But my father owned a brokerage firm in Palm Beach in the seventies and eighties. I grew up around it."

"Really? Now that's interesting. I always believed entrepreneurship was best learned at the dinner table. That's how they did it in the old days, through apprenticeship. I learned the business from my father, he from his father… I know Palm Beach a little — my grandparents had a house there, on Barton Avenue. And you?"

"Seaspray."

"What do you know…we may have passed each other in front of Bethesda-by-the-Sea."

She really liked him. Why would Alyson take up with Mr. Diamond Necklace, or anyone else for that matter, when she had Walter Strong? Would she ever understand what motivated men and women when it came to love?

"Perhaps," she mused.

"Back to business. You'll need a license. In order to get that, you'll have to take the real estate salesperson's course — it's offered in several places, but NYU and Marymount College are the best. The course takes six weeks; then you'll need to pass the real estate salesperson's exam and work for a licensed broker for nine months before you're eligible to be a broker yourself."

"Yes…" Alyson said.

"Don't worry. You can apprentice here, in my residential department. You'll add another dimension. We mostly sell apartments in buildings that I develop — although from time to time, my brokers do condo, townhouse, and co-op re-sales. I've noticed how lucrative those transactions are. Through you, West Coast Properties — under the Marry Well brand name of course — can build up the secondary market, re-sales, rentals, et cetera. I'll pair you with a top broker, so you can learn the business fast."

Camilla realized what Walter Strong was offering her, but she questioned his motives. He was, after all, Alyson's husband. Could he be setting her up? Making her so dependent on his operation that she would become just a cog in his machine? Her dream of autonomy was so close — only nine months away — that she could taste it. But she didn't want to be forced to give up control of her business idea, just to fulfill the bureaucratic requirement for a license. On the other hand, if she said no, it would be over before it had begun.

"I want to be completely honest with you. I hope to run Marry Well Realty for Alyson and myself — to be out on our own — as soon as we can. A line extension, a sub-brand, but…independent." From the look on his face, she could tell that he clearly hadn't expected her boldness. "Believe me, I appreciate your generous offer. But, you see —"

Walter Strong did see, without her having to tell him. "I understand. Here's what I can do. Do your best for Alyson and me for nine months, and then you're free to make your own decision. If you perform, you can change your mind and Marry Well Realty can find a permanent home here. If you go…Alyson still gets her cut, correct?"

"That's the deal. Fifty-fifty. Like a franchise fee — only larger."

"Good. Then you can see why I have an interest in making sure you learn how to be the best that you can be. Either way, I can't lose. The world is large, Camilla, but the circles are small — especially in real estate. This city needs smart, ethical people in the brokerage community — there are certainly plenty of the other kinds. You'll know about my projects and be better prepared than most to sell them — inside my organization or out. Who knows? Maybe we'll benefit each other as time goes on."

He was so balanced and self-contained; he must ground Alyson in some way. "Yes, Mr. Strong. I'd like that very much."

With a wonderfully warm smile, he signaled his assent and then buzzed his secretary on the intercom to come in. "Jennifer, this is Camilla Madison. She'll need a desk, a licensing sponsorship application, and send in Jayme Seagram — I want Camilla to meet her."

While Jennifer fulfilled her boss's order, Walter filled Camilla in on Jayme Seagram. "She supervises our on-site sales offices for all our residential buildings, Camilla, in addition to handling whatever re-sales come her way. Learn whatever you can from her. She's a tough cookie but she's been at it for 35 years and she can tell you the history of every major apartment in New York — who lived there, who died there, how many times it sold and for how much. She's a walking archive of Manhattan real estate."

There was a knock on the door and a small, boyishly built woman of about 60 walked in. She was wearing a gray pinstriped knee-length skirt, a gray silk blouse, and gray basket-weave flats. Her stick-straight silver hair was parted on the side. She was skinny and flat chested, about 5-foot-5, and projected an air of efficiency in the way she moved. In lieu of a handshake, she extended her fingers and clasped Camilla's in a vise-like grip.

"Good to see you," she said, using words to protect herself if, in fact, they had met some time in the past but Jayme just hadn't remembered.

"Jayme, Camilla's our new rookie. I want you to teach her the ropes, let her be your shadow for a couple of months, see how the pros do it."

Jayme raised a plucked eyebrow and let out a small sigh. Apparently she had been asked to play this role before and saw it as a chore. "I'll do it for you, Walter, but Ms. Madison's got to promise not to get in the way." Then she turned to Camilla, eyes bulging out slightly, thin lines extending from pursed lips. "Keep your ears open and your lips sealed and we'll get along just fine."

"She starts Monday. Anything planned for next week?" Walter asked.

"I've got a Mexican customer, a walk-in from Strong Place, scheduled for Wednesday; he's decided now that he wants a hotel apartment — she can tag along if she promises to behave. The Olafson apartment is closing Thursday at 10:00 A.M."

"Anything more…hands on?" Walter asked.

"I've got a board package due ASAP for 1022 Park Avenue. She can make the copies," Jayme said.

"Fine, fine. I'm sure she won't mind. Will you Camilla?" Walter asked.

Copies? "No, of course not. And thank you both for all your support."

Camilla enrolled in the six-week real estate salesperson's course at Marymount College on East 71st Street. Classes were held Saturdays from ten to six. After giving two weeks notice at Tiny Tots, for which she still hadn't been paid a month later, Chantal started working for Camilla.

Camilla approached the door to Marymount College full of enthusiasm. Being a student suited her, and the prospect of learning new information excited her. She had sharpened her pencils and bought a new pad at Staples for taking notes. The building had once been something else, a residence for nuns, or administrative offices, so the converted classrooms were long and narrow, with high ceilings and long, dirty windows. There were thirteen other students, twelve women and one man.

The teacher, Professor Marilyn D'Angelo, was short and plump, with glasses as thick as the bottoms of Mason jars, which made her soft yellow-brown eyes appear large and round like an owl's. She wore a Chinese-style caftan, with cloth-covered barrel-shaped buttons that tugged against her ample bosom when she inhaled.

Professor D'Angelo was trying hard to appear warm and concerned, calling the students "honey" and "darlin'." But she had taken an instant dislike to Camilla, for reasons Camilla could not comprehend, but imagined had something to do with her being blond and pretty, and bearing the carriage of privilege rather than that of persecution.

The faces around the table wore expressions of defeat, as if this real estate class was a depository for desperate seekers of last chances. One of her classmates had his ears plugged with cotton, and spoke softly in measured phrases. Another chattered incessantly, in a nervous way, as she jerked her head from side to side to brush her frosted hair from her eyes. They seemed a cast of misfits, in which Camilla felt she didn't belong. Perhaps that was what the teacher was sensing.

The first 20 minutes of the class elapsed pointlessly as Professor D'Angelo moved the students from room to room. The classrooms were all the same — deep, narrow, and airless — so Camilla wondered what the point of switching could be. The acoustics were appalling and Professor D'Angelo seemed to be procrastinating about getting down to the point, taking and retaking attendance, and then cross-referencing the students' names with those on her registration list.

"Well, darlins, now that we're settled, we will start with the basics of real estate law," she said, 40 minutes into the class. "There are three forms of ownership in New York State: tenants-in-common, joint-tenants, and —"

The neurotic hair flipper raised her hand, interrupting with her question without waiting to be called on. "Are we talkin' about ownership or rentals?"

"Ownership. We call owners 'tenants' in this context," the teacher explained. Sponsors, tenants, owners—it was confusing, Camilla had to admit. "To continue...where was I? Oh, yes. The third form of ownership is called tenants-in-the-entirety — this last form is reserved for husbands and wives only and is the only one with guaranteed rights of survivorship."

One of the older students, skinny with curly gray hair, burst into tears, disrupting the class.

"Are you all right, honey?" Professor D'Angelo asked, in a tone of pretending to care.

Camilla went over and put her arm around the woman. "What's your name?"

"June," she answered.

"Come on, June, let's step outside."

June's wrinkled face was slick with tears; her small blue eyes were grateful. "My husband of 40 years just died. I'm so sorry for creating a scene."

"Please don't worry. Everyone understands." As Camilla said it, she wondered if it were true. "Why are you here?" Camilla asked.

"I joined a support group, you know, of other recent widows. We meet at The Church of the Heavenly Rest on Wednesday nights. The minister said we should find a hobby, keep busy. And you?"

"My husband of two years left me. I need the money."

"What? You need the money?" Camilla wasn't sure if June was surprised because Camilla looked well off or because she thought selling real estate was a pastime, not a career.

"June, we'd better go back inside."

Professor D'Angelo glared at Camilla, instructing her to shut off the lights as she entered the room. Once she and June had returned to their seats, in partial darkness, the teacher continued her instruction. "Class, close your eyes and think of possible scenarios to which joint-tenants and tenants-in-common could apply." After a few minutes she turned on the lights and instructed the class to write their thoughts down without stopping. While Camilla reached into her bag to retrieve her pad, the teacher said: "This means you too, Ms. Madison, or do you have another appointment in the hall?"

Camilla looked up. "I was just getting paper..."

"Fine. Then get to work."

While Camilla attended real estate school, Rose helped Chantal hone her computer skills while they watched Merry. Rose taught Chantal how to put formulas into Excel and correct her own writing by using the spell-check tool. Spending Saturdays with Rose eating carrot soufflés and turnip timbales convinced Chantal to convert to vegetarianism, vowing to lose the 15 extra pounds she still carried from her ill-fated pregnancy.

When Chantal took Merry to the park or to Gymboree, Camilla began researching and writing her first column. The column was called "Madison's Avenue: Hot Properties for Sale." Alyson offered to arrange Camilla's access to the fancy abodes of her friends, beginning with Charlotte and Gary Kinnell's maisonette at 819 Fifth Avenue. Camilla also started a list of her own business prospects, hopefully beginning with Felix's friend Dennis Meehan.

So unfamiliar was Camilla with the vernacular of upscale living in New York that she asked the doorman where she should take the elevator to find the Kinnell apartment, only to learn that a maisonette was always on the ground floor. She decided then and there to create a glossary for her readers to accompany the columns she would write.

The Kinnells' maid answered the door, in a black uniform with a white lace apron. While Camilla waited for Charlotte Kinnell to appear, she surveyed her surroundings; she had seen beautiful homes in Palm Beach all her life, but never anything quite like this. Thanks to her days writing *Marry Well's* decorating column, "Pillows of Society," she knew the quality and value of what she was looking at.

The spacious foyer had a granite floor with a curvaceous staircase on its left. On the stairwell wall, there were dozens of small-framed silhouettes, eighteenth and nineteenth century, shadows of familiar profiles from Queen Victoria to Sherlock Holmes. They were hung close together, without any attempt at symmetry, and created a monochromatic relief from the glazed new-cherry red walls. The baseboards were faux painted like the feathers of a bird. A settee upholstered in zebra skin abutted the back wall, but it was smothered in throw pillows — in turquoise, apricot, crimson, and gold — allowing no place to sit if one were so inclined.

Charlotte appeared from the staircase as Camilla was examining the artful floral arrangement on the lapis table underneath the Napoleon III wooden chandelier.

"Are they real?" Camilla asked.

Charlotte looked down at the perfectly-shaped orbs beneath her sweater and then, realizing Camilla meant the flowers, said, "Fabulous, aren't they? You can only tell if you touch them."

"I'm Camilla Madison. I appreciate the opportunity to be here."

"Alyson and my husband are very close friends." Charlotte gritted her teeth as she said it. "He was a 'Him on Him' June of last year."

"Any place off limits?"

"No dearie, wander about, make yourself at home." Camilla heard yapping from upstairs; the cries were getting louder and louder.

"Don't mind them — they're just my bichon frises.

"I love dogs. What are their names?"

"Democrat and Republican."

Camilla stifled a laugh. "Well, thanks again. I'll call for you if I have any questions."

She descended two steps to an enormous living room, with distressed pine paneling painted emerald green. The rear wall of the living room was plate glass and outside was a garden, a famous garden, Alyson had told her, the largest private garden in New York. It was sandwiched between the buildings but generously planted with evergreens and ivy, augmented this early spring by creepers and rhododendron in bloom. The colors seemed to echo the green shades of the living room walls. There were small piles of dog feces everywhere in the otherwise lovely garden, marring the pleasantness of the scene, and a pooper-scooper in the corner, obviously waiting for the maid. To the right off the living room was a dining salon with a solid malachite table; Camilla counted 42 chairs.

The living space was cavernous, with ceilings 16 feet high. The dining room, living room, and study all faced east to the garden. Camilla turned left at the plate glass sliding doors and entered a square room more subdued and tranquil than the rest. The distressed pine was unpainted here and its natural sheen was a lustrous honey color. Around the doorframe hung framed boxes of plaster portrait medallions of English poets, most no more than an inch across in diameter. A chandelier shaped like an overgrown pinecone was suspended from the ceiling of the alcove leading into the room.

Camilla took notes as she moved through the rooms; everything in the study seemed to have a twin — a set of jugs, two portrait busts, matching gilt mirrors, Rigaud candles and miniature pairs of porcelain shoes. The bookshelves were lined with brand new copies of biographies and histories, none of which she suspected the owners had ever opened. There was a deep wine cellar at the end of the room; Camilla peered through the glass door and guessed that there were as many bottles on its racks as there were books on the shelves just outside.

The Kinnells had bought the superintendent's apartment next door, relegating the super to the converted suite of maids rooms on the thirteenth floor, and broken through to create a kitchen the size of a small ballroom. The walls were lined with custom made shelving on which were displayed Charlotte's collection of glazed pottery; Camilla recognized asparagus Barbotines, rich grass green Lunéville plates, and coppery antique vermicelli-patterned Faucon dishes from Aptes. Other groupings had sunflowers or leaves, butterflies or pansies.

When she tiptoed gingerly upstairs, to see what the six bedrooms were like, she bumped into Charlotte, who looked as if she was on her way out.

"Any questions? I have a lunch appointment at Le Cirque."

Camilla flipped through her pad. "Just a couple. What brokerage firm are you using and what's the asking price?"

"We've given the exclusive to Deirdre Cortile at Griffin and she's priced it at seven million."

"May I ask why you're selling?"

"Oh, dearie, can't you tell — we need more space."

"Are there apartments with more space?" Camilla asked, incredulous.

"Lots. But we haven't started looking yet…maybe a town house, or a penthouse. Anyway, we've decided to wait until we have an offer on this one. What time did you say the photographer was coming?"

"Four o'clock. His name is Rex." Camilla neither stated that he was just a summer intern nor that he was also Alyson's stepson. She simply assumed Charlotte would know if she was meant to.

"Good — after lunch and before dinner. I should be home."

When she got back to their place on 76th Street, Camilla told Rose every detail of her first viewing and how much she expected to enjoy this job. It would be so much more interesting than the decorating column had been, because here she would meet all kinds of people in their natural habitats, rather than just designers in studios showing only what they wanted her to see.

The Kinnell adventure was even funnier in the re-telling, causing them to laugh so hard that their sides began to cramp. The sheer audacity to think that an apartment the size of a mansion wouldn't be big enough for a couple and two little dogs struck both Rose and Chantal as absurd.

Then Camilla glanced around at Rose's more-than-adequate surroundings, comparing them to the Kinnells' enormous ones. She had read recently that the 13,000 richest families in America have as much income as the 20 million poorest, and those 13,000 have incomes 300 times that of the average family — whatever an average family might be. If that ratio could be expressed in space, it could be by the size difference between Rose's apartment and the Kinnells' maisonette.

Rose disappeared into the kitchen carrying the Pyrex dish with her. Camilla heard the clanging of steel against glass.

"What are you doing?" Camilla shouted.

"I'm transferring the red pepper, tomato, and cabbage gratin into a larger casserole."

"Larger? What for?" Camilla asked.

"It needs more space."

When Doris Sanger returned from her symposium, she immediately phoned Camilla, who told her about Marry Well Realty, prompting Doris to invite them all to brunch. "You know, Camilla — I may give you my apartment to sell. It's a fabulous little art deco jewel. I hate to give it up but I need a new place with terraces. I bought a little Moscow toy terrier who'll never be able to hold it in when I'm gone lecturing all day."

Camilla was thrilled that Doris was back, although she felt newly empowered and independent without her. She attributed her clarity to the invigoration of working again, the excitement of her new venture, and the pumped up feeling of just having put the Kinnell column — her first — to bed.

Camilla and Doris Sanger arranged to meet in the latter's art deco duplex in her non-doormanned prewar condo on East 57th Street off Sutton

Place at eleven, so she and Doris could talk business before Rose and Merry were due to arrive at noon.

As soon as Camilla stepped off the elevator onto the 12th floor landing, she smelled garlic and oregano wafting down the hall. She could hear the high-pitched barking of Doris' new dog, accompanied by the cooing of pigeons that were nesting outside on the window ledge. As Camilla rang the buzzer, she realized that this would be the first time she would enter the front door, rather than the office entrance, and actually see how Doris lived. The gravity of their changing roles hit her forcefully.

"Welcome," Doris said, kissing her baby's furry little mouth.

Like many childless women that Camilla had known, Doris treated her new pet to the affection she might lavish on a family of four. The dog's name was Chekarf, and the fabric on his four-poster bed, positioned center-stage in the large living space, was draped with fabric in a cherry orchard toile.

"Smells delicious," Camilla commented, referring to the homemade manicotti baking in the oven.

"Oh, thank you! Chekarf showers with me every morning. Nothing worse than a stinky dog."

"Who will watch him when you travel?" Camilla asked.

"I'm hoping to take him everywhere I go."

Doris's originality extended beyond her hair and her dog to her decorating style. The brushed steel casement windows in her apartment were very tall, and had been accented by simple moldings that looked like picture frames. Many of the original walls had been removed, to create a loft-like expanse, with highly polished walnut floors forming a continuous wooden sea between the textile-block covered walls.

There was a large sofa, covered in a chocolate and vanilla checked pattern, from which one could admire the view — a funny life-size replica of a Hereford cow that lived on the terrace belonging to an apartment across the street.

"It moos every hour on the hour, like a church bell," Doris explained.

"Don't the neighbors complain?" asked Camilla.

Doris shrugged. "This is New York. Anything goes."

There was a 1920s Pleyel piano supported by massive alate legs in the corner, and a pair of acid-green divans positioned in front of a 1930s white marble fireplace mantle inlaid with stylized floral designs. All the furniture was from the 1920s and 1930s, with strong lines and simple forms. It had been reupholstered in undiluted colors — acid green, rich blue the same cobalt color as Doris' hair, ruby red, and the yellow-orange color of reflectors on bicycle wheels.

"Did you use a decorator?" Camilla asked, scribbling in her pad.

"I tried. But I couldn't find one who could visualize what I wanted. A home should reflect who you are. So I did it myself."

"Why art deco?" Camilla asked.

"It was the greatest period of creativity in the twentieth century. Don't forget…the 1920s and '30s spawned not only art deco but psychoanalysis as well."

"It's terrific," Camilla said, thinking how little she knew about the private side of this woman who had contributed so much to her own self-understanding.

Camilla and Doris settled at the long stone counter that separated the kitchen from the living space. Doris poured a glass of Los Vascos cabernet for Camilla and one for herself. She opened the refrigerator door and produced a platter of beautifully decorated hors d'oeuvres — including patés with parsley garnishes and smoked salmon with crème fraîche and dill.

"So, have you heard from Robert?" Doris asked, as she tore romaine leaves into bite-sized pieces and tossed them in a silver-rimmed wooden salad bowl.

Camilla tried to come up with a clever response, but only one answer rolled off her tongue: "Not a word."

"You may think Robert's leaving was devastating — on a par with Rocky and your parents' death — but I have a feeling you'll come to view it as the best thing that ever happened to you," Doris said.

"What makes you say that?" Camilla asked.

"You've changed. I thought I heard it in your voice the other night, but I can see it for sure now."

"I do feel strong and optimistic…do you really think it has anything to do with Robert leaving?"

"More with your having survived Robert leaving. My husband left me too, but eons ago."

Camilla was stunned. "I never knew you were married. What happened?"

"One day, when I was just a little older than you, my husband and I were in a restaurant in Paris — Tour d'Argent. We were walking down a long hallway to our table and I caught our reflections in the mirrored wall. I thought 'Who are those people?' I'll never forget it. I knew it was over."

"Was he a psychologist?"

"He was a professor of psychology at NYU, wrote often for *Psychology Today* — Stanislas Sanger. Ever hear of him?"

115

"The name doesn't ring a bell. Are you still friends?"

"He's dead. Left me for an undergraduate who liked to party all night, and then he overdosed on amphetamines. He had to work, you see. He was so well-known, in demand; it's amazing you never heard his name. But, then again, we're all forgotten after our 15 minutes of fame, aren't we?"

Camilla sipped her wine slowly as she took in Doris's words. She knew Andy Warhol had coined the expression about fame; odd, she thought, to be immortalized by a soup can and killed by a masseuse.

"Do you mind if I see the upstairs before Rose and Merry arrive?" Camilla asked.

The staircase wound up in an elongated spiral to a hallway decorated with a stunning collection of posters from art deco and art nouveau expositions, promoting room settings by Eliel Saarinen, Joseph Urban, Raymond Hood, and Eugene Schoen. There were two high-gloss wooden chairs on bronze casters by Frank Lloyd Wright. The master bedroom walls were hung with patterned ivory damask, symmetrically dotted by wall sconces with fan-shaped alabaster shades. Doris had a period dressing table, its top inlaid with shagreen and ivory, its front veneered in amboyna.

The bed was simple and spare, with a black fur bedspread. The master bath had an octagonal window over the tub that echoed a mirror of the same shape above the sink. Even Doris's towels had a period look; they were brown and beige, with the monogram DS in block script. The buzzer sounded as Camilla finished her tour; she heard Chekarf yapping all the way to the door.

When Merry saw Chekarf, she let out an uninhibited howl. Rose sat Merry down by the cherry orchard bed, chubby legs in velvet tights crossed Indian style. Chekarf lathered her in licks, making Merry laugh some more, as she tried to catch his wagging white tail in between her pudgy little palms. But when Rose tried to teach Merry to identify the chess pieces, she seemed more interested in sticking them in her mouth than moving them across the board.

Doris had made a delicious meal — manicotti, gorgonzola salad, veal shank, and homemade zabaglione. Rose wrote down all the recipes, especially the zabaglione:

6 egg yolks, beaten

2/3 cup sugar

1 cup Marsala

½ tsp. vanilla

½ tsp. orange bits

1/8 tsp. cinnamon

1 cup heavy cream

"Then beat it all with a whisk," Doris told Rose.

"For how long?" Rose asked.

"The more you beat it, the sweeter and softer it becomes," Doris sighed heavily. "Pleasure can be measured in an inverse relationship to pain."

Camilla and Rose exchanged glances. "Doris, I'd like to use your recipes in a companion article to Camilla's. Is that OK?"

"I don't know…" Doris hesitated.

"The publicity will help move the apartment faster. We can give reprints of the articles to prospective buyers. Anything published has an implied third party endorsement," Camilla explained.

Doris digested Camilla's comments. "Fine." She smiled. "When do you expect the articles to appear in the magazine?"

Rose deferred the question to Camilla. "In August. The first column, on our editor's friends Gary and Charlotte Kinnell, is due out in July," Camilla said.

"And when do you think I should list the apartment for sale?" Doris asked.

"Statistically, you'd get the best price...and the highest demand... next spring...but it depends on how anxious you are," Camilla said. "I'm taking the test on Monday so, if all goes well, I should have my license within a couple of weeks. We could list it then...or wait."

Doris sighed. "I love this place. I'm in no hurry. Chekarf can last at least another six months peeing on newspaper."

"We'll plan for next spring then." Camilla embraced Doris, eliciting a growl from Chekarf.

When it was time for them to leave, Doris saw them to the door.

"Well, good luck with your test on Monday, Camilla. I think you'll be happy in your new career."

"Happiness is relative," Camilla responded, kissing both Doris and Chekarf good-bye.

Chapter Six

The real estate salesperson's exam was given every Monday morning at the Department of Licensing's office building on Centre Street. The test was multiple choice and so easy that Camilla finished in 40 minutes. A week later, she learned that she had passed. As she was reading her grade, Jennifer called from Walter Strong's office to let her know that the lawyers had received approval from New York State for a new division of West Coast Properties d/b/a Marry Well Realty.

Within two hours of the July issue of *Marry Well*, carrying Camilla's column on the Kinnell apartment, hitting the newsstands, her voice mail was flooded with calls from owners wanting their apartments featured. Camilla called them all back and chose two soon-to-be-bachelors-again, Mac Sanders and Sam Jacobs, whose apartments she would cover in her September and October columns respectively.

Deirdre Cortile called a week after that to thank Camilla for the great publicity. She congratulated her on landing such a terrific job. She said she wasn't a bit surprised; she knew Camilla had it in her the whole time. Then she confided that the column had sparked a bidding war and that the Kinnell apartment was under contract for $8.2 million.

"Wow," was all Camilla could think of to say.

"And the best part was no co-broker; it was a direct deal." At six percent, Camilla realized that the commission would be $492,000.

"Does that mean —"

"It sure does. The Griffin Group gets to keep it all." Deirdre cleared her throat. "Tell me how it happened? How did you go from unemployed single mother to celebrity columnist in six months?"

"It was you, Deirdre, who indirectly gave me the idea at our lunch."

"I don't understand…"

Camilla told Deirdre the entire story, from beginning to end. To Deirdre's credit, she bellowed with delight.

"So you're going to be a competitor now, eh? Well, there's always room for one more. Feel free to call me if you have any questions. I'd be happy to help."

Deirdre lowered her voice and began to pitch Camilla on writing columns on all of her exclusive listings — the television actress's triplex at The Majestic, the investment banker's pad on Beekman Place, the Park Avenue board president's 12-room apartment, which he was forced to sell because he had just been indicted. "Just say the word, and I'll set it all up." Camilla took notes, acknowledging to herself that Deirdre could be an excellent source for material for her column, and a good business friend as well.

When Camilla looked up after finishing her call she saw Rex, camera slung over his shoulder and blond hair in need of a trim. He proudly placed the July issue, open to the Kinnell's spread, flat on the desk before her. "Well, not bad for our first collaboration!"

Camilla liked this kid, although she didn't know why exactly. She thought she just responded to his naturalness, a respite from the artificiality of the world she now inhabited. Even though he came from money, he was so unassuming.

"The photos turned out great. Good job! I think I'll request your assistance on all of my columns — that is…until you go back to school."

Rex beamed. He sat with his knees apart; he tapped his left foot nervously, making his leg bounce up and down like a pogo stick.

Jennifer buzzed Camilla on the intercom to announce that a package had arrived for her. In the box was a rubber chicken from Alyson with a certificate that said: "Congratulations! The committee presents you with the Pullet-Surprise for your July column in *Marry Well*."

She was amused, but knew better than to count her chickens before they had hatched.

At dinner that night, Camilla and Rose celebrated. They talked excitedly about Camilla's future plans and gossiped about Alyson and Rex.

"She's even less discreet now that Rex is interning for the summer," Rose said, shaking her head as she whipped the potatoes into snowy peaks.

Camilla had noticed too. "Isn't she afraid Rex will tell his father?"

"It's as if she's testing us. Daring Rex. She was really specific this time; it's not funny anymore. She spoke to us in front of Rex about her last trip to Florida as if she were reciting a bad poem: 'lots of yachts, wine divine, irrational passion….'"

"Oh, God. That is bad," Camilla said.

Rose shrugged. "I think she's challenging her husband; I guess it makes her feel powerful. Here's Walter Strong, chairman of this and board member of that, much more successful than even she. Maybe by having affairs she proves who's got the upper hand."

"When I met with her to present the Marry Well Realty idea, she told me she makes the rules…" Camilla thought out loud.

"And she's telling a roomful of people who work for her, including her husband's son, ordinary folks with dull lives, how she watched her lover 'melting into his pillows, a fine line of drool running from the side of his mouth'. She didn't care, she said, because she had gotten what she went to Florida for."

Camilla and Rose sat in silence for a while as they heaped braised Brussels sprouts, sautéed spinach, and creamy potatoes on their plates.

"I feel sorry for her, Rose. What do you think she's looking for?"

"No idea. Alyson once said she could count her lovers in the hundreds if she ever cared to remember them all, which she didn't, only those who satisfied her. Chuck Maynard asked her what a man had to do to please her. She answered: 'Follow orders.'"

Camilla poured the last of the bottle of champagne they had been drinking into Rose's glass. She heard Merry, who had apparently woken up, and went into the bedroom to get her.

"It's easy to condemn her. She seems so...blatant and greedy. But I'll say one thing for her. Men seem to love her. What's her secret?" Camilla wondered.

"There was a woman at the office who started after you went on leave and quit a month later because of Alyson's flagrancy. She said it felt like sexual harassment, although she couldn't put her finger on exactly how — she asked her the same thing."

"Did Alyson answer?"

"She said that the secret to her success with men was that she cared little about pleasing them. She focused her erotic energies on her own pleasure, inadvertently driving them wild with her sensuality and excitability. Her capacity for orgasm and to lose herself in the sex act, combined with her lack of inhibition, fed a man's ego more than any tricks and techniques that she could perform, because they thought it was they who brought her to such heights of ecstasy."

Maybe Alyson was right, Camilla thought, as extreme as her ideas seemed. She remembered how hard she had tried to make Robert happy in bed, always trying to please him, to do what he liked. Then the sex was over, and it seemed her turn had never come. He had such a strong preference for oral sex; looking back, it was amazing she had gotten pregnant at all. "It sounds like autoeroticism, not lovemaking," Camilla said.

"She's proud of it too. But she told them that only selfish women could be good lovers. The others were nothing more than 'lubricated receptacles,' the kind that men filled, then tossed away."

"You could write a book about her," Camilla said.

"Maybe someday I will," Rose replied. "I could call it *Her on Her.*"

Merry was engrossed with the spoon in her hands. Camilla buried her nose in Merry's hair; Rose bent over and tickled Merry's toes. Camilla's mind was on Walter, intelligent, reasonable, gentle Walter. "What about her husband? He seems such a wonderful man."

Rose sighed. "Oh, she talks about him too. How much money he has, how successful he is..."

"How can she talk about all of these private things in front of everyone who works for her?" Camilla asked.

"We're her most rapt audience. Don't you see? It's verbal exhibitionism. It turns her on."

Camilla passed Merry over to Rose. The baby was wide awake and experimenting with tones and volume, trying to make words, but other than that one time she had repeated Aly-son, she kept just missing. Camilla was clearing the table when the phone rang. It was Alyson from her cell phone.

"What's that noise in the background?" Alyson asked.

Camilla tried to hush Merry but it was no use. "That noise is my daughter."

"How can you work at home with that racket?"

"Does it matter?"

"Maybe before. But not now. Not after that terrific column."

Camilla was relieved. She wasn't sure if she should mention to Alyson that she had passed her real estate salesperson's exam or remind her that she would be starting at Walter's office on Monday, not while she was so high about the column. "You shouldn't worry," Camilla said. "I have a terrific babysitter. Merry won't interfere with my writing the column."

"Mary? As in virgin Mary?"

"No, Alyson. MERRY."

"M-E-R-R-Y? Is her father's name Christmas?"

Camilla rolled her eyes, thinking that Alyson should stick to humor she understood — dirty jokes. "Glad you called. I was going to call you tomorrow. I wanted to know what you thought about my piece on Doris Sanger's duplex."

"Rex's photos are divine, and your writing is punchy and tight. I know you were under the gun to make the June 15th deadline for the August issue, but next time, pick a man. Remember who our audience is. And Doris Sanger — she's a nobody from nowhere!"

"I don't agree. She's published all the time. She's one of the country's experts on the psychological repercussions of rape —"

"Well, that's a penetrating subject."

Exasperated, Camilla said, "Alyson, did you ever think featuring a woman in your column from time to time might expand our readership? After all, men like to marry well too."

"No. Absolutely not. The *Marry Well* audience is women-only. Could you imagine a beditorial on a female? What would it be about? How to make perfect French corners?"

"There are many successful women, Alyson. Like you, for instance."

"I'm an exception."

Camilla decided the conversation was going nowhere, so she switched tactics. "Well, you'll be happy to know that I've lined up bachelors for September and October. They called me after the Kinnell piece ran. Do you have any ideas about whose home we should feature after that?"

"As a matter of fact, that's why I'm calling you. It's getting harder and harder to find men for my beditorials. The corporate scandals and stock market shakeout have decimated the ranks — I mean the Tech-Titans are more like the Tech-Titanics — sunk. And Kenneth Lay, always true to his name before, won't even come to the phone these days. Former publicity hounds are publicity shy. The only industry that seems to be an exception is entertainment but, then again, that's what they do isn't it? I've been toying with Dawson Landers for years—"

"Dawson Landers!" Camilla knew he was the creator/producer of *The Boondocks* and *The Suburbanites*."

"Shows you how desperate I've become. He's not perfect, because he's bi —"

"Bisexual?"

"Heavens no — although one never knows for sure. Bi-*coastal*. He lives mostly in L.A. Now he's finally come around but only because his townhouse has been on the market for eight months and he heard from Gary Kinnell how effective your column can be. He's offered us a package deal: he intends to take the house off the market for a few months — something about regenerating mystique before the re-run — then if we put him and his townhouse on the November cover, he'll grant a "Him on Him" interview, and here's the clincher — he'll give the exclusive to sell the house to Marry Well Realty!"

"Can we do that?"

"Listen, Camilla... West Coast Properties filed a d/b/a — doing business as — certificate for Marry Well Realty. It's approved, that means we're legal. I'll talk to Walter about it, but what I'm thinking is an upscale residential division of WCP — we can be to real estate what private banking is to Goldman Sachs — highly lucrative hands-on handling of high net worth individuals embarking on life changes."

"Alyson, that's great," she said, but her mind was working. Alyson was spouting Camilla's idea as if it were her own, which meant she believed in the concept, but the idea of Marry Well Realty being a division of West Coast Properties sounded a little too permanent for her. "Alyson...don't forget that this is temporary. In nine months, we're leaving the womb."

"Don't worry," Alyson assured her, in a corn syrupy tone. "I'm just being helpful. One businesswoman to another. Partners, right?"

Alyson did not strike Camilla as the helpful type. "All right, as long as everyone is on the same page," Camilla said.

"Onward. I've arranged for you to meet Dawson Landers on Saturday morning at his house. The address is 7 East 79th Street. Eleven-thirty sharp."

"Alyson, one question. Any idea why the house hasn't sold?"

"Well, for one thing, he's asking $21 million — I haven't seen it myself, so I can't tell you if it's worth it or not. For another, there's some sort of zoning thingy — it's not purely residential — it used to be the Lycée de Paris, so technically it's zoned as a school."

"How did he get around that?" She had just learned about New York's strict zoning laws in Professor D'Angelo's real estate class.

"The house is so enormous that he created a second entrance to a basement film school/television studio for budding screenwriters, actors, directors, and producers. And thirdly, he's got his buddy Jeffrey Ratchitt running interference."

"Jeffrey Ratchitt?" The name sounded familiar.

"Camilla. Jeffrey is…"

But before Alyson could elaborate, the signal went dead.

Dawson Landers' house was an Italianate limestone mansion located off Fifth Avenue. When Camilla entered his home office study, located to the immediate left of the front hall, Dawson was on the phone. She could see his balding pate and sharp profile as his head was stooped over, with his pointy chin practically touching his chest. His feet were up on the desk. She took a seat on an upholstered bench outside his office door, noticing a sign above the doorframe with Dante's ominous warning hand-painted in Bookman script: *"Abandon hope, all ye who enter here."*

"Damn it, Bruce," Dawson said into the phone. "Send over at least three. I hate this. Just when the audience was getting used to her, she quits. Now I've got to get a new one fast. We're supposed to start shooting the fall season next week. I'm putting my secretary on — she'll take the names. Oh, Bruce, one more thing… only send me blondes."

Without changing his position, he motioned for Camilla to come in and take a seat. Camilla extended her hand; he ignored it. "Mr. Landers —"

"Sorry," he said. "Actresses are flakes: It's the beauty. Beauty comes with no values."

"Mr. Landers —" Camilla started to say again.

"Dorothea!" Dawson shouted over her through the door that separated him from his secretary.

"Coming, Mr. Landers." Dorothea stood in the doorframe to his office with an old-fashioned steno pad in her hand, poised to record his demands.

"Order me a turkey club on rye. Extra bacon, extra mayo."

"Anything to drink?"

"Yeah. A Dr Pepper." He hadn't thought to offer anything to Camilla. "So you're the reporter, Ms. Madison. Ask away. My associate, Mr. Ratchitt, will be by soon to give you a tour of the house."

"I'd like your perspective on the house's attributes. Describe as best you can what you have enjoyed most about living here," Camilla said in her most professional demeanor.

He seemed speechless, as if he couldn't think of a single thing about living period that he liked. While he was mulling over her question, the intercom buzzed. Dawson picked up the phone. "Mrs. Landers is on the line. Calling from Santa Barbara," his secretary said.

He flipped on the speakerphone. "Darling, how's Santa Barbara?"

"I miss the smog in L.A.," she replied.

"When will you be home?"

"Well, that depends on you. Nicky is loving tennis camp and Robin met a boy at the club. I'm in no hurry, but if you need me —"

"No, no, lovey. Stay awhile," he said too quickly. "I'm swamped here in New York. I've got engagements every night this week."

"Well, that's no surprise," she replied.

"Listen. I'm in a meeting. Can I call you later?" But before she could answer, he disconnected her.

The coffee shop down the block on Lexington delivered quickly, and Camilla watched Dawson devour the sandwich, pickle, and slaw within minutes. He belched without inhibition and was picking the breadcrumbs off his shirt, disposing of them by popping them into his mouth.

"Any more questions?" he asked Camilla.

"Just one, Mr. Landers. Why are you selling?"

"Divorce," he said. "But you can't print that — my wife doesn't know." There was a tap on the doorframe. "Ah, Jeffrey — just in time."

Jeffrey Ratchitt was sparely built. His penetrating gaze through small black eyes looked past a cosmetically enhanced nose and a long, blunt-edged chin. His accent was raspy-Brooklyn, but his outfit was studied Brooklyn Heights — low-rise jeans, cowboy boots, Zegna shirt, and a new brown leather jacket. Jeffrey's hair was coiffed to look like silver spun sugar. Camilla watched his face convert to what she was sure he thought was charm but which she immediately detected was a fox-like felicitousness. He seemed familiar, though Camilla was sure she hadn't met him before.

The house tour began on the main floor, outside Dawson's office. As they left, she could hear Dawson talking on the phone in a coquettish way, making plans for later that evening with the person on the other end.

Jeffrey positioned Camilla in front of a bizarre sculpture, which looked like an old bottle drying rack with the bottles intact, a cheese grater, aluminum foil flowers, and an Indonesian mask, appearing like a household totem rather than the piece of art it was intended to be. It seemed to be the usual starting point for the tour.

"You will notice, Ms. Madison, that the house is decorated in a very theatrical style, providing insight into Mr. Landers' creative character."

If he was right, then Dawson Landers was more grotesque and self-indulgent than theatrical. But she could see the parallel with his work; wherever possible, he went for shock value over subtlety. She began to realize that the reason the house hadn't sold, despite its prime location, had little to do with zoning and more with the bizarre décor.

The hallway from Dawson's office to his living space was completely covered in mosaics set in cement. Every inch, including the furniture, was embedded with bits of broken glass, fragments of tile, pebble, and shell. The left wall boasted a mural of the horse-head-on-bedpost scene from *The Godfather,* and the right wall showed an amazing likeness of Hannibal Lecter biting off someone's nose.

As gruesome as these images were, they were but the appetizer for the main course — the "living" room — a misnomer if ever there was one. The grand salon could be described only as a domestic mausoleum; the furniture was draped in crushed black velvet, the cornice veiled in black eyelet strung with black satin bows. Amulets and crucifixes hung in a haphazard way throughout the room, and on every tabletop was a shrine-like arrangement of dead red roses and melted black candles.

Camilla's trepidation increased as they approached the master bedroom. It was trompe l'oeiled to look like the inside of a Pharaoh's tomb, with a nude replica of Cleopatra suspended from the ceiling. While Camilla searched for something that might appeal to the average townhouse customer, she noticed Jeffrey Ratchitt, out of the corner of her eye, caressing the collection of hardened plaster asps resting on the enamel painted window seat.

When he smiled, Camilla could see by their opaqueness that all of his teeth had been capped. "So, how long have you been writing about real estate?" he asked her.

She was stumped as to how much she should reveal. "Why do you ask?"

"I tried to find what else you'd written lately and, with the exception of that one column on Gary and Charlotte's maisonette, I came up with *nada*. Seems you wrote some decorating babble for a while and then — poof — gone from print for two years. Whad ya do — have a baby?"

"Correct." Honesty, she knew, was the best policy. She hadn't expected him to check her out, but it was inevitable that if she were to deal at this level of net worth, her rich and famous clientele and/or their handlers would want to know exactly who she was.

"And just how many real estate properties have you sold before? I called the New York State licensing bureau and they never heard of you."

"I come from a real estate brokerage family. It's in my blood. The shoes may be new but they fit perfectly," she said with more confidence than she felt.

"Well, well, well. You'll fit right in around here. Role playing is Mr. Landers' specialty." He gave a hardy laugh.

They finished the tour and Camilla realized she had taken more than ten pages of notes. She thanked Jeffrey Ratchitt again for his time and he responded with his fox-like grin. She stepped out onto the street where the normally rancid air of New York City smelled sweet as never before.

Camilla walked uptown two blocks to E.A.T. where she bought house-made salads and bagels and a sourdough baguette before hopping on the 79th Street cross-town bus. The temporary loss of appetite she suffered from her experience at chez Landers had passed and she was ravenous. She was pleased to find that she wasn't the only hungry member of her extended family, who attacked the food as if it were their last meal. Merry turned the hunk of bread she had been alternately gnawing and sucking on into a soggy mess while Camilla recounted her adventure for Chantal and Rose.

With a mouthful of lentils and pimentos, Camilla said: "Bingo! Jeffrey Ratchitt…beditorial subject, March 1999."

Rose dashed over to the living room credenza and fished out that issue. "I'm impressed. How can you remember them all?" Rose asked, leafing through the old issue.

"I don't. That one I remember because Alyson was unusually mute about him and sat on a pillow for a week."

"Him!?" Rose remembered the incident too.

"Lord — you don't say he got violent?" Chantal asked. Despite her own sad experience, she was a sweet innocent at heart.

"Alyson denied it. Said a tennis ball hit her in the wrong place," Camilla replied.

"You didn't believe her?" Chantal asked.

"Not unless the racket handle had a mind of its own as well," Rose snickered. "Not bad looking," she said, looking at the open magazine in her lap. "But the hair reminds me of a baked Alaska."

Chantal had a second helping of the eggplant with pine nuts. "Do you have any ideas about how to sell the house, Camilla?"

"In fact, I do. How late can you stay tonight, Chantal? And could you come in tomorrow? I've got a plan hatching and I want to get my strategy on paper. Monday is my first official day in the real estate business and I want to preempt Alyson, Walter, and Jayme with ideas of my own."

"I've got nothing special planned," Chantal answered. "And even if I did, I'd change my plans to help you out."

"Chantal and I can keep Merry busy while you work," Rose added.

Camilla worked all weekend. Fortunately, she had already secured an early slot on Walter's calendar, just prior to the meeting with Jayme and Alyson to discuss the new venture. His secretary, Jennifer, had explained that Mr. Strong always set aside an hour for any new member of his team, to make them feel welcome and to understand their goals. Goals Camilla had — goals galore — and she intended to use her time with Walter alone to her best advantage.

A summer shower had just started when Camilla walked into Walter's office with her laptop and four copies of her presentation. As she set up her laptop to the slide show function and pressed the F7 key, Camilla noticed her hands trembling. She didn't give him a chance to speak until after she had finished her enthusiastic pitch.

First, she presented her concept on Slide One — to found a high-end brokerage firm in Manhattan — with a twist. They would cater to individuals embarking on a life change — not unlike her — such as marriage, divorce, relocation, cohabitation, and upward or downward mobility.

Every customer/buyer would get a Timing Plan tailor-made for his individual needs, based on the template on Slide Two. A team of professionals would provide advice—such as John Confrere about mortgage options and Prissie Easton for decorating tips. Eventually she'd like to bring the services listed on Slide Three in-house, as well as an on-staff lawyer, a lifestyle consultant who would help with school applications, churches, and the location of such essential services as garages, grocery stores, and manicure salons.

Her own experience had taught her how complicated the process of buying a home in New York could be, embroiling a cast of dozens. She saw the opportunity in a one-stop shop, diagrammed on Slide Four — where the customer (not just his cash) would be king.

Each client/seller would receive a detailed Situation Analysis — like the one on Slide Five — that described the competition, assets and liabilities of the property, accurate recommended selling price, and marketing plan. She just happened to illustrate on Slide Six the one that she did for Dawson Landers' townhouse, (which, by the way, she could handle without Jayme), where she suggested offering the house with a $250,000 credit for interior demolition, to be done at the buyer's discretion either before or after the closing took place.

She explained that here was another exclusive she could sign up — now that Marry Well was legal — the psychologist Doris Sanger. As for re-sale, she mentioned she had just landed a movie star customer looking for a spectacular place to buy.

Camilla added that both customers and clients of Marry Well Realty would receive a free lifetime subscription to the magazine as well as an annual gold membership to E-male Dating Service, upon request. "Cross-marketing," she explained.

Camilla also had the idea to start a mini-management division that would pay the expenses for small buildings, such as real estate taxes, water and sewer bills, garbage pickup, pest extermination, and the like. For a multi-home owner, they could perform the same services plus water the plants, have the apartment cleaned, stock the refrigerator, etc., all for a monthly fee. For buildings such as her own on 76th Street — she was almost certain that she could bring them in as a client — she proposed adding maintenance services to repair, for example, torn carpet and damaged wallpaper.

Her projections, if she were to be made head of the division and named exclusive broker for listings she brought in, anticipated $1 million in gross commissions during her first nine months; once Marry Well Realty was spun off and staffed, she expected $3 million in year two, $5 million in year three, etc. Slide Seven looked like this:

	Gross Revenue (Sales and leasing commission plus management fees)	Net Revenue (Less commissions payable to MWR brokers)	Operating Expenses	Marketing (Adv., PR, color Brochures, Photography)	Profit
YEAR 1	$1M	$500,000	($200,000)	($150,000)	$150,000
YEAR 2	$3M	$1,500,000	($600,000)	($450,000)	$450,000
YEAR 3	$5M	$2,500,000	($1,000,000)	($750,000)	$750,000
YEAR 4	$7.5M	$3,750,000	($1,500,000)	($1,125,000)	$1,125,000
YEAR 5	$10M	$5,000,000	($2,000,000)	($1,500,000)	$1,500,000

Walter peered at her over the bridge of his reading glasses. He regarded her curiously, with a dash of admiration sprinkled in. "I see you've done a lot of work. Do you really think you can make those numbers?"

"I reviewed the sales reports of the Real Estate Board of New York as well as every brokerage firm that posts them online. Marketwide, high-end sales are down 6.5 percent, and it takes an average of 84 days, up from 66, for an apartment to sell, but my projections are based on a modest market share, and the firm retaining an average of 50 percent of collected commissions. Unless the market changes dramatically for the worse, piece of cake." She sounded confident but she secretly hoped the piece of cake wouldn't turn out to be the cookie that crumbled.

"I don't know… the economy… interest rates are expected to rise…" Walter said.

Camilla had anticipated his doubt. "Certain segments of the market will be affected for sure, but high-end co-ops and townhouses seem relatively stable —" And she pointed to Slide Eight, illustrating the average sale prices for prime co-op addresses to prove her point:

YEAR/RMS	4-5	CLASSIC 6	7-8	9 +
2002	$1,020,082	$1,553,831	$2,848,299	$5,579,750
2003	$1,160,995	$1,738,000	$2,547,503	$5,103,720
2004 YTD	$1,104,553	$1,626,775	$2,341,620	$4,900,879

They reviewed the numbers some more, with Walter asking cogent questions and offering suggestions. Then he looked up into her expectant blue eyes and said, "I admire your gumption, Camilla. And your timing is good — I really can't spare Jayme from the sales office at Strong Place — no matter what Alyson says. I'm willing to give it a shot. You've got the Landers exclusive, and you can run the show — with my help — for six months. I'm trusting my nose on this one; let's see what you can do."

"I won't let you down. I promise."

"Promise what?" Alyson asked, a faint scent of vintage Arpège surrounding her. She sidled up next to Jayme, who stood in the doorframe next to her. Alyson had on a Ménage A Trois sheer summer dress, in hot pink, and Jayme wore an Armani linen suit in silver gray. Their smiles were frozen in matching grimaces, and Alyson's face was so flushed it blended in with her outfit.

"I've given Camilla the assignment to grow the re-sale side of the business — under the Marry Well brand, of course. She'll use the Landers townhouse as her anchor client. Jayme, you'll concentrate on our sponsor units — specifically Strong Place."

Walter's tone was subtly defiant, almost challenging. Alyson stewed but didn't say a word. Camilla noticed their eyes dueling before she looked down at her own feet.

Jayme broke the silence. "I suppose congrats are in order," she said.

"Walter, may I have a word with you?" Alyson asked, voice strained.

Before he rose to attend to his wife's request, Walter looked at Camilla and said, "Why don't we all have lunch? To firm things up."

Alyson and Jayme looked at each other, to see who would protest first. But Camilla said sweetly, "I wish I could. But I'm closing on my own apartment today at noon. May I have a rain check?" And with that she returned to her new cubicle to grab her umbrella.

Jayme must have thought that Camilla had left the office immediately because Jayme left the door to her private office ajar and the speakerphone activated, enabling Camilla to overhear her.

"Has Alyson lost her marbles?" Jeffrey Ratchitt's Brooklyn accent was loud and clear.

"Happy Monday to you too," Jayme answered.

"How could Alyson assign little Miss Nobody to a $21 million house?"

"You'd have to ask Alyson that question. Seems she made the decision alone."

"What about Walter? Can't you get him to override Alyson's choice? After all, real estate is his domain, or has she pussy-whipped him out of that too?"

"Nobody 'pussy whips' — to use your unattractive phrase — Walter out of or into anything. He's tough, and straight as an arrow. If he ever knew about our arrangement—"

"So, what about our arrangement? I pushed Dawson to fire that insipid mouse from Pander, Martin & Horn and send the business your way. My share should be upwards of $120,000."

"What can I say? Dawson gave it to Alyson, who sent in Camilla, who in turn grabbed the whole pie."

Jeffrey was quiet. "Can't anything be done about her?"

"This girl has impressed Walter. It's useless ..."

"Unless he becomes convinced that she's a conniving little crook —"

"You mean like you, Jeffrey?"

He chuckled. "Takes one to know one, my dear."

"Look, Jeffrey. I don't like her. She's in my way, but Walter Strong is my boss. He's the best one I've ever had —"

"But what if the novice is after your job?"

Jayme tapped her foot while she pondered the possibility. "I don't think she is. This one is too independent. She'll be her own boss. If I'm patient, she'll be gone, and I'll still be Walter's right arm."

"That won't happen before this deal. I brought in that townhouse, Jayme. I brought it in for us…and I want my cut."

"We'll have to come up with some other way."

As she walked downtown to her closing, Camilla thought how like a video game her life had become. Obstacles, impasses, and treachery everywhere. If only one could buy a player's guide for life!

When Camilla returned to the office late that afternoon, it took her two hours to copy and collate the board package Jayme Seagram had left on her desk. It was several hundred pages thick and was comprised of a purchase application, employment verification letter, financial statement with hundreds of pages of bank and brokerage reports, checking accounts, retirement accounts, cash value insurance statements, schedules of real estate owned, art and jewelry inventories, and house rules pertaining to noise, smoking, cigarettes, household help, and the types of windows one could have.

There were eight letters of recommendation, four personal and four financial.

Camilla shook her head. It was ironic that the more one paid for a co-op, the more humiliation one seemed willing to endure. It was nothing more than a sophisticated form of frat house hazing.

Weary from the seemingly endless chore, Camilla deposited the finished board packages on Jayme's desk and grabbed a Snapple from the office kitchen. The iced tea tasted cool and sweet; she stretched, eager to pack up and go home. The telephone rang and she hesitated for a second before picking up the receiver. "Camilla, I've got someone I want you to meet. Come over right away," Alyson's voice commanded.

"I was just on my way home —" It would be at least an hour of subway travel, at rush hour no less, to get all the way downtown to Lafayette Street from Times Square and then all the way back home uptown.

"Good," Alyson said. "*Marry Well* is on your way home."

Everyone else had left the *Marry Well* offices by the time Camilla arrived. It was clear that the cleaners had not yet come. Clear plastic cups half-filled with flat Diet Coke, trashcans ripe with refuse, the white roses on the receptionist's desk wilting away, their snow-white petals outlined in brown fringe. Computer screens dark, phones silent, windows shut tight, and everything stopped dead in its tracks.

When Camilla approached Alyson's office and saw Rocky Faber sitting on the bidet chair, she nearly fainted. As she made her way down the hallway, she caught sight of him before he saw her. She considered bolting, down the stairs, out the window, onto a waiting horse. But then Alyson spotted Camilla standing there, a doe in a Hummer's headlights, and motioned to her to come in.

Rocky Faber stood up and turned to face her. Camilla thought there was a look of recognition in his eye, a fast-paced rotation of possibilities going through his brain like a slot machine deciding which fruit to land on.

The shark gray suit that he wore appeared silver in the waning light. The yellow smile she had remembered greeted her and was accompanied by an extended hand, one that brought chills when she recalled how it had touched her before.

"Ms. Madison, a pleasure to meet you," Rocky said.

If Rocky remembered her, he wasn't letting on. A little voice inside of her, sounding amazingly like Doris, nudged her and egged her on: "Here's your chance to confront him, your opportunity for revenge."

"Well, Camilla, are you going to shake our client's hand?" Alyson said.

Camilla took a tentative step toward him and clasped his dry hand. "Mr. Faber," she said, nodding her head.

"Rocky. Call me Rocky — everyone does."

Rocky and Camilla sat on the matching bidets as Alyson enthused about the marvelous relationship they would all have. Camilla smelled the scent of clove, an odor so loathsome to her that she avoided Christmas potpourris and Virginia ham as others would a dead skunk.

"So," Alyson began, "I had the wonderful luck to be seated next to Rocky several months ago at one of Walter's National Real Estate Forum functions at the Plaza Hotel. "The minute I met him, I just knew he'd be perfect for a "Him on Him." Don't you think?"

Camilla just didn't know what to say. Fortunately, Alyson didn't wait for an answer. "I'm moving people around so that Rocky — who might have been the archetypal man for *Marry Well* — will be featured in the December double issue." Alyson posed as if waiting for a round of applause. When it didn't come, she put her hands on her hips and said: "Have you nothing to say, Camilla?"

"Congratulations?" Camilla had had enough. It had been an exhausting day and she felt disgusting. The pants suit she had picked up at Bloomingdale's was wrinkled, her makeup had all but disappeared, and her ponytail was in disarray more like a feather duster than the clean professional look it had 12 hours before. Camilla stood up, about to politely say her good-byes, when Alyson glared.

"Sit down!" Alyson ordered.

Rocky stood erect and gave Camilla a small bow as well-bred men do when a lady is about to leave — or return to — the party.

"Camilla, Rocky has a pied-à-terre on Fifth Avenue that he's agreed to let you sell. He's about to become free — of wife number three — and has decided to move to New York full time. He's selling the place and will be looking for an appropriately posh condo with Park views. If you do a good job, he'll buy that through you too."

It took all Camilla's self-control to not lose it right there. The real Camilla saw a movie of herself screaming as loud as she could, pulling out all her hair, and gouging out chunks of her flesh with sharpened fingernails.

"Are you feeling all right, Camilla?" Rocky asked. When he touched her elbow, her reflexes jerked it away.

"Maybe I am a bit unwell…"

"Alyson, why don't we adjourn? You and I can speak tomorrow," Rocky offered.

"But —" Alyson started to protest.

Rocky glanced at the watch on his wrist. "I'm due at a dinner at eight." After walking around the desk to peck Alyson on the cheek, he brushed by Camilla and whispered, "Lovely meeting you."

And he left.

Camilla felt clammy and flushed.

"Listen, Camilla. I'm sorry if you're feeling ill, but before you go I just want to make sure you understand how important this is." So while Camilla sat catatonic, Alyson waxed poetic about the great opportunity that Rocky represented. Part of her speech had something to do with Alyson's investment in one of Rocky's developments in the south, but it might as well have fallen on deaf ears. After ten minutes, even Alyson realized she wasn't getting through.

"Do you take magnesium, Camilla? It does wonders for PMS."

As commanded, the taxi took Camilla to Doris Sanger's address. Chekarf licked the tears off her face as Doris embraced her and asked her, "What's wrong?"

After she told Doris what had happened, Doris said: "I know this is painful for you, but can't you see — he reduces you to a frightened child. You've got to fight it. Forget it. Move on."

"He's still so powerful, Doris. You should see the way Alyson tries to impress him —"

"It doesn't matter if he's powerful in the conventional ways the world measures. Only you can let him be powerful over you."

"He didn't even recognize me. It was as if he ruined my life and didn't notice — as if I were a bug and his shoe squashed me. He hasn't given it another thought."

"You don't know that —"

"Yes, I do."

"Even if you're right, it's him, his narcissism. It has nothing to do with you. It was just bad luck — wrong place, wrong time."

Camilla was crying again, gulping, gasping sobs. "Doris, it's just —"

143

"I know. There comes a time for each of us when we have to let go of the past and take responsibility for our own happiness. Think hard — what would make you get over this? What would set you free?"

"I don't know —"

Chekarf whined until he was picked up and held. Camilla wished she could do the same.

"Doris, there's something I haven't told you. Something that binds me to this man, makes it impossible to forget."

"Does he remind you of your father?"

The question perplexed Camilla, and she thought carefully about what Doris had asked. "No, it's not that. There was a child, a son, conceived from the rape. Rocky doesn't know."

Doris' normally placid face registered alarm. Camilla knew Doris would be shocked by the secret she had managed to keep to herself all these years, even during their doctor/patient time.

"The baby, Camilla, what's become of him?"

With a mixture of sadness and shame, she replied, "I have no idea."

Chapter Seven

Relieved by her confession to Doris, Camilla was calmer when she finally got home later that night. She found Merry rolling around the bedroom of Rose's apartment in a baby exerciser that looked like stacked fruit-flavored Life Savers; she was wearing a bright orange wig and a soft Hanna Andersen baby romper. She looked up at her mother and grinned as soon as she saw her, paddling and moving clear across the room, bumping into Camilla and bouncing off again. Camilla bent down to give her a kiss.

She heard a rustling noise coming from the closet. "Rose?"

Rose emerged from behind the louvered door, wearing black sweat pants and a T-shirt from Abercrombie & Fitch. "What happened to you? You look like you've been mugged."

"Sit down, we need to talk," Camilla said.

Rose found a spot on the bed and regarded Camilla warily, as if that tone of voice was prelude to the message. Merry rolled through the doorway and let out a cheerful chirp, breaking the tension in the room.

"Rose, you're not going to believe this. I just came from *Marry Well* and guess who Alyson's 'Him on Him' column will be on in the December issue?"

"Michael Bloomberg?"

"Cold." Camilla looked very serious.

Rose lifted Merry into her arms and kissed her all over. "Who then?" Rose asked.

"Rocky Faber, Florida Gold Coast real estate tycoon, will be *Marry Well's* cover story — and Alyson's column — in December."

"How could that be? How do they know each other? He's strictly Palm Beach — what..."

"Alyson met him at a real estate dinner. It appears that she's adopted him as her newest project."

"Uh-oh."

"I was summoned to a meeting in her office and there he was. He didn't recognize me."

"Oh, Camilla. Are you sure?"

"Either that or he's an amazing faker."

"What did you do?"

"I was stunned. The idea of Rocky the rapist in the same city as me made my memory ache. I just sat there, watching in disbelief, as he turned on the charm. He was very focused on Alyson."

"It's probably a good thing that he didn't recognize you. He'll go back to Palm Beach —"

"It's not that simple — Alyson said that she had found Rocky and that I would sell both his pied-à-terre and find him a new multi-million dollar bachelor pad now that I had my license. And that you humble Marry Well staffers should watch these transactions closely to learn how 'simple referrals can spawn a chain of fresh revenues'."

"She said this in front of Rocky?"

"No. After he left."

"Why do you have deal with him? Let Jayme Seagram do it. Yes, that's it — you can kill two birds with one stone."

Camilla was shaking her head. "Alyson wouldn't allow it. She only gets her money from me. Jayme has nothing to do with Marry Well Realty — thanks to my convincing presentation to Walter Strong this morning.

How can I explain my reluctance to handle a client like Rocky after my ferocious and successful sales pitch of today?"

"Tell her what happened between you and Rocky. Even Alyson might understand that."

"You know Alyson. If I refuse her, even with a good reason, she'll find a way to dump me. It's been 19 years since I've seen Rocky. I'm a grown woman now; he's an old man. Doris thinks I can handle it."

Rose took her hand. "I hate to say it, but you're probably right. If you squirm away from brokering Rocky's transactions, Alyson would consider you weak and incapable of the job."

"And, if I tell Alyson about the rape, Alyson would probably laugh and use the story as an anecdote in her column. Maybe it's time I face my ghosts…" Camilla said. "Doris said that until I do, I'd never be free."

But the humiliation of that afternoon on the boat stayed with her; she could feel him pawing her and forcing himself inside her as if it had happened that very afternoon.

On the other hand, nearly two decades had elapsed since she had seen him last — he hadn't attended the memorial service or even sent a condolence card when her parents had been killed — and she would have to confront him sometime if she hoped to get on with her life.

"Of all the potential interview subjects, why him?" Camilla asked Rose, as she turned Merry toward her and held her close.

"Who knows? Maybe he was sent to you by some divine intervention. Let's face it…you haven't exactly hit the jackpot with relationships."

Rose's words stung Camilla as only the truth from a close friend can. "It's not only Rocky — although he's a big part of my fear of men."

Secretly, she thought: *How could anyone love a woman who could abandon her own child?*

"I know what you mean," Rose said, misunderstanding Camilla's point. "Look around us. How often does some married man who seems perfectly happy with his wife hit on you? It happens to me at least once a week."

Camilla shook her head. "It's more the broken hearts and disappointments that discourage me. All those guys who didn't work out, for one reason or another —"

"I'll admit you have to kiss a lot of frogs before you find a prince, but what keeps me going is the idea that when I come out on the other side of love I'll be larger, richer, and more fulfilled — even if it ends badly. And you, Camilla...I think you are becoming who you are meant to be."

Camilla shook her head slowly. She thought about all the men she had known. Some she knew were fine — like her father — and some she thought were good, like John Confrere and Walter Strong, but she had never been *involved* with them. She had been in love with Robert; at least she thought she had.

"It will take a miracle for me to trust a man again, Rose."

"It's not men as a species who are untrustworthy, Camilla. It's certain people. I hate to keep using Alyson as an example, but she's the biggest philanderer I know."

"Oh my God, you don't think she'd sleep with Rocky do you?"

"Look, whether she does or doesn't isn't relevant to the fact that you need to rise above people like Rocky and Alyson, get past them, open up to the other kind — someone who can be a husband to you and a father to Merry."

Camilla instinctively offered Merry her breast, even though Merry showed no sign of hunger. Nursing comforted them both; it was a two-way pacifier.

Jayme woke them all up at 6:40 AM, shrieking into the telephone like a shrew.

"That board package you prepared last night is a piece of *gar*-bage. Get in here first thing and do it over," Jayme said.

Fortunately, Chantal was due at 8:00 AM. Camilla fed Merry, showered and dressed as quickly as she could, so she would have time to have breakfast with Rose. While she and Rose sipped coffee, and nibbled on Zabar's raisin pecan bread, they replayed the scene from the night before.

Chantal's key clicked in the door.

Merry had been standing unsteadily, holding onto Camilla's chair for support. When she saw Chantal, she took three tentative steps, arms out for balance, toward her. Chantal dropped her book bag to catch Merry before she fell.

"Did you see that?!" Rose asked.

"I sure did. Her first step! I'm keeping a spreadsheet on Excel, recording every milestone. This day will be highlighted in pink!" Camilla said.

Rose, Chantal, and Camilla formed a tight ring around Merry, praising her as if she had just won an Olympic medal. Merry lifted her arms toward Chantal, causing Chantal to beam with joy. Camilla noticed how much Chantal had changed since coming to work for her last May. She stood taller now, and took greater care in her appearance. Her figure was slimmer, thanks to Rose's high fiber, no meat diet, and her hair was neat and clean. She seemed to have a new, albeit modest, wardrobe from

The Gap, which she proudly proclaimed was assembled entirely from merchandise she had bought on sale.

"You look beautiful today," Camilla said to Chantal.

Chantal smiled. "You know why, don't you?"

"Another markdown at The Gap?" Rose asked.

"Naw. It's the love, from you and the baby. If I'm beautiful, that's why."

It was such a simple statement, but it touched Camilla in a deep and profound way. "It's easy to love you, Chantal. You give so much."

"Yes, Chantal. It's a two-way street," Rose added.

Then Camilla looked around her and said: "In our case, a four-way intersection."

"Camilla, you'd better get going. Jayme sounded mad as hell," Rose said.

Camilla had a hard time pulling away from Merry, who was feeling very proud of herself indeed. First steps didn't happen every day. It was becoming unbearable to part; the older Merry became, the more afraid Camilla was of missing something. She wondered if fathers ever felt the tug. "See you tonight?"

Rose and Chantal nodded their heads.

At the office, Jayme was standing by the reception desk, arms folded across her flat chest, in a threatening pose.

She was tapping her bottleneck toed patent leather gray shoe on the carpet.

150

"Re-Xerox every one of those pages on ecru résumé-quality paper now — even before you think about a cup of coffee," she said. "The copy paper you used just won't make the right impression."

"Good morning to you too, Jayme," Camilla remarked, wondering how many co-op board members even read the contents of these packages.

"And I may have a buyer for the Landers townhouse," Jayme declared to Camilla's back.

Camilla turned to face her. "That's good news. What time do you want me to show it?"

"You'll be too busy copying. I'll show it myself." Jayme pivoted on her heel and left.

"But…" Camilla said, as she watched the charcoal figure disappear around the corner like a cloud of dust.

As Dawson Landers' exclusive agent, Camilla knew she was supposed to be present during every showing. She wasn't sure if that requirement extended to members of her own office as well. The intricacies of real estate decorum in New York were confusing, especially as there seemed to be so many shady areas and unspoken rules.

Deep in thought, she passed by Walter's office on the way back to her cubicle. The door was open.

"Good morning," she said, poking her head through the crack.

"Camilla." Walter's face was hidden in shadow but she thought he seemed pleased by her intrusion. "Come in."

"Sorry to disturb you, but I have a question about propriety concerning the showing of the Landers property," she said.

He stood up and motioned for her to take a seat. Jennifer's voice came over the intercom, announcing that Walter's attorney from Strook, Strook

151

& Lavan was on the phone. "Excuse me," he said. "This will only take a second."

While Walter listened, responding mostly with "Um-hums" and "I sees," Camilla watched his every move. He was so graceful, the way he rested his arm confidently over the back of his chair, shoulders straight and legs crossed. The blue suit, white shirt, and red tie he wore were crisp and pressed; even his black socks were smooth and his wing-tipped shoes were shined. He was so attractive; she couldn't figure out why Alyson would ever stray.

Camilla watched the muscles in his jaw tense and his thigh muscles flex under his finely-tailored trousers as he took in what his lawyer had to say. When he hung up the phone, she could tell he was upset, but he forced himself to focus his attention on her. "Now, what's the issue?" he asked.

"If this is a bad time —" Camilla could sense that his problem was far greater than her own.

"Not at all. It's just business —"

She felt relieved that it wasn't about Alyson. "You do look worried," she said.

He glanced across at her. He had a way of looking openly into a person's eyes when he spoke to them that was disarming. "You know our project on West 56th Street?"

"Strong Place?" she asked.

"That's it." He seemed embarrassed by the name, which had been the invention of his marketing department. He struck her as too modest to name a building after himself. "The fallout from the stock market and all the economic turmoil has stopped the market for new condos cold. If you did one of your charts, it would look like the inverse of that co-op and townhouse table you presented yesterday."

"I've heard that we're in a slower, more cautious market for condominiums. But no one knows better than you that these things are cyclical…be patient, eventually it'll turn around, I'm sure."

"I'm afraid this time patience won't help. If we don't have signed contracts on 15 percent of the building — 63 apartments — in 60 days, and close on them within 90 days, the building converts to a rental automatically, subject to rent control and rent stabilization laws."

Camilla knew exactly how dire an outcome that would be. Rent control and rent stabilization were dirty words as far as New York landlords were concerned. A new condominium had a strict offering plan, closely monitored by the state attorney general, who could void the plan if sales projections weren't met.

"Couldn't you sell the building to the Roses or the Resnicks? They seem to have a monopoly on rental buildings in New York."

Walter laughed. "That they do. But this building can only be sold as a condominium. My father, Rex's grandfather, left the land to Rex in his will with a deed restriction that the land could only be developed as a condominium with the top five floors as residences for Rex and his children — to be passed down through the generations. So, you see, I have my father's legacy to protect, his wish for a Strong monument to uphold, and the guarantee that his heirs would always have a place to live."

"How far away are you from your sales goal?" she asked.

Walter eyed her cautiously, as if wondering whether he should confide in her or not.

"The on-site sales and marketing office, under Jayme's supervision, has been open for six months. We've closed on six apartments and have another ten contracts out. Another 47 apartments to hit the 15 percent mark — it's impossible..."

"Nothing's impossible," she said, and she meant it. "I'm going to think about a solution." She pointed to the Publius quote on the coffee table. "After all, no one knows what *she* can do until *she* tries."

He stared at her; his face became somber and his eyes sad. "You remind me of someone..." But he snapped out of his reverie as suddenly as he had fallen into it. "What can I help you with, Camilla?"

She told him about her confrontation with Jayme and asked for his advice. He confirmed that she should be present at every showing, whether the prospective buyer's broker was in-house or worked for another firm. In terms of priorities, the client needed to be serviced first and the board package could wait. He was angry, but controlled; the only evidence of his displeasure could be seen in the subtle pulsing of the muscles in his jaw.

Walter pushed the intercom button on the phone. "Send Jayme in here," he said. A few minutes later, the door was flung open, but by Alyson, not by Jayme.

"Jennifer said to tell you Jayme's left the office," Alyson said. She put her nose in the air and sniffed, as if she could smell the fondness that was growing between Walter and Camilla. "This is a cozy scene."

Camilla had never seen Alyson and Walter interact, except for a few minutes the day before. Walter stiffened when Alyson entered the room, reminding Camilla of a cat that arches its back when an enemy nears. Alyson pulled herself up, as if to appear larger than she really was. They glared at each other.

"Is there a reason for your surprise visit?" he asked, cautiously but politely.

Alyson appeared characteristically nonplussed. "I seem to have lost my key — you know, the one for the top lock to the apartment — that silly one that you had made unduplicatable, irreproducible, irreplaceable."

"For your protection —" he said.

"That's nonsense, I feel perfectly safe. Anyway, I need to go home and pack. My flight leaves at three for West Palm Beach. I don't suppose you remember, the American Publisher's Association conference in Boca?"

"I remember," he said, handing her the spare key he kept in a wall safe in his office. It was behind the Schnabel. "How are you getting to the airport?" he asked.

Alyson hesitated. "Rocky Faber's giving me a lift."

"Good. Then you don't need me for anything else."

Camilla observed Alyson's long legs stride toward the elevators, before she returned to her chore in the Xerox room. It was her plan to finish Jayme's grunt work as soon as she could and then to tell Jayme that she would be present at all showings of her exclusives. She would be friendly but firm, cooperative but uncompromising.

While she endlessly copied and collated, on spotless, ecru, Hammermill résumé paper, she thought about Walter and his marital woes. It was surprisingly pleasing to her that he seemed aware that all was not right. The idea of him hopelessly in love with Alyson, and being constantly deceived by her, was painful to contemplate.

She thought she could help him with his business problem. Strong Place was probably leveraged to the hilt with short-term debt. If the trend established in the late 1990s had continued, it would have been a breeze to pay down the loan before the balloon was due, but if the building converted to a rental, subject to tenant-favorable rent control and rent-stabilized leases, there would be no way Walter could make the interest payments, much less pay off the principal, during the required term.

Strong Place, and his hopes for a testament for posterity, would be sunk.

Camilla knew one bankrupt project wouldn't ruin Walter Strong, but it could sully his otherwise sterling reputation, making future deals much harder to finance. And she doubted he would ever recover from letting both his father and his son down. The importance of family succession in the insular world of New York real estate resembled that of European monarchies in medieval times.

The hairs on Camilla's arms were standing up from the static electricity being generated by the copying machine. The constant flashing of light that emanated every time she inserted a new page was beginning to make her see stars. The inky smell of the warm pages as she stacked hundreds of sheets was making her stomach queasy. By the time she was through, she would have gone through 20 reams of paper at least; she hoped that West Coast Properties bought in bulk.

Bulk! That was it. If paper could be purchased in bulk, why not apartments?

Hurriedly, she gathered Jayme's board packages in her arms, and arranged them on her desk. She passed by Walter's office deliberately, as she was leaving to go to lunch, and knocked gently. He looked up.

"How much is the brokerage commission on the Strong Place apartments?"

"The usual — four percent. Why?"

"I've got an idea."

Before he could ask what it was, she was out the door.

From the payphone in the lobby of the municipal building that housed the Office of the City Registrar, Camilla left messages for Walter and Jayme that she would be out for the rest of that day and the next doing primary research, which she hoped they would infer was for her column. She didn't dare tell anyone at West Coast Properties what she was up to yet; for one thing, she wasn't sure it would work, and if it could, she was afraid someone would steal her idea before it reached fruition.

Next, she checked her own voice mail; there were two requests to show the Lawson house on Thursday and a message from Jayme: "Where the hell did you disappear to?! Since you weren't here to be briefed, you've forfeited your opportunity to tag along on my customer showings tomorrow — not a smart move."

Camilla let the venomous tone roll off her back. She had bigger plans for her Wednesday than playing shadow to Spiderwoman anyway. But she did try to see things from Jayme's point of view. For as long as anyone could remember, Jayme had run all of Walter Strong's residential projects, as well as some choice pocket listings of her own. Then along comes Camilla — younger, hungrier, and unstoppable. She'd be threatened too, Camilla admitted to herself, if she had been in Jayme's gray patent leather shoes.

The Office of the New York City Registrar, where all real property deeds and mortgages were recorded, was on the 13th floor of 66 John Street.

It was the musty smell, more than the old-fashioned partitioned cubicles that contrasted sharply with the pristine offices of West Coast Properties.

Camilla entered the information office, where she passed a long wooden bench populated by a dozen blank-faced messengers, shoulder-to-shoulder, waiting their turns. The floor on which their sneakered feet rested was dirty gray with brown oblong speckles that so closely resembled water bugs Camilla had to look twice to make sure the pattern was not alive. She approached the long counter, topped with metal cages, and spoke through the index card-sized window with a teller whose eyeglasses were held together by masking tape, spelling out exactly what it was that Camilla needed to find.

She was directed toward a row of brown doors, pockmarked and scratched. Behind each door was a small room, more like a locker than a study space, each housing a vintage desktop computer. A soft-covered book the thickness of four telephone directories was chained to the leg of the hard metal chair; it contained the block and lot numbers for every piece of real property in the city of New York.

The entire borough of Manhattan had been mapped and divided into individual blocks and lots on a grid. Each block had its own number, and each lot on that block its own identifier too. In a condominium, Camilla quickly figured out, the building is the block and each apartment is the lot.

Camilla pulled from her briefcase some notes she had made on a Streetwise Map of Manhattan. She and Rose had strolled with Merry on the Upper East and West Sides of Midtown the night before after dinner, jotting down names and addresses of condominium towers they passed. Camilla had deliberately stayed clear of the ones she considered fancy — 515 Park Avenue, Millennium Tower, One Central Park West — considering them to be too expensive to attract investors who might buy in bulk. Armed with the buildings she had hoped would yield investors' identities, she began the onerous task of converting glamorous sounding names like CitySpire, The Belgravia, The Rio, and The Symphony into their more practical classifications of blocks and lots.

By noon, Camilla had completed her task. She had compiled a list of numerical combinations for 17 Manhattan condominium towers. After gulping her sandwich and swilling her bottle of Poland Spring, she logged on to the search engine for the City Registrar. It would be so much easier, she sighed, if this information had been available on the Web, but it wasn't — she had checked.

It took her nearly two hours to cross-reference the blocks and lots with the names in which title was held. Jotting down each owner next to the appropriate apartment, she amassed over 2,000 names, and while she could see some repetition, it would take time to study the list in detail. It was obvious at first glance that very few multiple ownerships were in individual names. Partnerships and limited liability companies seemed to prevail, with impersonal names like Hong Kong Realty Partners or Prometheus, LLC.

Next, she filtered her list, looking for deeds unencumbered by debt. The list shrank to 1,287 entities. Within minutes of finalizing her short list, she heard a knock. Camilla swung around in her chair and pushed open the door. It was the clerk with the masking tape frames. She squinted her eyes behind her glasses and said, "You can't eat in here, you know."

"I'm sorry, I didn't know. It won't happen again." She swept the remains of her lunch into the paper bag and stuffed it in her briefcase.

"It's 4:15. We close in 15 minutes."

As Camilla prepared to log off, she noticed an icon called Multiple Ownership. She quickly gave it a click with the mouse. Thousands of names popped up as she scrolled down the screen, with listings of blocks and lots immediately following. Some names had the numbers for six properties and some for sixty. It would take her a week to transcribe the numerical code back into real addresses and names so she could see how relevant they could be to her cause.

Knowing that she didn't have a week, Camilla started to scan the names as she heard the clerk's footsteps approach: Aadvantage Realty LLC (12), Abacus Partners (57), Barney Levine (6), Bosco Properties (22), Cara Mia Corporation (5), and then she saw it...Dawson Landers LLC (9).

It had to be the Dawson Landers she knew; the name was too unusual. Were these apartments he had bought to provide housing for his crews? Did he dabble in real estate? She shut down the computer, musing over all the questions she had, hoping that the answers would somehow be revealed.

Chapter Eight

Camilla headed straight for Jayme's desk on Thursday morning. The expression Jayme wore was one of bemusement, as if she had been waiting for Camilla to resume a game of chess.

"How did the showing of the Landers townhouse go yesterday?" Camilla asked.

"The customer rescheduled," Jayme said, rigid and unyielding.

"How fortunate! Next time I'll be sure to be there, as required by my role as exclusive broker."

"Really, Camilla, it's so tedious to have to teach you every little thing. The owner, or the owner's representative, can bring in anyone they want — without the exclusive agent."

Camilla knew Dawson Landers was out of the country, but then she realized that Jeffrey was the "representative" Jayme was referring to. Camilla decided that she would just have to beat them at their own game; she'd have to sell the townhouse before they'd get a chance.

"Oh, I see…" Camilla said.

"Of course, I respect your rights and would avoid scheduling snafus. Your last appointment there for today is at two, correct?"

The only way Jayme could have known that was by rifling through Camilla's diary. "How do you know my schedule, Jayme?"

"The real estate business depends on information, Camilla. It's my job to know."

"Really? Then you probably know that my first showing is at ten."

Looking at her watch, Jayme said: "Then you'd better get going. It's 9:30 now."

The broker from Douglas-Elliman and her customer from Taiwan were waiting in front of the Landers townhouse at ten minutes to ten. The woman accosted Camilla as the cabbie rolled to a stop. She wagged her knobby finger as she pulled her Burberry's raincoat tighter around her body with her other hand.

"You're late," she snarled.

Camilla looked at her watch. "No, I'm not. Our appointment is for ten."

"It doesn't matter. We've been waiting for 15 minutes." Her dark roots grew an inch from her scalp before meeting the greenish straw color of the rest of her hair. Camilla took the card that was thrust in her hand and said, "I apologize, Lauren, if I've kept you waiting."

Then Camilla strode past her colleague and extended her hand to the bristling figure huddled in the doorway of the house. As she was about to ask his name, Lauren jumped between them and said, "All negotiations will be conducted through me. Mr. T prefers that his identity be kept secret."

From the look of confusion on Mr. T's face, Camilla could tell that this was news to him. She surmised that Lauren was protecting her 20 million dollar customer the way a hyena would a pup.

"The owner is out of town at the moment," Camilla explained, "so the house is dark. Just give me a minute to turn on the lights."

"Mr. T is a world-renowned art dealer. He is looking for a site for a private museum for his collection." Lauren smiled at Mr. T as she spoke, baring a full set of cigarette-stained teeth. Her client backed away slightly and bowed to Camilla in a gesture that Camilla interpreted as an expression of his embarrassment.

In the entry foyer was a panel of switches that controlled the lighting in the house. Camilla flipped them all on at once. She heard Lauren, who had led her client down the darkened mosaic hallway into the living room, let out a gasp. "Who was his decorator? She must be very creative. I love black — it's my favorite color!"

"The décor is —" Camilla paused. "Very particular. It's not for everyone. But..." She was about to offer the credit for interior demolition, when Mr. T politely interrupted.

"Excuse me, Miss —"

" — Madison. She's new to the business but, don't worry, all negotiations will be conducted through me," Lauren reminded him.

Mr. T was beginning to get annoyed, but he was very self-controlled. "Any place I consider will be demolished to create space for my artworks. I am not influenced one way or another by interior design. I am interested in the bones of the space. Please, let us move on."

Camilla led the way through the rest of the large rooms. Mr. T extracted a tape measure from his pocket and measured the wall widths and ceiling heights. He nodded his head favorably. "Twelve and a half. Very good."

Lauren was fascinated by the asp collection, and borrowed Mr. T's tape measure to see how long each snake actually was. Mr. T shook his head sadly, as if it hurt him to see what passed for art in some circles these days.

The showing took an hour, which even for a townhouse, was a very good sign.

Camilla left the lights on after Lauren and Mr. T departed. Her next appointment, with Brooks Snow from Sotheby's, was two hours away. She placed the sheath of research from the day before on Dawson Lander's desk while she turned on the stereo to an easy listening station and went into the kitchen to look for something to drink. She pulled open the refrigerator door to find six bottles of Krug champagne, a container of diet Mazola, and a quart of Tropicana orange juice, which she sniffed before deciding whether she should drink it or not.

In the cupboard where she finally found the glasses, she found at least two dozen assorted bottles of vitamins, unopened, and a bottle of Viagra, half empty.

Camilla returned to the office with her glass. The night before, Merry had fallen asleep early and Rose had been working late. It had taken Camilla four hours, but she managed to enter all the owners' names into Excel. She had opted to back burner the multiple owner function in the City Registrar's database because most of those owners — including Dawson Landers — had a disparate collection of properties in locations that ranged from Chinatown to Washington Heights.

Now she reviewed her short list of 31 entities, each one owning 25 apartments or more in condominium buildings in similar locations to Strong Place. Her final short list included only buyers who had paid cash for a block of apartments in one building — and for whom she could find an address and phone number, via the Internet, somewhere in the civilized world.

A third of the entities were registered to owners in Hong Kong, India, Taiwan, Korea, or Malaysia; six were from Germany, Holland or England;

three were from Brazil; one from Argentina and eleven from the United States.

Camilla drew her laptop out of her bag and tapped out a draft letter, which she intended to e-mail later to each name on her list. She was scheduled to tour Strong Place at noon the next day, and would add floor plans, price lists, a description of views and finishes, and a few proposals outlining which apartments she would recommend be assembled as a bulk.

To sweeten the deal, she would offer to find tenants, collect rents, and pay the bills for six months for free. Camilla had no idea how she would do all of this — but if she got a nibble, she knew she'd find a way.

With the time she had left, she started to tap out her impressions of the Landers townhouse for her *Marry Well* column. She decided to write it as if it were a television review, calling the decoration "sets" and the furniture "props." She couldn't think of any other way to make the morose appealing, other than to turn it into the macabre. She did attempt to liken Dawson Landers to Julius Caesar — after all they did both share a fetish for Cleopatra — but somehow she couldn't make it work. Dawson reminded her more of Nero — and Jeffrey of Caligula, as long as she was going down that path — than of the great man himself. "Friends, Romans, countrymen —lend me your asps?" Nope, she admitted, it just didn't ring true.

Two o'clock! Camilla dashed outside to wait.

Thirty-two minutes later, just as she was sure Brooks Snow would be a no-show, a hunter green stretch limousine pulled up to the curb. An attractive brunette rolled down the window and poked out her head. "I'm Brooks," she said. "Hop in."

"But the house —"

"They're hungry. We'll come back."

Camilla checked the knob to make sure the house was secure. Then she slid into the limo, right next to Brooks Snow. Across the roomy passenger area sat a couple Camilla presumed were Brooks' customers.

"Jay and Sherrie Wolf," Brooks said, rotating her hand toward them, as a magician would to present his rabbit, "meet...what did you say your name was again?"

"Camilla Madison."

Jay Wolf had a long sallow face and deep-set chocolate eyes. He wore a small gold stud in his left earlobe. He appeared to be in his late twenties but Camilla still found it difficult to believe, despite the stories she had heard, that someone that young could afford a twenty million dollar townhouse. Camilla listened as he instructed his driver to find a pizza parlor nearby. "Pepperoni?" Jay asked.

Camilla realized she had forgotten to eat lunch. "Sounds great." She knew Rose would disapprove, but she said, "Can they sprinkle on some sausage too?"

"I'm really sorry we're late," Sherrie said. "I had my hair colored but Jay didn't like it so I had to go back and —"

"You looked like Britney Spears," he said, as if that explained it all. Sherrie let out a little growl, like a tiger, and nibbled on his stud. Then she pressed closer to his body and slid her hand between his thighs. He was a little overweight, and his black jeans were skin-tight. One of Rose's favorite lines, uttered at public overkill displays of affection, popped into Camilla's head: *Why don't you two get a room?* But naturally, she didn't dare say it to them.

While the driver went in to order and wait for the pizza, Jay got out to buy some fruit from a street vendor. Sherrie followed. Through the open door, Camilla watched as Jay bought a perfectly chilled bottle of Evian water for three dollars and used it to wash his $.75 apple, with at least $2.85 worth of the water splashing into the gutter below.

"What does he do?" Camilla whispered.

Brooks gave a throaty laugh. "Boiler-room," she whispered back. "He makes 30 mil a year," Brooks added, as if that would more than answer the questions that Camilla asked with her eyes.

The driver had returned with the food, and Jay and Sherrie settled back into the banquette of the limousine. A table folded down from a slot in the wall in between the two rows of seats. Sherrie served the pizza on paper plates while Jay popped the cork of a bottle of vintage Dom Perignon. He poured the champagne into plastic champagne flutes. Instead of eating, Sherrie turned into a human napkin, licking off every stray strand of mozzarella and wayward drop of grease that rolled down Jay's jutting chin. They polished off the pizza as the limo pulled up to the Landers house for the second time.

Frank Sinatra's voice was belting out "The Lady Is a Tramp" just as they entered the foyer. Jay and Sherrie paused to kiss in every room, making the showing stretch into an hour and a half. Brooks was a pro; she kept her mouth shut and let her customers use theirs.

"I don't mind the atrocious taste, honey. I want to gut the place anyway," Sherrie said.

"We're giving a credit for demolition," Camilla eagerly offered.

"I want to turn the school area into a separate apartment for the nanny and the children," Sherrie said. She purred at her husband. "You know, so we don't have to change our lives."

Camilla swallowed hard. How could a baby not change your life? And why would anybody want that anyway?

"There may be a glitch with the zoning, but Camilla here assures me there's a way around it," Brooks said.

"No sweat. There'll always be some poor schnook we can pay off," Jay said.

"Would you like to see the basement?" Camilla asked.

"Not now," Jay said, leading Sherrie by the hand toward the stairs. "We'd like to walk through alone."

Camilla and Brooks sat in the living room. They heard grunting and groaning, oohing and aahing, and the unmistakable sound of unoiled bedsprings.

"Why doesn't the owner do something about the noise?" Brooks asked.

"Maybe his lovemaking is a little more passive than theirs."

"I certainly hope the Wolfs buy something soon. This is getting tedious," Brooks said, yawning.

Camilla was about to ask if Brooks' clients had done this before, when she heard the front door click, and footsteps in the foyer, then familiar voices. She ran down the mosaic hall, panicking. "Jeffrey, Jayme — what on earth are you doing here?"

They were with someone who looked exactly like James Earl Jones — tall, black and bald.

"What are YOU doing here? It's five o'clock and your last showing was at two," Jayme said.

"They're still here," Camilla said.

Jayme shook her head. "Amateur, amateur. What have they been doing for three hours? Did they get locked in the bathroom?"

Camilla didn't know what to say. Her mind was skirting through numerous explanations. She was sure she would get fired as soon as Jeffrey figured out what she had allowed to happen. Fortunately, Brooks and the Wolfs appeared just at that moment, thanking her graciously for her time, as if nothing had transpired but afternoon tea.

"I'll be in touch," Brooks said, winking. She nodded at Jayme. It was clear that they had met before, although the relationship appeared chilly. Camilla gently closed the door and turned to face Jayme.

"Leave," Jayme commanded. "The ambassador is an important man. He doesn't have time for clutter." She led her guest toward the stairs. "Some say Cleopatra wasn't Egyptian at all, but pure African," Camilla heard Jayme tell him as she led him past Hannibal Lecter and *The Godfather's* beheaded horse.

Jeffrey followed Camilla into Dawson's office and stood over her as she packed up her things. She felt his gaze penetrate her back, as she felt like she imagined the leaf had when she set fire to it as a child by holding a magnifying glass over it to intensify the sun. She dropped her pen on the floor and it rolled toward Jeffrey, who kicked it back in her direction. After she picked it up, he escorted her to the door and, without a word, she heard him lock it twice from inside.

Jayme's appearance at the Landers house had come as a double surprise. If Jayme had been snooping through her diary, as Camilla knew she had, then she would have known that Camilla planned to visit Strong Place that very afternoon. Wouldn't Jayme want to be there to protect her turf? Or, would it be more useful to her if Camilla were otherwise engaged?

The 44th floor sales office for Strong Place was created from one of the corner three-bedroom A-lines that had unobstructed views of the Central Park Reservoir to the north and east, the Hudson River to the west, and the Empire State Building to the south. The original brochure had described the southern views as encompassing the Manhattan skyline from Midtown to the World Trade Center towers; it had cost a fortune to reprint all the sales materials to adequately reflect the world as it had changed.

Juan de las Heras had tastefully converted the three bedrooms into elegant private offices for the sales managers, with mahogany desks, sisal carpeting, and remote controlled blinds. The staff had been instructed to open the blinds every time a customer came through, despite the magnified heat of the afternoon sun. According to Walter, the view was everything in New York and "introducing a prospect early to the project's assets would ensure a higher closing price."

Camilla picked up a sales kit from the reception desk and started to leaf through it. The packet contained a set of floor plans for all of the apartments, a description of the building and the design, a blank sample contract, several disclaimers about equal opportunity and facts in the Offering Plan, and a price list. Camilla whistled.

The receptionist kept looking up at her, while she nodded into the phone. When she hung up, she informed Camilla, as politely as she could, that Ms. Seagram requested that Camilla reschedule the appointment directly with her.

"I'm kind of in a hurry. Isn't there anyone else who can show me around?" Camilla asked, observing three suits at desks idling away.

"Everybody else is busy," the receptionist said. The phone rang again as Camilla reached the door. "Yes, she's gone," she heard the receptionist tell the caller.

It made Camilla weary to contemplate all the possible reasons Jayme might have to stand in her way. Camilla hadn't known her long enough, or well enough, to fathom her personal motivations, but whatever they were, they distilled down to one fact: Camilla was competition.

In Camilla's short time in the residential real estate business in Manhattan, it became clear to her that every broker had access to the same inventory, every customer knew ten brokers and could meet five more tomorrow — while toning her quads at Lotte Berk, having her pedicure at Bliss, or powdering her nose in the ladies room at La Goulou — that to women like Jayme, every other person with a real estate license was The Enemy.

Now she had proof that Jeffrey and Jayme were working together against her —bringing a client in to her exclusive without her knowledge. Even if Jayme's explanation were true, there must be some law or rule to protect her. If anyone would know, it would be Professor D'Angelo. Camilla promised herself to stop by her professor's office early in the coming week.

Camilla devoted her weekend to preparing an electronic case for a Strong Place bulk purchase for the investors on her short list, which she finally e-mailed Sunday night, with a requested return response deadline of the following Friday afternoon. The movers brought her furniture into her new apartment while she had been at the City Registrar, placing it haphazardly about. But it didn't matter to Camilla, who viewed the studio not first as a place to live, but rather as a command post, from which to wage a battle for her dreams.

Chantal played with Merry, who was developing a penchant for dinosaurs and toy cars, while Rose helped Camilla by e-mailing an open house schedule for 7 East 79th Street to every brokerage firm in town. Camilla had decided that she would hold an open house for two hours every day until the Landers townhouse was sold.

She was frantic with activity, going in a dozen directions at once, keeping herself so busy to avoid the one thing on her list that she knew she did not want to do — interview Rocky.

When she called Rocky's secretary to set something up, she was treated brusquely, as if she had requested an audience with the pope. As it turned out, "Mr. Richard Faber," according to the secretary who had taken her call, "would be available to speak with her for half an hour in New York after lunch on Monday in the lobby of The Knickerbocker Club. "And," Rocky's secretary informed Camilla, "arrangements have been made to let you view his apartment anytime prior to the interview, so that you can use his time sparingly, to ask relevant questions only, pre-edited, please, to include only those necessary to facilitate a quick sale.

"Mr. Faber," the secretary emphasized, "likes his personal affairs to move quickly."

It was common knowledge, Camilla learned from asking Deirdre, that there were two buildings on Fifth Avenue that catered to the rich and private, who wanted the services of a hotel, without the transience of hotel clientele — 814 Fifth Avenue and One East 66th Street.

When Camilla walked into the lobby of 814 Fifth, the superintendent — who behaved as if he were Rocky's private valet — greeted her in person. She was shown the beautiful paneled library and restaurant only for the use of the apartment owners, located off the lobby and surrounded by planted gardens in the rear. The super/valet explained that owners had to pay $12,000 a year to maintain the kitchen staff, whether or not they ever used the facility themselves.

He let her peek at the private switchboard, concierge, and housekeeper's lounge that they had to pass en route to security. There Camilla received a magnetic badge that would allow her unsupervised access to the Faber apartment, until the residence was sold or her privileges revoked — whichever came first. She shouldn't worry about a key — all the owner/ tenants at 814 Fifth left their doors unlocked because, he bragged, "he ran an extremely tight ship."

The building even had a person on staff whose sole purpose was to walk and feed the eight-pound-and-under dogs of the owner/tenants — everyone who lived there had at least one or two. Of course, these dogs, like their masters, had passed the co-op board review. The recently discarded Mrs. Faber had had a miniature dachshund, named Nathan, who had an entire wardrobe of seasonal outfits all in varying shades of mustard yellow. The staff longed for him; they were very sad about the divorce indeed.

Armed only with her reporter's notepad, Camilla entered Rocky's apartment, not knowing what to expect. It was exquisite. Decorated by Bunny Williams, it was done in the chaste French classical style of Louis

XVI. The door opened immediately into a large living room with four elongated windows, all clad in restored ironwork, with Juliet balconies and window grilles, overlooking the bright changing autumn leaves of Central Park.

The soft melon color scheme of honeydew and cantaloupe was captured in striped silk on an upholstered settee. There were two antique prayer chairs, with beautifully carved mahogany backs, on either side of an ebony marquetry commode with gilt mounts in the corners so beautiful that they could have been sold in any jewelry store in town. Camilla would have sworn that it was an original by Riesener, the royal cabinetmaker of King Louis' time. She made a note to find out.

A chandelier comprised of 12 lustres, and bound by garlands of flowers in gilt bronze, hung from the living room ceiling. Little silk shades shaped like top hats but decorated like bustiers, with hand-sewn beading and bone stays, muted the light to a perfect pale peach hue. The baseboards and moldings were painted in the technique called *scagliola* — a form of marbleizing that even felt like the real thing to the touch.

The super's beeper went off, calling him away, leaving Camilla to view the rest of the apartment alone. There was a pigeonhole kitchen, she presumed to encourage the owners to use the dining facilities downstairs, and a tiny powder room, just large enough for a bowl and a sink. Through the living room was a door to the bedroom, which Camilla assumed must also view Central Park.

She sucked in her breath and turned the knob. She walked in and sat down on the bed. What perverse twist of fate had landed her here? On the actual bed of the man who, 19 years before, had raped her? If there was one thing Camilla despised, it was people who pitied themselves. But here she was, shakily on the edge, thinking how lucky her rapist was, to breeze through life, live in a beautiful place, and have an assortment of charming wives, who pleased him for a time and then were tossed away, while she had so much less — except for Merry.

Camilla bounced on the bed. It was hard and springy. Regardless of what had brought her here, she had a job to do. Looking back into the past only filled her with regret. She walked through the apartment once more, checking the commode for Riesener's signature, jotting down a few notes, and then she left — shutting the door behind her.

As she walked the few blocks from Rocky's place to The Knickerbocker Club, she knew she was depressed. The air outside was nippy and crisp, but she felt hot and disoriented, as though a flu was coming on. She almost got hit by a lumbering city bus but couldn't seem to care. Her legs felt heavy and slow to move; she had difficulty filling her lungs with the air she knew she was meant to breathe. Her eyelids felt weighty; they seemed to drag rather than flutter whenever she blinked.

The beautiful façade of The Knickerbocker Club appeared like a fortress, guarded by two mustachioed doormen in dark navy blue who stood shoulder to shoulder as she approached.

"I'm Camilla Madison from *Marry Well* magazine. Mr. Faber, please."

The taller one said: "Through the hall to the left. He's still having lunch but he's expecting you."

The grand hall of The Knickerbocker Club looked like she imagined a palace would. The ceilings were very high, and painted in rich bright colors like a summer sky. Long windows framed the view of the Park across the street, and the furniture might have been on loan from The Metropolitan Museum.

Rocky sat alone at a small table near the window. His hair fell on his forehead as he tilted his eyes down to read. It was a newspaper, folded in quarters, positioned to the left of his arm as it rested on the tablecloth. A fine china cup sat on his right. The nauseating smell of clove filled the space around him.

"Ah, Ms. Madison, there you are. Have you eaten?"

"Yes, I have." It was a lie.

"Then at least join me for dessert."

The few moments of silence that it took Camilla to find her courage seemed never ending. "Yes, of course."

Rocky flagged the waiter, who came with a tray full of pastries and sweets. Camilla asked for ice cream while Rocky chose rice pudding, into which he stirred a Sweet & Low. "You really must try the éclair — it's the Club specialty." Rocky smiled.

Yes, she was fairly certain now that he had no idea who she was. He had missed the connection with her name, but apparently he hadn't recognized her or her voice either. She must have been so insignificant to him.

"Did you see the apartment?" he asked.

"Yes, just this morning. It's lovely."

"So, what do you need to know?"

"How long did the decorating take?"

"Not long."

"Really?"

"I know what I want when I see it." There was a little creamy pudding curdling in the corner of his mouth as he spoke.

"Is that true for everything?"

Rocky straightened in his chair. "More or less, yes."

The arrogance of his attitude was the spark that ignited her.

"Are there ever any mitigating considerations?" Camilla asked.

"Like what?" Rocky regarded her oddly, as if he were trying to guess her game.

"Oh, I don't know…age, experience, morality, cost. For example, how much did the renovation cost?"

Rocky wiped the rice pudding from his mouth and placed his napkin by the side of the dish. His expression hardened. "None of your business."

"Why are you selling?" Camilla asked.

"Also none of your business. Listen, Ms. Madison, I'm doing this for Alyson. It's a quid pro quo — she's invested heavily in my new project and I've given her my New York real estate to sell."

So it was strictly a business deal; Camilla wondered if Walter was involved as well.

"Enough talking. I want action. I want this place sold by —" Rocky stopped in mid-sentence and stared as Camilla scraped the bottom of her bowl with the silver spoon in that idiosyncratic way that she had.

Rocky dropped his napkin on the floor. "Have we met before?"

By the feral look in his eye, she thought for a second that he had recognized her, not as the little girl that she had been, but as the woman she was, willing to take him on.

Rocky laughed. "My mistake, Ms. Madison. After all, where would our paths ever have crossed? If you think of anything else you need, send my secretary an e-mail."

The uneaten éclair stared Camilla in the face. She stabbed it with her fork. She stood to leave, passing the blue guards once more, as she headed toward home. With each step, she felt lighter and more alive. By the time she arrived on her block, she was singing: "Freedom's just another word for nothing left to lose."

As Camilla neared the door to their building, Rose came up behind her and Merry and Chantal arrived from the other direction. Merry's blue eyes were the size of quarters and her cheeks were as red as radishes from the cold.

She held out her mittened hands and yelled: "Mama!" for the very first time.

Rose stood leaning against the wall with her hands on her hips and a smile on her lips. Camilla covered Merry with kisses. Merry nuzzled back and repeated "Mama," now for the second time, prompting Camilla to give her more kisses and hugs.

"Oh, will you two get a room," Rose said, laughing, as she and Chantal went upstairs.

After Merry was down for the night, Camilla realized she had officially notified 62 real estate brokerage companies in town that there would be an open house from 12 to 1 pm every day next week at Dawson Landers' townhouse, but she had never hosted an open house before. She called Deirdre: "Do I need to do anything special? Or do I just show up?"

"Open houses are the most boring things in the world. First of all, anyone who's anybody has seen that white elephant of yours — or should I say white werewolf — it's been on the market forever. Second, people who have $20 million to spend don't look at houses in open view with other people who have $20 million — they're not buying ties at Saks. And, third, oh, never mind, you get my gist."

Camilla could hear Deirdre filing her nails in the background. "Should I buy cookies and flowers, just in case?"

"Waste of money. Just bring your knitting."

During the first open house, with the cookies and lemonade, the wood burning in the fireplace, candles lit on the dining room table, and Lauryn Hill singing "Killing Me Softly" on the stereo, only one broker showed up. She was about 80 years old, wore false eyelashes and used a walker, to which she had tied a leash attached to her equally ancient-looking papillon.

At 1:10, Camilla called Deirdre. "OK, you were right."

"Of course," Deirdre said. "It's ridiculous. Nobody ever sold a piece of real estate in an open house...or from an ad for that matter. Brokers promise these 'services' to sellers to make them feel taken care of. It's all about networking and creativity."

"How do you mean?"

"Did anyone who looked at the house since you've had the exclusive seem interested?"

Camilla thought Mr. T and the Wolfs both seemed to find something they liked about the house. "Two parties, in fact."

"Oh, goodie. Play them against each other. Tell Customer A's broker that Customer B looks like they'll be coming in with a bid. And tell Customer B's broker that you just talked to Customer A's broker and let her infer that they'll be coming in with a bid —"

"Deirdre, I don't know. Isn't that unethical?"

"Only if you lie, honey. What I'm suggesting is just... finesse."

Camilla called Lauren and Brooks as soon as she hung up with Deirdre. She did exactly as her friend had suggested. Then, in hopeful anticipation, she copied down the telephone numbers for Dawson Landers' cell phone, home phone, and mistress's phone that were boldly noted in magic marker and stuck up on the office wall.

The next day, right after she returned to the office from another open house where the only person to show up was the same past tense broker and her poor little dog, Camilla had offers on her voice mail from both Lauren and Brooks.

"What do I do now?" she asked Deirdre.

"Pray for a bidding war."

Camilla sat down and drank the cup of tea she had brought up with her from the corner deli. Mr. T had offered $18 million. Jay Wolf offered $18.2 million. Virtually the same, very respectable opening bids.

Contrary to Deirdre's advice, Camilla did not want a bidding war. She remembered vividly her father once losing both buyers in a bidding war, and overhearing how furious Rocky had been when her father had lost control of the deal. She decided she would determine the best buyer for this house and promptly returned calls to both brokers requesting full disclosure financial statements with proof of assets and a final offer sealed bid. She gave them until Thursday at noon.

Then her phone rang again. It was Alyson's secretary, informing her that Alyson had called a meeting for the following morning in the glass conference room at ten. "Be there," she said, hanging up without saying good-bye.

Chapter Nine

Alyson looked stunning at the head of the conference table, in a black crepe suit that made her appear even slimmer than she was. She wore her hair in a chignon and had diamond stud earrings the size of dimes in her ears. Her nails were medium length, in a pale pink French manicure; she drummed them on the conference room table while she watched the seconds tick by on the wall clock. At exactly ten, she began the meeting.

"The purpose for calling you all together is to discuss a new vision that I have for the magazine," Alyson began.

Six minutes after Alyson had begun the meeting, Harry Clark, the "Job Magnets" careers columnist rushed in, apologizing for being late because his train had derailed in Stamford. Alyson glared at him. "I attended two cocktail receptions, a dinner party, and a late-night theater revue, was working out at 6:30 A.M., had a breakfast meeting with the Tisch boys at eight, and I'm here on time, aren't I?"

Harry had reached that point of frustration that leads to poor decision-making. His face was nearly purple with rage as he reminded her, nearly shouting, that she had a chauffeur, an assistant, and a staff to do her bidding. Everyone around the table gasped, except Alyson, and the immediately apologetic columnist.

"I'll deal with you later," Alyson said to him, and continued with her agenda. She motioned for Chuck to flip the switch on the wall that dimmed the lights. "Now, as I was saying. The most popular new feature to come out of *Marry Well* in years is Camilla's real estate column. The response in terms of newsstand circulation and increased ad revenues has prodded me into thinking slightly differently about how we move the magazine forward." She took a breath. "I believe the secret to our past success has been our strong brand image and unique selling proposition — both geared to women. But..." She paused as she projected her first slide onto the screen. "...as you can see on the slide, both circulation and ad sales were flat for the first two quarters of this year."

"At first, we attributed this only to the slower economy," Chuck interjected. "Alyson, next slide please, you're doing the driving." He waited, then continued, pointing at the first of two graphs on the screen. "When the July issue with Camilla's first column hit the stands, circulation blipped. A month later, if you follow the green line there, ad revenues skyrocketed. And that blue line — that indicates an increase in circulation among men that we attribute to Camilla's piece on Doris Sanger."

All eyes were on Camilla. She was surprised at the credit she was receiving, and felt she had to say something in return. "The opportunity was just sitting there. I would just like to add that once the real estate transactions actually close, they'll dwarf the ad revenues." Both Alyson and Chuck shot her harsh looks.

"That may be so," Alyson said. "But it remains to be seen — especially after the earful I got last night. Also, I'd like to remind you that real estate commissions, even if you manage to close your deals, would be sporadic and unpredictable. I prefer to think of them as the gravy, and the ad revenues as the turkey dinner."

"Sounds like you're ready to talk about my column," Rose said, as always protecting her friend. Camilla wondered if Alyson was losing interest in the real estate part of the package.

"To continue...while I intend to be extremely careful not to undermine our existing franchise, I plan to expand into the arena of men who want to marry well," Alyson said. "On a macro level, we need to acknowledge changing lifestyles and family roles." Camilla nodded her head in agreement, thinking of how astonished she had been of late by the number of men pushing baby strollers around in the middle of the afternoon. Even the sandbox area looked more like a men's locker room than a children's playground at times.

"There's great potential in that direction for me, Alyson," Sally Reagan, the "Make-Up or Break-Up" beauty columnist piped in. "Forty-two percent of facials and fifty-four percent of massage appointments at the top salons are made by or for men. Also, hair transplants and acne scar laser treatments are almost exclusively male beauty services."

"Good. I'm adding a technology column on the latest in gadgets, especially to focus on personal area networks and wiring the home. These trends enable both men and women to work at home," Alyson added. "I'm planning to call it "Hot-Wired" — I can't say whom yet, but a certain editor from *Esquire* has agreed to jump ship."

Chuck signaled for her to change the slide. He was about to speak as Rabia Rubenstein, the "Flash in the Pan-ts" fashion editor, interrupted. "Listen, Alyson — what about a financial column? Tips on investing, interviews with money managers, analysts, etc."

"I'm already there," she said. "But I'll take suggestions for names if you know someone good."

"I've listed on the slide before you some categories of advertisers that I plan to target as we expand into these new areas. They include sports cars, beer, men's clothing manufacturers, gym equipment, financial service providers, and electronics —" Chuck said.

"These are all products that women buy too," Mindy Paar, the "Torts for Tarts" legal columnist pointed out. Camilla was thinking the same thing. In fact, she had just read in *Business Insight* that women were the primary purchasers in 85 percent of U.S. homes, contributing $3.5 trillion to the economy.

"Of course," Alyson agreed. "But when Chuck and I have tried that tack with advertisers and agencies before, we tended to hear the same line of resistance over and over again —"

"Alyson's right, folks. The advertisers always ask: 'If a woman consumer had the money to buy our product herself, then why would she be so interested in marrying well?'" Chuck explained.

Alyson cleared her throat. "My second idea, one also spawned by a comment Camilla made early in our negotiations…"

The word "negotiations" almost made Camilla laugh.

"It has to do with better coordinating our monthly columns around a theme. For example, Camilla's November column, due back from the printer's tomorrow, on Dawson Landers is fantastic. She's written it like a television review. Imagine if we had thought to make the November beauty column about how TV stars stay gorgeous, and Rose's column — nice touch by the way, Rose, including Doris Sanger's brunch menu and recipes — had focused on Dawson cooking for family and friends in his Manhattan kitchen —"

What might he make, Camilla imagined — a Viagra soufflé — guaranteed to rise? Homemade pretzels — with Dead Sea salt?

"It would have been so easy for me to trace the acting career of one of *The Boondocks* stars," the remorseful Harry Clark burst in, trying to redeem himself.

"Isn't Dawson Landers your 'Him on Him' for November?" Camilla asked Alyson.

"Yes, but it's a very short piece. He was, between us, deadly dull." She sighed and clicked the forward button on her PowerPoint presentation.

"One more slide on ad pages before Alyson takes over," Chuck said. "This chart from *ADWEEK* shows that ad pages in general have been on the decline for the past year. During a phenomenal run from 1999 through 2002, technology rose 38 percent and finance 17.9 percent respectively. But look at that red line there — that's real estate — the real estate sector alone, aided by low interest rates, has increased its ad spending in magazines in 2003 by a whopping 63 percent."

"Now, Camilla's December column will be on Richard Faber," Alyson announced cheerfully. And it's extremely important that you, Camilla, don't muck it up."

Camilla and Rose exchanged glances.

"For those of you who don't know who he is, Rocky is a major, major player in Florida real estate. He's been called the Donald Trump of Palm Beach." She paused for effect.

Silence leveled the room.

"That's meant as a compliment," Alyson said, rolling her eyes, as if they were all too dumb, rather than just morally discerning, to get it. "I want our December issue, our year-end issue, to be a Rocky Faber special. Oh, and I want a special box highlighting his newest development, Rocky Coast." Camilla realized that Rocky Coast was the project Rocky had alluded to at The Knickerbocker Club that Alyson had invested in. "Chuck, I want a color ad spread from every real estate developer within a 100-mile radius of Palm Beach —"

And then Alyson told Sally Reagan to get the skinny on Florida spas, Rabia Rubenstein to uncover the latest bathing suit styles for the upcoming winter season, Horace Buttons the travel editor to get down to The Breakers and turn out a fabulous feature on Palm Beach "The Resort," Mindy Paar and "Dish Wish" columnist Beth Tucker to do a joint feature on recent divorces and romances — "You know, like sugar baron Pepe Fanjul and what's-her-name" — and Rose to come up with something, maybe a cooking lesson, with the chef of Rocky's yacht.

"And will you be writing your 'Him on Him' about Rocky?" Camilla asked, hoping against hope that Alyson would say no.

"You betcha — you might say I'll be putting it to bed any day."

Camilla turned white as she made a beeline toward the door.

"Oh stick around, Camilla, I'd like to have a private word with you in my office."

Alyson was the first to leave the conference room, signaling for Camilla to follow suit. As soon as the door to Alyson's office closed behind them, Alyson said, "So what happened between you and Rocky?"

"When?"

"What do you mean when? The other night, you acted like a mouse at a cat show when I introduced you to him —"

"Sorry, I was under the weather," Camilla said.

"Oh, and what's your excuse for yesterday at The Knickerbocker Club? You were the perfect storm?"

"What did he tell you?"

"Not much. He just requested that I assign another reporter to the column and another broker to sell his flat."

"What did you say?"

"Frankly, Camilla, if I had another reporter or broker to assign I would have. After all, the customer is always right. But you're it, on both fronts, so I apologized on your behalf, said something about your having a baby who's teething, and begged him to give you a second chance."

"And he agreed?"

"Not exactly...but I'm having dinner with him tonight to discuss it further. I'm sure I can be persuasive. But I'm warning you, Camilla: Don't blow it. Rocky is big, very big. I'm hoping to get him to commit enough advertising dollars to *Marry Well* to more than make up for the IT pages we've lost. Chuck and I found some convincing numbers on the May/September second marriage thing where Mr. September just has to have a winter place in Florida to complement Ms. May's condo in New York."

Camilla took a deep breath. "I'll do my best."

No matter how she looked at it, Camilla couldn't convince herself that dealing with Rocky could be tolerable. Both Rose and Doris told her to just be professional. After all, she only had to write one column and sell one apartment (well, maybe two). It wasn't as if he would be an ongoing client she'd have to service month after month.

After the sale of the Landers townhouse was complete — and she knew it would be soon — Camilla would have Jayme and Jeffrey off her back, and she could concentrate solely on Rocky.

Camilla took another sip of her Starbuck's as she reviewed the bidder's score sheet she had devised. She decided to score the bidders 0 if the factor was negative, 1 if it was neutral, and 2 if it was positive. With everything tallied, Mr. T and the Wolfs came out exactly even.

	Mr. T	J.& S. Wolf
Able to Pay	2	2
Highest Bid	1	2
Zoning Problem	2	0
Demolition Credit	1	2
Total Score	6	6

Now she really wondered what to do. Camilla hadn't followed Deirdre's advice the first time around, so she couldn't call her back now. Both Alyson and Jayme, for entirely different reasons, were unlikely to come to her aid. She considered calling Dawson Landers — rolling the Post-It Note with his private numbers between her fingers while she mulled — but decided that he had hired her to bring him solutions, not problems, and therefore she abandoned that idea. Then she picked up her phone and called Walter's secretary — who put Camilla right through.

Camilla explained the situation to Walter who answered her as simply as he could: "If you're sure they both have the money, go for the higher offer — the other issues are your job to resolve."

Brooks was delighted to hear that the Wolfs' bid at full asking price would be accepted. "Thank God I won't have to listen to their squeaking beds anymore," she said.

And when Camilla reported the sale to Alyson, Camilla could tell Alyson was pleased, despite herself. "I'm telling you Camilla, it's a home run," Alyson said.

Camilla invited Rose, Chantal, and Merry to dinner to celebrate her first sale; even though Deirdre had warned her that the downfall of most brokers is that they spent their money before it was earned. "Anything can happen, honey, to make your deal not close — a stock market crash, divorce, death — usually in that order."

But Camilla was feeling euphoric, so they splurged on Russian caviar from the Caspian Sea at Foo King. P'nina always kept a secret stash hidden behind the moo goo gai pan.

There was nothing Merry wouldn't eat, nor for that matter, try to say. Camilla gazed upon her chattering and dabbling with the bits of food on her bread plate and leaned over to Rose: "I'm really happy tonight, Rose. To be with you and Merry and Chantal."

"The big check you're expecting doesn't hurt much either," Rose said.

Merry burped.

"I'm giving you a raise, Chantal. As soon as my deal closes. And you, Rose — I'll re-wallpaper your walls —"

"What's wrong with my walls?"

"They've got scuff marks from Merry's exerciser," Camilla said.

"That's true," Rose admitted. "And fingerprints too. But those marks are full of memories…"

"We can photograph them first." Camilla picked Merry up from her stroller. "And you little darling, will have the best first birthday party ever!"

"Wonderful idea! I'll bake the cake. Let's make our invitation list." Rose pulled a pad out of her purse to take notes.

"My, my, this is a joyous lot," P'nina said, joining them.

"We're celebrating Camilla's first real estate closing," Chantal said.

"What are you and Lee doing on November 1st?" Rose asked.

"Working, what else?"

"Can you slip away for a couple of hours to come to Merry's birthday party?"

"As long as it's after lunch but before dinner," P'nina said.

Camilla smiled. "You seem to keep the same hours as Fifth Avenue socialites."

"I wish I could keep their figures," P'nina said, shifting her weight.

To which Chantal said: "My Mama used to say: 'The bigger the cushion, the better the pushin.'"

Camilla was so busy Friday morning, finalizing details with Brooks, sending a memo to Dawson Landers about the accepted offer (since he was unreachable in Cannes), coordinating details with the lawyers who would draw up the contracts, that she worried she wouldn't have time for the most important project of all — Strong Place and the offering she had sent out.

Success was close, very close, and it propelled her through her day. Deirdre had heard about Camilla's deal from a friend of hers who had heard it from Brooks. Even Jayme knew within 24 hours that Camilla had an accepted offer on the townhouse and passed by her desk with congratulations.

"That's awfully big of you, Jayme. Thanks," Camilla said.

"Don't mention it. Beginner's luck is a wonderful thing. When's the closing?"

"We're shooting for mid-December."

"Good. See you there."

Camilla was about to ask Jayme why she would be attending the closing when she had nothing to do with the deal, but then she saw Walter walk in, head hanging uncharacteristically low. He caught her eye, and tried to smile, then entered his office and closed the door.

When Friday came and went with only one response to her Strong Place Bulk Purchase Proposal, Camilla became disheartened. She opened the e-mail from Sanjay Muttergee of Bombay, India: "Your offer sounds very interesting. I will contact you on my next trip to the U.S. early next year."

She thought she'd give it one more try, applying her new-found knowledge of competitive finesse, and sent another e-mail to her prospect list: "Other clients coming in with offers. Please respond one way or another by the extended deadline of Wednesday at noon."

Jennifer had left a message in Camilla's voice mailbox that Mr. Strong wanted to know if she might be free for lunch. Camilla replayed the message again because she thought she had misheard the name of the person Mr. Strong was inviting but, even twice around, she was unmistakably it.

At noon, he came by her desk to pick her up. She saw his reflection in the green glass of her monitor's screen but she had already detected his scent — a light salt air fragrance with a twist of lime. If she had only known that such an invitation would come, she would have dressed up. She was wearing her favorite periwinkle turtleneck sweater, and a pair of black cotton pants. She had her hair tied back in a piece of ribbon from the spool she had bought to decorate Merry's birthday presents, and her only jewelry was a pair of gold hoops that had once belonged to her mother.

"Let's walk, shall we?" he asked.

"I love to walk. That's the best thing about New York," Camilla said. "Where are we going?"

"Oh, just a little place I know."

They walked several blocks against the wind, with leaves and scraps of fast-food wrappers whirling around their legs.

"Winter is coming," Camilla said.

"Yes, remember seeing snow for the first time?"

They talked like that, casually and semi-personally, until they reached the doors of The Algonquin Hotel.

The lobby of The Algonquin on West 44th Street had dark square wood columns and paneled walls. Illuminated bookshelves displayed leather bound volumes and softly colored objets d'art. The atmosphere was cozily retro, although it had been newly updated. It still bore the air of a literary gathering place, the same one where writers and editors from *The New Yorker* had met as part of the famous Round Table and where *My Fair Lady* had been written.

Walter asked her what she would like to drink and she said, "A Lillet, with a slice of orange." He remarked that it was such an old-fashioned drink; he only knew it because it had been his wife's favorite.

"Alyson's?" Camilla asked.

"No," he answered. "Not her." He looked past Camilla to the glass bookshelves.

"I heard about the Landers townhouse. That's a remarkable coup."

She should have been grateful, but she was disappointed. This was to be a business lunch after all.

"Jayme calls it beginner's luck," Camilla said. She saw a dark scowl pass over his face, and then disappear as swiftly as a lone rain cloud on a sunny day. He smiled at her.

"Ah, jealousy, Camilla. It both drives and undermines the business world. I have ignored everything she has said to me about you and I suggest you do the same. Learn what you can from her and leave the rest."

The waiter arrived and, after consulting Camilla, Walter ordered pheasant for them both. He chose a French burgundy and before preordering the soufflés, he turned to her and asked: "Chocolate, strawberry or Grand Marnier?"

"Strawberry, please."

"Make it two," Walter told the waiter. "So how did you close the deal?"

"Exactly as you suggested — the highest bidder won."

"Were they both all cash?"

"Yes, why?"

"It's just that financing is getting harder to secure, appraisers are becoming more conservative, defaults are expected to rise, and that a cash deal makes it more difficult for the buyers to renege."

Camilla smiled as she thought how happy she was that he didn't say, "Cash is king."

They sat and ate the main course in silence.

"Walter, you looked distraught this morning. Is it about Strong Place?"

He leaned back against his chair, studying her. "Not entirely. Before I married Alyson, I lost my first wife to cancer. Today is the anniversary of her death."

"I'm terribly sorry —"

"It helps to be able to talk about her."

"I understand loss. My parents died in a car accident."

"How awful for you. Do you have brothers or sisters?"

"No," she said.

They sat awkwardly while the waiter cleared. "You remind me of my first wife, Camilla. That's probably the unconscious reason why I invited you to lunch today. You two look nothing alike — she was dark and petite. But you have the same spirit and sweetness."

"I've always wondered if men have a type, or if they marry the opposite of their first wife the second time around. I'm an Alyson fan — she's a dynamo — but 'sweet' isn't a word I'd use to describe her."

"Nor I." He looked unabashed; they both laughed. "Some women have a knack for seduction by flattery. Alyson had a way of highlighting those admirable qualities of mine in which I wanted to believe. She never went overboard. To tell you the truth, right now I don't know why I married her ..." He looked lost.

"She's gorgeous and successful, intelligent and fun. I can see why," Camilla said.

"Yes, I suppose you can...looking in from the outside."

"I have a business question," Camilla said, searching for safer ground. "Shoot."

"Why would Dawson Landers own a bunch of apartments in New York?"

"Is this a riddle?"

"No, I'm serious."

"There are lots of possible reasons. Maybe he uses them for cast members, maybe for grown children, perhaps investments —"

"They're not exactly in high-rent neighborhoods."

"Maybe he was in a hurry to fulfill a 1031 like-property exchange — "

"A what?"

194

"According to Internal Revenue Code, if a seller of real property reinvests within a certain time frame, he can defer capital gains taxes —"

It all sounded vaguely familiar. She thought it must have been a footnote in her real estate text. "So if Dawson Landers sold a building at one time in the past, if he rolled over the proceeds into a new investment —"

"He'd save a fortune in tax. The trick is finding the exchange intermediary and property in time."

"Interesting…"

"I would say delicious," Walter said, as he took his first taste of the strawberry soufflé.

Camilla noticed that he seemed more relaxed than he had been when they first arrived. She hoped it had something to do with her. "The whole meal was delicious. Thank you for inviting me. It's been such a treat for me."

"A beautiful woman like you? I would think you get to go to good restaurants often."

"I have a baby who keeps me at home — not that I'm turning away offers."

"Yes, Alyson mentioned her. How old is she?"

"Almost a year."

"Where is the father?"

"I don't know. He left right after she was born. It's probably for the best. Some people just aren't ready to change their lives when they marry."

"Yes, I know what you mean."

Camilla felt an aching in her chest. Just when she had decided only to yearn for things within her reach: Merry, good friends, her work, she felt the ache of desire deep in her chest for someone she couldn't have. Camilla couldn't stifle the feeling, so she embraced it instead. Love is dynamic and creative. She knew she must act.

"Walter, I have an idea."

Apparently, he did too. Her sea-blue eyes and lovely face drove him to act. He kissed her.

That kiss was new, promising, a miracle.

Chapter Ten

The kiss changed everything.

Camilla couldn't sleep. Everything made her laugh. Before, she had felt overwhelmed by the work she had taken on, now she felt energized and eager to take on more. When she looked in the mirror, she saw someone beautiful looking back at her.

On the night of Merry's first birthday party, Rose was making everyone laugh by telling a story about Alyson's escapades at a Halloween costume ball. Alyson had dressed in a white gown from Vera Wang, and had worn camellias in her hair. When someone asked her who she was — a bride, an angel? — she had replied, "No. A virgin. Can you think of anything scarier than that?"

Camilla laughed along with the others. No one seemed to notice how her cheeks blushed red as her thoughts were filled with images of Walter.

John Confrere arrived last. He brought a bouquet of pink spray roses and baby's breath for Merry and a Snugli baby carrier for Camilla. He kissed Deirdre on the cheek — Deirdre had recently sent a lot of business John's way. He shook hands with Cody, Felix, Doris, and Rose. John held onto Rose's hand.

"Have we met before?" he asked Rose.

"Don't think so. Care for a carrot?" she replied, holding out a basket of crudités.

The birthday cake was chocolate with strawberry cream filling and a border of flowers around the top. Rose had spent the day baking the large rectangular layers, getting them ready for Camilla to frost, sending the sweet scent of confection wafting though the entire building. Before the cake was cut and served, Camilla sat Merry down in the middle of the living room floor amidst a ring of gaily-wrapped gifts. Merry's face flushed pink, with spots like cherries on her cheeks, as she pulled plush stuffed animals and a musical book out of tissue paper filled bags and boxes. Felix sat with her on the floor, creating a procession of furry beasts whose names he was trying to teach her to pronounce.

Camilla had left the doors to both hers and Rose's apartments open so that the guests could roam freely between the two. She pulled John across the hall and lowered her voice to a whisper. "I've got an idea. If Dawson Landers were to use the proceeds from the sale of his house to buy — say, 47 condominiums — he could defer a bundle in taxes."

"It's not that easy," John replied. "The key is — he only has a limited time to identify the replacement property and a limited time to complete the sale. His best bet is to have one or more potential replacements in mind — even identified in the contract of sale — before the sale of his current property is completed."

"One more thought…Dawson said something about a divorce. But the title to the house is held in his name only —"

"Well, Camilla, I'm not a divorce lawyer but I do know that the IRS requires that the replacement property must be acquired in the same ownership as the relinquished. If the relinquished property is held as a spouse's separate property, the replacement property should also be held as his or her separate property. If his wife insisted on half, she might be liable at some point for the capital gains tax."

"So it's possible that this type of exchange might be protected from community property laws?"

"That I can't answer for sure. But I've often seen the spouses sign a written agreement that the character of the replacement property is separate of the other spouse and no gift has occurred — which, if legally drawn, I suppose would exempt it from community property."

"John, you've been a great help."

"What do you have up your sleeve this time?"

She confided in John how she hoped to sell 15 percent of Strong Place before Walter's deadline of 90 days. "I came up empty-handed on finding a bulk foreign investor for Strong Place…"

"I'm not really surprised. With what's going on in the States these days, it seems foreign investors are more interested in getting their money out than putting it into U.S. assets. The only motivation foreign investors have in this market is to sell.

But Dawson Landers…"

"I get it now. If he can shelter his gain from the IRS and his capital from his wife —"

"Exactly! He is doubly motivated. Only I don't like the idea of him possibly cheating his wife. What if I propose that he compensates her for signing away her marital rights to the bulk?"

"That sounds fair to me. After all, then he also assumes all the risk."

Camilla looked satisfied. "We're going to be missed. Let's go back to the party."

"Not before you tell me about Rose."

Camilla couldn't suppress her broad smile. "She's my best friend. She's beautiful, talented, and wise. She's a vegetarian —"

John held up his hand and signaled for her to stop. "That does it for me. Does she have a boyfriend?"

"Not now…but why do I have a feeling she will soon?"

It didn't take long for John to be seated beside Rose on the sofa, animated in conversation. They were intent on each other. Camilla was about to join Deirdre, who was busy reapplying her lipstick in a round mirror she held in her hand when Felix came out of the bedroom, where he had been playing with Merry, and slipped his arm through hers.

"You know the couple from Los Angeles I mentioned to you several months ago? They're finally coming to New York to buy an apartment. They want it to be in move-in condition, even furnished. They always eat out, so forget the kitchen. Dennis is loaded so spare no expense. But his movie starts shooting on the first of the year — so they're in a hurry," Felix explained.

Camilla reached for a pencil on the desk and jotted down Dennis' number. "How big a place?"

"A one-bedroom will do. It's really just a pied-à-terre but they'd like a beautiful view. They're keeping the house in Marina Del Rey — they'll be going back and forth."

"A one bedroom pied-à-terre?" Camilla immediately thought of Rocky's place. "I've got just the place for him — I'll call him on Monday."

Merry was exhausted from all the attention she had received and from playing with Chekarf all evening. She fell asleep immediately, on Camilla's old twin bed, fully clothed. Her face was flushed and her chubby lips were lax and soft.

Rose and Camilla kissed John good-bye; he was the last guest to leave. It was clear to Camilla that he didn't want to go. John had seemed so stoic and severe to Camilla, and Rose so loose and free. It wouldn't have been obvious that they should be together, but now she could see that they fit.

"How could you not introduce me to him before?" Rose asked, in a mockingly accusatory tone, as soon as the front door was shut.

"I don't know…no time to think about it."

Rose hit her over the head with a sofa pillow. "What do you know about him?"

Camilla kicked her shoes into the corner and put her feet up. "He's generous and ethical. Intelligent and kind. And a vegetarian —"

"That does it for me."

"Do you have plans to see him again?"

"Yes, next Friday night."

"That's great …you just reminded me that Friday is my deadline for proof changes on my column on Rocky. I want you to take a look."

"Haven't you finished that yet?"

"Not yet, I need to go up there one more time. I've been waiting for him to leave town. He's supposed to leave this weekend, according to his secretary in Palm Beach."

"Better get that one in on time, the whole December issue revolves around Rocky Faber. Alyson couldn't have been clearer. You know how she gets if her perfect plans go awry —"

"I know," Camilla said, wondering how to get things done for Alyson — and accomplish what she needed for herself at the same time.

In the morning, there was a message that Felix and Cody's friend Dennis returned her voice mail, so she called him again and got his. It was a perpetual suspended communication world — virtual speak and echo — she thought, as she pressed *88 to return: "Hello, Dennis. It's Camilla Madison again. Next Thursday afternoon at 4 P.M. is great. Come to 814

Fifth Avenue. I'll be waiting in the lobby. And no, sorry, I have neither a cell phone nor a beeper that you can reach me on."Not yet, she thought.

It was a glorious November day. There were still brightly-colored leaves on the trees that glowed like flames in a bonfire. The sky was clear and the air was so dry that it hurt to breathe.

Camilla hadn't prayed in a very long time. She had noticed that her prayers usually went unanswered while when she took matters into her own hands and applied strategy in place of spirituality, the payoff was immediate. However, she decided to hedge her bets and pray — she prayed that her strategy would work.

Rocky's secretary had said that Rocky would be in Paris all week, which was confirmed by the building concierge who said that Rocky had left town on Monday. Camilla had overnighted photos of 814 Fifth Avenue and Rocky's apartment, as well as a floor plan that she had found in the Register of Distinguished Cooperative Apartments, to Dennis. He had e-mailed her back that the apartment looked perfect.

Camilla arrived promptly and decided to wait for Dennis Meehan and his partner in the lobby. She thought she might show them the restaurant and library, as an appetite-whetter, before bringing them up to the apartment itself.

Camilla was leafing through a recent issue of *Marry Well*, the one with the columns on Dawson Landers, when Dennis walked in. She looked up to see a dashingly handsome man, and with him — her ex-husband Robert!

She dropped the magazine on the floor. Camilla and Robert stood face-to-face, mouths hanging open, mute.

"Do you two know each other?" Dennis asked.

"Camilla?"

"Robert!"

Dennis looked from one to the other.

Robert whispered something into Dennis' ear to which Dennis replied: "Come, come, boys and girls. This is New York — things like this must happen all the time."

Camilla plopped back down in the armchair. "Robert, why didn't you tell me?"

"I was afraid you'd feel rejected," he whispered.

"Rejected?" How could she tell him that it was infinitely more rejecting to think that he had left her for another woman than for a man? A woman would have meant that he found someone better. A man... was just something different.

He smiled. "How's the baby?"

Who did he think he was — her long-lost cousin?

"Robert —" Camilla started to say, but Dennis interrupted her.

"Listen, you two, I'm sure you have a lot of catching up to do, so why don't you make a date to have coffee or something? Right now, I want to see the apartment."

Dennis' suggestion came as a relief. Camilla felt a bit dizzy; she needed to digest the idea of the father of her child as gay before she could even think about "catching up." The three of them rode up the oak-paneled elevator cab, staring straight ahead at the rows of numbers above the door.

"We had an episode just like this in the soap," Dennis said, trying to break the ice. "Greg is gay but marries Katherine under pressure from his parents. They have a baby, but eventually his true sexuality emerges and he falls in love with Scott."

"But on TV, the baby gets to go home with its real mom and dad," Camilla said.

They were all silent as Camilla opened the door to the Faber apartment by waving her magnetic badge. She tried to retain her professional composure, but she was becoming increasingly upset. Here was the man she had thought she loved, the father of her child, returning as an open homosexual. Her mind kept recalling incidents that seemed innocent at the time but, in retrospect, should have been signs.

Camilla was preoccupied with these thoughts when she led Dennis and Robert to the bedroom first, because it did have the best view. A naked body, fresh out of the shower and facing the wall, was in a half lotus yoga position on the bed. Camilla saw the strawberry birthmark, shaped exactly like a heart, on his left shoulder, and knew it was Rocky meditating.

Camilla felt faint, Robert discreetly backed away, and Dennis let out a howl of laughter and said, "Not bad for an old guy," at which Rocky opened his eyes, turned his head to face them, and groaned.

"Get out of here, you imbecile!" Rocky shouted.

Robert took a dazed Camilla's hand and escorted her quickly to the door.

And Dennis sauntered casually behind, whistling the tune to *I Love New York*.

Camilla had to force herself to write her column the next day. The whole Rocky episode had been so upsetting that she had procrastinated, and the proof rewrite was already horribly late. She contemplated not turning it in, but then she realized that she still hadn't made a penny from real estate — in fact had spent several hundred dollars on cabs — and, while the prospects looked good, she knew that it was far from a sure thing that her deals would close and she would get paid.

Alyson had already warned her; Camilla just couldn't give Alyson an excuse to fire her now.

The column, titled *Rocky of Ages,* turned out to be one of her best. Writing was cathartic for her, and even though she couched her angst and passion in witty phrases, and hid her true feelings behind sofas and armoires, the underlying emotion shone through. She wrote about her youthful knowledge of Rocky from her now-deceased father, the edifices he had built over the years, the beautiful homes he had lived in, all culminating in a picture-perfect pied-à-terre on the best block in the greatest city in the world. It was subtly written as a memoriam, which in a way it was, talking about Rocky's importance to the world in the past tense.

Robert wasn't the only one who had come out of the closet that eye-opening November day — so had Camilla. With this column, Rocky would know exactly who she was. Camilla no longer saw Rocky as all-powerful, but as a sad, self-absorbed cad. He hadn't changed, but she had.

Dennis called her to ask if he could go back for another look, this time "when the theater was dark."

Robert called to see how she was doing. He asked if they could talk, about everything that had been left unsaid, and said that he wanted to see Merry.

Walter's secretary, Jennifer, called to inquire if Camilla could attend the Strongs' Christmas party on December 16th. Jennifer explained that the party was business — to thank those who had produced — not a family affair, as Camilla might mistakenly assume.

Camilla told all three that she was on deadline — in fact, the proofs were going to the printer the next day — but she would think over their requests. Then she made a few edits and e-mailed her finished column to Alyson Strong.

Physically drained and emotionally exhausted, Camilla and Merry relocated to Rose's bedroom for comfort, tucked chin-high under the yellow-flowered bedspread on the spare twin. Rose was out, but would surely provide the moral support Camilla needed after such a harrowing couple of days, as soon as she returned from her date. Merry slept contentedly, in the crook of Camilla's arm. She was so warm and soft that she felt like a fleece-covered heating pad, but provided little comfort to Camilla's shattered nerves and confused heart. Only Rose would be able to help her; Camilla couldn't wait until her best friend got home.

Camilla must have dozed off, because sometime around eleven she was woken up by noises in the living room. At first she feared burglars, but then it sounded more like a muffle than a scuffle, and then soft friendly voices and sounds. She gently cushioned Merry by putting a pillow in the spot she vacated on the bed before tiptoeing to the bedroom door. She reached her hand through the crack and flipped on the overhead track lights in the living room. "Rose?" she whispered.

It was Rose...and John Confrere. They were both disheveled and partially disrobed. She couldn't believe how much hair John had on his chest; she never would have guessed it from what he had left on his head.

"Camilla!" John said, blushing.

"Hi honey, how was your day?" Rose asked, nonplussed as usual. The freckles spread across her chest like a game of connect-the-dots.

Despite her own misery, Camilla couldn't help but be glad for her friends.

"I was just leaving," she said. Camilla moved quickly into the bedroom to gather up Merry and her toys. On her way out she kissed Rose and a flustered John goodnight, saying: "I'll see you both in the morning."

Chapter Eleven

It was Dawson Landers' habit to spend Saturday mornings in his home office, with his secretary nearby, to attend to his personal correspondence and private matters. He kept to this routine both in L.A. and New York. He was in a particularly grumpy mood when Camilla phoned him on the cell phone number she had scribbled down, but nonetheless he told her to stop by at 10 A.M.

A beautiful young woman in bare feet, whose slender hips and flat stomach were accentuated by low-rise jeans, answered the door. A gold ring with a single diamond pierced her exposed navel. She had wavy blonde hair and dimples. Camilla estimated her to be about 22.

As Camilla stepped into the foyer, Dawson's hostess smiled. She continued to blow on her fingernails, which she had just polished, rounding her glossy lips into a seductive aureole. "He's in there," she said, gesturing toward the office door.

Camilla watched her wiggle off in the direction of the master bedroom upstairs.

The door to the office was open but Camilla knocked anyway. "Mr. Landers?"

She heard a grunt, which she took to mean, "come in."

"I got your memo. Did Jeffrey call you?" he asked.

"No, why?" She felt a chill.

"Odd. Never mind. I see you've sold the house — good work."

"Yes. I never heard back from you, but since the final offer was at full ask/all cash, I assumed it was a go."

"You assumed right. Where I come from, cash is king."

Camilla was growing to hate that expression. "The lawyers have been working on the contract. It's supposed to be ready for your signature on Monday."

"Good. I'll still be in town. Then Bambi and I are off to St. Bart's. I don't want to be in the country when my wife is served. The press will be all over this like flies to a pile of horse shit."

Camilla didn't know Mrs. Landers, but Dawson's crudeness and cavalier attitude towards a woman with whom he had lived a life and had children seemed callous and cruel. For every Bambi that scampered in the forest, some family was pushed aside like a carcass on the highway.

"Mr. Landers, I noticed in the original closing binder that you paid $7.2 million for this house ten years ago. You're looking at a sizeable capital gain."

Dawson Landers looked at her as if she had used a vocabulary word incorrectly. "I have Ernst & Young working on my tax situation —" he sputtered.

"Yes, I'm sure you do. But accountants and lawyers—they're so conservative—" She took a deep breath. " — not creative, like you."

Dawson's shoulders drew back a few inches. He was wearing crumpled khakis and a soft blue-and-white checkered shirt. Little splotches of perspiration spread across his face while he took in her flattering words. She believed what Walter had implied other women did — found their way to a man's heart through a compliment.

He was batting his eyelashes! "Are you a closet fan of my shows, Ms. Madison?"

She had actually never seen *The Boondocks* or *The Suburbanites,* and was too young to have known his earlier work. "Of course. Everyone knows you're a genius." She gave him another few moments to preen. "Which leads me to my point —"

Dawson Landers took a plume pen from a leather holder on his desk and pulled a photo of himself — one that looked to be at least 20 years old — from an in-basket behind the phone. As he was about to inscribe something personal, Camilla cleared her throat and continued: "What if I could show you a way to defer the tax on your gain for this house and, through a small payment to your wife, exclude the proceeds of this sale from your marital property?"

He looked stunned. "You don't want an autograph?"

"Of course I do! But that's not the only signature of yours that I want."

Camilla took from her briefcase a set of Strong Place floor plans and her Strong Place Bulk Purchase Proposal for 47 apartments. She explained how, if Dawson Landers paid his wife $2 million to relinquish her marital rights to the townhouse and the new investment — also relieving herself of the risk — he could roll over the proceeds of the sale into a new, income-producing investment, with a higher tax base, that would appreciate over time, and be all his.

"Frankly, Ms. Madison, it sounds like a pain in the ass. I already own nine apartments around the city from the last exchange I did when I sold an old costume warehouse to the developers of Chelsea Piers. I know the tax angle works but... the management is a bore. My secretary Dorothea does it now and it's a mess. Who'd collect all those rents, pay all those taxes and expenses, and find the tenants —"

"I would," Camilla interrupted. "I'll even take on the nine you already own."

His eyes widened, as did his smirk. "How much do you charge?"

God, she wished she had anticipated this, done her homework. "Ten percent of the rental income? Management free until the whole Strong Place bulk is leased and my fees can be paid from cash flow?"

He started to review the floor plans she had laid out before him. "Are these the only units for sale?"

"No, but I selected the best values — and the ones that would add up to what you need for the exchange." And, she thought, what Walter would need to satisfy the attorney general.

"Let me think about it over the weekend."

"Okay. But…to make it stick with the IRS, we want to get these properties identified in the townhouse contract of sale and that's supposed to be signed on Monday afternoon."

Dawson opened another button on his shirt. He was perspiring profusely, even though Camilla thought the temperature was quite comfortable in the office. She watched him pick up his phone and press '0' with his pudgy finger. "Dorothea, I'm hungry. Tell them to send the usual." This time, he asked Camilla: "What can I get for you?"

"I'll have a vanilla milkshake and a chef's salad…" she waited for him to finish giving instructions to Dorothea "…Look, Mr. Landers. It's a wonderful solution for you, and I give you my word that I won't let you down."

"Nothing personal, Ms. Madison. But your word is worth diddly-squat —"

Dorothea's voice came over the intercom: "Mrs. Landers on line two."

Camilla listened to several "yes dears" and "soon dears," accompanied by eye rolling and jaw clenching. When he hung up the phone, Dawson Landers said, "What a nag — I can't wait to get rid of her."

"Mr. Landers —"

"All right, all right, I'll do it. Have them send me the contract on Monday — with the exchange clause and the..."

"Rescission of Marital Rights rider?"

"Yeah, that's it."

Camilla hand delivered the contract to Dawson Landers on Monday afternoon. She patiently waited while he explained to his wife on the telephone that she could be held personally liable for enormous gift tax if she didn't sign the document. He described how she might even have to sell her jewelry, if push came to shove, should the IRS decide to focus on her.

In the five minutes during which Camilla sat privy to their spousal banter, she could detect a lifetime of subterfuge and subtle intimidation. She was angry when she heard Dawson offer his wife $1 million, not the $2 million she had suggested, but within 15 minutes he had his wife's faxed signature on the agreement to rescind her marital rights to both the townhouse and the Strong Place bulk purchase package.

The exchange had a deep impact on Camilla, who swore to herself that no man would ever do that to her. Independence was the key to freedom; Dawson Landers' behavior fueled her motivation to secure her independence, and Merry's as well. It would make her next move easier to swallow.

Dawson Landers looked surprised when Camilla presented him with a second contract, this one to purchase 47 apartments at Strong Place contingent upon the sale of the house — but he signed it. She carefully explained the advantages of a simultaneous closing, which would leave him no loose ends between exchanges. "You are such a busy man that I want to keep things as simple for you as I can," Camilla explained.

He shook her hand with his moist palm. "Thanks again for your help, Ms. Madison."

"Will you be back for the closing in four weeks?"

"Not if I can help it. We won't start shooting again until March, so Bambi and I plan to stay out-of-touch until the hiatus is over and my divorce is old news."

As Camilla was leaving, Jeffrey Ratchitt arrived. He had a young blonde on his arm too, whom he introduced as Amber. He wore a pair of Armani A/X jeans, an alligator belt, and suede Stubbs & Wooten loafers with embroidered wild boars. "Congratulations on the sale, Camilla. Beginner's luck?"

"Luck had nothing to do with it," Camilla replied, as she walked out the door.

Camilla couldn't wait to tell Walter her good news. She found a payphone in a coffee shop on the corner and dialed the office. "I have something really wonderful to tell you," she said.

"Don't be coy. What is it?"

She thought about him sitting near her at The Algonquin and her lips grew hot with the memory of his kiss. "Not on the phone," she said.

"Where are you?"

She told him.

"Walk down three blocks to Bemelman's Bar at The Carlyle Hotel. I'll be right over."

While Camilla waited for Walter, she thought of the path that had brought her to this stool with a lucrative contract in hand. She realized that her life was taking off like the shooting stars she used to watch over the ocean in Palm Beach. She had followed the light. She only hoped the stars would not fizzle and fade, once she revealed what she had done.

Camilla watched for Walter through the windows facing Madison Avenue. She saw him pull up in a taxi seconds later and walk purposefully into the bar. He reached out to touch her hand and it felt as though they were surrounded by a magnetic field. He saw that she had a drink before her, an orange Lillet, and he ordered a scotch on the rocks. They were the only customers in the bar.

"So tell me something wonderful."

Camilla told him about her research at the City Registrar and her discovery of 1031 exchanges (thanks to him!). The words tumbled out of her like pebbles in a landslide, powered by feelings she dare not express. When she was done, she pulled the signed contract out of the envelope in her lap and proudly presented it to him like a report card with all A's.

Walter read through the contract, slowly recognizing what it was. "Where did you get this, Camilla?"

"It was in the sales kit. It was the sample."

He roared with laughter. "You're amazing. This is a sponsor-friendly one-sided agreement. You got him to sign it without a lawyer?"

"Is it legal?"

"You bet it is." He regarded her carefully, scanning every inch of her face. He leaned over and kissed her cheek. "Do you know what this means? Do you have any idea how grateful I am? You've saved Strong Place. You have a serious commission coming, a brilliant career in real estate. You'll make a fortune —"

She realized then that her reward wouldn't be the money. One hundred percent of her reward would be in pleasing him.

"There's a contingency clause. Dawson Landers insisted on it. He only buys the apartments if the sale of his townhouse goes through. The down payment is in escrow until then. I scheduled a simultaneous closing for four weeks from today. If the townhouse doesn't close as scheduled, the Strong Place contract becomes null and void."

Walter skipped through the contract to re-read the contingency clause. "We'll just have to make sure that townhouse closes, won't we?"

He looked into her Lillet as if it were a wishing well. Then he looked into her eyes and clinked her glass with his.

When Camilla returned to her office the following morning, there were two-dozen red roses from Walter. The card simply said: "Thanks." Careful of the thorns, she wrapped them in tissue paper and brought them home.

The roses from Walter filled the front hall of her apartment. As beautiful as they were to look at, they were 24 reminders of how lonely she still was. Not a word from Walter, who was on a business trip, nor comfort from Rose, who had been monopolized by John for the fourth night in a row.

Camilla never had the chance to tell Rose that she was meeting Robert at Isabella's for brunch the next day, hastily arranging the rendez-vous

215

the night before, more out of loneliness than conviction that it was the right thing to do. Now that the moment had arrived, she faced it with trepidation.

Camilla's greatest fear was that once Robert saw Merry, he would fall in love with her and sue for joint custody. It was a risk she had to take because both Robert and Merry were entitled to each other. The most precious being in her world was half him.

The fact that Robert was gay no longer bothered her. After all, he couldn't help being what he was. If only he had been honest — but then again, what good would that have done?

Camilla dressed Merry in baby blue, to accentuate her eyes, and put on her pink hat with the big pom-pom. She decided to forgo the stroller, and carried her baby against her chest in the Snugli that John had given them for Merry's birthday. Merry was facing out, mittens flailing and snow-suited legs protruding like powder blue sausages. Camilla was about to knock on Rose's door to say good morning and good-bye, but decided to let the lovers be; Camilla had no desire to intrude.

Robert was waiting on the corner of 77th Street and Columbus as Camilla and Merry arrived. Little puffs of steam against the cold air came out of Merry's mouth, like a teakettle just starting to boil. Robert's face broke out into a broad grin upon seeing her. "You were right. She looks like me," he said.

"Yeah, but she has my character." They both laughed.

Camilla let Merry sit in Robert's lap while they ate. Merry didn't exhibit any stranger anxiety, as she recently had toward those she didn't know. She was charming and content, and he was enchanted.

"Camilla, I am so very sorry for hurting you. There hasn't been a day since I left that I haven't wanted to phone —"

"It might have helped," Camilla admitted.

"Fate has brought us back together. Can we find a new relationship, a friendship? For Merry's sake."

He was right. Someday Merry would want to know who her father was. Every child had the right to know his or her birth parent…if it were possible. She understood Robert's need to know his child too. She would give anything to know the son she had lost long ago. Ever since Merry was born, her aching for her first child had grown more intense by the day.

"If we're starting over, then here are the terms: complete honesty. Frankly, Robert, I won't make room in my life for yet another superficial relationship. God knows there are enough of those. The least we can do is tell each other the truth."

"I agree. Ask me anything."

"How long have you known you were gay?"

As if on cue, the waiter came to take their orders. Camilla chose the French toast and Robert ordered quiche.

"It kind of snuck up on me. While I was in high school, I dated a few girls, but they were mostly friends. I like women, I really do. Then in college, I drank too much beer one night and ended up in a guy's bed. That really freaked me out, but I wrote it off as an experiment, a coming of age thing —"

"I remember when I was at Barnard, half the class proclaimed that they were gay," Camilla said.

"Where are they now?"

"According to the alumnae magazine, married with three kids and living in suburbia."

"That's what I thought would happen to me. I buckled down and concentrated on law school, the job. And then I met you…"

Camilla drifted back to that first meeting while Robert fed Merry little bits of quiche from a spoon. She had been a mess, beside herself with grief. Robert couldn't have been more sympathetic and consoling. Back then, he seemed to understand her loss better than anyone else she knew.

"You got me through my parents' deaths. I suppose I should be grateful for that."

"At that time, Camilla, I easily rationalized away my need for passion. I loved you, like a sister or a dear friend — so I told myself that I was just not that sexual a person, that eventually all marriages are based on friendship anyway, once the sexual heat subsides. As I remember it, you seemed as ambivalent about sex as I was. It all seemed perfectly normal, until —"

"Until?"

"Until I met Dennis."

"When was that?"

"When you were four months pregnant."

It was a small relief to know that it hadn't been earlier. "He's certainly good-looking. Are you in love?"

"Yes."

"How do you know? How does anyone know?" Camilla asked, thinking of Walter.

Robert chewed slowly before answering: "It may be different for everyone, but I would say you know you're in love when you are motivated more by another person's happiness than by your own."

"Is it because of Dennis' job that you're moving back to New York?"

"Yes. But don't worry about support payments — I'm transferring back to Irwin and Sanchez. Oh, before I forget…Dennis wants me to tell you that he really liked that apartment," Robert said. "Who was that guy, Camilla?"

"You mean the owner of the apartment?"

"He's more than that to you. Remember…I lived with you for two years. You looked as though you had seen a ghost."

Merry started banging her spoon rhythmically. Of course, Robert was right. She had seen a phantom from her past, one who had stalked her for years. "His name is Rocky Faber. He was my father's best friend. And he raped me when I was 14." There, it was out. Merry stopped banging and stared at her mother. There are some people who believe that babies understand everything.

"Why didn't you tell me?"

"I was ashamed…"

"Why are you telling me now?"

"Good question. Because…seeing him again made me realize how disgusting he is. That it was his fault all along, not mine."

Robert paid the bill and called Dennis on his cell phone to let him know that it was okay for all of them to meet at 814 Fifth Avenue at three o'clock. Robert covered the receiver and asked Camilla, "Are you sure you don't want to call first? To see if he's there?"

"This time I'll ask the concierge to announce us before we go up. I've got a job to do and the sooner I get it over with, the happier I'll be."

Fortunately, Rocky was not at home when they arrived. Dennis measured the rooms and examined the closets and bath. He commented on how breathtaking the view was and how he admired the owner's taste — in furniture — he was sure to clarify.

Robert and Dennis were not demonstrative toward each other, at least not in front of Camilla, but she noticed small gestures and private references that passed between them. Dennis touched his pocket, and within seconds Robert produced a pen. Robert glanced sideways and Dennis mentioned, without being asked, that yes, the hall closet was double-hung. They seemed able to complete each other's thoughts and phrases. She realized that she had never shared that type of intimacy with Robert — the invisible line of intimacy was one that she had never been invited to cross.

Camilla put her cheek against Merry, who was asleep in the Snugli but facing in toward Camilla this time. Her hat was untied and askew. The special intimacy she felt with her child seemed unique. How could she ever feel as close to a man as she did to her daughter? Many women go through life with much less. But in her new liberation, from secrets and self-deceit, she could lie to herself no more. Yes, she loved Merry, more than life itself, but she wanted more.

Dennis stood tall in front of the picture window and stretched. He looked like the movie star he was that day, with tousled hair and a chiseled square jaw. He wore jeans and a beat-up single-breasted brown suede jacket over a gray cashmere sweater and plaid scarf. He placed his generous hand on Merry's head, as if he were about to crown her Baby Miss, and said: "I'll take it — on two conditions. First, I want to buy it furnished, so I'll need an all-inclusive price —"

That would mean that Camilla would have to call Rocky, talk to him, and negotiate. Doris had encouraged her to confront him; to let him know that she knew he knew. Maybe this would be a good excuse. "And, second?"

"Merry has to have unlimited visitation rights!"

The most peculiar thing happened when Camilla called Rocky's office in Palm Beach the following morning to put in Dennis' bid. Camilla could hear Rocky in the background, instructing his secretary what questions to ask and answers to give. He was so accommodating that Camilla wondered if he had been sufficiently embarrassed by the scene in his bedroom that he'd rather get the apartment sale over with and go on to bigger things. But it became apparent to her, by his whining tone, and his effort to please her, that he was afraid. Just like a playground bully, all bluster and aggression — picking on the weak and vulnerable — until one of them chooses to fight back.

Rocky Faber, afraid of her. Imagine that!

No matter what his reason was, Rocky seemed to acquiesce with ease. The deal was agreed to — to sell the apartment and all that it contained. Just the closing date needed to be settled upon.

"Mr. Faber wants you to know that he won't be able to close until you've found him a new place to live," Rocky's secretary said.

"May I speak with him, please?"

After a few hushed words with his assistant, Rocky came on the line. "I only have a few minutes to spare."

"If I'm to find you a new place, I need to know what you want."

"Something large and needing no work."

"Water view?"

"I prefer the Park."

"Do you dine out...say, at your Club...or will you be entertaining at home?"

"That's an odd question."

"Is it? Let me try again. How many bathrooms do you need...or will you be using the 'head'?"

The line was so silent Camilla could hear the ticking of her watch. "Wait a minute...where did you say you were from?" Rocky's voice sounded strained.

"I didn't."

"Are you? Have we..."

"So you seem not to have Alzheimer's after all —"

"Is this a set-up? Blackmail? What do you have up your sleeve?"

"An arm. Listen, this is all an ugly coincidence; I certainly want nothing from you. But, to be honest, I have a lot at stake. I'm glad that we've met again. I can finally put things to rest. The column is done, and 814 Fifth is sold. If you'll just tell me what you're looking for, I'll find you an apartment so Dennis can close, Alyson will be happy, and we'll never have to speak again."

"Why should I do business with you?" Rocky asked.

If Rocky refused, Camilla was sure she would lose her job at the magazine and that Alyson would jettison her from Marry Well Realty too. "There must be some good in you, Rocky. Now is your chance to repay some of the damage you have done. I have forgiven myself; I've almost forgiven you. Don't you want to redeem yourself too?"

A snide snicker was his sole reply. "So you don't plan to tell Alyson about that ancient history?"

"Not unless I have to."

"Good. Neither will I."

Camilla knew that she and Rocky had struck a deal. Rocky's fear was of being exposed to Alyson as less than what he appeared to be and he seemed determined to avoid that at all costs. Meeting again was like a head-on collision in which Rocky and Camilla were the drivers who agreed not to tell the police, just to avoid the interrogation and stigma, and raising their insurance premiums for the future.

Looking out the window at the construction bridge across the street, Camilla took stock. If she could find a new apartment for Rocky quickly, and close on all the deals on her plate, both the column and her real estate idea seemed safe. But it all depended on Rocky keeping his word and being willing to move fast.

By now it was common knowledge around the office that Alyson was having an affair with Rocky Faber...that Rocky was Mr. Diamond Necklace. It wasn't Alyson's infidelity that piqued interest, everyone was used to that, but rather the longevity of the relationship. There had been a couple of the usual product samplings in-between, such as Dawson Landers, but it was unheard of for Alyson to stay committed to anyone other than herself for this long.

And that's what led Camilla to suspect that Alyson was planning to leave Walter for Rocky. It was the record length of their coupling — at least six months by her calculation — combined with Alyson's proprietary interest in Rocky getting a new apartment. Few businessmen were wealthier than Walter Strong, but Rocky had obviously cut Alyson in on a deal. He was promising her equity in his business and himself. To a woman of Alyson's ambition, this may have been the incentive to make such a drastic move.

Now it made sense to her why Rocky was so afraid of Alyson finding out about his dirty little secret. People like Rocky and Alyson wouldn't be vulnerable to love, but losing a business partner so close to the climax of a deal would pain them much more.

In the end, Rocky had described exactly what he was looking for in an apartment. It had to be grand, with views of the Central Park reservoir. Deirdre checked her database and insisted that there was only one listing on the market that would fit Rocky's — and Alyson's — criteria. It currently belonged to a department store heir, whose fortunes had taken a turn for the worse.

1051 Fifth Avenue had been an old pre-war rental, comprised mostly of cut-ups — a New York solution to contractions in the economy where grand twelve-room apartments were "cut up" into two or three smaller ones. It also had a dozen awkward storage rooms on the top floor.

The new owner managed to convert the air rights to development rights and built a penthouse floor on the roof that, when combined with the rabbit warren of storage rooms, created a 13,000 square foot duplex penthouse apartment with panoramic views of the Central Park reservoir. The asking price for the raw space when it first came on the market was $30 million.

"Is that what the owner paid?" Camilla asked, incredulous. After all these months, New York's real estate prices still astounded her.

"Are you kidding? Mr. Discount Merchandise?" Deirdre answered.

"So what did he pay?"

"Well, if you recall my telling you, this apartment came on the market at the peak of the last cycle, just after the current owner had been turned down by three co-op boards in a row. This was very appealing to him because it was a no-board-approval sponsor condo. But it was a tough sell, due to the price tag and all the work — rumor had it that he spent $5 million and three years building out the space."

Camilla was taking notes. "Who'd he use?"

"Juan de las Heras... with Karl Lagerfeld consulting. The raw space was strange — for instance, the living room had a glorious view of the reservoir but no other windows or doors. I'd be curious to see what de las Heras made of it."

"Come along then. I could use the company," Camilla said.

"Why not? It's deader than a cemetery around here today."

The first sign of Juan de las Heras' genius was apparent as soon as the burnished steel doors of the silver velvet-lined elevator cab opened directly into the living room. The view of Central Park was straight ahead. The upside-down duplex felt like a Soho loft — spacious, airy, and light. The windowless walls that Deirdre had referred to were lined with eight digital monitors, controlled by an elaborate computerized system kept in a hall closet, which played the owner's department store television commercials 24/7.

There was an electronic, red LED display with the words: You Are What You Wear, Design = Fashion, rolling by in a continuous flow.

The only furniture in the living room was four anthropomorphic chairs, upholstered in the same silver velvet as the elevator, and two oversized conga drums, animal skin stretched tight, in front of an undulating steel and glass wall housing a gas-fed fireplace.

"How would you describe it?" Camilla asked Deirdre.

"Oddly sexy," Deirdre replied. "I'm dying to see the bedroom."

A Filipino houseman appeared from behind the fireplace wall. He took their coats, which he passed to a pair of seemingly unattached hands. "Shoes, please," he said, holding open a new plastic bag he retrieved from his pocket.

In the background, Camilla heard the unmistakable snapping yaps of cabin-fevered Manhattan dogs. Two little pugs, with pudgy bodies and smashed in faces, ran out from behind the sheet of steel. They nipped at Camilla's stocking feet, puncturing the toe of her pantyhose and causing them to run.

Deirdre reached into her sweater pocket and retrieved two Milk Bones with which she staved off another attack. "It's the only protection," Deirdre explained.

"We'd like to see the downstairs," Camilla said to the houseman, who led them to a staircase behind the fireplace that looked like jagged slabs of ice connected by steel tubes. The steps felt cold on their shoeless feet.

The master bedroom was a study in tranquil sensuality. It was all white, but many different shades and textures. The diaphanous draperies were made from translucent gauze and the bedspread was angora. Two large globe-shaped lighting fixtures hung over the bed. They were covered in a nubby, fuzzy material that looked like cotton balls glued together and they were controlled by dimmers on the wall by the pillow. Facing the headboard, on one of those interior walls Deirdre had described, was a length of acrylic closets. Thousands of articles of clothing — suits, ties, shirts, sweaters, and pants — were neatly arranged by color, from light to dark, like a see-through box of Crayola crayons.

A wall safe had a glass front and was lit from behind, like a display box in a museum. In it were rows upon rows of gold and silver rings, with different colored stones and designs. On the night table sat a crystal bowl of condoms, wrapped in foil, and individually monogrammed JAW.

They peeked in the master bath and saw a double stall shower with all-glass walls. Next to the toilet, which looked like a throne, was a pile of magazines and newspapers, mostly *Vogue, Harpers' Bazaar, W,* and *Women's Wear Daily.* There was a basket with a cushion, where Camilla presumed the pugs slept. When she looked closer, she saw their names embroidered there: Wednesday and Pugsley.

"Everybody loves dogs," Deirdre said.

"According to Alyson, Rocky hates them."

"Never trust a person who doesn't like dogs," Deirdre said, rifling through the underwear drawer in the dressing room off the master bath. The houseman had left; they were alone. She held up a pair of boxers with pugs on them. "Having said that…this goes too far, don't you think?"

"At least he's a man you can trust," Camilla answered.

"Don't know about that but he does seem to have a sense of humor…" Deirdre said, holding up another pair of boxers, this time with Bugs Bunny tugging on a rope that disappeared over the waistband.

"Deirdre, do you really think we should be snooping in his drawers?"

"Was that an intentional pun? Oh, lighten up, Camilla. This is the fun part of being a broker. Besides, everyone does it."

Suddenly, the houseman reappeared at the door to the bathroom, with a large, brass disc strapped to his waist and two sticks with rubber balls at the end. The gong rang loudly. "Time's up," he said.

Camilla preceded Deirdre up the ice-slab stairs, lost in her own thoughts. The apartment did seem perfect. Rocky would have to make the trip to New York, like the place, and agree to move fast if Camilla hoped to get Dennis in to 814 Fifth on time.

She looked at her watch. It was too late to call Rocky today — she had to get home and feed Merry, draft her column (she was late again, but this time it was Alyson's fault), and type up her invoices for the Landers and Strong Place closings. Tomorrow would be the day she had worked toward for months. The day she would save Walter and the day she would finally get paid.

Chapter Twelve

The closings were held in a long conference room at Dawson Landers' lawyer's office — Wohlman & Tuck. Jeffrey Ratchitt was there, representing the absent owner Dawson Landers; Jayme Seagram was there, representing West Coast Realty and Strong Place; there was a title closer/1031 exchange intermediary who never introduced himself; the Wolfs both came with their lawyer; and Camilla and Brooks Snow were there, sitting in the back, waiting until it was over so that they could submit their invoices and collect their commission checks. The brokers' checks would be written last, from the escrow down payment, after the closings were over.

There must have been dozens of papers to sign and forms to complete. The Wolfs' attorney patiently explained everything to them, and they signed every sheet as husband and wife. The Wolfs may have been plunking down 21 million dollars, but they were still young and needed to have their hands held.

It was incredibly boring for the brokers — after all, their jobs were done. Brooks was completing the *New York Times* crossword puzzle while Camilla was daydreaming about the double commission she would receive and about how grateful Walter would be for saving his project with less than 24 hours to spare.

To Camilla's surprise, Jeffrey's friend Amber walked in. She had dressed up in a proper suit that looked borrowed and had her hair pulled back in a clip. She was so obviously high on something — her eyes were glassy and her mannerisms jumpy — that everyone stared at her, which made her simper even more.

"And you are?" the Wolfs' lawyer asked her.

Jeffrey jumped in to answer. "Ms. Feuer. She's the Seller's exclusive agent."

Camilla shot up from her seat. "No she isn't. I am."

There was a tangible silence in the room while all parties looked around for an explanation.

"Who's got the exclusive agreement for 7 East 79th Street?" the Wolfs' lawyer asked.

Jeffrey Ratchitt conveniently had copies for everyone. The Wolfs and their lawyer recessed to the hallway outside to confer. Brooks looked sympathetically at Camilla while Dawson Landers' attorney maintained a poker face. Camilla held the agreement before her and couldn't believe her eyes. It was an Exclusive Right to Sell Agreement drawn between West Coast Properties and Dawson Landers, LLC. It named Amber Feuer as exclusive agent. And, Jayme Seagram had signed it for WCP.

"It's a fake!" Camilla shouted. "Amber Feuer doesn't even work for West Coast Properties, much less Marry Well Realty."

"I'm relatively new," Amber explained.

"How new? Ten minutes?" Camilla asked.

"So you've never seen her before?" Barry Wohlman asked.

"Never in the office. Only in the..." her voice became weak "... house."

"Do you have an exclusive agreement also, Ms. Madison?" Barry Wohlman asked her.

Camilla turned toward her colleague with a desperate fury in her eyes. She practically knew the answer before she had asked the question. "Jayme, please, did you bring my Exclusive Right to Sell Agreement?"

"Would have, Camilla, if it had existed," Jayme replied, beads of perspiration gathering on her upper lip.

At that point, the Wolfs and their lawyer reentered the room. "My clients insist that the only brokers they dealt with were Ms. Madison and Ms. Snow."

"That may be so, counselor, but only Ms. Feuer has a written agreement, and both the Seller's representative and the real estate firm's head of sales confirm what's in it," Barry Wohlman said.

Everyone was still. It was obvious that Camilla was being cheated, but no one spoke up in her defense. Everyone had his own personal interest to protect, so Camilla realized she was all alone with hers. "Just a minute," she said. Then she walked over to the telephone on the conference room table and dialed Walter Strong.

"Jennifer, it's Camilla. Is Mr. Strong in?" Camilla spotted Jayme out of the corner of her eye, gloating.

"Oh hi, Camilla. No, he's on an airplane to attend lender meetings in San Francisco. He'll be back in the office next Monday. He did say I should e-mail him as soon as the closing for Strong Place was over. He checks his e-mail every night. Any news?"

Camilla looked at her watch; he wouldn't get her message for at least nine hours. "Not yet," she said, abruptly hanging up.

All eyes were on her. "We have to postpone the closing," she said. "This is fraud!"

Jay Wolf looked at his lawyer, then at Camilla. "Look, I believe there's something fishy going on here, but Sherrie and I want to close."

The Wolfs' attorney said that he was prepared to close as long as all parties indemnified his clients from brokers' claims.

"This sounds like an inter-office problem to me," Brooks said, quietly. Camilla knew Brooks liked her but ultimately would place her own interests first.

"Ms. Madison was never the exclusive agent. It's always been Ms. Feuer —" Jeffrey Ratchitt lied.

Amber started hiccupping without reserve. Her uncontrollable chirping noises stopped the conversation while everyone diverted their attention to her. Finally, the up-until-then quiet title closer spoke: "Unless we can come to a written consensus regarding this dispute, National Title recommends that we postpone the closings and the 1031 exchange —"

Jayme smirked: "Mr. Strong won't be happy about that, not with the attorney general breathing down his neck."

"Just a minute," Camilla said. She knew she was beaten. She had never actually seen an exclusive agreement with her name on it. She had just trusted that the paperwork had been done.

If the closings were postponed, then the Strong Place bulk sale would be cancelled and she'd probably still get nothing from the commission for the first deal anyway. But if they closed, then at least she would get her cut of the commission for Strong Place — half of five percent or $525,000 — enough to start her off on her own when the nine-month point had passed. And Walter — she had practically given him her word.

"I'll do it," she said. Everyone else at the table let out a collective sigh of relief.

It took another two hours to complete both sales. All the participants knew that something underhanded had taken place. They were somber, but polite. Brooks took her check and squeezed Camilla's arm as she passed her by. The Wolfs thanked her profusely for her time and effort on their behalf. The title closer shrugged and said, "You can't fight City Hall."

In the end, she was sitting there with Jeffrey, Jayme, Amber and Barry Wohlman. Barry handed Jayme a commission check made out to Marry Well Realty for the townhouse sale and another one to West Coast Properties for the Strong Place bulk purchase; Jayme held out a pre-cut Strong Place commission check to Amber, which Jeffrey snatched from her hand.

Camilla turned to Jayme and Jeffrey and said: "What goes around, comes around." Then she looked straight in Amber's eyes and asked her: "What do you have to say for yourself?"

"Hiccup."

It was tough to visit her old teacher, a bit with her hat in her hand. But Professor D'Angelo listened carefully as Camilla described the circumstances and asked her what, if anything, could be done. To Camilla's surprise, her professor seemed genuinely pleased and, more importantly, had the information Camilla had hoped.

"Here it is," Professor D'Angelo said, pointing to a section of New York Real Estate License Law. "Article 12, Section 442 on splitting commissions."

§442. Splitting commissions

No real estate broker shall pay any part of a fee, commission or other compensation received by the broker to any person ...unless such a person be a duly licensed real estate salesperson ... or a duly licensed real estate broker or a person regularly engaged in the real estate brokerage business in a state outside of New York.

"It's very clear, Camilla. If you have presented the facts accurately, something illegal is going on."

Camilla copied the legal language from the text, and then asked, "Is there any recourse I can take?"

"Let's read on:

"*The Department of State may revoke the license of a real estate broker or salesperson or suspend the same, if such licensee has been guilty of fraud or fraudulent practices, or has demonstrated untrustworthiness to act as a real estate broker or salesperson, as the case may be.*"

"So if a commission was paid to an unlicensed person by a licensed broker, the latter could lose his or her license?"

"Not only could, but should. It's known as a kick-back," the teacher said, owl-eyes wider and wiser than ever.

Camilla leaned over and kissed her. "Thank you. You have no idea how helpful you've been."

The professor put her hand to her cheek and smiled.

When Camilla confronted Jayme with the facts, it took Jayme all of 15 minutes to recalculate the commissions, revise the paperwork, and cut Camilla a personal check for the difference between what she was paid at the closings and what she was legally entitled to.

Chapter Thirteen

Equipped with her rightful portion of the Landers townhouse commission, Camilla had shopped with Rose and Merry for two entire Saturdays until they found the perfect dress, a blue chiffon cocktail dress by a new designer called Peggy Jennings, and matching slingback shoes by Jimmy Choo. A year earlier, it would have been inconceivable to her that she would spend so much on a pair of shoes and even more inconceivable that she would be able to afford them — but thanks to Strong Place, she could.

Being invited to Alyson and Walter's Christmas party was such an honor that it made Camilla feel heavy with anxiety. She wondered who else would be there and if she would fit in. Jennifer had hand-delivered one of Alyson's engraved invitations with the exact date and time. In the lower right-hand column, next to the word Dress, the card read: Sexy Lingerie Required. There was an embossed Christmas cupid, wearing a red lace thong, and devil's horns were where the halo should have been.

The hardest part of the shopping trip was to find the sexy lingerie that the invitation required. Camilla insisted that it would be a waste of money since no one would see it anyway. But Rose warned her not to put it past Alyson to place mirrors on the floor, just to make sure that the ladies followed her instructions, and if she chose not to heed Alyson's command, she risked being turned away at the door. That only increased her worry, but despite it, she indulged in a carnation pink lace panty with matching bra. She had hoped to buy a slip, because the chiffon of her dress was just a bit transparent, but quickly realized that slips just weren't worn, or it seemed sold, anymore.

The highlight of the day preceding the party was her haircut. Camilla had always worn her hair long and straight and parted in the middle. Her appointment at Kenneth's in the Waldorf Astoria was with Deirdre's hairdresser Victor, who gave Camilla a new, layered look à la Paula Zahn and who, at his suggestion, gave Merry her first haircut as well.

Merry scrunched up her brow in the mirror, and sneezed when the cut hairs tickled her nose; Camilla caught the virgin locks in an envelope, which she later marked "Merry's First Haircut." Then they both had their first manicures and pedicures, polished the same carnation pink as Camilla's lacey lingerie.

When Camilla called Deirdre to thank her for recommending Victor, she told her about what she had learned from Professor D'Angelo about Article 12 of The Real Estate Code.

"All kinds of sleazy stuff goes on. Last year, Puppi Springer met the assistant of some German movie star in the Viand Coffee Shop and handed him a $20,000 kick-back in a crumpled paper bag. Then you know about Stanley Towers? Well, no one passes the board there until his or her broker deposits $10,000 in the board president's offshore account," Deirdre replied.

A bottomless well of real estate gossip, Deirdre also told Camilla that after Alyson had married Walter and sold her apartment at the San Remo, they bought the penthouse triplex at River House. *The New Yorker's* Paul Goldberger had called it "Manhattan's most glamorous abode," describing how every major room had a panoramic water scene, with lower Manhattan visible to the south and the Triborough Bridge a glowing arc to the north.

The building required a Fidelifact Report on the purchasers and a signed copy of the House Rules. The normally stuffy board looked the other way when the Fidelifact investigator uncovered some of Alyson's indiscretions, in part because Walter was so rich, and in part because all seven board members were men.

Once past the army of uniformed doormen, Camilla entered the paneled elevator cab to be whisked up to the 26th floor. The elevator doors opened into the apartment's foyer, which had been rebuilt to be perfectly symmetrical, with an open doorframe providing a glimpse into the living room and to the East River beyond.

The foyer was simply appointed, with antique herringbone wooden floors and creamy colors to establish a neutral palette for the art — a large, colorful Helen Frankenthaler canvas, a Milton Avery portrait of his wife, and a Maillol Torse de Venus nude bronze statue. Many guests had commented on how like Alyson the sculpture looked; such comments irritated Alyson, who considered the Venus to be fat. The lighting was recessed and the only furniture in the room were two Regency benches and a lacquered Louis XV console table, on which were three-dozen champagne roses arranged in a Steuben bowl.

The only people whom she thought she knew other than the hosts were Jayme Seagram and Chuck Maynard, although she recognized Teddy Ruckensayer from his picture in *Town & Country* and spotted Rocky Faber from behind by his yellowed hair. As soon as Jayme spotted her, she turned the other way. Jayme was still furious that Camilla had overturned her plot with Jeffrey, who refused to contribute to Camilla's refigured share.

"But Jeffrey," Jayme had protested, "I could have lost my license."

"To quote my favorite super: 'Not my problem,'" he had smugly replied.

Just when Camilla thought she should turn around and leave, Chuck came up to her and took her by the arm. "Thank God they've invited someone normal. Come along, I'll show you around."

They walked through the immense living room, with walls upholstered in antique yellow moiré. There was a 25-foot-high neo-classical ceiling that Chuck explained had been created by Sir Richard Morrison — whomever he might be — in the 1840s, purchased by the Strongs from an estate in Ireland, disassembled, shipped, and reassembled and installed above where they stood.

There was surprisingly little furniture in such an enormous room, just a few cozy seating arrangements positioned to take in the view, and a celadon and gilt carved harpsichord that Chuck explained had once belonged to Johann Sebastian Bach. These items were spaced generously on a Persian rug, which echoed the palette of the room. The taffeta curtains puddled generously on the floor. On the eighteenth-century marble fireplace mantel were Sévres cachepots holding more champagne roses and a pair of Staffordshire unicorns, horns erect.

In the corner between the living room and library was a bartender, specializing in various martini drinks according to a calligraphied menu displayed in a silver frame. Chuck ordered a green apple Martini but suggested the Flirtini to Camilla, offering that it was Alyson's personal favorite.

As she sipped the delicious cocktail made of Absolut Raspberry Vodka, champagne, and Chambord, she remarked, "Now I understand what makes Alyson so seductive."

To which Chuck replied, "Believe me, Alyson doesn't need any outside help."

"Chuck, how can she invite Rocky Faber here?"

"Brazen, I agree. But he is a client of the magazine. And the star of this month's issue as well."

The dining room had been arranged banquet style, with a long table set for 24 along the expanse of the bay window facing the river. Because they were high up, the water vista gave the impression of being on a flying boat.

The tablecloth had been custom made from sheer Fortuny silk with gold threads woven throughout, reflecting the light from the dozens of shimmering votive candles floating on water in small Baccarat cut crystal bowls. Viennese mahogany chairs with cameos set into the backs faced place settings of Herendon china, antique English silver, and hexagonal engraved goblets of blown Bohemian glass.

Camilla peeked at the place cards, imprinted *Playing Footsie Is Encouraged*, to note that she had been seated between Chuck and Walter's son Rex.

She wandered into the library, with its thousands of leather-bound books, all catalogued by Christie's in a register casually left open on the Regency Gothic writing table situated beneath two moody portraits of Florentine noblemen. Teddy Ruckensayer was chatting with a woman in a black sheath, and Walter was leaning against the wall, near the red damask draperies, talking to a couple, Wall Street types, with perfect hair. He stopped talking when she entered the room. His eyes connected with hers.

A tuxedoed waiter came by with a small round silver tray; he offered tiny little potatoes, no bigger than ping-pong balls, halved and topped with dollops of crème fraîche, beluga caviar, and fresh chives. On the coffee table in front of the tapestry settee was a large silver platter filled with crushed ice, on which sat craggy Kumamoto oysters with garlic-tarragon crusts.

"I almost didn't recognize you," Walter said. But she couldn't answer because she had just popped a slippery oyster into her mouth.

Finally, she swallowed the oyster whole, and managed: "Thank you for inviting me."

"You are our guest of honor, our heroine, who saved the day. Without you, Strong Place would have gone up in smoke."

Camilla could tell Walter was studying her. She felt a warm flush rise to her cheeks and a stirring in her groin, both of which she tried to blame on the Flirtini.

"It was you who gave me the opportunity," she said graciously.

"Nonsense. I have a good eye for talent. Can I get you another drink?" But before she could decline, he had asked one of the servers to bring her one more. When the drink arrived, he led her to a hidden room behind the study so that they could talk without being disturbed. She sat next to him on a needlepoint love seat that faced the door. It was emblazoned with the Latin boast attributed to Julius Caesar: "*Veni, Vidi, Vici*" — "I came, I saw, I conquered." Along the wall on their left, Camilla noticed the only sure sign that Alyson lived there too — two dozen or so glass "passion testers" filled with brightly colored liquids.

He noticed her looking at them. "If you hold the bulb in your hand, you can tell how passionate you are by how fast the liquid rises. Want to try?"

"Better not," she said.

Camilla looked closely at Walter Strong in a way she hadn't dared before. Of course she had been keenly aware of her growing feelings toward him, especially since The Algonquin kiss, but she had set boundaries; after all, he was a married man as well as her boss, and her other boss's husband. The alcohol had suppressed her inhibitions, allowing her to view him without the restraint of reason, taking in the angularity of his nose, the lushness of his hair, and the smooth olive tones of his skin. She had to stop herself from stroking his cheek.

Walter seemed to be enjoying the caress of her eyes. He sat at ease in his body. "Camilla, I know you grew up in Palm Beach, and that you are raising your child in New York. But the time in between is a mystery," he said in a husky voice.

"I came up north for school and stayed," she said. "I haven't been back to Palm Beach since… for ten years."

He looked into her eyes while he spoke, as if searching for his own life in hers. "I remember visiting my grandparents in Palm Beach. People get dazzled by the stunning houses and famous names, but what I love is the way the island is sandwiched between the lake and the ocean."

"I know what you mean. Between the wild and the calm; I thought I would live there forever," she said.

"Why didn't you go back then, if you loved it so?" he asked, innocently.

Before she could think of an acceptable response, Rex walked in through the doorway behind them. His tall, blond good looks almost disguised the serious, quiet expression on his face. He lovingly touched his father on the shoulder.

"Camilla Madison, this is my son Rex." Walter beamed with pride as he looked back and forth between Camilla and Rex.

"We met last summer, at *Marry Well*."

"During your internship?" Walter asked Rex.

Rex stooped slightly, the way some very tall people do to avoid giving the impression that they are talking down to others in their group. He nodded, and a slight smile crept across his lips. "Yes... Dad, Alyson sent me to fetch you. Dinner is about to be served. And, Ms. Madison — I believe we're dinner partners! May I show you the way?"

When Rex led Camilla to the table, she noticed that the cards had been slightly rearranged and she was seated between Walter and his son.

Alyson glared when she realized that someone had altered her seating plan. She whispered something in the caterer's ear who, in turn, looked at Camilla and shrugged. As soon as everyone was seated, the wait staff removed the place cards and substituted a steaming bowl of asparagus soup in front of each guest.

"How are you enjoying Columbia?" Camilla asked Rex, remembering that he said he would be starting in the fall.

"It's great — except for the pathetic football team. I particularly love the Early Empires program — of course, that's not the empire Dad wants to hear about."

"Those empires are fallen — ours is still on the rise. I need you in the family real estate business when you graduate, to make sure it continues to grow," Walter interjected. "Rex had been a straight-A student at Collegiate, tennis star, captain of the soccer team, editor of the school newspaper —"

"Dad!" Rex said, reddening.

"Sorry, I certainly didn't mean to embarrass you in front of a beautiful woman." Now Camilla blushed, especially since the din of spoons against bowls and dining table chatter ceased at exactly the moment of Walter's compliment. Alyson, who sat at the head of the table on Walter's other side, heard every word.

Alyson stood up. She wore a strapless red raw silk dress, and emeralds in her ears. Her eyes were lit up like Christmas tree twinklers as she tottered slightly on her high spike heels from her numerous Flirtinis. She raised her wine glass while the staff cleared the bowls from the first course. "Since I know you all follow commands, I order us to go around the room and describe the sexy undies we are wearing."

Camilla waited for Walter to stop Alyson, but he sat stiffly silent.

"I'll start," Alyson said. "I've got nothing on." She drained her wine glass with the ardor of a thirsty athlete consuming a bottle of Gatorade.

As her guests watched their hostess imbibe, the entrée of roast duckling and wild rice pilaf was placed before them. Alyson announced that, on second thought, she would switch the game and everyone would *show* their sexy lingerie — and this time Camilla would start.

"Alyson, that's enough —" Walter warned.

Rocky sat on Alyson's other side looking uncomfortable. Camilla supposed that his upbringing usually relegated such public displays of aggression to private chambers — like yachts.

"Sit down, Alyson," Rocky said quietly. And she did.

"Is Miss Prim too shy to play in the big leagues?" Alyson hissed at Camilla.

"Alyson, I'm warning you," Walter said sternly, his hand on her arm. Only Rex, Rocky, and Camilla could hear what he was saying, but the others could sense the tension in the air.

"Rex, what are they teaching you in college these days — survival skills?" Chuck asked, defusing a blast.

There were several nervous laughs as Rex answered. "In a way, yes. I've been reading Euripides, Aristotle, Plato —"

Alyson interrupted, quite drunk now. "Who wants to know what I've been reading?" She slurred her words. Then she looked directly at Camilla and said, *"The Art of War."*

"By the Chinese general Sun-Tzu?" Camilla asked.

"Shih Tzu? Shih Tzu? The dogs? I have two," said one of the guests whom Camilla did not know. She was sitting down at the other end of the table.

"Not Shih Tzu," the man next to her said softly. "SUN-Tzu, now shhh..."

Camilla had had enough of Alyson's baiting. It was time to rise and fight back. "Wonderful book! Amazing how so little has changed since he wrote it 2,500 years ago. Didn't he invent guerilla warfare? Using strategy instead of intimidation?"

Everyone expected Alyson to explode. Instead she excused herself, claiming a headache from what she was sure must have been tainted wine. She regained her composure before she left the table, and insisted that the party continue. She was sure she would be her old self in the morning.

Walter signaled for the wait staff to clear her place. He discreetly moved his chair around to the head of the table, in effect closing ranks, under new leadership, after an impeachment. Soon after, Rocky excused himself, claiming an early flight in the morning.

"I thought I was going to show you 1051 Fifth Avenue —" Camilla was confused.

"Cancel the appointment. I think I've changed my mind about moving to New York," Rocky dryly replied.

As soon as Alyson and Rocky were gone, everyone relaxed and the conversation flowed again. A delicious selection of desserts was served — baba au rhum, fruitcake, and stollen — with the choice of coffee or tea. Smiles returned and faces brightened.

Walter was a charming and effortless host. He spoke to everyone, and told colorful anecdotes about his career and public figures he knew — just enough to be intriguing without being too revealing. Camilla could see that he was a master of rebound; a talent she knew could only be developed after a lifetime of recovering from difficult situations.

"Your father is magnificent," Camilla said to Rex, hoping to share her admiration.

"You were pretty terrific, too. Not many people would be brave enough to take on Alyson in public like that," Rex said. When the table broke up, they wandered together to the hidden room behind the library.

"It wasn't very smart. She *is* my boss," Camilla said.

"Dad says that's why I shouldn't have a boss, so I can always be free to say what I think."

"Your dad is very successful — he should know. Do you want to have your own business?"

"You know, you're the first adult who ever asked me what I want. Honestly, I don't know what I want, but one thing that Dad has always said keeps ringing in my ears every time I read the newspaper —"

"What's that?"

"He says: 'Business goes up and business goes down. If you work for someone else when business goes down, you get laid off. When you work for yourself, everyone else gets laid off.'"

"That's a harsh assessment," Camilla said.

"Maybe harsh, but true," Walter interjected, joining them. "Camilla, I want to apologize for Alyson's behavior. She was…out of control. As soon as Rex and I return from Christmas vacation in Palm Beach, I'd like to take you to lunch to make it up to you."

"That would be lovely…" She felt the warmth stirring in her groin again, but this time she knew why. "I'd better be going now," she said.

"I can't leave my guests, but Rex can take you home. You don't mind, do you, Rex?"

"It would be my pleasure," Rex said.

As they stood up to part, Walter took her hands in his and looked deeply into her eyes. "I'm glad we met," he said. He reached into his pocket to retrieve a small flat object. He pressed it into Camilla's palm. It felt smooth and sharp and warm. She closed her fingers around it.

From the doorframe, Camilla looked back, hoping to catch Walter's eye again, but he had turned away. Instead she spotted the prophetic words on the embroidered love seat: *Veni, Vidi, Vici*.

As she smiled to herself, she wondered if Julius Caesar had ever read Sun-Tzu.

It was too far to walk, from 52nd Street and the River to 76th Street and West End. It was clear across town, another continent, with a different population, separated by the vast snowy tundra of Central Park. Rex offered his arm, to keep Camilla from slipping on the icy sidewalks on her slingbacked Jimmy Choo shoes. They walked west, looking for a taxi.

At 18, Rex was still gangly. Camilla could feel the bone of his arm through his sleeve, and the energetic but awkward assertiveness with which he moved his limbs. He shaved unevenly, with small patches of shiny blond hairs in the few spots where he had missed with the razor. He had a fashionable goatee the size of a thumbprint just under his lower lip but it was a millimeter off-center. His Adam's apple bobbed when he spoke.

"Some party, huh?" Rex said.

Camilla shook her head. "It certainly was an interesting mix of characters."

"Oh, all Dad and Alyson's parties are like that."

"How do you mean?"

"They have a purpose. So-and-So has to meet Ms. This-and-That for some business reason that is so obtuse, you need a protractor to figure it out. Tonight was to thank everyone for their annual contribution to the Strong Fund — a.k.a the family checkbook."

Camilla wondered if that was why she had been invited — as a payback for selling the Strong Place bulk. But then she recalled the way Walter had looked at her, and knew it was more complicated than that, nipping her blossoming insecurity in the bud.

They walked in silence for several blocks, passing the Four Seasons restaurant, the Seagram's Building, the ornate gold-leafed façade of the original terminus of Park Avenue. They stopped and looked north; Park Avenue was adorned by lighted blue spruces and firs, beds of red poinsettias and golden bulbs that hung from the trees, which caught the moonlight the way mirrored balls in discos had when Camilla was Rex's age. She looked up at him. He was so much more centered than she had been at 18.

"Did you know Park Avenue was built over old railroad tracks?" Camilla asked.

"No, I didn't," Rex replied.

Camilla was shivering, not exclusively from the cold. Rex put his arm around her to warm her. "Close your eyes," she said. "What do you feel?"

"Rumbling." He opened his eyes. "It still looks like a track. Like a long flatbed train is passing through, bringing trees to the arctic —"

"Yes, yes. I see it too." Their frozen breath mingled as they spoke, looking to Camilla like the vapor from a steam engine.

"Where is your train going, Camilla?" Rex asked, wanting to continue the game.

She turned toward him. He stood there, not much older than she had been when her train had derailed before leaving the station. Since then, she had obsessed about where her train had been, but not about where it was going.

Rex still had his arm around her, but when she turned toward him, his hand slipped down to the small of her back. Large and splayed, his fingers pressed her toward him. She felt his impulsiveness, that freedom to follow one's instincts without thinking of the consequences — without thinking at all. He bent slightly and cocked his head; she pulled away but with just enough hesitation to enable him to plant his lips on hers, closed-mouthed but persistent. She was the one who broke the kiss.

Rex was blushing. "I'm sorry," he said. "That was out of line."

"It's all right," she said, gently patting his hand. She wanted to put him at ease, reassure him, because she knew what he had meant by the kiss even if he didn't. She felt irreversibly drawn toward him too — although not in a sexual way.

Camilla took his arm again and they resumed their journey west. They passed hotels and restaurants, turning right on Fifth Avenue, past Benetton and Disney, Tiffany and Bergdorf Goodman. They stopped in front of FAO Schwartz. They stood peering in the windows, like thousands of parents and children do, at the pre-Christmas abundance of toys guarded by gigantic toy nutcrackers four stories tall.

"Maybe we can buy a motorized toy taxi in there. I'm afraid it's our only hope," Rex said, charming her with his dimples and lopsided grin.

"Afraid it's closed," she said.

"Subway?"

Camilla remembered her mother's diamonds on her ears and said, "Better not." But her ungloved hands, particularly the one she kept tightly closed, were turning blue.

"I know!" Rex said, bolting diagonally across deserted Fifth Avenue with Camilla at his heels. He negotiated with a hansom cab driver, across from the Plaza Hotel, a man out of a Dickens novel, garbed in layers of tattered clothing in varying shades of soot, with fingerless gray woolen hand coverings and a top hat with more dents than a discarded tin can.

Rex delivered her directly to her doorstep, in a lacquered white chariot led by a dappled gray horse. The footman was true to his name more in odor than appearance, but this small detail did not detract from the pure magic of the effect. Any minute, Camilla expected her heirloom earrings would turn into pumpkins.

When Rex went to kiss her goodnight, she smiled fondly, and turned to offer him her cheek.

Camilla quietly turned her key in the lock, hearing the mechanism tumble. Robert had dozed off in the armchair with Merry deep asleep on his chest. Camilla stripped off her coat and scarf, suddenly hot from the steam heat that rose from the basement to her top-floor studio. She lifted Merry off Robert's chest, holding her close, drinking her scent in through her nostrils. "Mama," Merry mumbled.

"Yes, yes, it's me," she whispered in Merry's ear, as she laid her down on the bed.

She made Robert a mug of instant hot chocolate before gently shaking his shoulder. All her anger at him was gone; she felt only tenderness in its place. "Robert," she said, "I'm home."

Robert uttered something incoherent as he struggled to emerge from his coma-like sleep. She watched him, while the hot chocolate cooled, and realized sadly that during their two years of marriage, she had never observed him sleep. His eyelids fluttered and his lips quivered; he looked so much like Merry, how could she not love him? After a few minutes, she shook him again.

"Camilla? What time is it?"

"Two in the morning."

He sat up and shook the sleep out of his head. "Was it fun?"

"It was…it's so late, Robert. Do you mind if we talk about it tomorrow? I made you some hot chocolate."

Robert took the mug from her and sipped. As soon as her hand was free, it gravitated to her pocket where she wrapped her fingers around the treasure she had buried there.

"What's in your pocket?" Robert asked.

She looked down. Through her adventure with Rex, unlocking the door, removing her coat, hugging her daughter, making hot chocolate, she had never forgotten the object Walter had pressed into her hand. She unclasped and opened her fingers. It was some sort of a mollusk shell, but flat and worn shiny, and shaped like an ear. "It's a shell of some sort," Camilla said.

"Where'd you get it?"

"Someone at the party gave it to me." She removed the shell and held it in between the thumb and index finger of her other hand.

"It's left an impression on your hand," he noticed, tracing the ear-shaped indentation in her palm.

Her hand gravitated to her cheek. It felt hot. She combed her fingers through her hair and rested her palm over her own ear.

"What are you doing?" Robert asked.

"Listening."

"To your hand?"

"It's telling me something, but I can't make it out."

"How much did you drink at the party, Camilla?"

"You're right. It's probably just my pulse." Or maybe my heart beating, she added to herself.

"I'd better go back to the hotel. Dennis will be waiting."

"Won't he be asleep?"

Robert put his still full mug in the sink. "I doubt it. Love is like hot chocolate, Camilla. It's better hot."

After Robert left, Camilla couldn't sleep. She took a bath, steeped some tea. It was sweltering in the tiny studio, but freezing outside. A fog curtain formed on the windows, creating a cocoon feeling for her and Merry. She carefully placed the diamond earrings in a velvet sack to return to the bank vault after the weekend. On the floor, she spotted a paperback book, *Oedipus the King*, which must have been left behind by Chantal.

Camilla lay down on the bed next to Merry, stark naked against the heat, and placed the shell Walter had given her between her thighs for safekeeping. A nightlight burned brightly enough for her to read. She started the book, and found she couldn't put it down.

Jocasta, Queen of Thebes, was a woman who had lost everything — her husband Laios the King, and her young son, whom her husband had ordered killed in infancy because the Oracle of Delphi predicted that Laios would be murdered by his own child.

When thieves murdered her husband anyway, reputedly, Jocasta lamented the senseless loss of her innocent infant son: "*All these oracular voices meant nothing, nothing. The future has no shape. The shapes of prophecy lie. I see nothing in them, they are all illusions.*"

A young man, Oedipus, came into her life: "*He was tall, strong – built something like you.*"

And Jocasta married him.

Camilla paused to drink her tea, which had become tepid on the nightstand. She thought about Rose and Chakrapani and his predictions that there would be "a dark man" in her future and "an important figure from her youth would reappear in her life." Could Walter be the dark man? Was Rocky the important figure from her youth?

She read on: "*No mortal can practice the art of prophesy, no man can see the future.*"

Jocasta's warning: "*Ignore them.*"

Eighteen years. He was blond, and blue-eyed like her…but he was also a dead ringer for Rocky. Seeing them sitting across from each other at the party had given her a chill up her spine.

Now the words in the text were pleading: "*No more questions. For God's sake, for the sake of your own life! Isn't my anguish enough – more than enough?*"

Jocasta was right. Years of guilt and anguish had been enough. She was over-stimulated by the evening, by Walter, Rex, Alyson, the Flirtinis — Rex's kiss.

But there it was, in black and white: "*Why should the thought of marrying your mother make you so afraid? Many men have slept with their mothers in their dreams.*"

That was too much! It was four in the morning, a dangerous time, when the unconscious intrudes on the conscious. Maybe she was sleeping, and dreaming, or fantasizing, about the baby she lost long ago and would never get back. Yes, that must be it — the intensity of the feelings that she had felt that night, for Walter, for Rex, had opened the floodgates, and she was finally letting out the grief she had repressed for so long.

She was too wired to sleep and tried to distract herself from her thoughts with the book, in which Jocasta concludes: "*The griefs we cause ourselves cut deepest of all.*"

Merry shuddered and opened her eyes. She had that dreamy baby look that Camilla loved. She was hungry and Camilla offered her breast, but for the first time Merry refused. She sat up and looked bewildered; from the armchair to Camilla and then back again. She looked for her octopus, and having found it under the pillow, she twirled her hair around her finger.

"Hungry?" Camilla asked.

"Want egg-ie," Merry said.

Camilla carried Merry to the changing table and changed her diaper, then threw on the same mauve robe she had worn on the day Merry was born. While Merry watched from her highchair, Camilla cooked her an egg.

Merry ate her soft-boiled egg, swallowing slowly but opening her mouth fast for another spoonful, reminding Camilla of a baby bird.

Merry was here, Merry was hers, Merry was all that mattered.

Camilla took the book, *Oedipus the King*, and put it aside for Chantal.

As soon as the stores opened, Camilla dressed Merry in her powder blue snowsuit and pom-pom hat, and they went out. Camilla was tired but joyful, allowing the happiness she derived from Merry to propel her through the day. She held Merry's hand and let her walk, stopping to look in windows and at newsstands and at every dog that passed by. She would point and giggle, then squat on her haunches and let them lick her face. Finally, she crawled into her stroller and fell asleep.

They had arranged to meet Robert for lunch at a burger place on Seventh Avenue. Robert smiled when he saw them come through the door.

"Uh-oh," he said. "Who is he?"

"Who's who?" Camilla asked.

"I can see it in your face. You're in love."

"You can tell that by looking at me?"

"Of course! Remember...been there, done that."

Camilla smiled. She held up her treasure. "Do you know where I can get this mounted? So I can wear it around my neck?"

Robert looked at the shell. "Is it from him?"

Camilla nodded.

"Yes. I know a jeweler who can make you a setting. Is he available?"

"The jeweler?" Camilla teased, knowing exactly whom Robert meant. "He's brilliant, successful, handsome, charming, and straight."

"So he's not available?"

"No."

"Oh well, nobody's perfect."

Chapter Fourteen

Both Walter and Alyson were due back from separate Christmas vacations on January 6th. Alyson had e-mailed Camilla from Maui to schedule an emergency meeting at 10 A.M. on that day. Camilla also had a message that Walter had called her from Palm Beach, to confirm their lunch at noon.

Rose had taken John home to California for the holidays. "If he can tolerate my crazy parents for two weeks, then I'll know he really cares," she had said. Chantal had gone to Washington. She called from there to wish Camilla and Merry a great Christmas.

"How's it going?" Camilla asked.

"Fine," she said. "My mom and I are reconciled. She has a bruised eye like a pirate's patch, but at least the boyfriend's gone."

Dennis was in Cleveland visiting his large Catholic family, who had no idea he was gay.

Camilla decided to celebrate Christmas with Merry and Robert at Foo King, which was packed on Christmas Eve with Christians and non-Christians alike. In true New York fashion, a table had been erected in front of the window with a Christmas Tree; a Hebrew menorah; a chart showing the three Chinese teachings of Confucianism, Daoism, and Buddhism; and the traditional symbols of Kwanzaa.

There was no doubt in Camilla's mind that Merry was crazy about her father. She would reach her arms up to him whenever Camilla put her down and say, "Carry-you." Although Merry could now walk everywhere herself, she still preferred the physical contact of being held in someone's arms. She was calmer with Robert than she was with anyone else; she would wrap her chubby arms and legs around him as if she never intended to let him go.

And he adored her.

He had come back into their lives by accident but it was clear he intended to stay.

P'nina and Lee were fans of Robert's and supported his presence in Merry's life. They believed in accepting love however it was packaged. They explained that theirs was a relationship that seemed odder to the world than Camilla and Robert's looked to be on the surface. Everyone could see P'nina and Lee's differences before they could know them as people.

Two waiters approached the table, arms full of platters and stainless steel covered bowls. As each dish was presented with ceremony — a caviar nest on bean thread noodles, red chili chicken, sesame steamed pork, broccoli with anchovy and garlic sauce, and New Year's rice sticks — Camilla realized that Lee had prepared a Chinese Christmas feast just for them. The thought of a new year brought back Camilla's fear of what the future might hold.

"Do you think the other parents at school will speculate that Merry's father is gay?" Camilla asked.

"Speculation, Camilla, is like the slime trail that follows a snail," Lee responded. Alyson was tanned and rested from her trip, which most everyone assumed she had taken with Rocky. She was standing in the hallway, chatting with Rose and a few other *Marry Well* staffers. She stopped mid-sentence when she saw Camilla walk in, but then resumed, as if to signal that Camilla could not cramp her style.

"Good morning, Alyson," Camilla said, joining them. "How was your vacation?"

"A big snooze," Alyson answered, feigning a yawn.

The response was a surprise, causing Camilla to wonder if the romance between Rocky and Alyson had cooled.

Everybody gathered around, as people tend to do when the boss gets back from a trip. Alyson straightened her back and brushed her hair off her face. She raised her voice slightly. "Except for the plane ride home."

Rose and Camilla exchanged looks.

"Do tell," Chuck said, egging her on.

"Well, I've always wanted to do it in the lavatory at 30,000 feet," she said. There was a gloating glimmer in her eye.

"You'd have to manage standing up," Chuck said. Camilla observed that Alyson and Chuck bantered in the practiced way of a comic and foil.

"Or propped up on the sink," Alyson offered.

"Awfully small," Chuck responded.

"How did you know? Yes, he is." After which she pranced down the hall to her office, brown silk pleats sashaying behind her like the tail feathers of a duck. She raised her hand in the air and, without turning around, signaled for Camilla to follow.

Camilla took a seat on the left bidet. Alyson sat behind her bed-desk, staring at the CNBC website on her computer screen, and its stock ticker floating by. "Bond market's on the move," she said. "Must be the low interest rates — good for the real estate business."

"You wanted to meet? An emergency? If it's about my March column —"

"We're waiting for Chuck," Alyson said, cutting Camilla off. Her phone rang. It was her secretary, telling her that Rocky was on the line. Alyson said she'd take the call and told her secretary to buzz Chuck and tell him to hurry up.

"Uh-huh. Yes. The construction balloon is due January 15th? A capital call of $2.5 million? Where do you expect me to find that kind of cash on short notice?" There was a pause while she listened. "Forget Walter, I tried…. Bridge loan? ……You're sure I'll be able to pay it back when the units close? ……I'll look into it." She hung up as Chuck entered the room, closing the door behind him. He sat on the right bidet, looking uncomfortable.

"The reason I called you in today is to let you know that this is not working out —" Alyson said, coolly.

"What's not working out?" Camilla asked, bemused more than bothered.

"Read my lips." They were painted fire engine red. "YOU are not working out."

"You just sang my praises at the last meeting, talked about advertising revenues being up because of the column, great feedback —" Camilla looked toward Chuck for support. He was grim and staring at his feet.

"Oh, the column is working out — I've already lined up Ann Lowther to take it over. Let me start over…it's Y-O-U who's not working out."

Camilla was so stunned she was speechless. She listened in disbelief as Alyson continued her tirade. "You're not sophisticated enough for this job. That little episode at our Christmas party…didn't your mother ever teach you manners?"

Alyson uttering her mother's name in vain was enough to jolt Camilla back into finding her voice. "I'm not sure you're the best judge of appropriate behavior, Alyson."

Alyson looked about to lunge but Chuck intervened. "Perhaps we could explain the generous severance package to Camilla?" he suggested.

"Appropriate behavior? Rocky told me how you seduced him when you were a simpering teenager. He didn't even find you attractive. But you know how men are…they'll do it with anyone."

Even Chuck, who over the years must have heard it all, looked shocked. Camilla was shaking. Chuck put his arm around her shoulders as Alyson stormed out of the room, slamming the door behind her.

When he was sure Alyson had gone, Chuck said: "This is all about Walter you know."

Camilla was sobbing. "Walter?"

"Alyson hates to lose."

Camilla was confused but underneath it all, she understood what he was saying. Suddenly, she didn't give a damn about the column, or the $50,000 salary — she made much more money through her real estate sales. But she was panicked about what Alyson might do next. "What about Marry Well Realty?"

"She's pulling the plug on that as well," Chuck said, cautiously watching the closed door.

"What does Walter say?"

"I don't think she's told him yet. According to Alyson, he moved out the day after the party — to the River Club — then he went to Palm Beach. To the best of my knowledge, they haven't spoken since."

Camilla was strangely encouraged by the news. "Hasn't she called him?"

"Apparently, yes. But you know how powerful men can be. They have a cast of human armor around them; if they don't want to be reached they're impossible to find. According to Alyson's secretary, he never calls back…"

"Do you think he's discovered her affair with Rocky?" Camilla asked, suddenly worried about Walter.

Chuck put his hands on her shoulders and smiled. He lowered his voice: "I think he's discovered you."

* * *

Camilla looked in the mirror in the ladies room at La Grenouille. Her eyes were slightly puffy from crying, but there was something new in them that she had never seen before. She recognized it immediately, because she had seen it in others, mostly in the eyes of highly accomplished people. If she had to put a word to what she saw, she would have called it self-confidence.

She wore a slim-cut cranberry wool dress, against which her mother's pearls looked even more translucent. As usual, her makeup was spare. She pressed a compress of cold water made from a wad of Kleenex against her eyes to help the swelling go down. She took a deep breath, reapplied lip-gloss and blush, and straightened her spine, before walking into the dining room to meet Walter for lunch.

Camilla saw him, through a profusion of flowers, Sicilian white lilacs and long branches of pussy willows that seemed to transport them from January into spring. When she approached, he stood and held her chair, free open palm pressing against his jacket buttons in a gesture both elegant

261

and shy. He was very tanned, and had that new haircut look that always stays for a day until the style settles in.

The smile he wore when he first saw her faded quickly. "What's wrong?" he asked.

She was surprised that he could be so sensitive to her feelings. "She fired me this morning." Camilla saw the familiar dark scowl eclipse his expression. He pushed his chair back slightly and held tightly onto its carved wooden arms. Chuck had been right; Walter hadn't known. "Walter, Chuck told me she's withdrawing Marry Well Realty too. Can she? If it was all my idea?"

"It depends on your contract —" he said.

"I don't have one."

The waiter handed them large cream-colored menus with descriptions of the choices hand-written in black lettering. He suggested the *potage de potiron* and *langoustine grillée*. Walter ordered a dry white burgundy wine from the Carte du Vin.

"Camilla — you mustn't let her upset you." He paused while he seemed to be searching for words. "It's her, not you. Let it go."

"Walter, I have a child to support. If only she had waited, until the nine months were up —"

"You can always work for me —"

Camilla was already shaking her head. "That won't work. For one thing, Jayme —"

"There's a lot I want to tell you, Camilla. That's why I really asked you to lunch today. I've left Alyson. That may have something to do with what happened this morning."

"Do you know…?"

"…Know about her affairs? Yes."

"I'm so sorry, Walter. You deserve better than that."

"It took meeting you to realize that I do. You see... I was deeply in love with my first wife. We went through so much together — raising Rex, the deaths of my parents, the ups and downs of business, and her illness. I felt like a failure when I couldn't save her. And, then I felt guilty that I survived her. Her last words were asking me to marry again and, of course, to protect Rex."

"So when Alyson came along, you thought you were fulfilling your wife's last wish?"

"When Alyson came along, I was burnt out and exhausted from the ordeal of losing someone I loved so much. Now I see that marrying Alyson was safe, because she is incapable of love; I could never have loved her enough to get hurt like that again."

"Yes, that's true, isn't it? Real love has to flow both ways." She thought about her parents, and P'nina and Lee, and Rose and John. The equality of their love served to boost the power.

"After my wife died, I think I subconsciously never wanted to love like that again. But now I realize I can't be happy without that kind of love."

"When did you realize that?"

"When I met you."

Stillness embraced them. It was as if she had waited her entire life for this exact moment; to hear a man she could finally acknowledge she loved, say that he loved her back. Nothing had ever smelled as sweet as the Sicilian lilacs, or sounded as melodious as his voice, or tasted as intense as the salty tear that rolled down her cheek.

The waiter arrived to place their first course before them, suspending the moment. Neither one of them could eat.

"What do we do now? It's all new to me," Camilla said.

"There were actions I had to take first. That's why I went to Palm Beach. I couldn't expect you to take the overtures of a married man seriously. My uncle is one of the best family law attorneys in the country — he wrote my pre-nuptial agreement with Alyson and now he'll handle my divorce. In six months it will be over — and we'll both have her out of our lives."

"This is so much to take in," Camilla said.

"And we haven't even started the main course yet," Walter said, smiling again.

While they picked at their lunch, the conversation returned to Camilla's career. Walter offered Camilla any job she wanted at West Coast Properties — on-site, re-sales or even commercial leasing.

"I hope you won't mind, but I really want to be on my own."

"You've never wavered from that dream," he acknowledged.

"Do I have to start over? Another nine months?"

"I don't think so. Because so far, Marry Well is just a d/b/a — doing business as — extension of West Coast Properties. Let me talk to our lawyers and see what we can do. But I'm fairly certain that in another seven weeks, you'll be free to hang out your own shingle. In the meantime, let's figure out how to set it up best. Do you have a name in mind?"

"Not yet. How 'bout Merry Well Realty?" she joked, knowing that Alyson would sue her in a heartbeat for trademark infringement.

"Don't think so. But you've touched on something very much on my mind."

"What's that?"

"When do I get to meet Merry?"

It was inevitable, but she wished he hadn't asked. How would he feel when he walked up six flights to her single room, to meet her baby and her baby's dirty diapers, her gay ex-husband, and her friends Rose, John, P'nina, Lee, and Chantal? Would he love her still? She was ashamed of her doubts, but feared they were real. Instead of answering him, she reached into the neckline of her dress and pulled out the shell. Robert's friend had set it in a simple gold rim, and attached it to a fine gold chain.

"Tell me the story of this," she said.

"I found that shell on The Breakers beach when I was 21. I found it remarkable, so flat and oddly shaped. That evening, I met my first wife. I always thought that shell brought me love, and later luck. It has never been out of my possession…until now." He took her hands.

"And now I'll never let it out of mine," Camilla said.

For the entire afternoon following that lunch, Camilla floated. Thoughts drifted through her mind like poems, street noises sounded like music, and the only city smell she could detect was the wind-blown fragrance of sugared almonds from the street vendors' carts. It was all so unexpected that she couldn't be sure if it was true; Camilla decided to keep her blossoming feelings about Walter tucked inside. She shared the details of her meeting with Alyson with her friends when they met for dinner that night.

The taco shell dropped out of Rose's hand and onto the table as she reacted to the news: "She did what?" Rose screamed at the top of her lungs.

Everybody in Maya Mexicana turned around to stare.

"She fired me."

Camilla had suggested the dinner, with Rose and John, Robert and Dennis, Deirdre and Chantal. She sat close to Robert, with Merry on a bright, yellow plastic highchair in between. Robert was feeding Merry guacamole from a spoon.

"We had a scene like that on the soap once. Pamela is sleeping with Georgia's husband but Rachel finds out and blackmails her so Georgia fires Maria for reading Rachel's e-mails about Vitale," Dennis said.

Everybody looked at him.

"Must be the margaritas," Robert said, winking.

"Camilla, I wouldn't worry about it if I were you. You're a natural talent at real estate," John reassured her.

"That's right honey. You've got the perfect combination of moxie and class," Deirdre added, squeezing Camilla's hand.

"Marry Well Realty is being left at the altar. Alyson decided to ditch the idea," Camilla said.

The only sound at the table was the collective munching of tortilla chips. Finally, Chantal asked: "Can't that fellow, Walter, do something?"

Camilla saw Rose watching her carefully. "He's trying," Camilla sighed.

"You always wanted to start your own business," John said. "If you need financing, I could talk to our small business loan department." Rose caressed his arm.

"Thanks, John. I'll keep that in mind."

"I've just about had it with Griffin, honey. Take me with you!" Deirdre said.

"It's not so easy. I've still got another seven weeks before I've met my apprenticeship requirement to be an independent broker. Then I have to take another course, pass my exam, and apply for my license." Camilla looked at Chantal. "Walter's helping with all that."

"Then you've got to get an office, lease equipment, join the Real Estate Board—" John said.

"And she's got to set up her own company. She hasn't been around long, but the brokerage community associates her with the Marry Well name," Deirdre said.

"How complicated is it to set up a company, Robert?" Camilla asked.

"It's not a big deal. A Delaware LLC takes a few days…but Camilla, I just remembered something —"

A couple of out-of-towners, wearing fanny-packs and Yankees t-shirts, interrupted Robert's train of thought to ask for Dennis' autograph. Dennis obligingly wrote a note and signed two cocktail napkins — one To Debbie and the other To Al.

"What did you remember?" Camilla asked.

"Your father's will left the shares of Merewether Realty to you. We never dissolved the corporation. I'll have to check the minute book, but I'm sure we've kept it up to date — franchise fees, annual certificates of good standing, and such. Irwin & Sanchez's records department is good at that sort of thing."

"Wouldn't it be a Florida corporation?" John asked.

"Yes, I think so. But that's no problem. All we have to do is file a Registration to Do Business form in New York. That's much easier, faster, and cheaper than starting from scratch. And who knows? You might open an office someday in Palm Beach."

Palm Beach! The warm ocean breezes, Royal Palm Way, Worth Avenue. "Wouldn't that be like a dream come true?" Camilla asked.

While they feasted on baby shrimp with mustard and chile vinaigrette; *budin Azteca*, a tortilla casserole with chicken and cheese; and vegetarian dishes for John and Rose like *hongos*, sautéed wild mushrooms with garlic and Serrano chilies over cornmeal, Dennis did what Dennis does best: he entertained them. He told them about the affair the director was having with an extra, about the plot of the movie he was working on, and about his co-stars Harrison Ford and Anne Heche (How disappointing...she's not one of us after all!). He talked about the parties he had been to — the boozing, the snorting, and the pills.

As he spoke, in his baritone voice and enunciated diction, about the crowds who gawked while they filmed, and the admiring fans who followed him into restaurants and shops and theaters, Camilla knew she didn't belong in the milieu he was describing.

True, there were many tribes in the great nation of New York, but in one way or another, they all seemed to thrive on the energy and the action. She cared more for the ocean than the theater; she preferred quiet dinners at home to rowdy restaurants, bicycles to ballet, off-season walks on the deserted Lake Trail to fighting for jogging space in Central Park.

Camilla knew her fans were all here at this table. After all, what was life about if not human connection? And she had found it here in New York. They were chattering around her while she drifted off into her own inner world, fingering the shell pendant around her neck. She felt like Sleeping Beauty, the curse lifted, her seven loyal friends near — Rose, John, P'nina, Lee, Deirdre, Chantal, Robert — and Walter, at last, her Prince, had come.

When they got home that night, Rose came across the hall with an apple — which gave Camilla a start — and a cup of tea.

"So, what's with you and Walter? Word's out that he and Alyson have split," Rose said.

"I think I'm in love," Camilla said.

"You have been for months."

"And you?"

"Yes, me too," Rose said.

"Isn't it glorious, Rose? That it's happened to us both?"

Rose took a cautious sip of tea. "Be careful. Alyson's not one to roll over and play dead."

"I'm not afraid of her, Rose. I'm not afraid of anybody anymore."

Chapter Fifteen

Camilla was busy making plans, always conscious that God was watching, and always half-expecting him to laugh. She had seen Walter every night that week for dinner, spending as much time with Merry during the day as she could, before Robert would come by to baby-sit at night.

Robert would always bring Merry toys and books, one of which he read to her every evening as he put her to bed. Dennis's hours were brutal, so Robert was free, and loving every moment of getting to know his daughter.

"It's really nice of you to come every night like this," Camilla said.

"Are you kidding? How many gay men get to have a kid? I should be thanking you."

When Camilla got home from her dates, with stars in her eyes and lightness in her heart, Robert would sit and keep her company for a while.

"This man is right for you, Camilla. I can see it in your eyes."

"How can you tell? What do you see?"

"You're happy."

Because of their peculiar living arrangements — Walter at the River Club and Camilla in one room with her child — making love had been delayed. Their physical attraction was palpable, and was heightened by the anticipation of what lay ahead. Their bodies pressed close in restaurants and bars, and when they kissed goodnight in front of her house, she lost her breath and any sense of her independent self, for the moments that they lingered in the bracing January cold.

"Who's watching Merry?" Walter asked.

"Her father."

"Come with me…to The Four Seasons, The Peninsula, The Carlyle…"

How she wanted so badly to make love! "I can't," she said.

"Why not?"

"I'm not ready…."

Everyone knew about them in the office, although they tried to be discreet. The power of their love was like a fireball in a dry field — impossible to miss. Jayme seethed inside, but kept up appearances for her own sake.

Ten days after their lunch at La Grenouille, Walter flew to San Francisco for his mid-month meeting with his bank. While Camilla was at her desk filling out the forms for Merewether Realty's New York brokerage license, Rose called her at the office.

"The shit has hit the fan!"

"What happened?" Camilla was alarmed.

"I can't talk about it here. Can you meet me at Foo King tonight? By then I'll know more."

Camilla looked at her watch. "Dennis and Robert's closing is this afternoon. We had planned to pick up Merry and celebrate. Can they come?"

"Even better —besides, I have a feeling I'll need all the support I can get."

"We'll be there at eight."

In New York, closings for real property such as townhouses and condominiums are generally held in the office of the seller's lawyer. Co-op closings, which technically transfer a designated number of shares of a corporation and a proprietary lease for the apartment, are held in the closing department of the co-operative building's managing agent. Camilla met Robert and Dennis at the office of the managing agent for 814 Fifth Avenue, Brown Harris Stevens, located on Lexington Avenue across the street from Bloomingdale's.

The atmosphere in the large conference room on the fourth floor was quite congenial. Camilla sat in between Dennis and Robert. The seller's attorney had not arrived yet, but lawyers were frequently late. Robert was representing Dennis and while he laid out his papers, they were discussing the type of dog they should get.

Martha McIntee, the closer, reminded them of the eight-pound limit.

"What if your eight-pound dog gains weight?" Dennis asked. "Can he be evicted by the Board?"

"Every dog on Fifth and Park Avenues is on Atkins," Martha warned.

Camilla remembered Charlotte Kinnell, and other Avenue ladies she had met. "It seems their owners are too."

Robert was partial to chihuahuas, noting that they could get two and still be under the ceiling for freight, but Dennis thought they looked too much like hairless cats. Dennis wanted a Welsh corgi because that was the breed favored by the British queens.

"But we're not queens, Dennis," Robert protested. Martha's jaw dropped.

The intercom buzzed and Martha picked up the phone. "They're here."

When Rocky walked in, Camilla was stunned. Sellers rarely came to closings, preferring to avoid the nickel-and-diming over last-minute adjustments. He was elegantly dressed, like a New York businessman rather than a Palm Beach tycoon. He shook hands with everyone except Camilla, whom he ignored as if she weren't there. Robert and Dennis protectively moved their chairs as close to hers as they could get.

Camilla studied Rocky carefully as he signed the papers his lawyer put in front of him. His breathing was steady and shallow. He wore a black suit, like an undertaker, with a starched white shirt and yellow tie. There was a red handkerchief in his breast pocket. Camilla had learned in biology class at Andover that red, yellow, and black — in creatures including snakes, birds, and frogs — were nature's warning signs. Signals to other animals to avoid them at all costs.

Rocky's face was frozen in a smile; his teeth had yellowed even more with age. The only sign of tension was the subtle grinding of his teeth, which was noticeable by the infinitesimal shifting of the muscle in his jaw. The tasks — reading and signing documents, filling out forms — he performed with slow deliberation. Camilla thought it odd that someone who had been in real estate his whole life would need so much time for review.

"You all right?" Dennis whispered in Camilla's ear.

"Fine." Rocky didn't scare her anymore. But there was something insidious about him.

Because the apartment was being sold furnished, for an extra $250,000, a personal property rider had been drawn up by Rocky's lawyer and presented at the end. It listed all of the items included in the sale, the antique furniture, the precious wall coverings, rugs, and drapes. There was a little caveat, in fine print, that all items were being sold AS IS. Many a buyer and seller had argued over fingerprints and dog stains at closings, wasting everybody's money and time. Dennis, as the purchaser, signed it first, taking the opportunity to compliment Rocky on his exquisite taste.

Finally, after checking his watch, Rocky stood to leave. He thanked everyone except Camilla, and gave a slightly self-deprecating bow. His lawyer followed, then Martha, leaving Camilla, Dennis, and Robert alone.

"Now what?" Robert asked.

"Let's go to the apartment! I can't wait to move in. The truckers arrive with our personal belongings from California tomorrow," Dennis said.

As they were leaving, they ran into Deirdre, who had just finished a closing in the adjacent conference room. "What a coincidence," she said.

"We just closed 814 Fifth," Camilla said, kissing the air around Deirdre's head. "Sold and closed already? That place went so fast I never got to see it."

"We're going there now. Let's get a bottle of champagne to celebrate — your closings and our new home," Dennis said, euphoric. Robert had explained to Camilla that Dennis had grown up in a modest home in Cleveland, one of five sons; glamour was what he had always aspired to: the movies, New York, Fifth Avenue. With the Harrison Ford movie and purchase of this apartment — whose décor had been featured in *Architectural Digest* — Dennis's dream would be complete.

The superintendent was waiting in the lobby, with his indiscreetly outstretched palm. Dennis met it with a folded hundred-dollar bill; he viewed it as insurance that his movers would be met with cooperation, rather than a list of rules.

"Welcome to 814, Mr. Sheehan," the super said. "The plumbers left half an hour ago."

Dennis looked at Camilla. "Plumbers?" she asked.

"Yes. Mr. Faber sent them in."

Camilla knew that something was amiss the second they stepped off the elevator. There were strange smells: a metallic odor like rusty iron or old blood, and the toxic scent of burning rubber. None of the others seemed to notice, chatting amiably about chihuahuas and corgis. Deirdre was saying how she hated short-legged dogs, when the door swung open to reveal Rocky's revenge.

The striped silk upholstered settee had been sliced into shreds by a box cutter that lay on the floor. The two antique prayer chairs and Riesener marquetry commode had large black Xs spray-painted across their facades. The chandelier's silk shades had been set on fire, and then extinguished with orange juice, which had splattered sour pulp all over the hand-painted walls. The extent of the damage was appalling. Deirdre gasped. It looked as Camilla imaging a drug den would — devastated.

Dennis let out a guttural groan. He couldn't help it. "How could he do this? Isn't it illegal?"

"Sue the bastard!" Deirdre said.

Robert put his arm around Dennis, who sat on the shredded settee with his face in his hands, crying. "I'm not sure we can."

"Why not?" Camilla asked.

"Both the contract and the rider — the one you signed an hour ago — state the apartment is sold AS IS," Robert explained.

"But this is vandalism!" Camilla protested.

"C'mere honey," Deirdre said leading Camilla by the hand into the bedroom. Camilla covered her mouth; she felt like she was about to cry. Deirdre lowered her voice: "Didn't you bring them here for an inspection just before the closing?"

"I...I...we were here yesterday. Everything was perfect."

Deirdre was shaking her head. "It's customary to bring the buyers through just before the closing with instructions to the building staff that no one may enter the premises until the key has changed hands."

Camilla knew about inspections. But who could ever have anticipated this?

"What does he have against me?" Dennis cried, prompting Camilla to return to the living room.

"It's not you, Dennis. It's me he's after." Camilla knelt in front of Dennis and looked up into his forlorn face. "The decorator was Bunny Williams. I'll call her tomorrow first thing. Don't worry, Dennis. I promise I'll fix everything, and at my own expense." Repairing the damage would take at least her whole commission, which is exactly what Rocky must have intended.

Dennis looked hopeful and managed a smile. Deirdre popped the champagne cork and poured four glasses, "Good thing Rocky hadn't ordered those destroyed as well."

"What a monster," Robert said to Camilla, knowingly. "Has he no limits at all?"

The answer was obvious.

Steeling herself to keep going, Camilla felt some relief in knowing that Rocky would be gone. She believed by his actions, by his having had the last word, he was through with her now.

Deirdre and Camilla arrived home around six to find Rose in the kitchen preparing hors d'oervres. Chantal brushed the papers she had been working on into her backpack on the floor. She gratefully accepted their invitation to come to dinner. She had returned from visiting her mother changed, in ways that Camilla was still trying to ascertain. Superficially, she had gained a few pounds, ("Don't tell Rose I fell off the wagon!" she pleaded) confessing that the fatty fast foods she had grown up with were much too tempting to resist.

They had an hour to kill before it would be time to go. Deirdre poured herself a glass of wine from an open bottle on the counter, Chantal sat perched on the armchair, hands folded in her lap, while they both watched Camilla lay a blanket on the floor and play airplane with Merry by balancing her on her legs.

Normally Chantal would be eager for news, about Alyson, Jayme, Walter, and especially about Camilla's activities of the day. As much as she loved Merry, Camilla sensed that Chantal was starved for adult companionship. Her high school equivalency program online was convenient, but anti-social — she missed being with young adults her own age. She had often complained that there were no other sitters like her in Central Park; she noticed that nannies were like taxi-drivers in New York — they came in ethnic waves. At the moment, Chantal had reported, they were all Filipinas; and the playground she called "Little Manila."

"Even if I were from the same culture," Chantal said, "watching them, the nannies, all these months, has made me yearn to make more of myself."

Camilla sat up. She propped Merry between her legs and held her around the waist. "Are you quitting?"

"Oh no, Camilla. I'd never do that to you. So long as you need me —"

Merry broke loose of Camilla's grasp. She crawled over to Chantal and climbed up into her lap. Chantal held her close and sighed.

"We'll always need you, Chantal. But if you have a better opportunity, we'd never want to hold you back."

"It's not that...I want to go to college. I've been working on my applications this week." She looked hesitant when she blurted it out — as if it were such a preposterous idea that they would laugh at her for proposing it.

"That's wonderful," Camilla said.

Deirdre had been listening to the interchange. "I don't know you well, honey, but do you mind if I ask...what made you want a change? For years I've always had it in my mind to do something else, but I never do. I admit I hate change...the devil you know is better than the devil you don't. Guess I'm just stuck, like most people, in my rut. How'd you get inspired to get out of yours?"

"Lots of things, I guess. First, I see how Camilla has had all these bad things happen to her but she never gives up —" Chantal looked admiringly at Camilla. "Second, my mom. She's so beaten down despite being so full of love. She's cleaning people's toilets and letting men use her just for an hour of company. It broke my heart to see her again."

"You think if she had a college education she'd have been better off?" Deirdre asked.

"Don't know...but she'd think better of herself. She lives in the projects, a real slum. She's got nothing; everything was stolen or lost somehow. But she had one thing that she never let go. When I was five, she bought me a porcelain oven, about the size of a thimble. It was for Christmas. We couldn't afford any tree or turkey dinner, my daddy was long gone, but she found this oven in a thrift shop and she wrapped it up and gave it to me. Know what she said when I opened the box?"

Deirdre and Camilla looked at her expectantly. "What?"

"She said: 'Here's a lil' oven. That's all you need to be happy in this world, Chantal. A lil'oven...why's it so hard to find?'"

Deirdre looked perplexed. "An oven?"

"A little lovin'" Camilla explained.

"That's right," Chantal said. She smiled, "And I want Merry to have it now." She reached into her pocket and held out a tiny porcelain oven.

"Oh no, Chantal. That's yours. Your mother kept it for you all these years —"

"What good's a lil' oven, Camilla, if you can't pass it on?"

Camilla had tears in her eyes as she pressed Walter's shell to her chest. She watched Merry accept Chantal's gift, rolling it around in her fingers, squinting at it as if it were a precious gem. Instead of sticking it in her mouth, as Camilla feared she would, she held it up for the three of them to see. Then she acknowledged them, as a queen might in a knighting ceremony, and said: "Lovin', Lovin', Lovin'" When she was done, she carefully gave it to Camilla — for safekeeping, Camilla knew — and took Chantal in one hand and Camilla in the other and said, "Go now."

"What a day!" Camilla declared in the taxi. She gave Deirdre and Chantal the abridged version of Dennis's closing and then Deirdre described to Chantal the unbelievable condition that Rocky's thugs had left the place in.

"What's he so mad about?" Chantal asked.

"Somehow he thinks we got the better of him," Camilla said.

"Can't be just that. The violence of the act — it's too personal to be just business."

"Chantal's right. Most men might be angry if they feel they've been had, hire a lawyer or something, but to plot such an exacting revenge — for Christ's sake, to defile such a beautiful place — is a personal vendetta," Deirdre said.

Camilla didn't answer. She just looked out the window at the vagrants on steam vents and thought about all the lost souls of the world, and their counterpoints — the soulless — like Richard "Rocky" Faber of Palm Beach.

Rose and John were already there. So were P'nina and Lee. They filled four of the seven chairs around the big round table in the middle of the room. Everybody kissed everybody else, especially Merry, who made loud smacking noises with her mouth. She sat in Camilla's lap and Camilla whispered in her ear that Daddy was busy and couldn't come but sent his apologies. To Camilla's surprise, Merry opened her eyes wide and said, "That's OK, Mama." Then she refocused her attention on a stray grain of rice.

"Brace yourselves, everyone—" They each reflexively reached for the hands next to their own. "Whatever else you did today will look mild after you hear what I'm going to say," Rose said.

"I doubt that—" Camilla said, noticing that with lights dimmed and hands joined it must have looked like a séance was about to begin. In a way, it was.

John tried to help. "Anyone watch Financial News Network this evening?"

Camilla, Deirdre, Chantal, and Merry had been talking at that hour; P'nina and Lee had been working. They all shook their heads.

"Alyson got our marketing department to book her and Ann Lowther on as many shows as she could — CNBC, CNN, *The Today Show*, Jenny Jones, Conan O'Brien and FNN — to talk up the December issue with your column on Rocky in it."

"She wouldn't! Use my column to promote her magazine and Ann Lowther after what she did to me?" But Camilla knew she would.

"She would and she did," Rose confirmed.

"FNN was the last interview, and the reporter asked Alyson if she knew about Rocky Faber's arrest, to which she said, 'Impossible.' Then the reporter described the Ponzi scheme he had created by using a fictitious Palm Beach real estate development as the bait. Apparently he took pictures of the public beach from his yacht and told investors that this was the oceanfront parcel he owned and planned to develop. When the reporter told her that many of the investors will be bankrupted by the scheme..." John paused.

"...Alyson fainted on the air!" Rose finished for him.

Now it all fell into place. Camilla remembered the references both Rocky and Alyson had made to a joint real estate venture — Rocky Coast. But she couldn't be sure that Rocky Coast and Rocky's folly were one and the same. "Alyson didn't strike me as being so in love with Rocky that she would faint at the news of his arrest."

"You're right. In fact, Alyson's secretary told me that they broke up after Hawaii," Rose agreed.

"Here's the scoop," John said. "I called my counterpart at JPMorgan Chase in Palm Beach and he was happy to relate what he knew of the scandal. Apparently, Rocky had accumulated tens of millions of dollars in Euro loans to build a golf course in North Palm Beach. The town condemned the property under the Right of Eminent Domain—"

"Imminent what?" P'nina asked.

"Eminent domain means that a municipality can condemn property that they need for public use such as telephone lines or fiber optic cable. Then they pay the owner what they consider to be fair market value for the land," Camilla explained, secretly thanking Professor D'Angelo.

"Camilla's right," John continued. "So the town of North Palm Beach condemned Rocky's land to build a highway and agreed to pay him the assessed value which was peanuts, just five cents on the dollar, because he paid a bundle for the development rights to what was essentially useless swamp."

"And then?" Deirdre asked.

"Then the currency exchange rate changed dramatically, causing the interest due on his Eurodollar loans to skyrocket..."

"Why didn't he refinance here?" Deirdre asked.

"According to my friend, he tried. But when he started to run into trouble, he refinanced his yacht and then defaulted on the loan. Rocky destroyed his credit — he has no borrowing power here. So he cooked up the Ponzi scheme. He sold shares in a fictitious real estate project called

Rocky Coast and used fake capital calls to raise cash from newer investors to repay older ones."

"Oh my God!" Camilla exclaimed. "When I was in Alyson's office, I heard her commit $2.5 million to Rocky for Rocky Coast!"

"Where's the money now?" Lee asked.

"Gone. As soon as Rocky got it, he sent it to Liechtenstein, Bermuda, the Cayman Islands, you name it, to make interest payments before the banks foreclosed on everything and his empire came tumbling down," John replied.

"It gets worse," Rose said. "I called Chuck at home this evening after I heard the news, and he told me he knew about Rocky Coast too. What he knew that no one else did was that Alyson pledged the magazine as collateral for the loans —"

"How does he know that?" Camilla asked.

"Alyson made him secretary of Marry Well Enterprises last year. She needed his signature on the loan collateralization documents," Rose explained.

They were all silent while they let the gravity of the revelation settle. Rose said to Camilla, "It's not like you not to have a million questions."

"Well, I do have one…what happened to the…yacht?" That dreadful boat; she hoped it capsized and sank.

"It was repossessed," John said.

After a moment Deirdre threw her hands up in the air and said, "This sounds like a novel."

"It's too bizarre to be a novel. It could only be real life," P'nina said.

"'A likely impossibility is always preferable to an unconvincing possibility,'" Chantal quoted, impressing everyone.

"Now, I know that's not from Merry's books," Camilla teased. "Too many syllables."

"Confucius?" Lee asked.

"Aristotle," Chantal said proudly.

The phone was ringing off the hook when Camilla and Merry got home from Foo King. Camilla slammed the door behind her and grabbed it just in time. Merry woke up and howled. She was hot, and irritable, and wanted her mother. "Call back in ten minutes," Camilla said into the phone, hurriedly hanging up.

She undressed Merry, wiping the baby's face with a cool washcloth, then changed her diaper and put on her pajamas. Finally taking off her own coat and hat, Camilla crawled under the bed to locate Merry's octopus, which she dangled over her to try to get her to calm down. They sat down on the bed, as if they had run a marathon, and Merry stuffed one of her toy's eight legs in her mouth, looking mad as hell, when the phone rang again. Camilla reached over and picked up the receiver.

"Hello?" she was out of breath. Camilla felt for her shell. Thank God Merry was busy sucking on a tentacle. "Oh, Walter, what a day —"

"So you saw the news?"

Camilla was silent.

"I know everything, Camilla. She was brazen enough to boast. She even tried to get me to invest in the real estate project too — said she owed me one. I tried to warn her, but her greed was so enormous that she didn't listen; she never listened to anyone but herself —"

"Have you talked to her?" She bit her tongue as soon as she said it. It wasn't any of her business if he had talked to Alyson or not.

"No, but I spoke with Chuck. He's over there now with Alyson's doctor. She's sedated."

There's an oxymoron — a sedate Alyson. "How serious is it?" Camilla asked.

"I've heard from her banker. He wants to know if I'll repay her debt — there were several loans amounting to close to $10 million. I said no."

"What will happen to her?"

"Too soon to tell. When the dust settles, I'll see if I can help — but only through my lawyer. I'm finished with her. I hate to say it, but —"

"What goes around comes around," Camilla finished his sentence.

"What about you? I've missed you all day. I especially miss you now —"

The impossibility of her situation came tumbling down on her like a house of cards hit by a wrecking ball. How could she be where she wanted to be, in his arms, in his bed, wrapped up around him, when Merry slept beside her every night? Maybe Chantal would stay the night, if Camilla could buy a crib and wean Merry from her bed.

Why hadn't she done that yet? — moved Merry to a crib? She needed the warm body to comfort her, that's why. Merry had been her… lil' oven.

"Walter, I…I'm tired now. It's been a long day. It's midnight here."

"I understand. I'll call you tomorrow. We have all the time in the world."

Chapter Sixteen

It seemed to take forever, but it was only a matter of days until Merewether Realty's New York State license to conduct business as a real estate broker arrived in the mail. It was exactly nine months to the day from when Camilla had passed her salesperson's exam. Long enough, as P'nina had pointed out, to have a baby.

There were so many things that Camilla had to do that she made a list:

Buy: Crib

           Gift for Dennis

Call: Cushman & Wakefield RE: office space

           Doris RE: looking at penthouses

           Mac Sanders and Sam Jacobs RE: Selling their apartments

           Canon, IBM, International Furniture Rentals, Verizon, etc. RE: equip. leasing

           Madison Signatures RE: business cards

           Robert and John and Deirdre RE: getting business!

~~Buy: Crib~~

Send: Bunny Williams' final payment

*** Meet Walter 6 PM at The River Club, 447 East 52nd Street

Walter begged her to take her pick of any office suite available in West Coast Tower, so that she could be close to him, but she demurred, saying that she loved him as she had never loved anyone, ever, but that she needed to know that she could succeed entirely on her own. "I'll stay in the neighborhood," she said. "I promise."

"Camilla, spring break is coming up in a few weeks. Rex and I are going to Palm Beach," Walter said.

Her heart sank. It was hard enough missing him when he traveled to California for two days, but spring break she remembered was two weeks long. His eyes were a gorgeous color, like topaz, with swirls of gold. "I'll miss you…"

"I want you to come with us. You and Merry. I've already arranged it all."

An unsettled feeling crept through her; this was something new he was proposing. Not a weekend tryst, which she had assumed would come first, but something more…familial. "I don't know…"

"Why not?" he asked. The dark scowl started to creep across his face. Camilla could see that he was tiring of being refused.

She sighed. "Walter, this is all like a dream. It's what I've thought I've always wanted. But it's all so fast. I don't know what I'm more terrified of — loving you or losing you."

"We belong together, Camilla. Can't you feel that?"

"Yes, of course I do."

"So what's holding you back?"

Camilla looked out the picture windows of the main salon of the River Club, where they were sitting. The sky was clear and a barge was floating by. She knew once it passed that she would never see it again.

"There are many things about me you don't know," she said.

"So tell me, now. Get them off your chest. Nothing you could say would change how I feel."

"I was raped when I was 15." She looked at his face carefully, for signs of revulsion and disgust. There were none.

"Were you hurt?"

"Not physically, no, but I —" She stopped, and started toying with a matchbook.

"Camilla, what are you holding back?"

"You know him. It was Rocky Faber."

Surprise registered on Walter's face; his eyes widened slightly and the corners of his mouth tilted down in concern. "Oh no —"

"When Alyson met him last year, she convinced him to sell his apartment through Marry Well Realty, promising him that I'd not only get top price but write a column for the magazine on it as well."

"So you had to see him again." He moved nearer to her and protectively put his hand on the back of her head. He kissed her forehead, and then embraced her. "He's going away for a long time. He can't hurt you again."

Then she finally asked him the question that had been haunting her since that night on Park Avenue. "Walter, about Rex…"

Walter pulled away. "What about him?"

"I had another child, Walter, a son, 18 years ago."

They sat in dead silence. The barge blew its horn, like a long groan.

"What became of him?"

"He was adopted. I know this sounds crazy but did you notice a resemblance between Rocky and Rex?"

"Poor darling, you are distraught. Actually, I think they look nothing alike."

The comment made Camilla wonder if her mind had played tricks on her. "Didn't you say that your uncle from Palm Beach handled family law? Couldn't he have known my mother?"

288

"Anything's possible…but it's so improbable."

Walter concentrated his gaze upon her face. She thought he was looking at her features for similarities to Rex's. Then she asked the telltale question. The one she had been dying to ask.

"When was Rex born, Walter? What does his birth certificate say?"

"October 12, 1985 — the day Columbus's crew sighted the New World. We always thought that was significant."

She was relieved, but disappointed as well. "Ah, my son was born on Nantucket Island on August 31ˢᵗ."

"I understand you, Camilla — that you'd want to find your son. Maybe there's something we can do. There must be records —"

"I was supposed to find out on my thirtieth birthday. But when my mother died, so did any link to the adoption file. There were no papers in their estate, none at all. She handled everything…secretly with the aid of a lawyer from Palm Beach."

"Camilla, I know you'll never replace the child you lost in your heart but…you're only thirty-three. We can, if you're willing, if you'd —"

She stopped him before he said it. "There's more."

"More?"

"Yes. You know I sold Rocky's apartment?"

"You told me."

"I didn't mention that the purchaser was Dennis Meehan and —"

"The actor?"

"Uh-huh. Dennis Meehan and his lover…who's a lawyer…and my ex-husband."

"Let me get this right. Your ex-husband is a homosexual whose lover bought my soon to be ex-wife's ex-lover's apartment?" Walter laughed. "Is this ex-husband Merry's father?"

"That I can guarantee."

"What am I missing here?"

"Some of us are late bloomers when it comes to knowing who we are."

Walter ordered a scotch from the waiter passing by. "Lillet?" he asked Camilla.

"I think this time I'll have something stronger." She asked for Grey Goose on the rocks.

They sipped their drinks for a while. They held hands.

"Camilla, darling. None of this matters to me. It's the past. The past is unreal." He was resolute.

"There are things about the present that concern me too. You live a certain life, Walter. You are insulated by wealth and privilege. It is intoxicating to me, the idea of being protected by you. But I grew up a little bit that way and it backfired. I know the idea of being protected is an illusion. Each of us has to make his own way. I've finally found a place where I feel I belong. It's not here..." She looked around the perfectly appointed room, with not a speck of dirt or dust, no noise, no hardship. "...as much as I'd like it to be."

"Where is it then?" he asked her.

If it hadn't been for the fortifying effect of the vodka, she knew she'd never have had the courage to do what she did next. "Come. I'll show you."

Camilla knew that John and Rose would be having dinner at Foo King. She was sure that P'nina and Lee would be there as well. Dennis and Robert had picked Merry up from Chantal, who had to study for an exam on Greek tragedy, and taken her to dinner at Serendipity and then back to 814 Fifth Avenue to watch Dumbo on DVD. And, Deirdre, dear Deirdre, showing, showing, showing — to the hedge fund manager who'd only look at apartments after work — yet again.

As the taxi swerved off the Clarkson Street ramp, Camilla wondered if she were making a mistake. If by allowing her worlds to merge, she lost Walter, what would she do then?

"Where are you taking me?" Walter asked, squinting against the glare of the streetlamps as he looked at the seedy storefronts outside.

"You might say it's my club. No river view, but the membership is divine."

Camilla watched him carefully, for his reaction, before leading him to the center table set for eight. She was immediately struck by the contrast; Walter was polished and seemed to shine against the tired backdrop of Lee Ching's Foo King, like a shiny new penny in a pocket full of well-worn change.

She took him by the hand, and introduced him to John, who dropped his napkin on the floor as he stood to shake hands. Camilla noticed the gray stamped numbers from the laundry on the frayed cloth edge when she bent down to retrieve it for him.

"A pleasure to meet you, Mr. Strong," John said.

"Walter, please." He moved his head in a semicircle as he took in his surroundings. Then his eyes settled on Rose. "It's good to see you again."

Rose smiled. "When's your birthday?" she asked.

"March 6th," Walter said, seeming a little surprised by the directness of her question.

With arms folded across her chest and a smug expression on her face, she nodded her head once and said, "I knew it! He's Pisces like you, Camilla." Walter gave Camilla a curious look.

Lee emerged from the kitchen with P'nina in tow. She stopped in her tracks as soon as she spotted them there. Camilla observed her whisper something in Lee's ear then tug on his apron. She was trying to pull him back into the kitchen, but he resisted, and proceeded to approach the center table where they sat, leaving his wife standing there with an apron suspended from her hand.

"Lee, this is my friend, Walter Strong," Camilla said.

Lee laughed. In fact, he couldn't stop laughing.

"What's so funny?" Rose asked.

"P'nina thought Camilla's friend was an inspector from the City's Department of Health," Lee said, in a low tone.

"Health Department?" Camilla asked.

"You know — a 'mouse detective'."

Walter winced and Camilla swallowed her shame.

"It's not funny. I apologize," Lee said, stifling a snicker.

"No reason to," Walter said.

When P'nina saw Lee laughing, she cautiously made her way over to the table to join them. Camilla introduced her to Walter.

There was a little scuffle going on between Rose and John. It was mostly non-verbal, just nudges and gestures, but finally they heard John say, "If you don't ask him, I will."

And then Rose looked at Walter and said, "I'm worried, Walter. We all are. We haven't seen Alyson since Rocky's arrest two weeks ago. All sorts of people have passed through — accountants, lawyers, appraisers. Chuck and I have been acting as co-publishers, keeping things afloat. But everyone's afraid for their jobs. Word's out that Alyson used the magazine as collateral for money she borrowed to invest in a bogus real estate investment. Do you think *Marry Well* will fold?"

Walter looked at Camilla suspiciously. She shook her head. Once he accepted that he had not been set up, he said: "I'll tell you what I know, which isn't much. Yes, she used the shares of the magazine to cover her calls. She's in self-imposed exile while Veronis Suhler looks for a buyer for the magazine. So I doubt very much that the magazine will fold; it's highly profitable, but you should be prepared for a new owner."

"Veronis is an investment banking boutique that specializes in the publishing and communications industries," Walter explained.

"Do you know who they're talking to?" John asked.

Walter hesitated. "The usual — Hearst, Meredith, Hachette Filipacchi, Time Warner…" They all looked somber. "…and me."

All eyes were on Walter, boring holes, like a flock of woodpeckers attacking a tree. Everyone was very still.

Lee broke the silence: "This calls for a bottle of champagne!" He gave a hand signal to one of the black-clad waiters, who brought a bottle of Korbel and six short water glasses. There was a shadow of coral lipstick on Walter's glass that the dishwasher had missed. While all but Walter sipped the California sparkling wine, Lee and the waiter brought several of their favorite dishes to the table: timbale Chinoise, sweet peanut-filled rice balls, steamed vegetables with a spicy soybean dip, bean sprout spring rolls. Lee didn't have to ask them what they wanted anymore.

Camilla noticed that Walter pushed his food around his plate, which inhibited her from eating hardily, despite the fact that she was famished. He looked uncomfortable and twice regarded his watch when he thought no one was looking.

In the limo home, Camilla asked him: "Don't you like Chinese food?"

To which he replied, without looking at her: "I guess I'm a red-meat eater." She knew he wasn't talking about food.

"Are you really considering buying *Marry Well?*"

"My finance people are looking at it now. If it makes sense, yes. We're viewing it as a distress sale."

Camilla knew what that meant. He had more firsthand insight into Alyson's troubles than his competitors did; if he moved fast, he would probably get a good deal. There was something opportunistic and unsavory in this approach, something that irked her, but Snow White hadn't been asleep so long that she couldn't see that her Prince was a sharp businessman who would, when it behooved him, ruthlessly separate the chaff from the wheat.

"If you do buy it, Walter, who would take Alyson's place?"

"Chuck has been performing the role of behind-the-scenes publisher for a long time —"

"Yes. He'd be a good choice. For editor…Rose —"

"Forget it, Camilla. She's a food writer. I'd need to bring in a name from the outside."

His dismissal of Rose stung as deeply as if she herself had been swept aside. As wonderful as Rose was, she just wasn't high enough up the food chain to be considered for the job. The business world had strata, like a geological dig; the layers seemed as immovable as if they were set in stone.

"She's my best friend, Walter."

"I know, darling. She'll always be welcome in our lives. You can have lunch with her whenever you like and even dinner sometimes, if I'm out of town. Speaking of which, I'm starving."

And he told the driver to forget 76th Street and to take them to Smith & Wollensky's steakhouse instead.

Chapter Seventeen

Nothing was ever as simple as it seemed. Walter's clear reaction to Camilla's friends made her think twice about the relationship. She had just begun to taste true independence and it was even sweeter than she had imagined. Would she lose the intoxicating sense of freedom if she became hitched to Walter's star? She'd just have to wait and see. In the meantime, she had a baby and a business to nurture and grow.

Without hesitation, Camilla signed a five-year lease. Tad Shearer of Cushman & Wakefield, whom Walter had recommended, showed her 17 office spaces that might have worked. She chose 125 West 43rd Street because it was in move-in condition and because it was around the corner from Walter.

By week's end, she had rented all the furniture and equipment; hooked up the phone, fax, DSL Internet connection; printed stationery; and joined the real estate board.

Deirdre resigned from Griffin amid great fanfare to become vice-president of sales for Merewether Realty. To Barbara Corcoran's credit, she sent an enormous bouquet of flowers that graced Camilla's reception area for a week. The card was addressed to Camilla, not Barbara's ex-employee, and said: "Enjoy Deirdre," as if she were a gift instead of a person. Jayme Seagram sent a note wishing Camilla luck in her new venture; Camilla could read relief between the lines. And Walter had a rectangular brass block made for her desk, an adulterated version of Publius, which read: "No one knows what She can do until She tries."

Camilla had lined up Mac Sanders and Sam Jacobs, about whom she had written columns, as her first two customers on the sell side to launch her business with. Deirdre had brought a slew of exclusives with her from Griffin. And, Doris, dear Doris was ready to look at penthouses now that interest rates were at a forty-five year low.

The first phone call Camilla received on the day she became official was from the pug-owning department store heir.

"Do you remember my apartment at 1051 Fifth Avenue, Ms. Madison?"

How could she forget? "Of course."

"Well, I hear through the grapevine that you're on your own now and I was wondering if you would consider taking the exclusive?"

It was an unusual space, and wouldn't be an easy sell but, after all Camilla reckoned, Fifth Avenue was Fifth Avenue. However, there was nothing worse than a seller with grandiose ideas about how much his property was worth; the result was invariably a waste of everybody's time. Camilla had learned that the buyers dictated the price, not the sellers, no matter what anyone might think. "The market is inventory heavy right now, more sellers than buyers…it depends on the price you'd be willing to accept."

The prospective client lowered his voice, despite the fact that he was in his own home, which Camilla knew because she could hear Wednesday and Pugsley barking in the background. "I'll take whatever you can get Ms. Madison, and as fast as you can get it. The retail business hasn't been this bad since the Great Depression."

From the desperation in his tone, she could tell he needed the money. "I'll do my best for you. I'll have my secretary fax you an exclusive agreement right now." Camilla took down his fax number.

Deirdre's first task in her new role was to populate the database with real estate listings, most of which she derived from her network of broker friends. Within days, she managed to get Merewether Realty on the co-broker list of every major brokerage firm in town, no small feat for an upstart company like Camilla's. Ninety-seven percent of Manhattan listings were selectively co-brokered in this fashion, with the other three percent accessible from the Web, independent listing agencies, and the most reliable source — word of mouth.

Camilla concentrated her efforts on developing her vision for Merewether Realty: to create a vertical real estate firm that offered turnkey services to her demanding clientele. Prissie Easton quit her job at *Marry Well* to start a design firm of her own based on Camilla's assurances to send all referrals her way. As a result, Prissie named her practice Priscilla Easton Interiors, An Affiliate of Merewether Realty.

John opted to stay at JPMorgan Chase, despite Camilla's urging that he start his own mortgage brokerage firm. He explained that not everyone can be an entrepreneur; some people are risk adverse, especially those planning to marry and settle down. Camilla let out a whoop of joy when she heard his rationale and said, "Darn that Rose, she hasn't said a word."

To which John replied, "She doesn't know." And he pulled out of his pocket a turquoise box from Tiffany's that contained a ring with five diamonds, "One," he explained, "for each glorious month that I've known her."

Camilla brightened at his declaration of his love for her friend; no one deserved it more than Rose.

"I've got more good news," he said.

"More?"

"P'nina and Lee have found a house. And, they're taking a mortgage through us. It's a lovely house, Camilla, in Little Neck on the border of Queens and Long Island. P'nina brought me pictures and a floor plan. Plenty of room for them, a baby… and two more."

It warmed Camilla to hear it. "Pretty soon they'll be getting a dog."

"I doubt that, Camilla. In China, they eat dogs and revere children… even though in Manhattan, it's the reverse."

Into her computer Camilla typed: *Penthouse, terrace, six rooms, midtown,* then clicked SEARCH. Fourteen apartments popped up; only seven allowed dogs, less than eight pounds of course. Camilla made appointments to show them all to Doris Sanger.

The first one was too small; the second one was too big. Another had no view; a fourth had no kitchen. Of the two that Doris liked, only one met with Chekarf's approval, which he indicated by wagging his tail and barking twice. Fortunately, Deirdre represented the seller for the apartment of Chekarf's choice.

The penthouse Chekarf favored at 557 Park Avenue belonged to Dawn Marsh, who had been the director of fashion at Brooks Brothers and then moved to London on short notice to accept the position of president for the renowned haberdashers Ashton & Tate. It was bright and cheery, decorated in the understated Classic English style.

Deirdre put on a show, adopting an uptown accent as she described what she hoped to sell: "The living room is generous and beautifully *pro-por-tioned*. The seating is as comfortable as it looks. Don't you just love the subtle blend of bold red and faded pink? The Penelope toile curtains, with fan edge and silk swags, hang from pewter pelmets across tall and graceful

French doors that lead to the planted terrace. Those period chairs by the eighteenth-century English furniture makers *Chip-pen-dale*, Hepplewhite and Sheraton are covered in coordinated cut velvets with matching wool *bull-ion* fringe." Above a mahogany sideboard was an assortment of oil paintings of dogs.

"The furniture *could* be included," Deirdre said, although Camilla could have told her it wasn't Doris's taste. After the showings, Doris invited Camilla back to her duplex on 57th Street for a drink, and to discuss how they should proceed.

"It needs work," Doris said. "I'd have to gut the place..."

Camilla had thought the apartment was in perfect condition. She estimated that the traditional décor — Jacobean paneling in the library, Bosanquet & Ives bordered carpets, silk moiré *fleur-de-lis* wall coverings — had cost a fortune. But, as she suspected, it clearly wasn't Doris's style. There's a business idea, Camilla thought, a secondhand shop that specialized in recycling the magnificent installations from apartments that the next owners whimsically tore out.

"...And then there's the problem of selling this place — I'd need the money to close and to pay rent. I'd need a place to live while the renovation is going on."

"Doris, the house rules at 557 Park Avenue only allow construction for four months. After that, you'd be fined $1,623 per day."

Doris shook her hand as if she'd touched a hot stove. "I couldn't do it myself then. Not with my travel schedule."

"Don't worry about that. Prissie Easton could do the job." Camilla was proud; her idea was working.

"For four months, I suppose I could stay at the Kennel Club," Doris said. Chekarf yapped in agreement. The Kennel Club was the only hotel in New York that encouraged canine guests. It even had a doggie bar in the lounge.

While Doris retreated to the kitchen to prepare some hors d'oeuvres and open a bottle of wine, Camilla looked around her at the beautiful home Doris had created. True, there were a few dog stains on the carpets, but most of the natural stone and wood materials that Doris had chosen were animal-proof.

"You have an extraordinary eye," Camilla said, when Doris returned. Camilla thought how she would love to own an apartment like this. It was large enough for her and Merry, perfectly located, and she felt sure she could afford it. Even after self-financing Merewether Realty, she still had enough cash left over to put down 20 percent, which would be all she'd need to get a mortgage, since it was a condo and not an all-cash or 50 percent co-op building. "Doris…"

"Um," Doris's mouth was stuffed with a chunk of pepper brie.

"What if I bought your apartment?" As soon as Camilla said it, she regretted it. If her relationship with Walter continued on the path they were on, they might marry… she had seen his and Alyson's apartment — it made Doris's look like a dollhouse.

"That would be ideal. Are you in the market?" Doris asked.

Camilla picked up a mushroom cap filled with crabmeat. "There's just one thing holding me back. Walter…I'm not sure where it will go."

Chekarf leapt through the air, like a mini-ballerina in a fur coat, and pounced upon Camilla's mushroom cap, pulverizing it between his jaws.

"I'm sorry, they're his favorite," Doris said, kissing his head while she called him *bad dog*. "Camilla, what I'm about to say may sound self-serving, as if I want you to buy my apartment..."

"Don't worry, Doris. Speak your mind."

"It's just that I've been there and done that — altered my life waiting for a man. It's not in your best interest..." Camilla listened keenly. "Go forward independently, make your own way; whoever he is, if he's worth his salt he'll love you more for it."

Camilla wondered if Doris's situation fit her own. Doris had been divorced; but so had Camilla. Maybe Doris was just bitter? Or maybe she was right.

"Go on..."

"I'm sure you're thinking that if I know so much, how come I'm alone?"

That was exactly what Camilla had been thinking, so she picked up another mushroom cap and stuffed it in her mouth quickly, noticing the look of envy on Chekarf's face, to avoid having to confirm.

Doris continued, "When Stash left me, I was angry. I had organized my life around his, catered to his every need, adored him — and, he bailed anyway. So I made my own life, focused on my own career, became completely self-sufficient, my own person, not Stash and me, just me — and you know what?"

"What?" Camilla asked, on the edge of her seat.

"The men swarmed like bees to honey."

Camilla couldn't help but think of Alyson. Maybe that had been her secret too. Maybe men really did want an independent partner after all, rather than an attendant to their needs. At least the men she'd be interested in. Men like Walter.

"Doris, why did you never re-marry?"

"I was older than you when Stash left; I was 40 and childless. My needs were different. The older I got, the less I needed a man, except for sex of course. It's the opposite with men you know."

"What do you mean?"

"The older they get, the more dependent they become. The more they need a woman. I'm 55 now, I'm not interested in taking care of an old man."

"What about companionship?"

"I've got tons of co-workers, friends…and Chekarf. And my sexual needs are taken care of as well." After swallowing her stick-full of beef satay in spicy peanut sauce, she opened her purse, which was on the floor near the sofa. In it was a leather picture frame holding a photo of a smiling Indian man, about 28 or 30. "This is Jitan. He takes very good care of me, indeed."

On her way to meet Walter at the River Club the next morning, she decided not to tell him about the offer she had made. Why upset him? So many variables had to fall into place before she could buy Doris's apartment that it was far from a sure thing.

It was beginning to become a habit, breakfast at the Club. The French Toast was divine and the company was becoming indispensable. Walter was waiting at their usual table, reading *The Wall Street Journal.*

"My lawyer got a call from Alyson late yesterday afternoon," Walter said, almost as soon as Camilla sat down.

The first thing Camilla thought was that Alyson wanted Walter back. She imagined Alyson would be sorry for all her unconscionable behavior. If he took her back, she'd behave, worship him, have parties with him, have children with him (gasp!).

"What did she want?" Camilla asked coolly.

"She asked if I would agree to sell the River House triplex. She needs her half of the proceeds to help pay off her debts."

"And?"

"I said yes."

The apartment was one-of-a-kind and would fetch a mighty sum, even in a recession. There were always people immune to recessions. "Oh, Walter. Won't you miss it?"

"I love the water view, but not the time I spent there," he said, biting into his English muffin. He drained his water glass.

"There are many beautiful buildings with water views, One East 79th Street, One Sutton Place —"

"Then let's look at them, as soon as you sell River House."

"Me?! Alyson will never allow it, Walter, no matter how much you insist."

"It was she who expressly requested that it be you, Camilla."

"But why?"

"Why don't you see her and find out?"

Walter's attorney had fixed the meeting for ten A.M. the next day. Alyson answered the door herself; she wore no make-up and had lost weight. She was still stunning, and the bluish-white pallor around her naked eyes reminded Camilla of the color of mother's milk.

Camilla entered the apartment warily, prompting Alyson to ask her, "Is there a problem?"

"It's just a bit awkward being here..." Camilla said, cut off mid-sentence by Alyson.

"Whatever may have transpired between us personally, you're the best man for the job. Plus you have a vested interest, don't you? The more you get for this place, the bigger the one Walter will buy for you. He does have his asset allocations, you know."

Camilla wondered what had made her so hard. From what she knew of Alyson, she'd had everything go her way — until recently, but that was her own doing. A pampered Southern Belle upbringing, Princeton, Columbia Business School, a successful enterprise, any man she wanted, a remarkable, wonderful (soon to be ex-) husband. What could make her throw it all away the way she had?

"If you can put the past behind us, then so can I," Camilla said, pulling herself up to her full height.

"Good. Here's the deal. I want this place sold fast. The timing's right; we're just at the beginning of the spring market. Ask $14 million, but let's negotiate any offer over $10 mil — as long as it's a cash offer. Cash is —"

If Camilla heard that expression one more time, she'd blow a blood vessel. "River House is an all cash building, Alyson."

"Oh. I'll only give you three months to sell it. If you fail, I'll try someone else." The phone rang. Alyson picked up the portable handset and said to Camilla, covering the mouthpiece, "It's my divorce lawyer, and I've been trying to reach her for two days. Go in the study. I'll join you as soon as I can." Then she walked in the opposite direction with the phone to her ear.

For the first 20 minutes, Camilla sat quietly, planning a sales strategy in her head. The volume of objects Alyson and Walter had amassed during such a short tenure astonished her, and she wandered about the room, wondering how they would determine who would get what. On the bookshelves alone, there were hundreds of valuable tomes; she touched their spines as she read the titles. There was Alyson's copy of *The Art of War*, as well as other books Camilla assumed belonged to her: *The Feminine Mystique*, *The South Beach Diet*, and *Lysistrata*.

Walter's section seemed segregated by the subject matter, if not by the shelf. A biography of Napoleon near one about the Duke of Wellington; *Skyscrapers of New York* dwarfed its neighbor, *Short Men and Power*.

There were a few recent photo albums, bound in green leather and dated in gold leaf. Camilla didn't dare open the ones that might have contained pictures of Alyson and Walter together, but she spotted an older one, with a worn black binding, which she hoped might have mementos of Walter as a child. It didn't; it appeared to be a photo album from Alyson's youth.

The snapshots of Alyson were ordered chronologically and labeled by the year. She had been a chubby infant, which would be hard to imagine if one knew her now. Her eyes glistened with intelligence and joy. In every shot, she was dressed in perfectly matched outfits, like the ones Camilla had seen on Madison Avenue in the windows of Bon Point, and her soft blond hair was held in place by ribbons and bows. Even her white anklets had lacy tops and her shoes were spic and span. Young Alyson had had a blinding smile.

During these early years, she was never shown alone. There were pictures of her mother and father and another golden girl who looked like

Alyson's twin, only younger. Camilla presumed she must be her sister, although during the many years of having known her, she had never heard Alyson mention the existence of a sibling at all. Camilla turned each page slowly…1965, 1969, 1973, until she reached 1977.

There was a remarkable change on that page, when Camilla calculated that Alyson would have turned 12. Her smiles were gone, and her father too. In the few family photos that followed, there was a new man, tall and dark, but with a vacant stare. The album ended just as Alyson returned.

"Is this your sister?" Camilla innocently asked, pointing to the younger child.

Alyson closed the cover and returned the album to the shelf. "Yes."

"How come you've never mentioned her?"

Alyson shrugged. She sat down on the sofa and lit a cigarette, even though Camilla had never seen her smoke before. "Gone." And, then as an afterthought: "Drugs."

"I'm sorry," Camilla said. "You were a beautiful child, Alyson. You grew up in Louisville, yes?" She was trying to divert the conversation away from Alyson's sister.

"Mostly. But we moved to Nashville when my mother remarried."

"The tall man in the photo?"

Alyson scoffed at the question and smashed her cigarette stub in a lovely Limoge ashtray that rested on the coffee table glass. "That's him all right — Violator Vic," Alyson said, accompanied by a sarcastic laugh. "Enough small talk, Camilla. I've got more problems than him right now. Did you bring an agreement?"

"Yes, it's right here." Camilla took a pen from her purse and changed the term from six months to three. Then she filled in the price — $14 million — and watched Alyson sign her name just below the line where Walter had signed his.

A plague of sympathy consumed her as she finally realized what she had always wanted to know. Alyson had been hurt, Alyson had been damaged, Alyson's life had been changed, practically before it had started — just like her own. At that moment, the truth hit her: It's not what happens to you in life, but how you handle it that counts.

That night, she told Rose what she had seen.

"You think she was molested?" Rose asked. She was pensive; Camilla could tell she hadn't considered this before.

"It was a different face in the photos before and after 1977."

"Maybe it was just her parents' divorce?"

"She called him Violator Vic, Rose."

"Could she have been referring to his traffic tickets?"

Camilla made a disapproving face. "This is no time for humor. I've been thinking about it all afternoon. If a girl is molested, there are many ways she might react." It was a painful subject but fascinating too. "I suppose she could decide that she would never get hurt again. That when she grew up, she would hold the power over men."

Rose was silent while she snapped the ends off the string beans she was cleaning. "It makes sense, Camilla. She didn't just shut out her conquests emotionally over the years — she publicly denigrated and humiliated them. I always thought it was a kind of titillating exhibitionism but, now that you pose the possibility, it could be plain hatred of the opposite sex."

"Like Tom Cruise's character in *Magnolia* — 'seduce and destroy.'"

"Yes, I remember. Seduce and destroy," Rose agreed, as she loudly snapped the end off the last bean.

It was Saturday, and deliciously spring-like outside, so Camilla invited Robert to join her and Merry for a stroll through Central Park Zoo.

"Can I have her tonight?" Robert asked.

"Not tonight."

"And why not?"

"Tonight Walter is coming over to have dinner with us."

"Are you crazy, Camilla? If he sees how you live, he'll run for the hills."

Robert's comment hurt her deeply, because it played into her own fears as well. It had been a long time since she'd dated, but she remembered the shifts in her feelings toward certain men when the context suddenly changed. "He's got to meet Merry sometime, Robert. And I want it to be before Palm Beach."

The light turned red and Robert stopped the stroller three feet from the curb, prompting Camilla to turn around and look for them.

"You can't be too safe you know." Robert said. Parenthood had brought out his protective side. "Palm Beach?"

"Walter has invited Merry and me to go."

"When?"

"If I go, we'd leave on February 25th."

"The day before your birthday."

Camilla was touched that Robert had remembered. "And nine days before his."

The green light signaled for the walk down Fifth Avenue to continue. "That's a coincidence. Dennis and I are going to Florida as well. We leave on the 28th, but we'll be at The Delano on South Beach."

Camilla had read that the men at The Delano's pool had pierced nipples.

Robert stopped at a hot-dog cart and bought Merry a warm pretzel. "Listen, Camilla, I have an idea. Why don't Dennis and I keep Merry until the 28th? Chantal can watch her during the day, and we'll bring her to you in Palm Beach before continuing on to Miami?"

"Why would you do that?"

"Mostly for selfish reasons. ...Just kidding. If you want this relationship to work, spend a few days with him without Merry, just the two of you —"

"His college-age son is coming too."

"That's different. He'll be out at night chasing girls...Or?" He raised his eyebrow in a mischievous way.

"No, I think you were right the first time..." she said, recalling the kiss. "...I think he likes girls."

"Then you two can still be alone for romantic nights. Nothing like a full diaper to kill the mood, if you know what I mean."

Camilla laughed. "You're probably right."

"It's only four days. The Big Apple Circus is coming to town, we'll go to Serendipity — she loves the frozen hot chocolates."

Merry looked up from her stroller and clapped her hands.

"I thought hot chocolate was better hot," Camilla said, teasing.

"There's always an exception to every rule. So, what do you say, are we on?"

They had arrived in front of the seal pool. "Let's see how things go tonight. Then I'll let you know."

A sleek, gray bull was barking and slapping his flippers as the person who would feed him approached. A couple of seals were wrestling under water while another pair lolled about on the pool's deck, soaking up the sun.

"I feel like a peeping Tom," Camilla said. "They have no privacy."

"We all live in a fishbowl, Camilla. There are no secrets," Robert said, lifting Merry up onto the fence for a closer look.

"Yet, I lived with you for two years and never knew the obvious."

"We see what we want to see, Camilla."

Merry and Camilla kissed Robert good-bye and left to meet Rose at Fairway to shop for the evening's supplies. Camilla had enlisted Rose's aid; the seductive effects of a deliciously prepared meal are well-known in the circles of sisterhood, so the women did not need to discuss the importance of the selections they were about to make. They approached each luscious display before them with the reverence one might in nearing an altar; the discernment they exhibited in planning the menu would normally be reserved for choosing a college or a first home.

"*Cuisine du terroir...*" Rose explained to Camilla, "...means cuisine of the soil — the best of which is located in the south of France. You wouldn't put anything else in your mouth unless you knew where it came from, why would you do it with food?"

Merry, who was in the habit of putting everything in her mouth, looked highly offended by the comment.

The mushroom department at Fairway appeared like a Provençal winter wood. There were a dozen varieties of the delectable fungi, including cremini, chanterelle, portobello, enoki, white, button, and ones with exotic names like trumpet-of-death and hen-of-the-woods. Rose suggested that as a first course they prepare *cassolette de champignons aux noisettes* — a medley of exotic mushrooms with hazelnut oil.

"Sounds good," Camilla said. "...If we can leave out the trumpets-of-death. What else do we need?"

"Organic butter, hazelnuts, peanut oil, and chives."

"I think I'll roast a chicken, with parsley, sage, rosemary, and thyme, for the main course."

"Planning to play Simon and Garfunkel on the stereo?"

"Very funny. What else?"

Merry turned her head and pointed at a dog through the window. "Look! Pet doggie, Mommy?"

"That's a pit bull, Merry. Very dangerous. Pit bulls bite."

This seemed to perplex Merry more than scare her and she continued down the dairy aisle muttering to herself: "Spitballs bite, spitballs bite, spitballs bite..."

"You'll need potatoes for balance — fingerlings, for shape — and...I know, new spring peas à la Francaise! Balance, shape, color...the only thing missing is texture." Rose added a whole grain loaf of bread to their cart.

The fruit section burst forth like a kaleidoscope of color and shapes, inspiring Rose to offer to make the dessert. She gently lifted each box of berries toward her nose, closing her eyes so she could smell for ripeness, choosing only the ones that she thought were best. She placed each box in the cart — raspberries, strawberries, blueberries, red and white currants, and blackberries — as if each were an egg laid tenderly in its nest.

"Berry soup?" Camilla asked.

Rose gave her a condescending glance. "*Craquelins au crème citron, fruits rouges* — lemon cream and fruit tuiles to you!"

When they returned to the apartment, Camilla gave Merry a bath and put her down in her crib for a nap. They left both doors open between their apartments and did the prep work in Rose's kitchen, which was much better equipped than Camilla's. While Camilla rinsed the mixed mushrooms and set them aside to drain, Rose shelled the bright green peas and threw them into a pot of salted water to boil.

"Guess who's in hot water?" Rose asked.

"Other than Rocky and Alyson?"

"Yup. Your old friend Jeffrey Ratchitt."

Camilla looked up in surprise while she beheaded a white mushroom with one swift slice of the knife.

"I saw it in *New York* magazine today. He's positioned himself as some money-management genius, although he has no bachelor's degree, and he's suckered in millions, mainly from Dawson Landers and his Hollywood pals. The reporter asked around, and no one in the wealth management world seems to know what he does. The probing started trouble and now the SEC's stepped in and Dawson Landers is suing Jeffrey Ratchitt for fraud."

Camilla broke off the chicken's neck and threw it in the trash. "There's hope for us yet. I was beginning to think his type never got their just desserts." She placed the chicken in a shallow roasting pan with four springs of rosemary and a dash of fresh thyme. Then she rubbed olive oil into the skin, topping it with sprinkles of butter to seal the flavor in, adding the chopped carrots, parsley, sage and onion to the pan.

"I would say his goose is cooked," Rose concluded, tossing a garlic clove into the poultry pan.

Camilla plucked the garlic out. "Unh-uh, not a good idea," she said, scrubbing the fingerling potatoes.

When the potatoes were clean, she brewed some peppermint tea and settled down on the top of a red three-rung stepladder that had been propped up against the wall. She watched Rose combine 1½ cups of confectioner's sugar, 1/3 cup of flour, and seven tablespoons of organic butter in a bowl, mixing the ingredients until they were smooth. Then she folded in the fresh juice from an orange, and its finely-chopped zest, as well as ¼ cup of slivered almonds that she kept in a tin by the stove.

"Can I help?"

"You relax. I have a feeling you have a long night ahead of you."

"Robert thinks when Walter sees how I live, he'll run for the door."

"That's nonsense, Camilla. If he loves you, why would he care?"

The tea burned her tongue. She was fascinated by the efficiency with which Rose now made the lemon cream, watching closely as she measured ¾ of a cup of heavy cream and squeezed ½ cup of lemon juice into a saucepan, bringing the mixture to a gentle boil. Then she combined ½ cup of sugar, five large egg yolks, and 1½ tablespoons of cornstarch, and whisked the ingredients until they were pale and smooth. All of this she covered and put aside to cool.

"And if he doesn't love me?" Camilla asked.

"Then you have nothing to lose."

Camilla weighed what Rose had said. "That's not entirely true."

"What's worrying you?" Rose asked, pulling up a chair.

"I always thought true love would fix it all. My marriage was a disaster. But then things started looking up — I have Merry, and you, and now Merewether Realty, and all our friends. What if Walter usurps all that? …I'm not sure I'd be getting more than I'd be giving up."

Rose walked to the sink and started to wash and drain the berries. She whipped a bowl of chilled heavy cream until soft peaks formed. Then she married the whipped and lemon creams into a perfectly blended new whole. "It's not a quid pro quo, Camilla, an all-or-nothing sort of thing. Part of growing is accepting change and making room for what's new in your life, while keeping the good parts of the old. If you can't figure out how to do that, then you're perpetually stuck and, I predict, you'll be miserable as well. You're a powerful personality; it's time you realized that. That's probably what Walter loves about you. No one can overpower you unless you let them."

Camilla had never thought of herself as a powerful personality before; her life had seemed about overcoming cataclysmic events — but maybe that ability to surmount them was the power Rose meant.

"I can't see Walter changing diapers or hanging around with us at Foo King…"

"True. But we're all moving on as well. Merry's diaper days are short-lived, and then she'll be going to school. P'nina told me that with the move coming up, they're thinking of relocating the restaurant closer to where they're planning to live. Chantal will be going to college. John and I, who knows where that one will lead —"

Camilla knew, but she didn't dare spoil the surprise. "You and John are the perfect match."

"I know. And so are you and Walter. Remember who you are, Camilla…Palm Beach, real estate family, a born entrepreneur —"

"Just the same, it would be so much easier if things didn't have to change," Camilla sighed. But then she remembered Deirdre, who had always resisted change, and how unhappy she claimed her life had been — stuck in a rut. Maybe the shift to Merewether Realty would give Deirdre the new start that she needed as well.

"To cease to progress is to regress. To cease to grow is to die."

"Keats or Yeats?" Camilla tried hard to remember.

"Neither. It was on the back of a card someone handed me on the subway."

The flowers Walter brought — protea, hydrangea, and wild cherry tree blossoms — were as complex and unusual as he. While Camilla unwrapped the cellophane from around the stems, she noticed Walter taking everything in. With arms folded across his chest, wearing an ivory shirt, azure sweater, and casual pair of charcoal slacks, he walked once around the small room as a surveyor might a plot of land.

She had set the table in front of the window, covering it with a piece of brocade silk, using the antique family silver, Bernardaud china, and Baccarat crystal that her mother had left her, some of the only treasures she had not sold. Two director's chairs, covered in caramel canvas flanked the table, with Merry's highchair — like the Broadway star — reigning in between. The rest of the decorating was a hodgepodge: the Lucite coffee table, sofa and pillows from The Future and, in the alcove, her bed. Next to it was Merry's crib, so stuffed with toy animals that it appeared more like a circus train than a place for a baby to sleep.

In her nervousness, Camilla had changed Merry's outfit three times, settling on a blue turtleneck and a pair of Oshkosh denim overalls. Although she was walking, Merry still liked her Life Savers exerciser, which she rolled to within an inch of Walter's knee, parking there to look up and stare. She cocked her head and studied him, eyes thirsty, cheeks bountiful, beautiful mouth a slash of indecision.

Walter bent over. "Hello, Merry," he said, reaching in his pocket to pull out a present.

Merry hesitated before accepting it, looking at Camilla for permission. Finally, she took the gaily-wrapped box from his hand and tugged on the curled ribbons on top. Walter helped her open the gift — a harmonica. He took it from the box and showed her how to blow.

While Merry was busy with her harmonica, Walter placed his cool palms on Camilla's cheeks and kissed her. He brushed the blonde strands from her eyes and met her gaze with his own.

"I told you it's not much," she said, referring to her modest surroundings.

"It's the gem that makes the jewel, not the setting," he replied.

They sat on the sofa and Camilla poured two glasses of wine, a dry Kendall-Jackson chardonnay. Framed photographs of her family and friends graced the side table and Walter methodically picked up each one, tracing his long fingers over the faces, as if by doing so he could bring the flat figures to life.

"That one was taken just before I left home for Andover in 1985. That's my mother, and my father —"

"Where was it taken, Camilla?"

"On the porch of our house, 115 Seaspray in Palm Beach." Camilla regarded the Christmas cactuses wistfully, comparing them to the view out her window, a dirty brick wall.

Walter picked up another frame. "I recognize Dennis Meehan…is that your ex-husband with him?"

"Robert. Yes, that's Robert. We've actually become the best of friends."

Merry rolled over in her walker and Camilla lifted her out, settling her in a cross-legged position on the couch. She held her harmonica out toward Walter and broke into a grateful grin, and then she banged the instrument on the coffee table edge.

"Daddy?" Walter asked Merry, pointing to the photograph of Robert.

Merry smiled. "My Daddy," she said proudly. She started tooting on her harmonica again.

Camilla refilled Walter's wine glass, then slipped away to finish preparing the meal. She melted three tablespoons of butter in a large skillet over medium heat, watched it sizzle, and thought how much like the butter she felt every time Walter was near. She sautéed the mushrooms, sprinkled in the chives, and drizzled hazelnut oil over the top. Then she threw a few in the Cuisinart for Merry, while she divided the rest, generously garnishing the portions with chopped hazelnuts fresh from the shell.

Camilla slid Merry into her highchair and handed her a plastic-tipped spoon. She fed herself the gray mushroom mush with great dexterity and determination.

"You have no idea how much I appreciate a home-cooked meal," Walter said. "Since I moved out it's been nothing but restaurant cuisine." He savored his bite of the buttery mushrooms. "Delicious!"

Camilla loved him more for his graciousness; especially since she knew her competitors were the best chefs in town. "I must admit, Rose helped me out."

"Speaking of Rose, Camilla, you can let her know that her job is secure —"

"Does that mean…?"

"Yes. West Coast Publishing will be buying *Marry Well* magazine. It rounds out our portfolio nicely — we've got a newsweekly, a literary journal, a couple of daily papers and now…I'm not actually sure how to define *Marry Well.*

"It's a glossy monthly with an entirely different audience than your other publications. I think it's a brilliant strategy."

He brightened at her approval. "Chuck suggested trying to get Tina Brown to be editor-in-chief."

"Great idea! What's she been doing since *Talk* folded?"

"Not much." He looked at Merry, who was watching him. "What is that stuff she's eating anyway?"

"The same as you, just blended."

"Don't babies eat Beechnut anymore?"

"Not if they have a godmother next door who's a gourmet chef."

Camilla cleared their plates. She returned to the kitchen and heated an inch of peanut oil in the bottom of a pan before spreading out the potato slices to brown. The peas she had parboiled were now ready to be sautéed as well, with tiny bits of translucent onion and shreds of lettuce leaves. Walter and Merry were deep in conversation about dogs, and Camilla heard Walter confess that he loved them, but big dogs — golden retrievers, Irish setters, German shepherds — not those little ones that, where he came from, could pass for lunch. Camilla smiled.

"What's your favorite kind of dog, Merry?" Walter asked her, lifting his glass to his lips.

Merry concentrated hard. "Spitballs!" she declared.

Walter was laughing so hard, Camilla thought he would spill his wine. Instead, he leaned over and kissed Merry on the top of her head.

Camilla removed the chicken from the oven and placed it on the platter her mother had reserved for special occasions. She surrounded it with potatoes and branches of fresh rosemary. Into the Cuisinart she tossed a slice of chicken, a few potatoes and a handful of peas. The resultant color was disgusting, but it didn't seem to faze Merry a bit.

Walter dug into the succulent chicken with unrestrained delight, raising his wine glass in the direction of the front door. "My compliments to the chefs," he said.

Merry imitated him and lifted her juice cup as well.

"Camilla, Chuck had an idea I'd like to pass by you —"

Her mouth was full so she said, "Um —"

"We've been talking about *Marry Well* spin-offs, maybe special issues four times a year. Naturally, one idea was *Live Well*, on real estate. Then *Think Well* on continuing education, *Look Well* on beauty, and of course, *Eat Well* on cooking."

"I think it's a splendid idea. Are you considering Rose for the food spin-off?"

"Actually, Chuck recommended her to run the whole shebang. She'd be editor-in-chief of the spin-offs, reporting only to Tina Brown, or whomever we end up hiring to run editorial at *Marry Well*."

The potatoes were eaten, the peas consumed and the poor chicken had been reduced to bones. "And what is to become of Alyson?"

That dark scowl came out of nowhere. "To steal a line from *Gone With the Wind*: 'Frankly my dear, I don't give a damn.'"

Walter stood up and helped her clear. While Camilla brewed Vanilla Kiss decaf, Walter rinsed the plates. Merry banged the harmonica on her high chair tray for attention, and it was Walter who walked over and lifted her out. She pulled away from him and squirmed in his arms. Without discussion, Walter took her over to the changing table and freshened her up. Camilla almost fell on the floor. "Thank you," she said.

"Glad I remember how. When did they start making Pampers in pink?" he asked.

"I thought they always had."

Walter spread a woven blanket on the rug and put Merry down there, surrounding her with her stuffed toys. "What's this?" he asked.

"Octopus," she answered.

"And this?" he asked.

"Elephant."

"And this one?" he asked, holding up an armless bear.

"Bear-bear," Merry said, shaking her head and lowering her voice. "She's sick."

"Sorry," Walter said.

"That's OK, she'll live," Merry assured him, in a most matter-of-fact way.

The *tuiles* with lemon cream and berries were like ambrosia to the tongue, and looked like architectural masterpieces. Each layer of *tuile* was baked to a golden brown and filled with lemon cream. Perfectly quartered strawberries alternated with raspberries, blueberries, blackberries, and currants around the edges of each story, and a dollop of cream topped off the whole tower with coulis drizzling down its sides. "Amazing," Walter uttered.

"Rose did this one alone. It took her all afternoon."

After coffee and dessert, Camilla cleaned up the kitchen while Walter put Merry to bed. He read *Runaway Bunny* and *Goodnight, Moon* to her, stories he had remembered from baby days with Rex. Camilla appreciated how hard he was trying, and she knew what it meant. She was relieved and happy that Merry had taken to him so — one more member of her large extended family whom it would never occur to Merry not to love.

"I was thinking of you when I read *Runaway Bunny* to Merry," Walter said.

"How so?" Camilla asked, mulling over how funny it was that diapers had changed, and the food that babies ate, and the shape of bottles as well, but books, good books, became classics, and never seemed to go out of style.

"Because Camilla, even though I'm not your mother, and you're not a little bunny, I would change shape and form if I could to keep you in my realm." He put his arms around her and kissed her deeply, in a way that blew her away, like the wind does to the runaway bunny in the book.

They stayed like that, in each other's arms, talking, until they both nearly fell asleep. "You'd better go," Camilla said.

"Have I passed the test?"

"I'd say so."

"Then you'll come to Palm Beach?"

Oh yes, oh yes, oh yes... "I'd love that very much. Robert offered to bring Merry on the 28th."

Walter hesitated. "Is that OK with you?"

"Yes, I'll tell him yes." She could see that made Walter happy.

"Three nights alone with you..." he said in parting. Camilla lingered in the doorway, listening to his footsteps wane, until she heard the heavy front door thud closed behind him.

Chapter Eighteen

It had been nearly a decade.

Ten years should have dulled the memory, but it didn't. The second Camilla's toe touched Palm Beach soil familiarity overwhelmed her. She stood rock-still outside the automatic doors of the airport and closed her eyes. The moist air enveloped her, as it filled her hair, nostrils, and pores with the tangy fragrance of the sea and the citrus trees. The coming and going of planes was drowned out by the rustling of the coconut palms in the breeze.

Walter touched her fingers with his but said nothing. When Camilla opened her eyes to look at him, he had a small smile on his lips that bespoke his understanding.

Once they crossed the North Bridge onto the island of Palm Beach, it was as if they had entered the iris of an eye. Before them an outburst of color and symmetry unfolded, seemingly radiating from that great all-seeing black pupil of the earth — the Atlantic Ocean.

They drove slowly up Royal Poinciana toward The Breakers, passing Chuck & Harold's and Testa's, the North County Road Post Office, and the new stores in the spots where stores had turned over every year since Camilla could remember. There were ostentatious Rolls Royces and Bentleys, all baring vanity plates — X-IPO, PASHA, WIFE 3 — glistening in the sun.

The vista from the road to the hotel took in acres of golf course dissected by a long driveway lined with ancient queen palms 50 feet tall. Dozens of wild parrots nested there, in the crooks of palm tree branches, beyond the reach of the armies of gardeners to whom the care of the trees was entrusted. The insistent squawking of the birds was like the cheering in an arena, melting together to form a unified chant. They would swoop down from their branches in graceful arcs, fraternizing in the airspace between the rows of palms. When she had been young, Camilla would feed the parrots fruit cocktails of papaya and watermelon, lovingly cut by her own hand.

There was a secret garden, with a hedge-maze to get lost in, topiaries shaped like animals, and a gazebo. It was a little paradise, and hadn't been there when she had been young, but it was here now — waiting for Merry to discover.

Walter was watching her closely, she presumed for signs of pleasure or distress, the two faces of remembering. He took her hand and led her into The Breakers baronial lobby, which had been copied from a Genovese palazzo, with its rich fabrics and antique rugs, and a vaulted ceiling at least four stories high. He had booked the two-bedroom Imperial suite; it was the size of a field, with grass green carpeting and curtains of yellow dotted Swiss. The bellman put their luggage in the master bedroom and Walter walked her out onto the balcony to admire the Atlantic view.

"We have another room, for you or for Rex, whatever you're more comfortable with," Walter said.

"When is Rex arriving?"

"Late this afternoon."

"Then I don't have to decide now." She smiled smoothly but was nervous just the same.

Walter entwined his fingers in her hair and kissed her ardently, passionately, as if to let her know where he stood. But since telling him about Rocky, and Robert, and all the pain she'd had to endure, he had never pressed her to rush. He soothed her emotions the way one might a healing muscle, compensating for its limitations with patience and care. She knew he loved her, and he was everything, everyone she had ever wanted before.

Still she felt reticent. There were compromises she would have to make, sacrifices as well. She realized that he would supplant her friends, and his demands — to travel with him, be with him — would interfere with Merry too. And as loving as he could be, Camilla knew that his power might consume her; she was a supple shoot growing, yes, growing. And he was a redwood, elegant and strong. Could she thrive in his shadow? Did she want to be in his shadow at all?

Would he love her more, as Doris had predicted, if she remained completely independent of him? Or less? Or not at all. Then she realized that even having these thoughts, about whether he would love her or not, made her dependent, on his judgment and his love.

It came down to power, again. He had it all. She wanted to run, away from him, and Palm Beach, the illusions of happiness, because she knew that's all they were. She was on the verge of exploding, the butterfly bursting out of the cocoon with great expectations, only to find that it was safer inside after all.

But maybe all these doubts reflected the doubts she had about herself. That she was damaged, couldn't really love, or be loved in return.

Then she buried her nose in his neck, recognizing his scent of salt air and limes for what it meant to her, home at last, and she let it permeate her pores as if it were a tangible thing, alive, saturating her, and she knew she was hooked — she was in love! The doubts were pushed beneath the surface once more.

"There's a place I want to take you," Walter said.

Camilla stirred slightly but remained with her chin resting on his shoulder. "Now?" She was ready to make love.

He ran his hands down her sides and took her hands. His face touched hers, as he hesitated, so that their noses were aligned. She could feel the roughness of his beard like sandpaper, or a cat's tongue, caressing her cheek, although it had only been a few hours since he had shaved. "Now," he whispered in a croaky voice, into her hair.

Walter retrieved something from the bedroom and then returned. He led her out the door, down the hall, through the lobby, without a word of resistance from Camilla. Only the sun stabbing at her eyes woke her from her trance. They still wore Northeast March clothing, and she felt hot in the rays of the sun. They left the hotel through the side door to the south, trespassed across the putting green, and slipped through the wrought iron gates that separated the white-shingled houses where the workers lived from the rest of the hotel grounds.

The service road ran parallel to the ocean. It not only provided access for the hotel but for the Estee Lauder estate as well. Armed guards protected the white ocean-facing mansion from gawkers and passersby. They turned the corner onto Barton Avenue and, half a block ahead, faced the brilliant blue-black of the ocean, punctuated by the frothy whitecaps crashing arrogantly at its feet.

When they reached the oceanfront, they descended a rickety staircase to the beach below. Then Walter surprised her; from his pocket, he retrieved a long dark expanse of cloth, like a scarf, the type a magician might use more than a person would wear, and tied it across her eyes. The world was black.

"Where are you taking me? Not swimming I hope?" Camilla asked.

"No, of course not. Be patient."

It was much harder to walk in the sand without seeing. Her feet replaced her vision; every tiny shell and crab claw, pocket of tar and grainy sandy spot that she felt sent its images to her brain through the heightened sensitivity of touch in her toes.

At first they walked at a playful pace, stopping to kiss now and then. But suddenly, after about half a mile Camilla estimated, Walter hastened his gait. With quiet determination he guided her now, away from the beach, up the stairs, and across South County Road. He held her waist tightly from behind as he protected her from the cars whooshing by.

"Do you know the game called Trust?" he asked her.

"How could there be a game called Trust? Trust is much too serious to play with."

"It's *de rigueur* in business school orientations and corporate indoctrinations. Random partners are selected and one is blindfolded while the other stands behind her. The blindfolded partner falls backwards into the arms of the other, who presumably catches her when she falls."

"Is that what we're doing?"

"No."

As he said it they stopped walking. Camilla concluded that he had told her the trust tale to distract her from their destination. Everything felt so familiar — a place where comprehension and apprehension became one. "Where are we?"

"That is for you to figure out. You get ten questions." She heard a gate swing open. It creaked and moaned and then twanged when it slapped shut behind them.

Walter gently led her up four steps to what felt like a porch. She waited while he took a key from a lock-box near the door. She heard the turning of the dial and the tinny scrape as he closed the cover after removing the key. Camilla ran her hands over the smooth stucco walls. The flowers on the vines that grew there were soft and dense, like lamb's ear lettuce leaves, only thinner. "Bougainvillea?"

"You have nine questions left."

"What color?"

"They are the same color as your cheeks when you blush — magenta, I would say." He was laughing as he kissed her cheeks.

She blushed as she stepped inside. "What shape is the foyer? And how big?"

"It is almost a perfect square, about four by five," he said. Then he walked a square around her and lifted her in his arms. He carried her over the threshold into a room and rested her on a sofa so stuffed with goose-down that she sank deeply in it. She heard music playing, although there was none.

"That melody…do you hear it?"

"The ocean?"

"No, it's sweeter, soothing, not fierce. Like a child's lullaby."

Walter became very still. They were both so still that Camilla felt the air move around them. "Yes, I hear it too," he said.

There was a bowl of candy on the table in front of the couch. The foil paper crackled as Walter unwrapped one. Camilla opened her mouth as he slid it in. "Lillet! Where did you find them?"

But instead of answering he kissed her again, slowly, longingly. He took off her shoes and her stockings, and caressed her bare legs. "Do you know where we are?"

"Your uncle's house?"

"Not even close."

The house had a new smell. Not the house exactly, but the furnishings. There was the scent of fresh paint, and polyurethane, and the lingering fragrance in the air of flowers that had just been there but no longer were.

"New construction?"

"Let me take you upstairs. Maybe that will help."

At the top of the stairs, she thought the turn felt familiar. She pictured herself running around the bulky banister at that exact angle before. The smooth wood felt polished, but she could make out subtle indentations from prior wear. "Are we alone here?"

"Yes."

There was a bedroom, with thick cut pile carpet crushing beneath her toes. She felt a dresser, made of solid wood, the stacked slat louvers of a closet door, heavy silk draperies with knotted fringe as soft as Merry's curls. She felt her way all around the room, resting her palms against the plate glass. "I see the ocean," she said.

But when Walter checked, her blindfold it was tight.

We see what we want to see…

"Trust me?" he asked, standing behind her, flicking his tongue against the top vertebra of her spine.

She fell backwards, automatically, without the slightest bit of resistance, into his arms.

At last, Walter undid her blindfold.

Camilla squinted and looked out the window, noticing that the sun had traversed past them on its journey west. She was disoriented. The wallpaper was aquamarine and white, the curtains striped shades of sea, the carpet pliant, plush and unknown. She ran barefoot into the hall, with Walter following. Her fingertips traced the curves of the walls as she was driven toward her destination. She stood before the door and pulled on the brass knob. It was her room, the one she had known as a child.

Camilla braced herself in the doorframe while she devoured the scene. The room had been painted lavender, but it was still a girl's room, with a white carved single bed and eyelet curtains filtering the view. "How…?"

"It's for sale," Walter said.

"But the Ramsey family bought it when my parents —"

"I know. Then a year ago, they sold it to the Archers from New York, who spent a fortune renovating. After he was laid off by Merrill Lynch, they decided to sell it. Say the word, Camilla, and it's —"

She threw her arms around his neck and kissed him. "Am I dreaming? Are you real? Is this the house I lived in as a child? Are we even in Palm Beach at all?"

"I've lost count, but I think you've used up your questions."

Camilla slowly wandered through the rest of the house, opening every cupboard and closet door. There were no signs of her parents, her lost innocence, anything from her past. All she had left were her memories.

"Let's go back to the hotel," she sighed.

Walter didn't ask her why, or push for other answers, which was a relief, because she would have hated to tell him how disheartened she was. It wasn't the house she had missed, or even Palm Beach, but the people who had lived there. And it sickened her to see how easily their vitality had been wiped away like dust.

Since the island was only three blocks wide between the ocean and the lake, Walter and Camilla returned to The Breakers on foot along the Lake Trail. The large orange globe was still high, illuminating the translucent feathers of the ibis and heron that were feeding on the lake.

The villas with water views were hidden by walls and fences covered in lush tropical vines. Dozens of cold-blooded chameleons and black-footed lizards clung to the walls to soak up the last hours of sun before the source of their sustenance sank into the horizon for the night.

"Do you ever wish you were a lizard?" Camilla asked Walter.

He laughed. "Never. Do you?"

"Look at them. Life is so simple. It's about flies and sunshine —" She caught a chameleon in her hand just like she loved to do when she had been a girl.

"Survival, Camilla, just like us," he said, prompting her to let it go.

The Flagler Museum was on the Lake Trail just before the turnoff through the Breakers property to the hotel. The cats that she had remembered from years ago were still there, or their offspring. They were surviving too, on the largesse of tourists who brought them scraps of food from the restaurants nearby. The felines lurked under cars in the parking lot, camouflaged by their own shadows.

Before the elevator doors had opened to their floor, Walter started with the buttons on her blouse. In place of each one that became undone, he traced a shape with his finger on her skin and then planted a kiss, like a gardener-lover who carefully sows the seed in anticipation of the fruit that will grow there in time. With each touch of his lips, Camilla felt the layers of doubt peel away. By the time she lay on the bed in their suite, with only her mollusk shell, she was ready to receive him, to have him love her, at last.

The hours of eager, tender lovemaking seemed to evaporate. Every word he whispered sounded like a dozen snatched from sonnets invisibly floating by. The blindfold had awakened her ability to taste, smell, and touch in ways she had never known before. Seeing as much as she had, in fact, had blinded her; finally being free of the shackles of sight enabled her to feel — and to love. There was no violator here, or a victim fallen prey — just two willing bodies filled with yearning and desire.

Walter and Camilla dressed quietly. Walter moved nearer to her once he was done and started to say something, but she didn't want to dispel the magic with mere words, so she preempted his query by moving closer to him and blocking his lips with her own. They stayed like that, breathing in a synchronized way, not deliberately, but in step on a convergent path.

Both sets of eyes were closed; both pairs of lips were parted. She felt him mouth the words: I love you.

To which she silently replied: I know.

"It's time to pick Rex up at the airport," Walter said, glancing reluctantly at his watch. They arranged to meet by the pool near the spa when he returned with Rex. The West Palm Beach Airport was only seven miles away so he estimated that he'd be back by six.

"Hurry," Camilla said.

The first thing she did when Walter left was phone Merry. Robert picked up on the first ring. "Camilla! We had a wonderful time. We bought a dog."

"Corgi or chihuahua?"

"Neither. A toy French poodle. Merry picked him out from a litter of apricot puppies at American Kennels. He's a ball of fluff."

Camilla could imagine Merry's delight in the puppies; she could hear her squealing as the little tongues licked her face. "Did Merry name him too?"

"Dennis did. We're calling him Quasimodo." Robert started to chat about the snow, and the ringside circus tickets Dennis managed to get through his agent, and how much Merry could eat, when Camilla interrupted, "May I speak with her, please?"

"Hi, Mama."

"Merry, baby, are you having fun?"

"Lots and lots of fun." A dog yapped in the background.

Camilla was happy to hear it, but she ached for Merry just the same. The absence of a person you love seems so much larger than the space they actually fill. "There's a secret garden here, little darling. It has creatures made out of leaves. There's a squirrel, and a goose —"

"Mama?"

"Yes, darling?"

"Gotta go now."

Camilla's mood deflated. "Okay, baby. I love you. See you soon."

As Camilla changed into her bathing suit, she realized that Merry would grow up someday and leave her too.

Palm Beach is best in the late afternoon. The sun journeys from where it rises over the Atlantic Ocean in the east, going south out of sight when it passes below The Everglades and Bath & Tennis clubs, to where it sets in the west over Lake Worth.

The spa pool faced the ocean. Most of the bathers had left once the sun moved away, but Camilla found it the most beautiful part of the day. The waiter took her order for a Lillet on the rocks while she looked over the ledge onto the beach below, where a blue-gray fish twisted and turned, trying to get back home to the sea. She stretched out on a chaise and sipped her drink, listening to the subtle cadences she had buried under the city noises she had come to know so well. She missed the spontaneous sounds and sensuous smells of nature.

For her, the slides down the chutes had been fast and deep. And the way back up the ladder was climbed one rung at a time. She was nearing the top; she had Merry, her own business, and the prospect of true love. She had to let go of the past, the regrets for those things she couldn't get back, and move on. Or else her perch would be too precarious.

Walter loved her. He had awakened in her a sexuality that had always been there, hidden under the debris of failed hopes and dreams. Yes, she loved him — but she couldn't, if it meant she'd lose herself again. As soon as he returned, she would tell him. No I can't go back, we can't stay here. The past doesn't exist, except in our memories.

At that moment he returned. She felt his movement behind her, unwavering, self-confident. He said, "Camilla, you remember Rex."

Rex looked a little sheepish. He gave her a complicit smile. "Hi," he said. "Mind if I change for a swim?" He pointed toward the men's locker room near the spa.

"Not at all. Enjoy," Camilla said.

"Why do you love me?" Camilla asked Walter as soon as Rex was gone.

"That's easy. You are my other half," he replied.

"Aren't you afraid that I'm damaged by all the things that have happened to me?"

"Life is like that. The degree to which you can feel happiness is directly proportionate to how much you have felt pain."

Camilla smiled sadly as he stroked her cheek. "Based on that theory, I've got unimaginable joy coming my way."

"Horrible, unfathomable things can happen to each of us, in differing degrees, of course. And then you turn the corner and something wonderful and unexpected comes out of nowhere…"

Rex came running from behind, in his royal blue and white Columbia University T-shirt and knee-length cargo-style trunks. He paused before diving into the pool to flash them a smile that rivaled the setting sun and to strip off his shirt, which he tossed on top of a chaise.

And then she saw it.

On his left shoulder he had a strawberry birthmark, the size of a dime, but shaped exactly like a heart.

Camilla's skin grew hot, and the only sound she could hear was her own blood rushing through her veins. Love denied welled up in her when she realized Rex was really her son. The guilt and self-loathing, over giving up her child — her flesh and blood — had been slowly dissipating with her own success in the face of adversity and Walter's love.

Rex was proof of her redemption.

Merry and Rex and Walter were her rewards.

About The Author

Jessica Dee Rohm holds a MBA from Columbia Business School and is currently working on a MFA degree in creative writing. A former intern for The New York Times, she started a public relations agency at the age of 21 and sold it to the largest independent advertising agency in the United States when she was 30. She also started and ran a real estate firm serving foreign investors. She currently is the vice president of communications for Thomson Learning in Stamford, Connecticut.

Make Me An Offer is her first novel. Her second book Love Lessons .is expected out within the year.

The author lives with her husband, two children and numerous pets in Greenwich, Connecticut.

Printed in the United States
28429LVS00003B/46-111